# THE
# PEOPLE
## OF THE SKY

Also by Walton Golightly

*AmaZulu*
*Shaka the Great*

# THE PEOPLE OF THE SKY

## WALTON GOLIGHTLY

*Being The Many Diverse Adventures Of The Induna & The Boy*
*Among The AmaZulu,*
*During The Afternoon Of Shaka's Reign,*
*When Even Though The Bull Elephant Has Secured*
*Hegemony & Trade Routes For His Children,*
*& All Should Be Content,*
*Conspirators Are Honing Their Blades*

Quercus

First published in Great Britain in 2013 by

Quercus
55 Baker Street
7th Floor, South Block
London
W1U 8EW

A CIP catalogue record for this book is available
from the British Library

ISBN 978 0 85738 331 0
EBOOK ISBN 978 085738 334 1

10 9 8 7 6 5 4 3 2 1

Typeset by Ellipsis Digital Limited, Glasgow

Printed and bound in Great Britain by Clays Ltd, St Ives plc

*For my mother*

. . . and all the excitement had induced a kind of vertigo, a youthful intoxication tasting of gunpowder, glory, and exaltation. That is how, 'fore God, a lad the same age as the number of lines in a sonnet comes to witness a war when the goddess Fortuna decrees that he will not play the part of victim but of witness and, at times, of precocious executioner. But I have already told Your Mercies, on a different occasion, that those were times when a life, even one's own, was worth less than the steel used to take it. Difficult and cruel times. Hard times.

From *The Sun Over Breda* by Arturo Pérez-Reverte

# Contents

# Main characters

**Zulus**

| | |
|---|---|
| Shaka KaSenzangakhona | *King of the Zulus; born in the 1790s; seized the throne in 1816* |
| Senzangakhona KaJama | *Son of Jama, and Shaka's father; allied the Zulus with Dingiswayo's Mthethwas while King* |
| Sigujana | *The son Senzangakhona chose as his heir* |
| Mbopa | *Shaka's prime minister* |
| Mdlaka | *Commander-in-chief of the Zulu army* |
| Dingane Mhlangana Mpande | *Three of Shaka's brothers* |
| Ndlela | *Induna in the service of Mnkabayi* |
| Mgobozi | *Shaka's most trusted general* |
| Njikiza (the Watcher of the Ford) Phepho Namasu | *Men of the Fasimba regiment* |
| Sola | |
| Nolaka (the Leopard Man) Bamba | *Indunas in the service of Mhlangana* |
| Nkulukeko | *A district head* |

| | |
|---|---|
| Thenjiwe | Shaka's chief body servant |
| Pampata | Shaka's favourite concubine |
| Nandi | Shaka's mother |
| Mnkabayi | Sister of Senzangakhona KaJama and hence one of Shaka's aunts |

**Others**

| | |
|---|---|
| Henry Fynn | |
| Francis Farewell | } English traders |
| James King | |
| Jakot Msimbithi | Their Xhosa interpreter; called Hlambamanzi, the Swimmer, by Shaka |
| Mzilikazi | One of Shaka's favourites, who betrayed him and fled north with his people, who became known as the Matabele |
| Soshangane | One of Zwide's generals, who Shaka spared and who established his own 'tribe' – the Shangaan |
| Dingiswayo | King of the Mthethwas; became Shaka's mentor and helped him seize the Zulu throne |
| Zwide | King of the Ndwandwes; killed Dingiswayo; defeated by Shaka in two wars |

# Prelude

We have heard how Malandela's son Zulu, whose name meant 'Sky', took his extended family and settled in among the green hills between the Pongola and Thukela rivers of the south-east coast of southern Africa, where the grass was sweet and the herds grew fat. After Zulu came Gumede KaZulu, who was followed by Phunga KaGumede, then Mageba, then Ndaba, then Jama, and along the way a clan became a tribe: the AmaZulu, the People Of The Sky.

★

They were Abantu – Human Beings – and all other tribes they regarded as wild beasts, savages, izilwane.

★

We have heard how an heir to the Zulu throne, Senzangakhona KaJama, made a female of the Langeni tribe pregnant. It was Ukuhlobonga, he said, the Pleasure of the Road: a dalliance between clenched thighs; if both of you lost control and pene-tration occurred, a fine of a few cattle would appease the girl's father and she'd still be regarded as a virgin.

With Jama ailing and close to death, his brother Mduli all but ruled the small tribe in his stead. And there was now a problem.

As the enraged elder told his nephew, this was not a matter that could be resolved with a few cattle. For the Langeni were the home tribe of Senzangakhona's mother and, in getting one of their females pregnant, the young fool had committed incest in the eyes of Zulu law.

Mduli's only recourse was to deny everything. 'You say she is

1

pregnant,' he told the Langeni delegation that had been despatched to the Zulu royal kraal at Esiklebeni. 'I say impossible! You say her belly is swollen with the seed of a Zulu King. I say rubbish! This female is ill.'

Her swollen belly, he declared, was caused by a stomach beetle called a 'shaka'.

'That is what's in her gut,' sneered Mduli. 'A shaka!'

Fine, said Nandi – the 'afflicted' maiden in question, whose name meant 'Sweet One'– and when her son was born she named him 'Shaka'. Now here is your Beetle, said her family. Come and fetch him! And his mother too, for they were only too happy to be rid of the wilful girl.

Senzangakhona was by then King and was told by his uncle that he no longer had any choice in the matter; it would be better to hush up the affair. Reluctantly, the new King took Nandi as his wife. No lobolo, or bride price, was asked for or paid – a mark of shame; a sign of how little Nandi was valued even by her own family.

Years of abuse and cruelty followed. And things didn't get better when Nandi and Shaka were sent off to live with his mother's people. As if the scandal of the 'banishment' wasn't bad enough, Shaka's insistence on his being the heir to the Zulu throne saw him mocked and bullied by the other local boys, while their parents shunned Nandi. She had brought this all on herself, they said. She had tried to seduce a Zulu prince and failed – and yet still acted as if she were a queen. Finally it became too much and they left the Langeni, to live like beggars seeking succour wherever they could.

In 1802 came the great famine of Madlatule – Eat and Be Quiet – and they almost starved to death as they roamed the dying land. Yet always, amid these hardships, their bellies howling, Nandi would hug her son tightly and tell him: 'Never mind, my Little Fire, never mind. One day you'll be the greatest King in all the land.'

Finally, when Shaka was eleven, they went to live with a clan of the Mthethwa tribe – and their fortunes began to change for the better.

★

Meanwhile there was one other who joined Mduli as the power behind the Zulu throne. This was Senzangakhona's elder sister, Mnkabayi – and it was said that, aided by her loyal induna, Ndlela KaSompisi, this wise and powerful woman had been dabbling in Zulu politics – such as they were – even while her father Jama was alive. Whatever the case, she and Senzangakhona were particularly close and she could be counted upon to make sure that, as far as possible, her brother lived up to his name as The One Who Acts Wisely.

She was also feared by the tribe's sangomas, who were led by a certain Nobela at that time and who constantly sought to exert their influence on the Zulu Kings.

Aiee . . . that old crone, Nobela! Even though she never sought to exercise her authority over the others openly there was no doubting she held them in her thrall, and Mnkabayi's hatred of her knew no bounds. Which wasn't surprising since Nobela was one of those who had wanted Mnkabayi dead before she'd even suckled her mother's breast.

It had to be Nobela told Jama, if he was to save himself – and the tribe – from the curse that accompanied twins. In an act of courageous obstinacy, however, Jama decreed that Mnkabayi, who had left her mother's womb first, and her sister Mmama would both be allowed to live. Anyone who sought to harm them would have to face his wrath.

Mmama died while still an infant and, although her immediate family then treated her just like any other child, Mnkabayi would never forgive the sangomas.

Ironically, this very antipathy saw some seek her patronage. And these creatures made good spies.

★

We have heard of the warrior Godongwana, who at a young age revealed the traits that would one day make him a great ruler, and how his jealous brothers managed to persuade their father Jobe that Godongwana was plotting to overthrow him. Upon receiving a summons to Jobe's kraal, Godongwana chose to flee rather than see his father shame himself by believing the lies of others.

Finding himself among the Hlubis, people of Xhosa stock, he soon distinguished himself through his bravery and initiative and became a headman in the tribe. One day, a White Man came to his kraal who was likely the last survivor of an expedition despatched from the Cape in 1807 to find an overland route to Portuguese East Africa. Having heard that Jobe had died and deciding it was time to return home to claim his birthright, Godongwana agreed to guide the man to the coast, but en route the stranger contracted a fever and died. Godongwana never forgot the White Man, never forgot the things he'd spoken about as they sat around the fire of an evening.

For, coming from the Cape, the White Man could speak Xhosa, a Nguni language Godongwana understood, and the young prince could grasp most of the concepts he raised – trade, empires, wars of conquest. It was the sheer scale of such concepts that awed him. And got him thinking.

It was the White Man, Godongwana later said, who gave him the idea of uniting the tribes in the region. But it wasn't to be conquest for the sake of conquest, for Godongwana envisaged what was in effect a commonwealth that would be able to deal with the White Men on their own terms. For that was something else the White Man told him: the Long Noses *were* coming, and in greater numbers than he could ever imagine. And their actions would gradually begin to impinge more and more on ways the tribes thought were timeless and immutable.

After burying him, Godongwana took the White Man's gun and horse and returned home. He was a dead man come to life, reborn and renamed – for he now called himself Dingiswayo, the Wanderer, and cut a fine figure with the horse and rifle. It mattered not that the horse soon died, for these were not healthy environs for naked zebras, or that the gun was next to useless, lacking ball and powder. They were still powerful talismans, and few had the courage to dispute his claims. Here was a man truly blessed by the ancestors.

The year was 1809 and it was Dingiswayo, not Shaka, who first set about uniting the tribes and clans on the south-east coast of Africa, organising something approaching a standing army, and fighting wars not only to increase his herds but to gain – and hold – territory, so as to secure the trade routes with the Portuguese in Mozambique. The Zulu King merely completed what his mentor had started.

A brave warrior with some outspoken notions as to how battles should be fought, Shaka would have come to Dingiswayo's attention sooner or later. That their relationship should soon deepen into something beyond mere respect and admiration, however, wasn't surprising. It's likely that Dingiswayo saw in the young Zulu a kindred spirit, a fellow outcast.

And in 1815, the ruler of the Mthethwas persuaded an ailing Senzangakhona to acknowledge Shaka as his heir. When, on his deathbed, the Zulu King reneged on his promise, selecting his son

Sigujana as his successor instead, Dingiswayo sent the elite Izicwe regiment with the twenty-eight-year-old Shaka to help set matters right.

In this, Dingiswayo, Shaka and Nandi were assisted by Mnkabayi. Sigujana had already proved himself to be a dissolute ruler whose reign did not bode well for the future of the tribe, and Mnkabayi's endorsement of Shaka's claim went a long way to assuaging any doubts the people might have.

At the same time she persuaded Nandi to stay Shaka's hand, should he contemplate removing his other brothers – especially Dingane who, as next in line, could be expected to plot against this usurper who had spent so much time among the Mthethwas that he could barely speak Zulu.

In turn, following his aunt's orders, Dingane surprised everyone by acknowledging Shaka as King and swearing fealty when the two finally met. This was the final endorsement the nation needed and, that day, cries of 'Bayede, Nkosi!' *Hail to the King!* 'Bayede, Nkosi, bayede! Bayede!' rang out around the sacred cattlefold.

★

A short while later Shaka set about slaughtering those who had been unkind to Nandi. Mduli, the cantankerous uncle who had sent Nandi's relatives packing, was among the first Shaka saw put to death. But it's said he asked to die like a warrior, with an assegai thrust, and went to join the ancestors praising Shaka's greatness, for he had looked into Shaka's eyes and seen there everything Senzangakhona's other sons lacked.

Chances are that Mnkabayi herself would have been spared even if she hadn't played an active role in helping Shaka to seize the throne. Her noble upbringing – a willingness to grit her teeth and endure Nandi's tantrums – had seen her treat Nandi far better than her brother's other wives had done. And Shaka came to treat her as a veritable queen, second only to Nandi, entrusting to her the care of his great northern ikhanda, or war kraal, which was the Sky People's most important settlement next to KwaBulawayo.

When his impalers had finished with the members of the Zulu court, Shaka took his wrath against the Langeni, Nandi's home tribe, punishing those who had shunned Nandi and mocked him.

At the same time he set about reorganising the Zulu army.

★

And we have heard how he introduced his men to the iklwa – a short stabbing spear used in an underarm motion, much like a Roman broadsword. Why, he asked his men, would a warrior want to divest himself of his weapon in combat? That each man might be equipped with four or five long spears mattered not a bit. All were for throwing, which meant *throwing away*, thus leaving one with nothing with which to defend oneself. Aiee! What foolishness!

With the help of Mgobozi, the Mthethwa warrior almost twice his age who had fought alongside Shaka in the Izicwe legion – and who had decided to remain behind to serve the King – Shaka set about training his men in how to use the iklwa.

What they *could* throw away, he decreed, were their sandals because, invariably ill-fitting, these made a warrior clumsy. From now on Zulu warriors would march and fight barefoot, and Shaka sent his men back and forth barefoot across thorns to toughen their feet. (In later life, though, whenever he came upon a shattered terrain littered with sharp rocks, Shaka would order a pair of sandals made for him.)

Following Dingiswayo's example, Shaka also proceeded to

reorganise the Zulu amabutho, or regiments, according to age-sets, as a way of improving discipline and defusing any potential threat the army would have for himself, or his plans.

Previously, local chiefs had been responsible for sending men to the King whenever the need arose. If they were opposed to a campaign, they'd send fewer men than were actually available, claiming that's all they had. Even if a chief condescended to despatch all the men he could muster, they remained primarily loyal to him. They were still his men and therefore more likely to do his bidding than the King's.

By creating his regiments according to age rather than region Shaka changed all of this. Males born within the same four-year period would be summoned to Bulawayo from across the kingdom and formed into a fighting unit with its own name and unique shield markings.

Regional and clan loyalties were thereby negated. While in training or on active service the regiments were stationed at the amakhanda, the war kraals sited in areas of strategic importance. Thrown together, each far from home, but of the same age, the men were soon referring to themselves by their regimental rather than their clan names.

However, Zulu custom threatened this cohesion. Once a man married he was allowed to leave his regiment and return to his clan lands to establish his own homestead. This, of course, brought him back under the sway of the local chief. Shaka's solution was to withhold permission for his warriors to marry while he was consolidating his own power.

The Ufasimba – the Haze – was the first regiment trained in Shaka's methods from the start of its career, and it would become his favourite ibutho.

★

Warriors at this time were expected to forage for themselves and therefore another important innovation the new King introduced was having twelve- and thirteen-year-old boys accompany the soldiers, carrying rations, water gourds and sleeping mats. One boy would look after three or four warriors, while indunas – senior officers – would have an udibi to themselves.

*

We have heard how the uneasy peace that gave Shaka time to begin training his men and form his new amabutho ended when Zwide, King of the Ndwandwes, fell on Matiwane and his Ngwanes, killing men, women and children and burning their kraals. Only the precious cattle were spared. When Dingiswayo angrily demanded the meaning of this massacre, wily Zwide claimed he'd received news that the Ngwanes were plotting against Dingiswayo and had attacked them before they could bring their plans to fruition.

The Wanderer wasn't fooled, and Zwide sent his sister to soothe the Mthethwa monarch's anger. She also stole his seed, it's said, and the Ndwandwe medicine men went to work. For a King's semen was regarded as the source of his power, and thus Dingiswayo was cursed.

Meanwhile, Dingiswayo called upon his allies and moved on the Ndwandwes. Although he had bested a few clans who saw in the Zulus easy pickings, Shaka felt his army wasn't ready and his powerbase still insecure, but he had no option but to obey his mentor's summons.

However, the curse was already working. The Mthethwa army halted close to KwaDlovungu, Zwide's capital and, while waiting for his allies to join him, Dingiswayo went out scouting, accompanied by five female bodyguards, and was duly captured by a Ndwandwe patrol. The small group was escorted to

KwaDlovungu, where Dingiswayo was cordially received by Zwide, who slaughtered an ox in his honour.

The following day, the ruler of the Mthethwas was executed, and his head was removed so that Zwide's mother, Ntombazi, could add another King's skull to her collection.

Left in disarray, the Mthethwa army was easily defeated. The only reason why the Zulus did not become involved was because Shaka and his men were intercepted by a messenger from Dondo of the Khumalos, who told them what had happened and enabled Shaka to withdraw his army.

Zwide, who knew of Shaka's achievements, especially against his own legions, and also knew he was Dingiswayo's favourite, saw this as an act of cowardice and resolved to leave the People of the Sky until last – when he had finished devouring Dingiswayo's other allies.

★

When Zwide finally sent his army against Shaka, the Bull Elephant was ready for the clash. 'Know this, my children: we fight for our lives!' he told his regiments shortly before the battle. 'Death is the only mercy we can expect!' Zwide was coming for their women, their children, their cattle! 'But we have his measure,' said Shaka. 'Let him come, and he'll encounter a tempest the like of which this land has never seen. This land . . .' The King spread his arms. 'Do this, defeat these lice, and *this* awaits you! These green hills, these plains and swollen rivers! Standing shoulder to shoulder, you have the power to win this land. To rule this land!'

The Bull Elephant then had his greatly outnumbered amabutho encircle Gqokli Hill. In due course they were in turn surrounded by the Ndwandwes, who were led by Zwide's son Nomahlanjana. But, so great were their numbers, the Ndwandwe soldiers found themselves trapped among each other, struggling for space – unable to throw away their spears, as Shaka would put it. And the Zulus attacked, then returned to their position on the slopes of the hill. And so it went for most of that day – the Ndwandwes would attack, struggling uphill in their sandals, the Zulus would repulse them, then counter-attack as they fled down the hill, before returning to their positions.

Soon thirst began to take its toll. Shaka had ensured waterskins were stored on the summit of the hill, while the Ndwandwe warriors began to wander off, ignoring their screaming officers,in search of something to drink.

The Zulus themselves had suffered many casualties – and were still outnumbered – but a final charge shattered the exhausted Ndwandwe ranks, and a slaughter ensued.

Gqokli Hill was the end of the beginning. It announced to the world – the growling, quarrelsome relatives who surrounded them – that the Sky People were no longer going to be vassals.

Other successful campaigns followed once the Zulu regiments had regained their strength, and new regiments were created and trained. At home, Shaka consolidated his power by embarking upon a campaign of a different sort against the Zulu sangomas. Because they had the Calling and so could commune with the ancestors, they enjoyed a special status and were as revered – and feared – as the King himself, who would do well to ensure he had their support. Shaka, however, made sure they knew things had changed and he was now ruler of all. All had to obey him or else have the King's Impalers find them a new perch.

*

And we have heard how Zwide sent his men against the Zulus once again. This time they were led by a more able commander-in-chief, since Soshangane had been at Gqokli Hill and had learnt a lot. It was thanks to him that of the three assegais Ndwandwe

11

soldiers carried, one was a short stabbing spear much like the Zulu iklwa – and their flimsy wooden shields had been replaced by tough oval cowskin shields similar to the Zulu isihlangu. He'd also tried to instil in his men a sense of discipline, so that columns and troop movements were now more orderly. He wasn't sure the men were ready yet, but he had no choice but to obey his ruler.

Shaka had a spy in Zwide's court, though, and was ready for the Ndwandwe invasion. His force easily defeated, Soshangane was allowed to go free, while the Zulu amabutho went rampaging through Ndwandwe territory. But Zwide eluded them, fleeing north with his sons, but Shaka was able to ensure his mother Ntombazi's death was painful and prolonged.

The Sky People now controlled the trade routes – and hence the trade – with the Portuguese.

★

And the praise-singers, the izimbongi, sang of Shaka's greatness: *He is Bull Elephant! He is Sitting Thunder! He is Lightning Fire! Hai-yi hai-yi! I like him when he wrapped the Inkatha around the hill and throttled Zwide's sons. I like him when he went up the hill to throttle Ntombazi of the skulls. Bayede, Nkosi, bayede! Blood of Zulu. Father of the Sky. Barefoot Thorn Man! I like him because we sleep in peace within his clenched fist. Hai-yi hai-yi! I like him because our cattle are free to roam our hills, never to be touched by another's hand. I like him because our water is sweet. I like him because our beer is sweeter. Bayede, Nkosi, bayede!*

★

We have heard how, before Gqokli Hill, Zwide ate up most of the Khumalo tribe. Led by Mzilikazi KaMashobane, the survivors had fled to Shaka. Time and again Mzilikazi proved his courage in battle, and he soon became one of the Zulu King's favourites.

In June 1821, after defeating Soshangane's invasion and consolidating his power south of the Thukela River, Shaka turned his attention to the north-west. 'Go!' he told Mzilikazi. 'Go to the land of Chief Ranisi, go in my name and offer him the compliments of the Bull Elephant, then impale him on the bluntest pole you can find, let his screams ring out across the valleys as a warning to the others who would spurn our protection!'

If successful, decreed Shaka, Mzilikazi could lead his people back over the White Umfolozi to the rolling hills below the Ngome forest . . . They could go home! Could return to the land of the Khumalos!

This duly happened, but then some in the Bull Elephant's inner circle, believing Mzilikazi to be too much of a favourite, whispered in Shaka's ear that Mzilikazi hadn't handed over all the cattle he owed Shaka as a tribute after the campaign.

Mzilikazi kicked the emissaries Shaka had sent him out of his kraal, saying: 'If Shaka thinks I owe him cattle, let him come and fetch them!'

And still Shaka stayed his hand. But finally he gave in to the warnings of his councillors that such flagrant mocking of his authority could not, must not, be allowed to go unpunished. Finally, he sent his army against Mzilikazi and his followers, who'd left their home village to take refuge in a mountain stronghold.

And there are those who say Shaka stayed his hand yet again and allowed his favourite to make his escape. And, before finally settling in what is today Zimbabwe, Mzilikazi and his people – who would come to be called the Matabele – roamed the land to the north; a tribe of nomadic bandits practising the total warfare favoured by Shaka.

★

Nandi, meanwhile, wasn't happy, for she wanted her son to find his Ubulawu.

Since the days before Malandela, the father of Zulu, one of a King's most powerful weapons was a potion called Ubulawu – or the Froth. He'd mix the muthi in a sacred vessel at sundown, while praising the ancestors and speaking the name of the enemy he wanted to defeat.

The King always used the same vessel. But when he died it was destroyed and the heir had to 'find' his own vessel; a process which could take years. It was said, though, that the King would know it as soon as he saw it. Emissaries from all over the kingdom would travel to the King's kraal with a selection of pots, hoping he'd 'recognise' one of them, for it was a great honour for a clan to be the one who guided the King to his vessel.

Over the decades, the vessel itself came to be called the Ubulawu, the 'froth' becoming of secondary importance. Eventually the Ubulawu stopped being a pot and became any artefact the King deemed a bringer of good luck – and so a potion became a talisman.

Senzangakhona's Ubulawu had been destroyed on his death and Sigujana hadn't had time to find his before Shaka had him assassinated.

And Nandi kept pestering Shaka to find his own talisman, but he professed disdain for the tradition. 'Let my mighty army be my Ubulawu,' he said.

Of more importance to him was the fact that, as Soshangane had demonstrated, the remaining tribes had begun to organise themselves better and adopt Zulu-style tactics, and even versions of the iklwa. Far more cunning would be needed in future campaigns, and it was cunning that saw the Bull Elephant destroy

14

the Thembus which, next to Faku's Pondoes on the coast, was the last tribe that posed any real threat to Zulu hegemony.

★

Meanwhile another tribe of barbarians, of izilwane, had arrived on the scene: White Men. They established a trading station on the shores of the sheltered bay they called Port Natal, and which the Zulus referred to as Thekwini. It was an ideal anchorage sheltered from the worst of the storms that made sailing along this coast so hazardous, and was marred only by a sandbar which was covered by less than a metre of water at low tide.

They claimed to serve a distant King called Jorgi who lived far, far away, but who might be a valuable ally to the Zulus. But the truth was, as members of the Farewell Trading Company, they were there to make money, trading in ivory and, it was hoped, gold.

But Lieutenant Francis Farewell, who had first conceived of cutting out the Portuguese at Delagoa Bay and dealing directly with Shaka, had a rival. Lieutenant James King – who captained (and, with his mother, co-owned) the ships Farewell had hired to explore the littoral – also recognised the potential of Thekwini.

As soon as the expedition returned to Cape Town on December 3, 1823, King got to work by writing a letter to Earl Bathurst, Secretary of State for the Colonies, seeking to broach the idea of establishing a British settlement at the bay.

He made no mention at all of Lieutenant Francis Farewell or the Farewell Trading Company.

Not surprisingly, Farewell was incensed. But then, clearly believing he could raise more money there, King set sail for England. Suddenly, Farewell had time and proximity on his side. He raised money from the wealthier businessmen in the Cape's Dutch community, won over by his tales of cattle kraals made entirely of elephant tusks, and had an advance party on its way to Port Natal before King was anywhere near England.

And early on the morning of May 10, 1824, the sloop *Julia* slipped over the sandbar and anchored in the northern sector of the bay. Henry Fynn, who had arrived at Cape Town in 1818 at the age of fifteen, was the group's leader. He was tasked with ensuring that dwellings for the main party were built and also establishing contact with Shaka.

He set about the latter with alacrity and would become one of the Zulu King's favourites among the White Men.

★

Then Nandi died, and we have heard of the horrors that followed.

Over the coming months Shaka took to slaughtering whole villages of people he felt weren't showing sufficient sadness at the passing of his mother. He forbade fornication, and had holes torn in the huts so that his slayers could come round at night and make sure this law was being obeyed. Another ukase allowed that the cows be milked but no one was allowed to drink that milk; instead, it would be thrown onto the ground.

It was as if Shaka wanted to see everyone join his mother on the Great Journey. These weren't sacrifices, all those people put to death for failing to show sufficient sadness; it wasn't about reminding the ancestors of her greatness. Instead, it was as if all of those who still lived were an insult, an affront – how dare they eat and drink and fuck while she lay curled up in a hole! If she couldn't live, then neither could they!

Shaka even shunned Pampata, his favourite concubine, while Mnkabayi and the King's prime minister, Mbopa, and others loyal to the King did their best to ensure some form of governance was kept in place. Aiee! And see how Shaka rewarded Mbopa! Just when you thought his actions couldn't get more depraved or more spiteful. Aiee! Dingane, Mhlangana and the other brothers had trembled and slept with their spears, thinking Shaka might use this as an opportunity to thin their ranks, but see where Shaka's madness had led him: to the kraal of one of his most trustworthy servants!

And then it was over. It was as if Shaka had been ill with a fever – because that's how sudden the recovery was.

There were still lapses, when the King disappeared into his hut, his indlu, for days on end and no one dared disturb him, or times when every utterance of his condemned some unfortunate to death, but these became less and less frequent.

The insane laws were repealed, and the nation rejoiced.

But there were those such as Mnkabayi who, observing the King closely, came to suspect that the terrible fever had merely been the birth pains of something infinitely worse.

★

And we have heard how, in 1826, Shaka decreed that the Umkhosi, the First Fruits, would be conducted differently henceforth. Traditionally, the final rituals of the Zulu harvest ceremony were carried out by the various village chiefs around the kingdom as well as by the King, their ceremonies mirroring his, but Shaka announced that, henceforth, only the King would conduct the rites that concluded the First Fruits.

This would serve to centralise his power even further. Mnkabayi could appreciate that and therefore she supported the ruling, despite the disgruntlement it caused among the abanumzane, or headmen.

But why invite the White Men from Port Natal to witness these sacred rituals? That's what she couldn't understand. That's what vexed her. It was sacrilegious and reinforced her belief that

Shaka's 'recovery' after Nandi's death had been temporary, merely the prelude to further, more dangerous madness.

But there was more to the Umkhosi, more to the First Fruits, than a mere harvest festival. It also involved the King going into seclusion for several days beforehand. Doctored by his inyangas with Imithi Emnyama, Black Medicine, he would commune with the ancestors, seeking their blessing for the year to come. And Shaka intended to use the ability this afforded to move between worlds, to divine the strange power he had discerned in the White Men. It was a sign of his desperation that he had resorted to sorcery to seek out this power, but he had become obsessed with discovering the nature of this otherness, the taming of which would enhance his own supremacy. Or so he believed.

★

And so they came, the People of the Sky, leaving their swollen crops to journey to KwaBulawayo, Shaka's capital, the Place of He Who Kills. And the regiments came in what was the largest mustering of the Zulu army to date, so that all might see for themselves the might of the nation. It was truly a momentous time that few would forget. But, even as the people feasted and celebrated, there were those who tried to disrupt the First Fruits. They too resorted to sorcery and, had they succeeded, they would have brought about a disaster – the ultimate sign of the ancestors' displeasure – from which Shaka might never have recovered. However, then irony took a hand. Shaka was stabbed while watching his warriors dance, and the would-be assassin escaped in the ensuing chaos.

★

A terrified Fynn was called upon to treat Shaka. In truth the wound wasn't all that serious and the White Man managed to save the King, but the consequences were. After he had recovered, the Bull Elephant took to skulking in his royal compound for longer and longer periods, causing Mnkabayi – and others – to fear for the future of the nation . . .

★

And we have heard how the Induna and the udibi moved through these events, these tragedies and triumphs, incidents and accidents, agonies and ecstasies, always, always loyally serving Shaka, the King of Kings. Now let us hear how the story ends.

★

*Izindaba zami lezi* . . .

These are my stories, of long ago and far away.

*Uma ngiqambe amanga* . . .

If I have lied, I have lied the truth.

If this is not the way things were, it's the way they should have been.

# PART ONE

## *Devils In The Dark*

I am very far from being certain that the Zulu is on an inferior evolutionary stage, whatever the blazes that may mean. I do not think there is anything stupid or ignorant about howling at the moon or being afraid of devils in the dark. It seems to me perfectly philosophical. Why should a man be thought a sort of idiot because he feels the mystery and peril of existence itself? Suppose, my dear Chadd, suppose it is we who are the idiots because we are not afraid of devils in the dark . . .

From *The Club of Queer Trades*
by G. K. Chesterton

'Take some more whiskey and go on,' I said.

From *The Man Who Would Be King*
by Rudyard Kipling

They come for him in the afternoon.

The wind of earlier has died down. The day is as still as a lion in repose, the cloudless sky as blue as only an African sky can be on days like these. Not that they notice, for the enormity of what they're about to do numbs them.

They're oblivious to the children playing around them, the adults going about their chores, making pots and shields, beer and maize meal.

It's as if they've passed over to the other side – the world of the amadlozi, the ancestors – and are invisible as they make their way between the domed huts.

There are four of them. Each man is, of course, barefoot and wears the isinene and ibeshu that comprise the Zulu loin covering. Each also carries the short stabbing spear the People of the Sky call the iklwa, an onomatopoeic word imitating the slurping, sucking sound the broad blade makes when it's withdrawn from a dying man's torso.

To avoid undue suspicion – and who knows who suspects who, and who's watching who, in this climate of doubt and dread – they approach the royal compound from different directions.

One takes a wide detour that brings him to the black isigodlo – the walled compound that houses the King's harem. The man's younger brother serves with the regiment currently tasked with guarding the seraglio, and that's his pretext for venturing so close to this forbidden section of KwaBulawayo.

He wants to make sure the full complement is still there, and that some men haven't been redeployed and are now lying in wait to ambush them.

For the four of them could well be walking into a trap, with Mdlaka having withdrawn the royal guard – at Shaka's prompting – so that those

23

who plot against him might be goaded into revealing themselves by doing something rash.

(And decades later, the young men will ask the old general: 'Is it true? Is it?')

*The second man — the leader of the four — approaches the royal compound through the section housing the King's izilomo, his advisors and councillors. Quite a few others have found excuses to visit their home kraals, so as to escape Bulawayo before the King's brooding erupts again into a storm of anger. And they have no doubt that this will happen, for Shaka's unexplained seclusion is like a thundercloud growing darker and darker.*

*The man, however, notes nothing to arouse his suspicions in the behaviour of those who've remained here at the capital. They greet him with the deference owed his rank, ask after his health, ask him if he wants to share some snuff. He knows, from past experience, that this is their way of initiating attempts to discover if he knows anything new about the King's current state of mind. Today, as always, he politely refuses the snuff, claiming an important errand, and then moves on.*

*Would they know — would they have heard — if Shaka was setting a trap for him? But surely, if that's the case, they wouldn't be their usual sycophantic selves — and someone always hears something, don't they?*

*Which is why they must seize this chance! For who knows how long it is before they're betrayed? Or, if already betrayed, who knows how long before the Bull Elephant, having watched and witnessed enough, decides to crush them?*

(And, decades later, they'll ask the old general: 'Is it true? Is it true Shaka survived?')

*There's no time to lose! Let the bitch conspire and connive. But many of the izinkosi will be happy to see Shaka go merely because he long ago decreed that they would no longer be referred to as 'inkosi' or 'chief'. Henceforth that was to be a title reserved only for the King; and hence-*

forth they would be addressed as 'unumzane' – a term of respect, yes, but one previously used merely for the head of a family.

As for Mdlaka withdrawing Shaka's bodyguard . . . he was only the King's second choice for commander-in-chief. Shaka had originally offered the post to his old Mthethwa crony, the late unlamented Mgobozi, who said he preferred fighting in the front line instead. Yet more often than not it was Mgobozi's counsel Shaka sought, which had to rankle over the years with Mdlaka. Rankle and fester.

And how do I know about that! From scars that never heal, but instead multiply and widen. Every day a new affront: having to grin and bear it, gritting your teeth to stop yourself from clenching your fists, and thereby betraying the rancour and humiliation you feel.

How I know about that!

Although amply rewarded, Mdlaka has never really received the credit he deserves for ensuring that the new regiments are well trained and that discipline is maintained; thus ensuring they're always where Shaka wants them to be.

And perhaps Mdlaka has at last decided to, if not cast his lot in with them, then at least leave the gates open. Is that such a far-fetched assumption?

Certainly, it's one reinforced by the third man, who's ambled all around the perimeter of the royal compound. As far as he can see, there are no signs anywhere of a large force of men hidden and waiting, he reports when the four of them converge again near the entrance to the isigodlo.

The fourth man has approached through the regiment's lines – the dwellings allocated to them when they're stationed at Bulawayo – and can confirm they too are deserted except for the udibis who look after the huts and ensure they remain habitable during the regiment's absence.

The leader nods. There is no longer time for vacillation. For one thing, you don't want to be seen lurking near the royal compound with a spear in your hand.

('Is it true?' they'll ask him. 'Is it true Shaka survived and was spirited away by those loyal to him?')

*The fourth man is to remain here to act as a lookout. If it turns out to be a trap, there'll be little he can do, of course. But, if it's not, he can prevent others from entering the compound, while his three companions are going about their business.*

*The others exchange glances, then look left, look right, to make sure no one's around, before darting through the entrance quicker than rats.*

*As if mimicking its inhabitant, the royal hut seems to sit there brooding and scowling. Crouching even though it's broad daylight, they approach the hut, two coming from the left, the leader moving in from the right, so that anyone looking out through the entrance can't see them.*

*At the hut, the other two look to their leader. He can't strike the killing blow, so they have to — and he understands the need to urge them into action promptly, as even now they're likely to be having second thoughts. He tilts his head, while indicating the doorway with the tip of his spear.*

*The first man takes a breath, then ducks through the door, followed quickly by his companion, their spears ready to feast on Shaka — that sickness which started as a beetle in Nandi's womb and has grown to have a malicious, destructive life of its own.*

*He imagines them striking like cobras, and his impatience sends him also into the hut, after just a few heartbeats. And he sees why there's been no sounds of a struggle, or of someone crying out in shock.*

*The hut is empty.*

*Shaka isn't there.*

# 1
# Dark Days

*A frightfully forbidding countenance: a killer's face and a manner that shows a disposition for murder.*

This is how Fynn describes the Induna in his *Diary*. He also says the man's name was 'Msika'.

He's wrong about the name.

And this morning, in early June 1828, the Induna looks especially forbidding, especially murderous. Rage tightens his blood vessels, fills his muscles, flares behind his eyes.

He's tall and broad-shouldered, with heavy arms and strong thighs. His duties take him far and wide, so he's had little time to enjoy the numerous rewards the King has bestowed on him. His herd has grown, but he has yet to acquire the paunch and heavy buttocks that signify nobility among the People of the Sky.

To stop his hands from trembling, he adjusts his isinene, pats the calfskin pouch which he wears around his waist. The front covering of the Zulu kilt, the isinene comprises skins cut into circular patches and strung together on sinews to form tassels weighted to prevent the apron from opening in the case of sudden movement. The pouch itself contains flints and a smaller bag of beads.

He breathes in deeply, exhales. Then raises his face toward the sun, lets its warm rays caress his cheeks, press against his eyelids, and calm him.

As much as it pains him he'll have to exercise restraint. His iklwa will stay hungry; words must suffice for now. To do otherwise, and go charging among them like a ravenous lion, will only exacerbate an already parlous situation.

For they are, after all, Mhlangana's men . . .

Aiee! He bows his head. That thought turns the sun cold, causing him to clench his fists, curling his toes as though to anchor himself to this same spot. Because that thought brings with it a presentiment: the carrion stench of something bigger, stronger, moving ever closer. The creak of armoured scales, the sinuous sweep of shoulders and hips. Snorting nostrils. Yellow teeth. Horns sharper than a wizard's spite. Inexorable, unstoppable. So that issuing a dressing-down to a contingent of disobedient warriors will be like spitting at a charging rhino.

But their transgression is serious. Something has to be done and, with Mbopa still indisposed, it's up to him.

Having finished securing the amashoba below the Induna's knees, his udibi rises. A long bulging scar resembling a large centipede stretches from just above his navel to his left hipbone. The assassin's blade had left him in death's grip for a long while; even Fynn had despaired and all the White Man could do was close the gash and see it was kept closed – and clean. By contrast, Shaka's wounds had been much lighter. But, in the end, thanks to Fynn's ministrations, and the muthi from a few trusted inyangas, the udibi had overcome the fever and the pain.

A head shorter than the Induna, and slimmer, he's in his early twenties and therefore much too old to be an udibi carrying extra weapons and food and water for a warrior. But, shortly before the First Fruits celebration of 1826, Shaka had ordered him to work with the Induna again in order to find those trying to sabotage the harvest festival, which for the first time was going to be officiated over by the King, and only by the King.

Since the Induna serves as Isithunzi SikaShaka, the Shadow of Shaka, the King's emissary, who is allowed to wear the blue crane feather and who speaks and acts with the Bull Elephant's authority, his udibi has come to be called Mthunzi, a shortened form of the 'Shadow of the Shadow'.

In common with others his age and many older males, he hasn't yet taken the isicoco. Made by plaiting a fibre around the skull, then smearing it with black gum to harden it, the head-ring is one of the most important adornments in Zulu society. Only once the isicoco is assumed is a male recognised as an indoda, a man. Before that, no matter his age, he's regarded as a boy, an insizwa, or hornless ox.

The Induna glances down and shifts his feet, causing the leggings to rustle. 'Ngiyabonga!' he says. *I thank you.*

Mthunzi moves over to the mat where two more amashoba lie. He picks up one – a leather thong with long fringes made from a cow's tail – and returns to the Induna's side. The older man extends his left arm.

Around them sprawls KwaBulawayo: the Place of He Who Kills. This is Shaka's Komkhulu, his Great Place, where he spends most of his time, thus making it, to all intents and purposes, the kingdom's capital. Situated between the Mhlathuze and Thukela rivers, and built on a slight slope for better drainage, it's laid out in typical fashion. Round as the full moon, it consists of a series of concentric circles. First, there's the stout outer fence of poles lashed together; about four kilometres in circumference, this palisade is patrolled day and night. Along the curves of the left and right hemispheres, extending from the main gate to the royal enclosure, are the huts of the regiments.

There are also the homes and workplaces of the artisans who make shields and assemble spears. Regiments receive their shields from Bulawayo when they're first given their names by Shaka, and they must come here again to ask for replacements when such are needed. Although weapons are manufactured throughout the kingdom, an iklwa from Shaka's Komkhulu is highly prized, and often handed out by the King himself as a reward for bravery.

The isigodlo, or royal enclosure, fills the upper arc of the city, farthest from the main gate. When Nandi, the King's mother, was still alive, the largest house here – and in the isigodlo of every other war kraal – was hers; after her death every indlunkhulu was pulled down. Shaka's hut is much smaller and occupies its own compound.

In the isigodlo are also to be found the huts of the King's councillors and servants, a communal cooking and eating area, as well as storage huts for the King's provisions. Traditionally, this is also where the monarch's wives reside, in a section known as the 'black isigodlo', where trespassing means instant death. Shaka, however, will never marry and, in each of the amakhanda, the war kraals, spread across his kingdom, the black isigodlo houses members of his harem– who were watched over by Nandi when she was alive and are now overseen by Pampata, the King's favourite concubine.

Hidden deep within the black isigodlo is the Enkatheni – the hut that houses the sacred Inkatha. Constantly added to, it comprises muthi made from substances such as the King's vomit and shit, and other materials culled from wild animals so as to co-opt their magical powers. All of these ingredients are smeared over a coil of grass rope which is in turn covered by python skins. Shaka has further strengthened the Inkatha by adding fragments from the izinkatha of vanquished tribes and flesh from the bodies of the chiefs that his impis have slain. Some say the coil has grown so large and is now so wide that the King can barely straddle it.

In the centre of the ikhanda, as in the centre of all Zulu settlements, is the sacred isibaya, or cattlefold. It is here the beasts are brought in at night, and there are a collection of smaller pens for calves, or cows about to give birth and also those which belong to the ancestors.

It's also here that the regiments parade and supplicants gather. At the top of the isibaya, near the isigodlo's main entrance, is the ibandla tree, under which Shaka holds court.

Pausing to listen to the low hum of activity around them, it's easy to assume all is well, but the Induna knows better. Look closer, move among the huts, and you see the people wear furtive, shifty expressions. Laughter is rare, and when anyone in authority is spotted, there's a scurrying to avoid crossing his path.

Hai, what with the trade routes firmly under Zulu control – and a new outlet having opened up at the place the White Men call Port Natal – also with their herds increasing, the cattle being able to roam the hills in safety, you'd expect Shaka's children to be happy. But they're not, because the bloodshed hasn't stopped. Ever since the assassination attempt, Shaka's amabutho – his regiments – have almost constantly been at war as he's embarked on campaign after campaign. And has this been to gain yet more territory? No. For after destroying this or that chieftain's army, he's simply ordered a withdrawal and sent his men rampaging off somewhere else.

*And now the war is coming home, isn't it? Frail men with hollowed cheeks, shaking knees and shattered minds roam the paths of the kingdom, begging for food or water, and then lying down in the long grass, ready to*

*make the final journey, happy just to have made it home. Once brave
warriors, but now left to rot, their final resting place will be the gut of the
vulture or the hyena . . .*

This fear, this sense of a nation cowering, while waiting for
the blow to fall, brings to mind the terrible days and months that
followed Nandi's death. That was a time of spiteful laws and mass
executions. Now the King skulks in his hut once more; and,
although longed for, his reappearance is also dreaded, for now
all know what he's capable of.

Having finished tying the amashoba to the Induna's arms, the
boy who is no longer a boy steps back. He is done.

The Induna thanks him.

'I'll be accompanying you, of course.'

The Induna grins, but shakes his head. Mthunzi will wait here
– and he already knows why. The repercussions that could result
from the Induna chastising men from Mhlangana's regiment will
be bad enough for the Induna and he won't countenance others
risking themselves.

'Besides,' he adds, 'I may yet need rescuing . . .'

The udibi bows his head. 'And I will be ready should the need
arise.'

'Good. Now, let us finish here, so that I can go and seek out
those jackals.'

He dons the civet collar and inserts the tail feather from a blue
crane in his leather headband – these show he is Isithunzi
SikaShaka, the Shadow of Shaka.

He doesn't today have the King's permission, and one may
only wear the blue feather and serve as the King's Shadow in
Shaka's absence. He earlier sought an audience with the Bull
Elephant, only to be turned away and told that waiting will be
futile, as Shaka hasn't seen anyone for days and days. Under

normal circumstances, therefore, for such presumption the Induna would be facing a serious rebuke, or worse.

But these aren't normal circumstances. These are dark days, perilous times.

# 2
## Spear Red To The Haft

Blood! Let blood flow like the Thukela – with the frightening suddenness that gave the river its name. Blood for blood. Blood of vengeance. Blood of retribution. Blood like phlegm choking the world. Assegais in the elephant grass; blood-soaked loam. Bare feet, tougher than rhino hides, on the march; the Bull arisen and on the march; rage on the march. A brown river in flood, carrying along cattle-hide izihlangu – shields – and short stabbing iklwas.

A black bull is slaughtered bare-handed, its meat roasted on green mimosa, treated by the war inyangas and distributed to the men in strips. This is black medicine intended to strengthen them and bind them together like the Inkatha – like the fragments that create isihlangene, the full moon. Then the regiments, the amabutho, were sent forth, their bladeseager to feast.

★

After the assassination attempt, Shaka had at first been dilatory, lingering in his hut, sticking to the isigodlo long after his wound had healed. He scarcely roused himself when his would-be assassin was captured. He didn't even question the man, merely glanced at him and returned to the isigodlo, leaving Mbopa to order the execution.

★

But the river was rising; the drums only Shaka could hear amid his pain were beginning to beat faster and faster . . .

★

Some said the assassin's blade had been doctored with muthi and that the King was now bewitched. Kept pinioned in his hut by evil forces, he was a mere husk, they said. And, when they have finished with him, these same baleful forces would turn on the King's children. So it's only a matter of time before the curse spreads to them all, crippling their cattle, devouring their crops. Not even the sangomas could help, because Shaka's ill-considered culling had left their number too weak.

★

Higher and higher; storms upcountry – as in the King's head – causing the river to swell, and test its banks. Faster, louder, more insistent, the drums helping the King to tame his wound, now focus his mind.

★

Some said Fynn had done the bewitching, while purporting to heal Shaka. He had merely been biding his time, waiting for the right moment, this izilwane – this savage – from across the Great Waters. And, as a result, now Shaka was on his way to becoming the White Man's creature.

★

And then Shaka, King of Kings, left his hut . . .

★

*Blood.* The remnants of the Qwabe tribe had tried to take advantage of the assassination attempt, by sending the King's indunas packing when they came to ask why their tributes were overdue. One ibutho was all it took to send the Qwabes fleeing southwards, along the coast, to crowd up against Faku's Pondoes.

★

*Blood.* The Chunus in the north-west were broken up. It was an easy victory which saw the survivors pushed southward, just like the Qwabes.

★

*Blood*. Shaka pointed his war axe to the north and his amabutho were sent after the Ngwanes. Feigning flight, they tried to ambush the Zulus. A desperate battle ensued, Zulu casualties were high, but the Ngwanes were beaten. Abandoning their cattle to Shaka's forces, they fled over the Drakensberg.

★

After a period of relative peace, an assassin's blade had prompted Shaka to sweep away all the tribes who had refused to join the Zulu kingdom – as far as the Drakensberg in the north and the Mzimkhulu River in the south. However, the great northern war kraal, about two days march from the mountain range, remained the main bastion up there, as the People of the Sky lacked the capacity to maintain a permanent presence in the region. Or in the southern highveld, where the Griquas and other mounted gun-men were becoming a growing problem, even if they were merely in quest of cattle and not looking to occupy Zulu territory.

★

*Blood*. Sikhunyana, another of Zwide's sons, had gathered together an army and was coming to reclaim Ndwandwe territory. Shaka's amabutho caught them in the hills north of the Phongola River. The White Men, and those of their servants versed in the use of firearms, accompanied the regiments and took part in the battle. No quarter was given, and even the women and children who had accompanied Sikhunyana were slaughtered.

★

With the annual First Fruits approaching, it was to be hoped that Shaka's hunger for vengeance had been sated. The Bull was tired now, so let there be peace. Besides, although the campaigns had been successful, the pickings had been slim, as they involved harassing tribes already struggling to survive due to the turmoil Shaka had created elsewhere.

Most of the regiments were duly summoned to KwaBulawayo for the great mustering, and it seemed as if no more blood would flow for a while. Especially as it emerged that Shaka was planning a different kind of campaign in consultation with one of the savages based at Thekwini.

For some reason, even though Fynn had undoubtedly saved his life, Shaka had begun to shun his company, and Fynn – who the Zulus called Mbuyazi – rarely visited Bulawayo these days. It wasn't that the Bull Elephant was angry with him; all would have known if that was the case. But something had clearly happened between them.

On the other hand, Shaka *was* angry with Francis Farewell.

First, the savages continued to harbour criminals and refugees at Thekwini – and, as the unumzane of the settlement, Farewell was the one Shaka held responsible for this transgression. In the past the King had vacillated between lambasting either Farewell or Fynn (who would visit Bulawayo more often) for disobeying his orders or else ignoring the whole matter. But it was said the assassin, when he was tracked down, had been heading for their settlement, clearly expecting protection there. Farewell must learn to stop sheltering crocodiles.

Second, the flow of gifts has petered out, since Farewell's company is now in financial difficulties. Too many ships with cargo holds full of ivory have been sunk in storms on the way to the Cape, putting off potential investors. The settlement at Port Natal has even begun bartering for food, and Shaka has had to resume trade with the Portugiza. Where now were all the exotic commodities and weapons that Farewell had promised him?

Third, when Farewell had had the chance to redeem himself a little in Shaka's eyes – by helping the Bull Elephant defeat Zwide's spawn once and for all – he'd been 'injured' on the march, and conveniently near to an umuzi where he could recuperate in relative comfort.

And suddenly the smooth-talking James King found himself Shaka's favourite. He wasted no time in taking advantage of this unexpected boon, starting with breaking Farewell's monopoly on trade with Shaka. Realising he was 'in disgrace with Fortune', at least in some men's eyes, Farewell reluctantly allowed King to operate independently.

And it was James King who was now busy persuading Shaka to embark upon a campaign of a different sort.

# 3
## Two Nights Ago

'Do you have anything to tell me, Ndlela?' she asks her induna.

'Yes, Ma, it seems as if he and the boy were sent on an errand by Mhlangana.'

'Mhlangana! Doesn't the fool know only Shaka or Mbopa may do that?' asks Mnkabayi.

'Perhaps the prince feels that with things as they are, there's little chance of his impudence reaching the King's ears. Also his servants are saying Mhlangana was extremely anxious about something.'

'Regarding which matter he sent the Nduna to investigate?'

'We can send out messengers to find him and recall him, Ma.'

'No, let my nephew remain unaware that we know of his transgression.'

'A wise strategy, Ma.'

'Aiee, that one,' says Mnkabayi, thinking angrily of her nephew Mhlangana. 'And what of Mbopa,' she continues, 'how fares the old cannibal?'

'I have spoken to the inyanga who's been treating him, Ma, and he says the worst is over. The prime minister will survive.'

'Good,' says Mnkabayi. 'That's as it should be.'

A dutiful pause, then: 'Will there be anything else, Ma?'

'No,' sighs Mnkabayi. 'You may go.'

Infuriating man, thinks this sister of Senzangakhona. Mnkabayi is about fifteen summers older than Ndlela, and they were lovers, once, when he was only a herd boy and she the experienced guide who taught him the warm secrets of a woman's body. But there was something about him, the glimmer of promise, that saw her take an interest in other aspects of his education, as well as his advancement, long after she'd found new cubs to pleasure her. Now their age difference doesn't seem so great, and the induna is her most trusted advisor. They have healed the rift that developed between them as a result of Mnkabayi's action that fateful First Fruits two years ago – the reconciliation taking place without words but merely in a resumption of their interaction – but things still remain somewhat strained.

Infuriating man! I knew you'd have qualms and try to stop us, and so I tried to protect you. Was that a mistake? I'll own up to that. Perhaps I should have told you what was going on, thinks Shaka's aunt.

But, no, the method here was immaterial; it was the effect that mattered!

'And it's the method that angers you, Ndlela,' thinks Mnkabayi. 'But do you honestly think I believed Mhlangana and his pet sangoma would succeed in their demented scheme? of course not! Kholisa was deranged, and had beguiled Mhlangana – and that was what led me to give my tacit consent to their machinations, for it was how things would stand once it was all over that mattered to me.'

That business with the impundulu, the zombie – that was merely the snare. And it had worked, for it had trapped Mhlangana and delivered the prince to her. And while he may dream of the day he gets to sit on the throne and can see her sent to the impalers, he doesn't realise that he too has become an impundulu who will be used to lure a bigger, more important predator.

★

Floating on a fever, Mbopa opens his eyes and sees his mother crouching next to him.

40

*No!*

Grimacing, as the simple movement sets off a fresh series of spasms in his stomach, the chief minister rolls over, stares at the wall of his hut, but sees – and smells – burnt thatch. A smouldering . . . smoke . . . dead cows in the spear grass . . .

They'd even killed the dogs.

*And you, Mother!*

Strange, though, that he should remember seeing smouldering thatch, orange caterpillars atop black stalks – for he had only arrived several days later. By which time the cattle had become carcasses fed upon by scavengers.

And Vakashi, his friend with a homestead nearby, had arranged for the bodies to be buried. He'd also sent the messenger to Bulawayo after the slayers had departed and it was safe to emerge from hiding.

That's what you did in those terrible months following Nandi's death: when the slayers appeared in your district, you fled. They'd arrive late at night to pounce upon those who had been singled out, and all the surrounding homesteads would be deserted before they had finished sating their bloodlust.

Aiee! His stomach! Torrents have flowed from his mouth and arse, leaving his hut smelling of shit and vomit, even though he's lying on a fresh layer of large green leaves which his servants have replaced three times already tonight. But, while that first storm seems to have abated, something remains in his gut. It has claws and is trying to scratch its way out.

His sweaty feet slide against each other, he's having trouble breathing and he's very, very thirsty. The pain is relentless, and there seems to be no position he can lie in that will see it ease.

And these thoughts . . . these thoughts have claws too.

'What of Mzilikazi? Consider Mzilikazi,' he says to Shaka, who's taken his mother's place alongside him.

'Yes, Mzilikazi – the one whose name we dare not mention. Your favourite, remember him?'

Mzilikazi KaMashobane being one of the few survivors of the Khumalo clan which Zwide mauled before coming after Zulu blood, who subsequently brought his people over to the Zulu camp and who proved fearless in battle. Who became Shaka's favourite. Who the King allowed to return to his clan's old territories.

'But he wasn't satisfied, was he? For Mzilikazi wanted to be recognised as a King in his own right. He wanted to be treated as an equal.'

Eventually Shaka couldn't ignore his favourite's grumbling, or his little acts of disobedience, which were likely to give others similar ideas. He sent an ubutho to punish Mzilikazi, but even then . . . Mzilikazi's own brother had betrayed him, offering to show Shaka's men a secret way up onto the plateau where the wayward favourite and his followers had sought refuge. But, even then, Shaka stayed his hand long enough to give Mzilikazi a chance to escape northwards.

'Hai, your actions dismayed some of your advisors, but not me. For it was all the same to me. Yet now I have to say something,' says Mbopa, his eyes on Shaka, who remains conveniently quiet. 'You allow Mzilikazi to go free, while I – who have only ever shown you loyalty – have my family slaughtered. Why?'

And why . . . why does recalling that sweaty night when he seized the assassin's discarded blade, and before he even knew what he was doing . . . Why does that memory bring with it terror, guilt even, when there should be exultation? But guilt! Why guilt?

He knows he owes his life to Shaka. Accused of cannibalism, he'd been sentenced to death, and was saved only when Shaka intervened. Almost immediately Mbopa had been able to show the new King how easily the art of diplomacy came to him, and thus began his ascent to the position of prime minister.

'I owe you my life,' continues Mbopa, 'but is that not a debt I have repaid time and time again? Why kill those who had done you no wrong? Why do this to your most loyal servant?'

Usually, when preparing to put an unpalatable, but necessary, proposal before the King, he rehearses the exchange beforehand – considering what he'll say, what Shaka is likely to reply. But tonight the King remains mute. Mbopa just cannot imagine what the Bull Elephant might have to say to him, or what explanations he'd offer.

Hai, but then again a King doesn't have to explain anything.

Pampata's tried to speak to him already, but Mbopa doesn't know what to make of the royal concubine's sorry attempts to excuse Shaka's actions.

★

She doesn't understand, just doesn't understand.

Knowing he won't be able to sleep, Ndlela has come to watch the izinkomo, the cattle, in Bulawayo's large central isibaya.

They, at least, seem at peace.

Unlike myself, thinks Ndlela watching the quiet izinkomo.

And unlike the others dwelling in these huts: rows upon rows of huts encircling the cattlefold. Look closely and you'll see eyes peering out of the doorways, frightened, anxious. No songs, for even the children are glum, and the dogs no longer bark; they're as silent as the drums and the praise-singers. Aiee, even the praise-singers have fallen silent.

'It's started,' Ndlela whispers.

And she doesn't understand . . . more than that, she won't be able to understand.

*It's started.*

She condoned their actions. That she might not have realised the enormity of what they intended to do is neither here nor there. No matter how long he talks, he won't be able to make her *see*. Won't be able to make her realise that, no matter what she thinks, it's started.

*It's started.*

She'll say Kholisa failed, and she'll think that matters. But it doesn't and, anyway, the sangoma didn't fail. Ndlela's been able to establish that Kholisa did in fact raise an impundulu – a zombie. He can't be sure about what happened next, but suspects the creature had, for some reason, attacked its own creator.

The conspirators then resorted to other means so as to disrupt the First Fruits – but the madness had already infected them and begun to spread.

And this is what Mnkabayi needs to understand. Raising an impundulu is a horrific act that will have dire consequences for all involved. The forces she's now set in motion won't stop with the fall of Shaka. There'll be ripples and reverberations and the way things are will never be the way they should have been, and that which is still to come will never be what it could have been.

★

When Shaka had retreated into madness as a way to mourn his mother Nandi – and began issuing his insane laws – as prime minister Mbopa had quietly, and as far as possible, taken over the day-to-day running of the kingdom. He and the others who remained loyal to Shaka had to do anything to keep things as normal as possible, so as to reassure the people that the

King's sudden hatred of them, his children, was only a temporary malaise.

Of course Mbopa was aware that Shaka knew what he was up to, and saw the King's silence on the matter as a sign that some part of the King was still the King and that part of him realised the need to maintain law and order.

But he had been wrong . . . Or perhaps not totally so. Given the King's irrational state, it was just as likely that Shaka would condone Mbopa's actions the one day, then see treason in his endeavours the next.

Whatever the case, the King decided Mbopa needed to be taught a lesson in not allowing his ambitions to become too rapacious.

Pampata told the prime minister she had begged with Shaka to reconsider. But even she was finding it hard to get through to the King during those days, and her position as his favourite concubine had been far from secure.

She had pleaded with him to reconsider, but Shaka had remained adamant. All the same – and here Pampata became almost frantic, because Mbopa had to believe her, he just had to! – the King had never intended for Mbopa's homestead to be destroyed and his family slaughtered. He had merely ordered his prime minister's cattle to be confiscated.

'And he would have returned them to you,' Pampata had insisted. 'Of that I'm sure.'

★

*What she didn't tell him was how Shaka had sent for her and wept in her arms when he heard what had happened. 'I who have lost my mother know how he feels, and how will he ever forgive me?' he had said.*

★

Mbopa writhes and rubs his feet together, and addresses Shaka once more: 'I do not doubt your beloved was speaking the truth. But, wise as she is — and I have noticed that, of late, you have begun to ignore her again, and that's not a good sign . . .'

Where was he? (His stomach! His poor stomach! It's as if he's swallowed handful after handful of long Devil's thorns.)

Ah, yes . . . 'Wise as she is, and persistent as she is in her efforts to seek my forgiveness on your behalf, Pampata doesn't understand that some things should never happen. They should never be allowed to happen. And if they do . . . aiee!'

# 4
## Spirits Of The Living Dead

The thing is, old cucumber, King tells Shaka through the interpreter he's brought with him from the Cape, you're quite right to be disgruntled with Farewell. At the end of the day, he's a businessman, a trader. At the end of the day, Your Highness, profit is all that matters to him. Simply profit. That means he wants more from you than he's willing to give.

Also, and I'm sorry to have to be the one to break this to you, continues King, but Francis has no official standing, none whatsoever. King Jorgi? He knows nothing about this.

If Shaka wants to open up a dialogue with King Jorgi, he needs to make contact with one of King Jorgi's official representatives. And the head pasha, the top nawab in these parts, is the Governor of the Cape.

★

And so King gets Shaka to sanction a diplomatic mission to Cape Town. In February 1828, a document is drawn up by King and signed by Shaka. It reassures King George IV of Shaka's friendship and suggests a treaty be negotiated between the Zulus and the British. Representing Shaka will be Sothobe KaMpangalala. He's a giant of a man, almost the size of Njikiza, who wears his isicoco on the back of his head. He is, of course, accompanied by a retinue of retainers. But, says the document, Shaka's 'friend James Saunders King' is actually in charge of the undertaking.

The mission leaves at the end of April on the *Elizabeth Susan*, a ship the traders have built at Port Natal and named after Farewell's wife and King's mother. The weather is bad for most of the voyage to Port Elizabeth, and Sothobe and King are among the few passengers who aren't seasick. Zulu praise-singers will celebrate the former's bravery in sailing 'the uncrossable sea, which is crossed only by swallows and white people'.

A short while later, Shaka sends his army against Faku's Pondoes.

★

It's an action which confuses Mbopa and the King's other advisors. In going after Faku, Shaka is in effect sending his amabutho towards the Cape frontier; so how does this square with his assurances of goodwill to Britain? Why does he seem to want to undermine his own diplomatic mission?

★

Four days after leaving Port Natal, the *ElizabethSusan* arrives at Port Elizabeth (formerly known as Algoa Bay). King immediately sends word to Cape Town that the Zulus are coming. The response is for him to remain there for the time being, with Sothobe and his party being entertained at government expense until arrangements can be made to convey them to the Cape. As it happens, that's as far as they will get, for King's dubious charms appear to have no effect on the local authorities.

Quite the opposite: he's raised their hackles and their suspicions.

It also doesn't help that just a few years earlier, while trying to raise funds for an expedition to go and 'rescue' Farewell, Fynn and the other White Men at Port Natal (and thus to start trading with the Zulus himself), King had exaggerated Shaka's 'barbaric' nature and the threat he represented to the Cape Colony's eastward expansion.

Consequently, one day while King's away, Major Josias Cloete, the commanding officer of the Port Elizabeth garrison, settles down to have a chat with Sothobe, using one of his own interpreters. The chat soon becomes an interrogation, and Sothobe – who's been well treated until now, having been fêted and taken on tours of the burgeoning port city and shown all manner of desirable goods – suddenly feels like a prisoner of war.

Can Sothobe produce anything to prove he was actually sent by Shaka?

They are here with Lieutenant King, isn't that enough? It is their custom to send cattle as a gift, but there was no room in the ship's hold, explains Sothobe. But there is still the ivory tusk Shaka gave them for that purpose.

Seeming satisfied on that score, Major Cloete asks Sothobe what Shaka's intentions are? What does he expect from this mission? What does he want from the Crown?

Sothobe's answers are vague. It could be that he's confused by this sudden change in attitude on the part of his hosts, or because he really doesn't know – as it's King who will be doing the negotiating when they reach Cape Town, with Sothobe and his retinue there merely to prove that King has Shaka's ear.

That this might be the case is evident when Sothobe steadfastly refuses Major Cloete's suggestion that he and the other Zulus proceed on to Cape Town without King.

King himself is furious when he learns that the Zulu has been interrogated behind his back. He claims it's an insult to him as a British subject, and a pathetic display of 'petty authority'.

For their part, Major Cloete and various officials at the Colonial Office wonder – if the delegation is here to reach an understanding with Britain, and if its aims are as innocuous as King claims – why King is so pissed off about the major having had a 'private' chat with Sothobe . . .

Meanwhile, Shaka's regiments are rampaging along the coast. He isn't with them, though, for he's established his base of operations about 130km away from Port Natal, on the bank of the Umzimkhulu River, where Fynn has built a kraal. Fynn himself is there, as is Jakot. In fact, the former is serving as a hostage to ensure the safe return of Sothobe and the other Zulus, although he's hardly being treated as such.

The army is now split into two, with the one wing moving inland to deal with the tribes there, while the other continues along the coast. It has become total warfare, as Shaka seems to show no interest in gaining more vassals.

He will not play with them, as the White Men have done at the Cape, yes – even as these crocodiles have continued to defy the British by stealing their cattle and killing farmers. Instead, the tribes will be obliterated, made to vanish. And Shaka urges his amabutho onward, ever onward, with further plundering, burning and killing.

★

And, in early June, word duly reaches the Cape that the Zulu King is heading their way in person. Panic ensues, whereupon all available forces are mobilised and the frontier posts manned. Meanwhile, a small contingent under Major Dundas is ordered into the tribal lands beyond the frontier, to see what the situation is like.

Dundas eventually tracks down Faku, who tells him the Zulu regiments are accompanied by armed White Men. After leaving Faku, Dundas and his men attack a group of warriors in the vicinity of the Umtata River, believing them to be Zulus. They're not, but instead the remnants of one of the tribes Shaka's men have all but destroyed. Though outnumbered,

Dundas manages to chase them from the area. He then returns to Simonstown.

In the interim, Major-General Richard Bourke, the Lieutenant-Governor of the Cape, has ordered the HMS *Helicon* to take King and Sothobe's party back to Port Natal. The *Elizabeth Susan* follows a few days later.

★

The reason why Dundas can't find any Zulus is because Shaka has suddenly ordered their withdrawal and he has retired to the war kraal that protects the kingdom's southern reaches, to await them there. When the advance parties arrive, they are jubilant, for they deem the campaign to have been a success, having captured many cattle. Shaka has these men beaten with sticks.

When the regiments arrive, he refuses to allow them to undergo the cleansing ceremony. Angrily, he berates them as cowards, and says the only way they can redeem themselves is to march immediately against Soshangane KaZikode, who has established himself along the Olifants River, to the north-west of Delagoa.

The men and their officers are aghast, because that's a long way off. Are they not to be allowed to return home and rest a while? But there's no going against Shaka's orders. Wearily, resentfully, they set off again.

Shaka sends messengers carrying orders for two more regiments to reinforce them. Dingane and Mhlangana are to accompany these, he adds.

★

King returns to face Farewell's enmity, for he's now destroyed all the hard work Farewell has done to maintain good relations with Shaka, and to keep alive interest in the settlement among investors in Cape Town. As the final twist of the knife, King opens the sealed case General Bourke has sent to Shaka, hoping its contents might help ameliorate Shaka's anger – only to find it contains a few sheets of copper, some cheap knives and a piece of scarlet broadcloth.

Sothobe returns to advise Shaka to have nothing more to do with the White Men, whose King is much inferior to himself. In addition, he says, James King is not even trusted by his own people.

'See these paltry gifts, Father,' he goads an enraged Shaka. They are so inferior because they were unpacked at Port Natal, where King took the best things for himself.

Shaka examines the case, then tosses the contents on the floor. No one present can remember when last they saw him so angry. Even Sothobe fears for his life and everyone agrees it's just as well that King has been taken ill and can't leave Port Natal (where Fynn has diagnosed pleurisy).

★

And now, as the month of June reaches its end, the regiments are returning. Or at least the remnants of them, drifting back in ones and twos.

The amabutho are being eaten, whisper these ghosts of the living dead.

All those regiments, their war songs have become screams.

They've defeated the tribes they've come across, but these have been mere skirmishes. The real enemy – the fetid swamps, the disease – has cut them down.

The Bull is stuck.

The Bull is dying.

And Shaka does nothing.

Instead he hides in the darkness of his hut.

Hai, he has been there so long that he and the darkness have become one.

★

*See these paltry gifts, Father!*

His hands trembling, cold fire in his veins, burning ice behind his eyes, he examines the contents of the case, then tosses them away.

The thing is, Shaka doesn't care about the copper and other trinkets, but King has forgotten the one thing he's specifically asked him for – a bottle of the macassar oil that Farewell once told him about, which apparently removes the grey from one's hair.

# 5

# The Confrontation

'Eshé, ndoda!'

'Eshé,' grunts the Induna.

A faint smile playing across his lips to show he's noted the insult implied by the Induna's truncated greeting, Nolaka allows his gaze to rest on the warrior's civet collar and the blue feather.

'To what do we owe this pleasure?' he asks.

'Is it true your generals are elsewhere, and you command this contingent?'

That is so: the generals are back at the prince's home kraal, along with the bulk of the regiment, says Nolaka, the Leopard Man, so named because he once caught a leopard singlehandedly and presented it to Mhlangana so that the prince could use its pelt.

From the corners of his eyes the Induna sees how two, three, then five men have drifted over to form the beginnings of a circle around him. Some are carrying spears.

'I would ask you a question,' he says.

Nolaka parts his hands. 'Ask, Shadow of Shaka!'

'Do you know the penalty for stealing cattle?'

Not bothering to feign perplexity as to why the Induna should be asking such a question, the Leopard Man grins and says: 'I do, and it's not pleasant!'

The Induna doesn't even need to look to know that more men have moved up behind him, to complete the circle.

'Why then,' he says, 'did you allow your men to do that very thing on the way to Bulawayo?'

Nolaka's face hardens. One or two of the warriors surrounding the Induna hiss.

'What nonsense is this?' asks the Leopard Man, taking a step closer. This is a regiment, which has proved itself in campaign after campaign, how dare the Induna cast aspersions on their honour!

The Induna refrains from pointing out that claiming distinguished service in battle when this is an exaggeration bordering on outright falsehood is scarcely honourable. Instead, adopting a tone of mild inquiry, he asks if this means Nolaka denies having taken Zulu cattle from Zulu stockmen in umuzis situated outside of the prince's own assigned territory.

Nolaka's laugh is a dismissive bark. 'Of course, I don't!' But it wasn't a matter of 'taking' or – he sniggers – of 'stealing'.

'Then how would you describe this transgression of the King's law?'

'The King . . .' A soft sneer. 'No, not the King.' A softer murmur. 'Not this King, but,' says Nolaka, raising his voice, 'orders. We were following orders, Nduna.'

'Who issued these orders?'

Nolaka scratches his left elbow, his fingers continuing upwards to scrape the stubble on his chin.

'No,' he says at last, then stretches and yawns. 'No, I don't think so.'

Meeting the Induna's angry glare, he adds: 'I don't think you need to know that, Nduna. To quench this unwarranted curiosity of yours, it should suffice for you simply to know that orders were given, and orders were obeyed.'

'Who issued the orders?' repeats the Induna, knowing that only Shaka himself can issue instructions for his men to requisition cattle from Zulu stockmen.

The Leopard looks to his left, then to his right, as if appealing to his comrades to bear witness to this display of obtuseness.

'Answer my question,' says the Induna, tapping the blade of his iklwa against his knee.

'Hai, first tell me this. Has the Bull Elephant left Bulawayo?'

Knowing where this is heading, the Induna answers only with a scowl.

'No, I didn't think so,' continues Nolaka. 'That being the case, you tell me the penalty for appearing as the Shadow of Shaka, claiming to speak and act with the King's authority when, in fact, the King is still present here, and able to speak and act on his own behalf.'

Raising his left haunch slightly, Nolaka launches a long fart. He pushes his fingers through his ibeshu and raises them to his nose.

'Ahh,' he says, 'I am fragrant today.'

'Who gave the orders?' demands the Induna once more.

'Hai, Shade of Shaka, now you begin to try my patience' – Nolaka glances at his grinning men – 'and to test our hospitality.'

'Would you add treason to your theft of cattle?'

'And now you begin to insult us! Come, come, Nduna, you should know how dangerous it is to come into a man's kraal and insult him.'

The Leopard takes another step toward the Induna, his eyes hardening like the tips of assegai blades. 'And you should also know this is not *your* regiment. You should know you cannot come here and issue commands to us, or ask impertinent questions. You should know, Nduna, that you have no authority here!'

'But *I* do!'

Startled, Nolaka looks past the Induna, who turns to see Mbopa pushing his way through the gathered warriors. The prime minister clearly hasn't fully recovered from his illness, for sweat speckles his brow and he's moving gingerly, almost shuffling, and leaning on an iwisa, a stout walking stick with a large rounded head that also makes for a good weapon. But his ability to brandish his authority remains undimmed.

'I have the authority!' he declares. 'And I tell you, Nolaka, and these tittering maidens you dare call warriors, that you will pack your belongings and be ready to depart before the sun reaches its zenith.'

The prime minister goes on to inform them that they will return to their own district, fetch izinkomo from their own herds, deliver the animals to the villages they have taken cattle from. Then they must make haste to the war kraal that lies on the border with the Xhosas, where a certain 'necessity' has arisen that requires their presence.

'But the prince—' interjects Nolaka.

'Dare you challenge me? Or perhaps you would like to spread out your concerns before the King. That can be arranged.'

'No, Master!' says Nolaka. 'It's not that.'

'What is it, then?' inquires Mbopa.

The Induna watches as the Leopard flounders, his eyes darting here and there, his teeth burying themselves in his lower lip. 'This, uh, necessity you speak of – are we not to know what it is?' he finally asks.

'But of course,' says the prime minister. 'The necessity here is that of ensuring that you and your comrades remain on your hindlegs for a little longer. That can only be achieved if you get out of my sight, and then stay out of my sight until my cows grow pizzles!'

His swagger obliterated, Nolaka stands there like a leopard slowly coming to the conclusion that swallowing the springbok's horns may not have been such a good idea after all.

'Nolaka?' says Mbopa, moving up alongside the Induna.

Swallowing the rest of the animal, meaning the squishy stuff, yes, but the horns, no.

'*Nolaka!*'

'Yes, Master?'

'You are still here. Why are you still here?'

★

'Stealing cattle! I couldn't believe my ears,' says Mbopa after they have left the regiment's lines.

'And I . . . I couldn't believe my good fortune when I heard your voice,' says the Induna with a chuckle. 'And for that I thank you, Master.'

'Think nothing of it! If anything you have Mthunzi to thank,' says the prime minister. He had come looking for the Induna and found his former udibi instead, who told him what had happened – and where the Induna had gone.

'I would have come to consult you first, Master, but I heard you were ill. And the King . . .' The Induna lets these awkward words fade away.

'The King is indisposed, and one now gets the impression that it's an illness that induces symptoms of desertion in others.' Mbopa immediately pats the Induna's forearm, grinning ruefully at the younger man's startled expression.

'But do not listen to me! My stomach still pains me and I appear to have acquired an old man's legs. However, I must ask you to say nothing more about this incident.'

The Induna nods, for the people cannot know that Shaka's laws are being broken by the princes – or by one of them, at least.

'Yes,' murmurs Mbopa as they continue walking, 'let us say nothing of this, until we find a way of dealing with the prince.'

Hai, interjects the Induna, but there's always a chance Shaka may have found out on his own, as is his knack.

'As he demonstrated to me this morning,' says Mbopa, grinning tiredly. 'Yes, you heard right. I had an audience with the King.'

The Induna waits for the prime minister to elaborate. Is the King well? Does he look healthy? What was his mood?

Instead, Mbopa says: 'Something is vexing him, and he requires your services.'

'Yes, you said you wanted to speak to me, Master,' replies the Induna, struggling to accommodate Mbopa's slower pace.

★

Quite how Shaka got to hear about it is a mystery. Certainly it's not the first time he's surprised a member of his inner circle with information seemingly plucked from the air. But on such occasions he hadn't been spending most of his time merely skulking in his hut and refusing to see anyone.

Whatever the source, Shaka has received word that imikhumbi wokuthwala – slavers – are operating inland to the north-east, close to Zulu territory. The Induna is to take some men and go and kill them.

'You are to leave as soon as possible,' adds Mbopa.

# INTERLUDE
## The Man Who Would Be Prester John

*He knows they'll be coming for him soon.*

*Day and night have become meaningless. All he knows now is Before, During and After. And he knows that Before is about to begin.*

*He also knows this: the room he lies in is circular, with a thatched roof rising high above him. It captures the darkness and holds it over him like a threat. The wall is lined with beaten copper that shimmers in the light of the blazing torches.*

*If he lets his left hand drop off the side of the bed, it will encounter the wide mouth of a large clay pot. If he thrusts his hand inside, it will be submerged in diamonds.*

*Diamonds of all shapes and sizes. Diamonds still embedded in crusty kimberlite. Blue-ground diamonds wrenched from deep within the earth. Diamonds plucked from rivers. Small diamonds, large diamonds, diamonds that will make a rajah weep with envy. Yellow diamonds. Brown diamonds. Blue, green, orange and purple diamonds. Black diamonds.*

*If he lets his right hand drop off the other side of the bed, it finds itself amid a cornucopia of rubies, emeralds, bloodstones, red, yellow and blue jasper, chunks of onyx the colour of fingernails, jagged amethysts; some blue stones he reckons might be garnets, because they resemble pomegranate seeds, but can't be because they're blue; and a whole lot of other precious stones that even one such as he, who has roamed far and wide in search of wealth, can't identify, but which he assumes are valuable simply because they've given them to him.*

*In the next pot along there are gold bracelets and necklaces; ankhs and crosses; crowns and diadems; lapis lazuli amulets, scarabs and elephants; as well as darics and sigloi, drachmas anddinars, sestertii and aurei, and* a profusion of other coins bearing the heads of the gods and emperors of forgotten dynasties, whose only remnants are now galleys rotting on the seabed, or armoured skeletons in a cave, blocks of stone buried beneath the shifting sands.

He calls out to the darkness above him, to the barred door beyond the foot of the bed:

> Brave Benbow!
> Brave Benbow!
> Lost his legs by chain shot,
> By chain shot!

Let them know he's waiting for them!

> Brave Benbow lost his legs by chain shot!
> Lost his legs, lost his legs,
> But on his stumps he begs,
> On his stumps he begs:
> 'Fight on, my English lads, fight on,
> For 'tis our lot,
> 'Tis our lot!'

Far and wide he's travelled, from the Leeward Islands to Ceylon, from Cape Town to Rajputana, from Trinidad to Calcutta. He's tilled fields, whipped slaves, drilled native levees, roamed those 'burning zones'. He's speculated and peculated, run guns and rum, conned and swanned his way through salons and cesspits. He's fled the ire of an Ashanti chieftain and escaped many a town just one step ahead of the authorities. He's stabbed to death a pimp who tried to rob him in Kingston – and cut up the fellow's drab for good measure. He's strangled a man on the road through Peshawar, because they were both trapped in a hut for days while a blizzard raged outside and the mountains wailed, and it was cold, so cold, and the fellow had possessed a better coat than he did.

Far and wide he's travelled. Far and wide. ('Tis our lot! 'Tis our lot!) *And see where his travails have delivered him!*

He's rich now! Richer than Prester John. Richer than Croesus.

'Didn't I tell you?' he asks the shapes who come to stand around him – old travelling companions, partners-in-crime, with avaricious eyes set in granite faces. They are bearded, pockmarked, scarred and – in the case of Ben Snood who contracted leprosy and died on Saint Kitts – even noseless.

'Didn't I tell you? I told you, didn't I?'

Gold, silver, diamonds, jewels . . . He always knew, always knew, how this would be his lot!

And he knows this, too: he knows the room is circular, knows the time of day before it is upon him, also knows there's nothing he can do about it, knows he can't reach the torches, or move far from the bed, for he wears a steel collar and a chain disappears up into the darkness above him, trapping him here in the midst of all his treasure.

'Farewell and adieu to you!' he bellows . . .


Farewell and adieu to you, ladies of Spain;
  For we've received orders to sail for old England,
  To sail for old England!


He knows they'll be coming for him soon, because the effects are now waning of the thick, greasy lotion they rub down there whenever they bring him back here – and his prick is starting to feel as if someone's hammering nails into it.

And it will get worse.

Much worse.

# 6
## A Conversation With Dingane

INDUNA: I am pleased to see your ankle is better!

DINGANE: Yes, the rest suggested by my nyanga did wonders for it but, alas, he has no muthi to cure my disappointment.

INDUNA: At missing the chance to lead our brave men into battle against Soshangane?

DINGANE: As well as sharing the many diseases they must face. Let us not forget those, Nduna!

INDUNA: No, we mustn't, and I'm sure our men won't.

DINGANE: And my disappointment at not being able to follow my brother's orders to go and die in some swamp up there, that haunts me. It haunts me, Nduna!

INDUNA: And might one presume such disappointment haunts your brother as well, for he was taken ill on the road, was he not?

DINGANE: So he was! But who can say, with Mhlangana, when it comes to his feelings!

INDUNA: Nonetheless, I'm sure there must have been some disappointment.

DINGANE [*chuckling*]: Yes, perhaps at not having the forethought to get injured *before* joining the march and eating up all that distance.

INDUNA: But you hailed me, Brother. Is there something you wish to discuss?

DINGANE: You have recently spoken with Mbopa. He is well?

INDUNA: Let us say he is better.

DINGANE: Ah! And did he share any suspicions he might have as to who tried to poison him?

INDUNA: No, why should he?

DINGANE: Come now, Nduna, this is no time for false modesty. It's precisely in matters like this that you have proven so invaluable to my brother the King, and to Mbopa.

INDUNA: Hai, but we had important things to discuss.

DINGANE: More important than the old cannibal's well-being and the fact that someone tried to poison him? [*Holding up a hand*] I see your point, however. Perhaps Mbopa meant to raise the topic but was distracted by these other important matters. But, then again, being poisoned is not something one can simply forget, is it? Always assuming, of course, he was in fact poisoned.

INDUNA: There is some doubt?

DINGANE: Well, this is why I wanted to talk to you, old friend. We have been thrown together many times, and I have watched your ways, and listened and learnt from you. And looking at this . . . this poisoning through your eyes, it has me scratching my head.

INDUNA: How so?

DINGANE: You have often spoken of Sky Knowledge – of knowing without knowing how you know – whereas in Earth Knowledge the truths are tangible, yes? You can hold them, feel them. Yet here I find myself caught between the earth and the sky. There's the porridge Mbopa had been eating. There's the dead birds. Yet the sky . . . the sky is asking me why. Or rather, it's asking me to ask why!

INDUNA: Aiee, old friend, this mist is too thick – you have now lost me.

DINGANE: I am sorry! But the mist envelops me too. Sometimes it's all clear – and the implications are frightening – but at other times I'm left thinking, 'You have been at Bulawayo too long. You're seeing things that aren't there.' And, Nduna, you have to admit there are many people here who are *seeing* things. Who have become *adept* at seeing things! Could it be that some now want others to see things, too?

INDUNA: I'm listening . . .

★

They'll be leaving at first light tomorrow, and there will be six of them. Aside from the Induna, Njikiza and Mthunzi there'll be Phepho (whose name means Tornado), Namasu (the Resourceful) and Sola (the Grumbler).

Phepho and Mthunzi collect – and parcel out – the provisions they'll be taking with them, while Namasu and Sola see to their weapons and shields.

Njikiza, meanwhile, questions the messengers who brought news of the slavers to Shaka, identifying landmarks and rivers and so reducing the area that needs to be searched. Fortunately, it seems as if the slavers are few in number and do not stray far from the camp where they keep their merchandise until it's time to return to the coast. This means they are always split in two, with some of their number being required to guard the captives.

They're also searching for gold, and so have wandered some way from the territory of the tribes who normally protect them and sell them slaves, who are invariably members of other nations they have defeated in battle. And their pickings have been slim on both accounts. The rivers they've squatted by to pick through wet gravel haven't given them the strange yellow substance that these and other foreign savages lust after, while they've had to rely on waylaying travellers or falling upon small settlements in order to acquire slaves.

★

DINGANE [*running a hand over his face*]: Let me tell you what happened, or what they say happened. [*Looking at his companion*] Do you not know any of the details?

INDUNA: No, but do not interrupt yourself, old friend. Just tell me what you know and what you think you know.

DINGANE: It's soon told. Mbopa eats his porridge, and has a bull goring at his gut before he's even finished. His cook goes looking for an nyanga, but first he meets Ndlela – who's on his way to see Mbopa. Ndlela sends the cook off to fetch his own nyanga, while he himself goes to see what he can do for Mbopa. There follows a lot of shitting and vomiting and, after the nyanga has arrived and has given Mbopa some muthi, there is more shitting and vomiting. While this is going on, Ndlela retrieves the bowl of porridge, and makes sure the pot it was served from is also preserved. These are not to be emptied, he instructs, and sends one of Mbopa's other servants to fetch some of his men, who will watch over the pots – and Mbopa – until the morrow.

INDUNA: This you know, because . . . ?

DINGANE: I have spoken to the cook, who was afraid he'd be suspected of trying to poison his master. Which is highly unlikely, by the way. It is true that Ndlela had him taken into custody, but one of the first things Mbopa did when he began to rally was insist the cook be freed. So even the old cannibal doubts his man was involved.

INDUNA: He might be wrong. After all, this is how men come to be poisoned, through trusting those around them too much. Years of obedient service blinds them to the possibility.

DINGANE: Agreed, but let's leave the cook in the clear for now. I also spoke to Mbopa's servants, and to one of Ndlela's men who stood guard over our prime minister that first night.

INDUNA: And something bothers you?

DINGANE: Indeed. For I find myself wondering why Ndlela happened along at that very moment.

INDUNA: Perhaps he had something to discuss with Mbopa.

DINGANE: And, given the time – which is when men can expect to fill their stomachs without rude interruption, safe in the knowledge all the day's tasks are done – his mission would have to have been urgent, agreed?

INDUNA: I'm listening.

DINGANE: Then why did this urgent matter vanish with the discovery of Mbopa's illness? If the matter was *that* urgent, if something was genuinely wrong, surely we would have heard about it by now. [*Holding up a hand*] Hai, and don't tell me this was two friends getting together to share some snuff and beer! Mbopa and Ndlela gossiping and laughing together? I think not.

INDUNA: Aiee, you are right there!

DINGANE: And why . . . tell me this, why was it Ndlela's first reaction that Mbopa had been poisoned? Why was *that* the first thing he thought? And, whereas anyone else would have wanted to escape the stench, he was seeing to it that the remains of the meal were kept safe.

INDUNA: You mentioned birds? Am I to take it that pellets of porridge were left out for the birds the next day?

DINGANE: Yes, and one of those birds was found dead a short while later.

INDUNA: So . . . ?

DINGANE: Ndlela was right. There *was* poison!

INDUNA: He is wise . . .

DINGANE: This is so, old friend. And so the mist begins to close around me, and I start to think I'm seeing things that aren't there. Preserving the tainted food so that there can be no doubt — that's just the thing Ndlela *would* do. It's one of the things that make him Ndlela!

INDUNA: But then you wonder *why*?

DINGANE: Why did he happen to be nearby just at that moment? Why was poison his first thought? Why didn't he assume the old cannibal had merely been over-indulging? *Why?* And why . . . and I keep coming back to this, Nduna: *why* was he there?

INDUNA: I have another *why* for you, Brother . . .

DINGANE [*grinning*]: Now it is I who must confess he is listening.

INDUNA: Why does this torment you?

DINGANE: Maybe it's because I've been stuck here too long while waiting for my brother to awaken from his stupor. Will he emerge from his hut and become our King again? Or will this be just another day of sucking our teeth impatiently. Hai, and if he *does* emerge, maybe he's been plotting our punishment . . . and now it's time for the pain to begin. All the waiting. All the watching. And I'm not telling you something you don't already know when I say Shaka's not the only brother who needs keeping an eye on. Mhlangana also needs watching. And he has become very smug of late. But what has he to be smug about? Aiee!

INDUNA: Easy, old friend, easy. You are right about one thing, at least — you *have* been stuck here for too long. So come with us! We go to kill some slavers! That will settle your mind, for killing has that effect. Other things become insignificant. The moon becomes brighter. Life tastes a little sweeter.

★

Dingane laughs in a way he hasn't laughed for a long while, and thanks the Induna for his offer. But, while the prospect of once more risking his life in the service of Shaka is certainly enticing, as he admits, he had better remain here at Bulawayo.

Because, he tells himself as he walks away from his friend's hut, there might be mist, there might be uncertainty, but he might also be right.

For there might be more to this poisoning business than meets the eye.

'Hai, think about what you're considering, mfowethu!' Dingane tells himself. 'Things have come to a pretty pass when a poisoning isn't strange enough in and of itself!'

But there you go – that's just another reason why he needs to stay and watch and listen.

After all, his own life might be in danger. If there's something underhand going on, if a plot is coming to fruition, he hasn't yet been told about it – and that means he's likely to become one of the victims.

# 7
## Telling Tales

Broad-leaved aloes and lala-palms are scattered amid the thatch grass on the slopes. Slabs of rock define the summit, making access difficult except towards the south, where a path makes its way through a breach in the rampart. Dotted here and there are low bushes long ago tamed by the wind, and the skeletal remains of trees, one with its trunk singed and nearly split in two by lightning.

Looking north, you can see KwaBulawayo's huts like upturned bowls encircling the cattlefold; with threads of smoke hanging from the pewter sky. Here at their vantage point, only a few paces in from the rocks, lies an isiguqo, a circle of stones where one can come and kneel and commune with the Great Spirit.

Mnkabayi is standing at this circle when Mbopa approaches her.

When he calls out a greeting she turns, nods and asks him if he is well.

The prime minister shrugs and steps off the path to allow Mnkabayi to pass. He is well, he says, deciding it's everyone asking after his health that's likely to precipitate a relapse. (It's the eagerness in their voices that gets him, for it's not his state of health they're interested in. They're merely hungry to know what happened, and seem to expect a full and vituperative account from the victim.)

A few steps later, Mnkabayi wheels round to face him.

'Aiee, Mbopa, I do not understand you!'

The prime minister bows his head. 'Perhaps that's because there's really very little to understand, Ma.'

Her right arm rises, palm upward. 'There! That's exactly what I'm talking about.'

'Now I'm the one who does not understand, Ma.'

'This obsequiousness! With all that's going on, you still play these games with me, I do not know why. Your motives remain obscure as ever.'

Mbopa lowers his head once more. 'I thank you.'

'For what?'

'The compliment.'

'Do not try my patience! It's bad enough that you've been avoiding me.' Her right arm comes up again, the palm facing Mbopa this time. 'And do not echo me and question "avoiding me", as if you don't know what I'm talking about.'

'But, Ma, I was *not* avoiding you! I was merely attending to affairs of state. What with the King indisposed, and I myself being ill, and with all the rest that's going on . . . well, there's been a lot to do.'

'Then tell me, did one of these tasks involve despatching runners to call our men back?'

Mbopa shakes his head. He doesn't have the authority to do that, as she well knows . . .

'I merely thought, with the King indisposed, as you put it . . .'

'There's the thing,' interjects Mbopa, explaining it is merely his opinion that the King is indisposed. For Shaka may simply have retreated to consider where next to send his army.

Mnkabayi regards him with narrowed eyes. 'That is a frightening thought.'

'I'm afraid I don't . . .'

'Because if proper consideration preceded this current campaign, then truly the King has gone . . . well, is not himself.'

A neutral expression, as bland as the White Men's tobacco, is Mbopa's response to this.

'Don't think I mean to impugn my nephew's abilities,' adds Mnkabayi.

'No,' says Mbopa, allowing his eyes to meet hers, 'you are merely concerned about his well-being.'

'That is so,' agrees Mnkabayi. 'And I'm also concerned about your own well-being.'

'Rest assured, I am well.'

'Hai, perhaps I should have said your *continued* well-being.' She turns, gesturing at some rocks nearby. 'Come, let us sit. After all, neither of us is getting any younger!'

'I find that hard to believe when one is looking at you, Ma.'

Stifling the urge to rebuke him once more, Mnkabayi makes her way over to the rocks.

'Where were we?' she asks, after getting herself settled, facing Mbopa.

'The King—'

Mnkabayi leans forward to wag a finger in Mbopa's face. 'Oh no – we were talking of your well-being.'

'Ah yes,' says Mbopa dutifully. 'My well-being. Specifically, my *continued* well-being.'

'Doesn't it worry you that someone tried to poison you?'

'But they clearly didn't, Ma, for here I now sit!'

'You know what I mean. You *were* poisoned, of that we can be certain.'

'Thanks to Ndlela.'

A raised eyebrow.

'His foresight, I mean,' adds Mbopa, 'in preserving the porridge.'

Silence descends while the prime minister examines his toes

and Mnkabayi examines him, like a mother debating whether or not to slap her child.

Village weavers soar overhead, spots of yellow against the blue sky. From somewhere nearby comes the cackle of the green wood-hoopoe, called Nhlekabafazi by the Zulus because the bird sounds like an old woman. A breeze rustles the threadbare grass.

Mnkabayi sighs. 'Come now, Mbopa! Exchanging sweet nothings is a luxury we can no longer afford. You know it and I know it: my nephew is acting as bad as he was in the months following Nandi's death. So far, the only thing that's different is he has yet to unleash his rage. And all that says to me is that, when it comes, we will see horrors far worse than those he visited on his children back then.'

Tilting her head, she lowers her voice: 'And, back then, who was the one who sought to ensure the kingdom endured? It was ever loyal Mbopa!'

Mnkabayi pauses, waiting for a response. When none is forthcoming, she continues, keeping her voice soft and soothing: 'And how did the King repay this loyalty?'

Now she pauses to give Mbopa a chance to remember . . . He only saw the aftermath, but she's sure he can imagine the huts burning, hear the screams, see his mother dragged out into the long grass.

Let him dwell on this betrayal, on the spite involved in a son, grieving for his own dead mother, ordering the slaughter of his most trusted and most loyal advisor's mother.

She waits, watches the hoopoe rise up and turn its long curved red bill in the direction of Bulawayo. She thinks of Ndlela standing guard at the foot of the path that leads up here. Cha! Shaka's not the only one to misuse a trusted advisor!

'And now?' she asks. 'The King . . . the King goes away again, and once more loyal Mbopa steps forward. But why should your reward be any different this time round? Hai! On seeing you remain unchastened, even after the great injustice he visited upon you, the King might even choose to go further and . . .'

'Poison me?'

She shrugs, as if to suggest, *You're the one who said it, not me.*

'We are, of course, merely musing aloud, fabricating tales,' declares Mbopa, with a grin.

'This is so,' agrees Mnkabayi.

'But neither are we wasting words,' adds Mbopa.

'This is so.'

'For that is a luxury we can no longer afford.'

'Do you mock me now?'

'No, never, Ma,' says Mbopa contriving to look shocked at her suggestion.

'For, even if you are, you speak the truth.' The mere fact that the bulk of the Zulu army is now dying in disease-infested swamps, leaving the nation vulnerable, should tell him that, adds Mnkabayi.

'And do not say we don't have any enemies left,' she continues, 'for we will always have enemies.'

'I do not dispute that, Ma. Far from it, I see enemies wherever I look.'

'Precisely,' says Mhlangana, 'and I am here to warn you.'

'Warn me?'

'Yes. What would you say if I told you that Ndlela saw Pampata near your hut?'

'Pampata? When?'

'At about the time your cook was preparing your meal.'

'Which is to say *that* meal.'

Mnkabayi inclines her head.

'And Ndlela saw her?'

'So he says.'

'Pampata?'

'Yes, Pampata, who we know lives only to do the King's bidding. What do you say to that?'

'I would laugh, Ma, and say no.'

'No?'

'No. For, as I was about to say . . . since we are here to tell tales, swap stories, let me tell you *my* story. Let me tell you what *I* think transpired.'

Mnkabayi's response is the indulgent *please-yourself* shrug of one smug in the knowledge that there is – and can be – no other side to this tale.

Mbopa pauses a moment, then says: 'Mhlangana.'

The merest twitch of her lips is evident and, smiling to himself, the prime minister mentally compliments her on her self-control.

'Whether he meant to kill me or not, I don't know. Doubtless, news of my demise would have brought joy to his ears, but he could have intended to guide me down the same path as you would, and have me believe the King wants to see me gone for good.'

The prime minister scratches his chin, enjoying the emotions flickering across Mnkabayi's face, and her struggle to suppress them.

'Are you well, Ma?'

'What? Yes, of course!'

'Only you seem a bit . . . light-headed.'

'I am merely trying to digest your revelations.'

'Ah! A touch of constipation, then. Aiee, how I longed for my vent to be blocked while I writhed around in my own shit, thanks to your nephew.' He holds up a hand. 'of course, this is mere speculation. A tale told to pass the time. Simply my humble opinion – which you yourself asked for, Ma.'

# 8
## Port Natal

Led by Henry Fynn, the Farewell Trading Company's advance party landed at the bay the Zulus call Thekwini on the morning of May 10, 1824. Sheltered by a bluff of high ground from the worst of the storms that make sailing along this coast so hazardous, it's a near-perfect anchorage. There's just that sandbar at the entrance, which is covered by less than a metre of water at low tide. Crossing it can be a nerve-racking affair, but worth it considering the tranquillity that awaits on the other side.

Aside from Fynn, the advance party comprised a Hottentot servant called Michael, a Xhosa interpreter named Frederick and three 'mechanics' – handymen who would construct the buildings that would store the deluge of ivory Farewell had promised his investors.

Fynn, meanwhile, was to make contact with Shaka, a task he undertook with alacrity. He soon became a firm favourite of Shaka's, and the King was happy for the White Men to build a kraal at Thekwini so that they might trade with the People of the Sky. (Resembling Robinson Crusoe, his attire a mix of cowskins, torn European garb and shrubbery, Fynn would divide his time between sojourns at Bulawayo and long, long tramps down along the southern coast, where he befriended Faku and his Pondoes.)

Although Lord Charles Somerset, Governor of the Cape, had insisted this was to be a *private* venture, Farewell duly raised the Union flag and claimed the bay for the Crown. However, one would have thought that if he was going to risk the ire of the

Whitehall mandarins by annexing a beach and some mangrove swamp for the empire, he would at least have attempted to spruce the place up a bit.

Instead, with entrepreneurs and adventurers coming and going, and Farewell and his investors more interested in getting ivory from the Zulus and panning for gold in the region's many rivers, Port Natal currently comprised a wattle and daub barn-type structure without windows, and with only one door made of reeds, besides some lean-tos, the vague beginnings – a short ditch and a low mound of weed-infested soil – of a mud fort, a cattle kraal and several mounds of ivory – although not nearly so much of it as the White Men were expecting.

The refugees the White Men insist on sheltering all vanish into the long grass as the two Zulus approach the man dozing on a shady hammock strung out under a couple of trees.

★

Jakot had found himself seized as part of the booty following a cross-border raid occurring while he was still a child. He then grew up on a White farm, where he learnt Dutch and a smattering of English. When he eventually escaped and returned to his people, they used him as an interpreter in their dealings with the settlers. He was also a useful guide to be taken on rustling expeditions. Captured on one of these, he and a companion had only avoided being shot when Jakot had revealed he could speak Dutch.

In July 1823, he accompanied Francis Farewell on the lieutenant's first expedition to establish a trading station on the south-east coast. There he saved Farewell from drowning during a botched landing attempted during inclement conditions near the estuary named Santa Lucia. But an altercation on the beach then saw the Xhosa stomping off to find Shaka on his own. The fact that he would be able to tell Shaka all about the devious ways of these arrogant White Men would surely see him secure a position of some prestige in the Zulu King's court.

Though Shaka knew a conman when he saw one, he reckoned Jakot's knowledge might just come in handy, if only to help him in deciding what *not* to do. And if, as Jakot kept insisting, the White Men were coming whether Shaka liked it or not, he could do with an interpreter able to reveal the hidden meanings that lurked behind their words.

He also found Jakot's stories entertaining, and called him Hlambamanzi, the Swimmer, after hearing of his escape in the waves.

As for Jakot, the realisation that these Zulus weren't about to be so easily duped after all was somewhat unsettling; a sign that he might not turn out to be as indispensable as he hoped. As a result, after Fynn and then Farewell arrived, he began dividing his time between the White Men and the Zulus, through favouring the former until he had become all but a permanent member of the settlement at Port Natal.

★

Not for the first time during his sojourn in these parts, Jakot comes awake at the prod of the Induna's assegai blade – and wishes he was still dreaming.

'Aiee,' he says, shading his eyes and looking up at the Induna. 'You!' Gazing past the warrior, he continues: 'Shadow of the Shadow, you are well, I take it. That terrible wound not plaguing you?'

The Induna extends a hand, which Jakot accepts, allowing himself to be pulled out of the hammock.

'Where are the savages?' asks the Induna.

Things remain strained in the wake of the failed diplomatic mission. Ogle and Cane have retreated to their kraals and wives, on the other side of the bay. Fynn is at Ogle's kraal, trying to do something for the ailing James King, who's lodging with Ogle.

As for Farewell and the other White Men: 'They have gone looking for the kraals of gold they know you are hiding from them,' explains Jakot.

'Again?'

'Again.'

'Gold,' sneers the Induna.

'I know,' says Jakot, with a shrug. 'They are just like children, but what can one do?'

'You can come with us.'

The Xhosa narrows his eyes. *No! Oh, no!* Feeling his throat constrict and his chest tighten, he tries to imitate the Induna's grin. Instead, his lips part in a grimace.

'Ukuvakasha,' murmurs the Induna.

The hammock twists to catch him as Jakot sags backward. 'Walking,' he whispers.

The Induna nods.

Jakot's eyes drift to the reeds where he knows the refugees are hiding. If only those ingrates had warned him of the Zulus' approach, he too could have disappeared.

'We are going walking,' says the Induna.

'We?' asks Jakot.

'You, me, him,' says the Induna indicating his former udibi. 'And a few others.'

'And the reason for this, er, excursion?'

'Thengizigqila!' says the Induna. *Slavers!*

Jakot draws himself up and endeavours to sound reasonable. 'As you know, Nduna, certain episodes in my sorry life mean that no man may compete with me in my loathing of these monsters.'

'However . . . ?' probes the Induna.

'However,' says Jakot with a watery smile, 'I'm not sure how I can aid you here.'

'Come now, that should be obvious!'

Jakot shrugs, like a humble man humbly admitting his deficiency. It's a performance that earns him a guffaw from Mthunzi.

Come now, the Induna persists, it stands to reason that certain circumstances might arise wherein understanding the babble emitted by these savages might come in handy.

But, interjects Jakot, hoping he doesn't sound too relieved by this; he doesn't speak the language of those who . . . well, live up there (a very, very, *very* long walk away).

He's not lying, either. The Xhosas and Zulus are of Nguni stock and so, with a little concentration, one can understand the other's language. However, those who have settled in what is today Mozambique belong to other ethnic groupings.

This is so, agrees the Induna. But since these intruders are slavers, it's safe to assume some of their number will be savages from across the waters – whose language Jakot *can* speak.

'But those savages speak many different languages, Nduna. What if I cannot decipher their tongue?'

'There will still be some killing to be done – don't forget that. Your journey won't be wasted.'

'Killing is something I prefer to leave to the experts, Nduna. And who is more expert than Shaka's lions?'

'Nonetheless, the King himself has suggested you accompany us. You do still serve him, don't you?'

Jakot swallows, takes a deep breath, forcing himself to meet the Induna's gaze, then says he'll go fetch his things.

# 9

# A Sennight Passes

It suddenly strikes her what a perilous path Mbopa has had to tread since Shaka had the prime minister's mother killed. Having had no time to grieve, he's been forced to swallow his pain – and, yes, his anger – while at the same time keeping a wary eye on Shaka . . .

*Then why doesn't he join them?*

Surely he must understand a wait-and-see attitude won't do him any good. If they fail, suspicion will still fall on him, because how could the prime minister not have known about the plot? For this is Mbopa, who's proven so adept in the past at spotting sedition and disgruntlement, and at moving in to quietly smother these sparks before they spread!

And, if they succeed, where will neutrality get him? What will it avail him when the fields must be weeded, as inevitably they must, to get rid of those still loyal to Shaka?

Hai, Mbopa, you are valuable to me, thinks Mnkabayi, for you will help me when the need to restrain a certain young bull arises. But do not think this will save you if you choose to hide away in your hut.

Of course, things aren't quite ready yet, which is fortunate for Mbopa since she's likely to give him a second chance to join them.

Meanwhile, she's been busy stamping out certain dangerous rumours. Very busy, indeed.

★

For a few days they follow the coast, allowing the sandy shores with their long, low, languid dunes to guide them.

Everywhere grow strand aloes, their yellow tubular flowers rising out of clusters of large, fleshy leaves resembling tentacles; and the disarrayed foliage of silver-oaks glint in the sun; and the shiny mauve flowers of beach beans add specks of colour to the shrubs coating the back dunes. And over there extends the warm, warm Indian Ocean, and in the opposite direction a flat expanse of estuaries and salt marshes.

When they're on the move, Mthunzi and the Induna each carry a sleeping mat and a cowhide cloak tied in a bedroll suspended diagonally across the chest. Slung crosswise from the other shoulder are a food satchel and two waterskins. Both men carry an iklwa, with four more of these short stabbing spears – as well as two or three longer hunting spears – affixed to the inside of their shields.

As for Jakot, he wears sandals and klapbroek, which are trousers made from cowskin, with a front flap that hides the belt and folds downwards when unbuttoned. He carries two waterskins and his pack bulges with a peacoat wrapped around a dagger. A grey blanket is rolled up and secured to the top of the pack.

★

The King's absence from public life has created . . . well, an absence which the unscrupulous and conniving are attempting to fill with calumnies meant to sow discord.

What kind of lies? Good question. If Mnkabayi happens to be talking to older councillors and generals – those likely to remember how it was back then – she'll say she's referring to the tales about Shaka's paternity.

Yes, these have resurfaced – will they never go away? They'll recall the stories she's talking about, she'll say, but she elaborates just to make sure. Don't they remember how, at the time Shaka claimed the throne, people wondered if Senzangakhona really was his father? Where was the proof? Surely the fact that Nandi had spread her legs for him meant she'd done the same for others – so who was to say one of these other men wasn't Shaka's father? Who was to say Shaka was really of the Blood? Aiee, who could say for certain he was even a Zulu?

Don't they remember how such rumours had raced from camp-fire to campfire?

Well, it's happening again, and it's their duty to see they're stamped out before they can spread too far, or are believed by too many. It's crucial that such gossip be suppressed because, after all, there really is no proof that Senzangakhona was Shaka's father, is there?

★

Eventually, they move inland, skirting the mangroves that lie along the coast here. Soon they're in the sand forests, a rolling landscape of ancient dunes now far away from the sea. Here are the green-apple trees whose branches are used in building huts, the leadwood bushwillow which provides excellent, slow-burning firewood, and the Lebombo wattle with its thirty-centimetre-long seed pods, wine-red now that they're maturing. There's the ordeal tree, once used by sangomas to determine guilt or innocence. The unfortunate accused was made to drink a muthi that included powdered bark from this tree and was therefore poisonous, whereupon vomiting was considered a sign of inno-cence. There are ravines made impassable by thorny-rope creepers. Zebra and impala herds stick together, the former eating the longer grass, the latter the shorter stems. One afternoon, as the sky turns orange, the three men are forced to go to ground in the shade of a podberry and watch as a wildebeest tries to beat off a lioness clinging, improbably, to its snout. When the gnu, with its humped back and upward-curving horns, finally frees

85

itself, the lioness doesn't renew its assault — and the Induna and the udibi agree it's shame that sees the feline slink away, leaving the wildebeest to return to its herd. After picking some of the podberry's thin-shelled fruit, which tastes like sherbet, the three continue on their way.

★

If she happens to be addressing younger advisors or officers, who are flattered at being taken into her confidence, Mnkabayi then suppresses a shudder and speaks of the pernicious claims some have made regarding Dingiswayo's death — rumours which continue to do the rounds from time to time, like an illness.

'It pains me to recount it,' she'll say, 'but you must know this animal so you can recognise its spoor and hunt down and kill it!'

They have heard of how Dingiswayo recognised Shaka's greatness, she'll say. They have heard how the King of the Mthethwas loved Shaka like a son.

And they'll have heard of the dark day Dingiswayo decided to march on Zwide. Of how Dingiswayo neglected to send word to Shaka telling him where exactly their forces should meet. Of how Dingiswayo then blundered into Zwide's arms while out scouting.

Aiee, she'll say, some claim that the King of the Mthethwas was bewitched. That his semen was stolen and delivered to Zwide's medicine men.

And they'll have heard of how Shaka saved the nation by refusing to attack when he learnt his mentor had been beheaded by Zwide. The Mthethwas were thrown into confusion by the death of their King, and Zwide's forces were able to eat them up, while Shaka withdrew with a few of Dingiswayo's remaining allies to bide his time.

*This is what they say, but . . .*

She'll shake her head and contrive to look old, frail . . . as if these heinous rumours are assegai thrusts invading her very flesh.

But there are those who say that when Dingiswayo went to war against the Ndwandwes, ordering all his allies to join him, it was the chance Shaka had been waiting for. His mentor had helped him claim the Zulu throne, but now he wanted to be his own man, free of the shackles of gratitude that would keep him as Dingiswayo's vassal.

So, even though he loathed Zwide, he sent emissaries to the Ndwandwe capital to tell Zwide of Dingiswayo's plans . . .

Mnkabayi gives a world-weary sigh. Yes, they are right to look shocked, but there you go . . . there are those who actually say Shaka betrayed Dingiswayo!

And then she'll send them away, these young cubs. They'll start off by being conscientious in their efforts to obey her instructions, but they'll also be mulling things over and, despite their promises of secrecy, they'll soon speak to their friends . . .

She'll send them away, then move on to the next batch of youngsters, just doing her duty, and trying to protect her nephew.

★

A sennight passes before they come upon the first rendezvous point. Having been along here before, Njikiza chose it and described it to the Induna. It's an overhang in the ridge that can be seen from the path and, once he's standing directly opposite it, the Induna takes three steps off the track, towards the ridge – and starts to dig.

Soon he comes upon a small leather pouch. Opening it, he finds two pebbles. That says Njikiza and the others have been here and moved on to the second rendezvous point; three stones would have meant they're going to return here, and that the Induna and his party must wait for them.

They reach the second meeting place at mid-morning the following day. Sola is waiting for them. They have reconnoitred and found the slavers, he says, as he leads the Induna and the others to their hidden campsite.

Where there's a surprise waiting for the Induna: Dingane has decided to join them after all.

It's late July, in 1828, the time of Uncwaba, the New Grass Moon.

# INTERLUDE
## The Time Of During

*They come for him, four fat, flabby mollies, their bald pates gleaming in the torchlight. He's worked out they must be eunuchs, but he calls them mollies for it's clear they're also bumboys. And hasn't he kicked the teeth out of a few of those in his time!*

*'Oh, a drop of Nelson's blood wouldn't do us any harm, wouldn't do us any harm,' he bellows by way of greeting.*

*Quicker than thieving monkeys, they've got him untied and upright, lashed to a pole stretched across his shoulders that keeps his arms extended.*

*And all the while, barely able to stand, he sings:*

> *Oh, a drop of Nelson's blood wouldn't do us any harm*
> *And we'll all hang on behind.*
> *And roll the old chariot along.*

*The effects of whatever they smear down there have now almost completely worn off, and it feels as if his prick has been skinned. Which it has been in a way, if you think about it.*

*He's pushed sharply forward, having to do some fancy footwork to stop from landing on his face. Which doesn't help the pain down there.*

*'Oh, me cullies, give me five minutes without my hands tied,' he tells the mollies. 'That's all I ask for. We'll see who draws the claret then.'*

*But his hands have to be tied, because there's no touching the precious cargo, is there? That's one of the few things he's managed to work out, amid all the chirruping and clicking that comprises their language.*

*Sweat speckling his forehead, pain biting his cock with every step, he staggers forward.*

'And it's all for me grog, me jolly, jolly grog,' he sings. 'All for me beer and tobacco!'

When one of the eunuchs tries to shove him from behind, to make him move faster, he grits his teeth and swivels his upper body. But, long used to such a response, the molly leans back, out of the reach of the pole, and the four giggle like milkmaids.

Panting now because of the pain, he moves out of the big hut and down a walkway lined with animal skins on either side. The first few times he was taken along here, there had been a bevy of wenches trying to peek through the gaps, shrieking with laughter whenever the eunuchs tried to shoo them away. For a while now there have been no eager faces peering through the openings, and he can only hope this is a sign his torment is almost over.

And then . . . think of the gold! No more pockets to let! No more punting on the River Tick!

The thought gives him the strength to burst into song again:

> Farewell and adieu to you, Spanish ladies,
> Farewell and adieu to you, ladies of Spain;
> For we've received orders for to sail for old England,
> And I hope never, no never, to see you again!

'Think I'm touched in the upper works?' he says, turning to address the molly waddling to his right. 'Queer in the attic? But I'll not be sticking my spoon into this wall! You'll see! I ain't dying here!'

Taking a deep breath:

> Farewell and adieu to you, Spanish ladies,
> Farewell and adieu!
> And, oh, a plate of Irish stew wouldn't do us any harm!
> So haul away, Joe, haul away.

Into the smaller hut. A slap to shut him up; then two of the eunuchs guide him to the foot of a slab of stone covered with a thick layer of hay. One places his hands on the prisoner's chest and pushes him backwards. As he falls, the other two each grab an end of the pole to slow his descent, and gently lower him onto the straw.

The time of During. He swallows.

Comatose After, giving way to the dread of Before, giving way to this, the unspeakable agony of During.

A cord is wrapped around his penis – an action which almost causes him to pass out, since it involves lifting and fiddling with his prick. Next, and none too gently, the loop is forced down to the base of his penis. Two of the eunuchs take up position, one either side of him, each holding an end of the cord.

Initially, when he could no longer produce an erection, one of the mollies had stepped into the breach with a willing hand. Actually, they used to take it in turns, sniggering as he writhed and cursed them. Now, though, with his cock reduced to raw meat, the job is left to only one of the eunuchs, who clearly has a taste for such things.

He now takes the man's prick into his mouth and starts sucking.

Pain and revulsion and those horrid slurping noises.

When the prisoner has something resembling an erection, the eunuch moves away and the cord is pulled tight. A command is issued, and the first of the plump, roly-poly women scuttles into the hut. Helped by one of the eunuchs, she straddles him. More and more often of late, a certain amount of pushing and squeezing has been needed to get him inside the woman, but then it's haul away, Joe, haul away!

He never knows how many of these females he has to service each time, but there's no stopping until he's filled his quota – something which has been taking him longer and longer.

# 10
## The Turncoat

Jean-Christophe, who is the son of slaves transported to the island of Saint-Domingue from Benin and who, as a teenager, first fought the Spaniards and then the French with the army of Toussaint Louverture and who, having long ago fled that island, is now a slaver himself, emerges from the bushes a few metres away from the stockade, still savouring the sublime afterglow of a morning shit.

He wears a French infantryman's habit-veste, breeches cut off at the knees, and leather sandals. The coat is a grubby, faded greyish-blue, the red collar and cuffs a pale pink, and the white lapels have long ago lost their pipe clay and are spattered with mud, food stains and blood. Made of a woollen material, the breeches were also once white but are now a dusty brown.

Jean-Christophe carries a Baker rifle and, pushed beneath the red sash around his waist, is the sixty-centimetre-long sword-bayonet that British riflemen were equipped with to compensate for the short length of the Baker. He doesn't have his powder horn or pouch of loose ball with him, but the rifle is loaded.

Stepping into a shaft of sunlight, he stretches and yawns, enjoying the sudden warmth after the cold night shadows that lingered in the bushes he's just left.

Then he starts, gapes, and brings his rifle up across his chest, his finger in the trigger guard.

The stockade is set at the edge of a clearing covered by long grass and some low bushes. Early-morning mist lingers here, but he's sure he's seen a man at the far side of the glade.

He squints, tightening his grip on the rifle.

Yes! *There!* A man.

The figure stands immobile, as if he wants to be spotted.

Jean-Christophe moves sideways, trying to get himself closer to the stockade. He keeps his eyes on the man, then almost trips over a root and glances down. When he raises his head again, the man is gone.

He scans the mist, as if looking for signs of disturbance.

Nothing.

He looks over his shoulder at the stockade, hoping one of the others may be up and about, but there's no sign of anyone at the low wall of logs they've constructed. Two men should be guarding the merchandise, which is confined in a sturdy cage made of tamboti trunks lashed together, several paces in from the barricade. But right now the sentries are nowhere to be seen.

Jean-Christophe killed his first man, a planter's son, at the age of thirteen and no one will ever accuse him of having a nervous disposition; nonetheless he feels his heart clench when he looks back at the mist . . . and sees the man again, several paces closer this time.

It's as if he's leapt forward. Only the fact that he remains immobile, with his arms fixed by his sides, prevents Jean-Christophe from shooting at him.

There's also the fact that he can now see the stranger is wearing European clothes: a white shirt and cowskin trousers.

*Henri! Get out here!* he calls in French, keeping his eyes on the stranger.

Now one of the sentries appears. With skin the same crow-black as Jean-Christophe's, his name is Bertrand and he's also from Saint-Domingue. *What is it?* he asks.

*Fetch Henri!*

Henri is actually Hendrik, a half-caste they picked up at the Cape. Having worked for a family of Huguenot stock, he can speak French as well as Xhosa, and a smattering of Zulu. Yawning and scratching his stomach, he joins Jean-Christophe. His grey trousers reach his calves and he's carrying a long spear with a heavy blade.

Trailing after him comes Bertrand, with his Brown Bess. He wears the remains of an old black frockcoat and the cowskin kilt and leather sandals favoured by the tribe they've been dealing with.

*Do you see him?* asks Jean-Christophe.

Hendrik nods.

*Go and see what he wants.*

Hendrik studies the man for a moment. He certainly doesn't seem to be from these parts, so they might be able to communicate – although he's long ago given up trying to explain to the others that, while he can make himself understood most times, he doesn't speak every one of the dialects they're likely to encounter.

*Bertrand and I will cover you*, adds Jean-Christophe, by way of encouragement.

The stranger doesn't move as Hendrik approaches him. The latter is intrigued to see the man's wearing those strange trousers, with the flap over the front, which are favoured by Dutch farmers at the Cape.

Could it be . . . ?

*Greetings*, says Jakot, in Xhosa.

Hendrik grins. *And greetings to you, Xhosa. You are a long way from home.*

*As are you!*

*This is true, but sometimes a man must roam far and wide.*

94

*And these you are roaming with now? Are they your masters?*

*Let them think what they like, it will not change the way things are. But why are you here?*

*I am here with some Zulus,* says Jakot.

*Zulus?* says Hendrik, drawing back. They are aware that a Zulu army is somewhere in these parts but, by coming so far north, they've been hoping to avoid them.

*They have come seeking you and your friends,* continues Jakot. *Shaka has sent them to kill you. But they are just a few, and no match for your weapons, and I have grown tired of their company. So I have come seeking to make a trade: my Zulus in return for the freedom to return home.*

*A long journey, Xhosa!*

*Indeed,* agrees Jakot. *Then let me say I merely seek my freedom – even perhaps the freedom to join your company. After all, two are better than one when it comes to controlling those who think they're one's masters!*

★

Hendrik conducts Jakot back to where the others are waiting and tells them what Jakot proposes: how he'll show them where the Zulus are camped so that Jean-Christophe and his men might catch them unawares.

Ordering Hendrik to keep an eye on the Xhosa, Jean-Christophe leads Bertrand out of earshot so that they can discuss the scheme in private.

The pickings have been slim this trip. There are just four of them and they have a deal with a chieftain on the coast who, like so many others on the continent, sees slavery as a lucrative way of getting rid of his rivals. However, with Shaka's impis on the rampage, they've had to move further inland than normal. (Of course, they don't know how the Zulu ranks have been decimated; all they know is Shaka's lions are best avoided and the contingent of twelve men the chieftain has lent them, who are armed only with flintlocks, will avail them little should they encounter a Zulu ibutho.)

After more than a month, they've only been able to round up fifty or so creatures, ranging from young children to an old woman. That the latter has been kept alive at all, along with some of the weaker males, is an indication of how desperate they are. Right now they're picking up anyone they can.

But some Zulus might see them make something approaching a reasonable profit.

*Can we trust him?* asks Jean-Christophe, meaning Jakot.

Bertrand shrugs. *What have we to lose?*

*What if it's a trap?*

*If their numbers are sufficient there would be no need for a trap. See how he has found us. They would merely attack and overrun us. So let us go and see. If he speaks the truth and they are few in number we can overrun them and leave this accursed place at last. And if he isn't speaking the truth, we can come back and make him suffer.*

★

It's decided, then. Jean-Christophe, Bertrand, Hendrik and four of the tribesman they've been lent will go and fetch the Zulus – taking Jakot with them, of course. Afonso, the fourth member of the group, will remain behind with the rest of the tribesmen, to guard the other captives.

# 11
## The Biter Bit

'You!' snarls the Induna. 'We thought you had run away back to the savages at Thekwini. But this . . . this is something I thought even you were incapable of!'

Jakot shrugs. 'A man must do what he must to survive in these dark days, Zulu!'

*What are they saying?* asks Jean-Christophe, now speaking French. Chuckling, Hendrik translates for him. Then Jean-Christophe is also laughing. *I don't blame him for being a little annoyed*, he says.

The Zulus were camping in a narrow ravine and, after disarming them and tying their wrists, the first order of business was to shift them to a more open piece of ground, so that Jean-Christophe could better evaluate their haul.

And he likes what he sees – an assessment shared by Bertrand. If only there had been a few more! He's not unaware of the irony inherent in that thought, given his earlier apprehension, but these Zulus proved remarkably easy to capture. Clearly, stories of their martial prowess have been exaggerated. Not that this will affect their captives' value, because they certainly look ferocious.

See the tall, broad-shouldered one, how he's eyeing the Xhosa. Still seething.

For a moment Jean-Christophe considers letting him loose to vent his anger on Jakot. Maybe later, though, because the Xhosa might still be of value to them.

'You,' says the Induna addressing Hendrik. 'Can you understand me?'

Hendrik nods.

'Then ask the fat one: he came here seeking human beings, but how would he like to leave with tears of the sun?'

*What's he saying?* asks Jean-Christophe seeing Hendrik stiffen.

*He . . . Wait!* Addressing the Induna, Hendrik asks if he knows where these tears might be found.

'Of course,' says the Induna. 'And, with us to help with the digging, there'll be more than you can carry.'

*What's he saying?* asks Jean-Christophe more urgently this time.

*He says he can show us where to find some gold.*

Bertrand's suddenly there, eager as a hunting dog. *Gold?* he hisses.

Hendrik nods.

Jean-Christophe and Bertrand exchange a glance. *Gold,* says the former. *Gold,* echoes the latter.

*Gold,* adds Hendrik.

*Hmm,* says Jean-Christophe, scratching his belly and eyeing the Induna. *I don't suppose we can torture that one until the others tell us where the gold is, just to end his suffering.*

Bertrand snorts.

*Just a thought,* grins Jean Christophe. *Ask him what he wants in return for showing us where the gold is,* he instructs Hendrik.

While Hendrik is speaking to the Induna, Jean-Christophe examines the Zulu's face closely, hoping to be able to gauge whether he's telling the truth. Noticing their attention has begun to wander, Bertrand barks at the tribesmen to watch the captives. Of course, they can't understand French, but they pick up the import of his bellow.

It's too late, though. Seizing his chance, with his hands still bound together in front of him, Phepho barges past one of the warriors, knocking aside his flintlock, and throws himself on

Jakot. They go crashing backwards into a bush. Twisting, Jakot throws the Zulu off him. But, as the Xhosa struggles to disentangle himself from the branches of the bush, Phepho folds an arm around his neck and pulls him free.

Jean-Christophe waits until panic and the struggle for breath seem about to make Jakot's face explode, before signalling to Bertrand to end it. This he does with the butt of his Brown Bess. He has to hit Phepho three times before Jakot can breathe again. And, even then, Phepho remains on his feet, swaying but upright.

Handing his musket to Jean-Christophe, Bertrand checks the cords binding Phepho's wrists together, then shoves him back towards the other captives.

Jean-Christophe passes Bertrand the Brown Bess, and turns his attention back to Hendrik. *So? What did he say?*

*He said they will show us where the gold is if we let them continue on their way and also take the Xhosa with them.*

Jean-Christophe nods. That makes sense. No one likes a traitor.

*Tell them,* he says, *that we agree. But any trickery and they die.* Looking at the Induna he runs a finger across his neck. *Tell them, Henri.*

Before Hendrik can address the Induna, however, Jakot is there, grabbing his arm. Before being attacked by Phepho, he'd heard enough of the exchange between Hendrik and the Induna to guess what the latter has in mind.

'No!' he says. 'You cannot do this!'

Which is all the Induna needs to hear to know the slavers have accepted his offer.

Hendrik pushes Jakot away, and Bertrand steps between them, the butt of his Brown Bess raised, forcing the Xhosa even further back.

Taking in the Induna's grin and the ashen expression on Jakot's face, Jean-Christophe laughs. *So both know*, he says. *Henri, when you have the chance, tell your new friend I have no intention of keeping my word. It will keep him more docile for now.*

And there's one more thing, he adds. He's to tell the Zulus they will now tie their hands behind their backs.

Hendrik begins to translate the order, but is interrupted by the Induna.

*What now?* asks Jean-Christophe.

The Zulu has told him they will need to traverse very rugged terrain, and therefore progress will be quicker if their hands are bound in front of them. That way they'll be better able to climb and prevent themselves from slipping.

That's why their wrists were tied in front of them in the first place, to make getting them out of the ravine easier, and to enable the slavers to keep their weapons trained on the Zulus from a greater distance.

Bertrand intervenes. He doesn't like this at all, he says. Getting them from their camp to here is one thing, but quite another is leaving them able to use their bound wrists as clubs, over a longer distance.

Anyway, he adds, why don't they simply take one of the Zulus to show him where the gold is?

*But remember what he said*, says Hendrik, indicating the Induna. *They will be able to help us move more gold more quickly.*

*Yes*, adds Jean-Christophe, *and you yourself said the quicker we can leave this shit-hole the better, Bertrand. Besides, we outnumber them and we have these*, he says raising his rifle.

★

All the same, progress is slow. Where the ground permits it, Hendrik leads the way, followed by the Induna, behind whom comes Jean-Christophe with his Baker at the ready. Then come the other Zulus, flanked by the tribesmen, with Jakot and Bertrand bringing up the rear. Where the bushes close in, or they're forced to enter a kloof, all the Zulus are herded together and each forced to place his bound wrists on the left shoulder of the man in front of them. Where they need to climb out of erosion furrows or scramble over rocks, Jean-Christophe and Hendrik move ahead, then stand guard as the captives make their way towards them.

# 12
## The Stream & The Stockade

The stream lies in a kloof reached by a narrow trail that runs through bushes and low-standing trees. The water is shallow, coming up to a man's ankle, but seasons of excess rainfall have seen the current undercut the bank at the point where the path ends. The undergrowth opens up here, and this is where the Induna, Sola and Jakot have halted. Keeping an eye on them are Hendrik and three of the tribesmen. Because there's no space for him, Mthunzi stands in the water by the overhang; beside him is the fourth tribesman, his flintlock aimed at the udibi.

Jean-Christophe and Bertrand are a few metres upstream. The water is even shallower here, and a wide island of sand takes up most of the watercourse. Phepho is here, too, bent forward, watching the channel that crackles past his feet. Jean-Christophe stands opposite him, right on the bank of the stream, which is merely a narrow strip of dried mud in front of a wall of reeds. Bertrand is squatting a few paces away, where the bank widens, examining his own stretch of water. Reeds line the opposite bank, with trees peering over the top of them.

Annoyed at being left with the prisoners, Hendrik keeps pushing past the Induna to see how his companions are doing.

The next time he does it, the Induna grabs him and shouts, 'Ayi hlome!' *To arms!*

Jakot reaches up to the branch of a tree, where an iklwa has been hidden . . .

Sola charges into two of the tribesmen . . .

Mthunzi grabs for the barrel of the flintlock, pushing it aside just as the man pulls the trigger . . .

Njikiza rises up out of the rushes behind Jean-Christophe, and brings his club down on the slaver's head . . .

Phepho throws himself sideways and Namasu rises up out of the reeds on the opposite bank to throw a long hunting spear at Bertrand . . .

The Induna twists Hendrik's head sideways, snapping his neck . . .

Jakot drives his iklwa into the stomach of the tribesman next to him, who falls away from him, pulling the trigger of his flint-lock, only to have it misfire . . .

Sola wrestles the gun away from one of the two tribesmen he sent crashing into the bushes . . .

The Induna throws himself at the second man, who's dropped his gun . . .

Namasu's spear hits Bertrand in the chest, and Njikiza's club shatters his face as he collapses backwards onto his ankles . . .

And Jean-Christophe's body hits the water with a splash . . .

And the udibi head-butts his man, then retrieves the spear hidden in the overhang . . .

And Jakot throws the iklwa to the Induna . . .

And the current pulls red streamers out of Jean-Christophe's broken skull, and sends them unravelling downstream.

★

The Induna, Phepho and Namasu are already about two paces into the clearing, when Afonso finally spots them. Calling out to the remaining tribesmen, he takes cover behind the logs form-ing the low barricade. The Zulus have spread out, running fast and they know what to look out for. As soon as smoke rises from the guns facing them, they hit the ground. Then they're up and running again. Afonso realises the mistake he's made – he should have had every second man fire, then the rest, while the first batch reloaded – but it's too late for that now. As he fumbles with his powder horn, two of the tribesmen rise to their feet, having decided they're not sticking around. They don't get far, though.

Afonso has his Brown Bess at his shoulder when he hears shrieks behind him. Some of the Zulus are attacking them from the rear. He wheels, his finger curling around the trigger. Leaving Dingane and Njikiza to finish off the pair escaping, the udibi charges forward and throws his spear. Instead of firing, Afonso uses his Brown Bess to parry the iklwa. Bad mistake. In doing so he accidentally pulls the trigger, wasting a shot. Then the udibi's onto him . . . and the Induna and the others are leaping over the barricade.

★

From the group of prisoners, an isalukazi, or elderly woman – who's either younger than she looks or older, it's hard to tell – pushes her way forward, saying she can speak Zulu.

'And am I to assume you have killed them all?' she asks, referring to the slavers.

The Induna nods.

'Good,' she says. 'That saves me from having to exert myself.'

The Induna chuckles and regards her more closely. She has gaunt, angular features, with prominent cheekbones giving way to a small, narrow-lipped mouth. At first glance, you might assume she's been forced to miss too many meals, but that would be a false impression. She's slender rather than skinny, lean rather than underweight. And she doesn't carry herself like someone who's seen as many seasons as she clearly has.

She's dressed in a fashion similar to that favoured by elderly Zulu women: wearing an isidwaba, a skirt that reaches to her knees, and an ingubo, a large leather apron.

Her name, she says, is Duthlle. She was captured with two younger females — both tall women who go bare-breasted and wear skirts adorned with tassels made from zebra tails. They had wandered far from their home kraal, seeking an overdue hunting party.

The Induna can just imagine this one taking charge, insisting on going to seek the missing men herself. But what of the tribe's other menfolk, are they so timid they leave such things to their women?

No, no, says the isalukazi, they were needed to protect their land and cattle, for Mzilikazi's Matabele are on the march.

'One of yours, not so?' she adds.

'Not any longer,' says the Induna. Although there's no doubt that Shaka's former favourite has learnt his lessons well and is every bit as ruthless as the Zulu King himself.

They want to get going as soon as possible, continues Duthlle. Can they now collect some provisions?

The Induna nods.

Calling Phepho and Namasu to him, he instructs them to move out into the bush and circle the clearing just to make sure they really have killed all the slavers. Then they are to find a vantage point from where they can observe all the approaches to the clearing. They can return here at nightfall.

Next, the Induna instructs Sola to guard the path that Njikiza and Dingane followed in order to attack the compound from the rear. He's also to keep an eye on the old woman and the rest.

Jakot and the udibi had gone to retrieve the Zulus' baggage. They've now returned, and Njikiza has gone over to help them sort out the various shields and pouches; it's important they're fully armed as soon as possible. As soon as that's done, Njikiza and the boy will go to fetch water and firewood.

When each man's belongings have been placed on top of his shield, Njikiza stretches, yawns and slaps Jakot on the back. 'Hai, but you had me worried,' he says, as the Xhosa staggers a step forward. 'For a moment I thought you really had decided to join up with those crocodiles.'

His shoulder blade stinging, Jakot straightens up, and the Induna sees a look cross his face the like of which he's never seen before. It's an expression that narrows Jakot's eyes and hardens his features.

And, just as the Induna realises that something unpleasant is about to happen and he should intervene, Jakot turns and moves up closer to Njikiza.

'What did you say?' he asks, and his tone and the fact that he's showing no sign of fear causes the Watcher of the Ford to step back.

'What did you say?' asks Jakot again.

Despite himself, Njikiza feels his lips twist into a silly grin. 'I merely . . .' But before he can continue – and, truly, he's not sure what he's going to say next, being more used to intimidating than explaining – Jakot throws up his left hand in a dismissive gesture.

'Cha! What do you know, you overgrown baboon?' Twisting around, he points to the scars on his back. 'Where do you think I got these?'

Wheeling to address the others, he continues: 'You Zulus say you have stamped the thorns, but what do you really know? Your King – who now sulks like a maiden whose swain has filled her ears with sweet promises and her cunt with his cock, and then abandoned her – this mad tyrant demands total obedience, but his harsh discipline is tempered by rewards!'

Jakot approaches Njikiza once more, glowering up at the big man, who is now beyond being nonplussed. 'You know nothing of the horrors that await those stolen by others. *Nothing!* They too must toil under a tyrant, but for them there is no reward. Hai, even the one who wipes your King's arse is envied and regarded as an important man. Those stolen from their own people are simply beasts of burden and their toil doesn't end with the setting of the sun. You people are called upon to risk your lives, but your King sees to it that you are well armed. In the constant battle that is their lives, what do slaves have to defend themselves with?'

He steps away from the Watcher of the Ford, haranguing all of them again. 'You are warriors,' he says, 'but after you return from your campaigns you become husbands and stockmen once again. Those who have become slaves know only the agony of servitude. They can never be anything else. Never!'

He eyes each one in turn – the Induna, the udibi, Dingane, Njikiza. 'And I ask you again: what do you know? Do you know the terror of the child snatched away by bearded albinos? I do. Have you heard the crack of their guns as they shoot women fetching water? I have. Have you been dragged behind a horse until your legs give way and the stones gnaw at your stomach? I have.'

He laughs. 'And learning more of the ways of these savages, who eat their god and seek to steal our land, was simply to understand the depth of their brutality. But then so did my hatred grow. And I have marshalled it, kept it safe, let it increase like your precious herds. And you are fools – absolute *fools*! – if you think you have nothing to fear from them. These ones we killed today are merely their creatures, like the impundulu you Zulus speak of. They are little more than slaves themselves. But do not judge their masters by *their* behaviour. Never do that.'

Addressing Njikiza once more: 'So, yes, Zulu, you may doubt my loyalty to your insane King.' A chuckle. 'But,' he continues, his tone menacing, 'do not ever doubt my hatred for those who steal away our people. Do not think I would ever ally myself with them. And it's only because of your ignorance that I choose to ignore this affront and leave you standing upright.'

There follows a stunned silence. Even the birds are still and the branches motionless; the hubbub from the stockade has faded away, and it's as if everyone is waiting for that ominous noise they think they've heard to be repeated, so they can be sure death has come sniffing around them.

Then Njikiza coughs.

'I was just joking,' he says.

Appealing now to the Induna: 'That's all, just . . . joking.'

Walking away, Jakot ignores him.

★

Not counting Duthlle and the two girls with her, there are fifty-two captives. A group of these appear especially agitated, notes the Induna. Duthlle says she believes these ones were among the first captured.

It turns out they're Lomwes, whose territory adjoins that belonging to the chief who is collaborating with the slavers. They have the shortest distance to travel and are eager to leave – doubtless so they can urge their own people to punish the chief who set the slavers on them. So why not let them go, suggests Duthlle.

'That one is not afraid to interfere in the affairs of menfolk,' Dingane will remark to the Induna later. 'She reminds me of Mnkabayi.'

The Induna shrugs, saying he is of a mind to let them go anyway, for their fidgeting and shuffling is beginning to annoy him. As far as he's concerned, they can all go.

Night has now fallen and Dingane, who wasn't present at the stream but was instead watching the stockade, examines the remaining group huddled around one of the campfires. Yes, there is that, he murmurs, recalling the way all of them, except for Duthlle and her girls, simply . . .

'Stood there?' asks the Induna.

Dingane nods. 'Yes, they kicked and clawed at their captors when they were down, but it wasn't long before they were meek and docile once more.'

# 13
## A New Kind Of Madness

Something happened at the First Fruits – at those fateful First Fruits – but what? Knowing the answer to that question might yet save them, save the whole tribe. Not that Shaka's children are even aware that anything out of the ordinary occurred at that time. They merely revelled in those momentous days when they could see for themselves the greatness of the nation their Father had forged for them in the fires of war.

*But something had happened!* Something that had nothing to do with the assassination attempt. Mnkabayi is certain about that, just as she's certain it had nothing to do with the insane plot hatched by Mhlangana to disrupt the harvest festival, and to do who knew what else. That same plot she had allowed to play itself out, for her own reasons, and not because she thought it had much chance of success.

*Although the results were bloodier than you anticipated, weren't they?*

Would she have let things escalate if she could have foreseen all of that: the deaths of innocents, the mutilations . . . ?

Probably. *(I will not lie to myself!)*

Because looking the other way, letting Mhlangana think he had her acquiescence, was an important first step in her own plan.

Which, at this stage, can still be laid aside, if need be.

*Liar!*

No, wait . . . Think of it more as a tactical retreat. Shaka has elevated her; his power is her power. Let his rule continue and her power will likely increase still further. She might yet replace his beloved mother as his most trusted advisor.

*But the tribe . . . what of the tribe?*

Hai! She will see the tribe protected, for is she also not of the Blood? Everything she does is solely for the tribe.

*Which is why you are a liar, old woman! You think you can heal the King, and then things will be as they were. Hai! Suddenly this is an option? Are you now a coward, too? You know that, if the tribe is to survive, Shaka must go.*

*You wanted him to come – or someone like him. You willed him into being. But now you must see that he sets like the sun, for his day is done.*

True, all true. But it's also true something happened to her nephew during the First Fruits, and it worries her that it might yet affect the welfare of the people, just as the fate of the regiments in the swamps to the north also worries her. That's a sizeable portion of the Zulu army up there and, if it isn't withdrawn soon, the nation will be left vulnerable to attack from other directions. As it is, replacing the soldiers lost might take several seasons. But what happened during the First Fruits might be even more dangerous, because there might be nothing they can do, no muthi capable of fighting off the sickness.

And isn't Shaka acting very like a defeated chief who knows there's nothing more he can do to save his people?

★

Although it only reaches its climax in January, the First Fruits begins in the month of the September–October moon, with Ukutatamageja – The Taking Up of the Hoes. First the men clear the fields; then come the women to sow the seed.

Ummbila, maize, predominates; sorghum is grown mainly for use in the making of beer; then there are the ipuzi, a large, light-yellow pumpkin, and the imfe, an indigenous form of wild sugar cane, besides various melons and different varieties of sweet potato.

The women are feeding the nation, their efforts in the name of Nomkhubula, the Princess of the Sky, and this planting is accompanied by numerous ceremonies performed to entreat her to keep away drought and protect the plants from pests.

The planting season then gives way to the month of the October--November moon, the fecund month of Uzibandela, the Pathfinding Moon, when everything begins to grow and the new grass hides the trails and tracks.

Next comes Umasingana, the Peering-About Moon, whereupon the second phase of the First Fruits starts. This is Ukunyathela Unyaka, the Stepping into the New Year, when the women start searching the fields and gardens for the emergence of new crops – namely the First Fruits.

The Umkhosi reaches its climax during the month of the December–January moon. Traditionally, the final rituals were conducted by the various village chiefs all around the kingdom, as well as the King himself, their ceremonies mirroring his, but in 1825 Shaka decreed that from that year on only the King would conduct these rites.

Lasting for several days, these involved the King going into seclusion and being doctored with Imithi Emnyama, Black Medicine – to protect him and enable him to move beyond this world to seek strength and sustenance for the whole nation.

Meanwhile, contingents from the various regiments visit KwaNkosinkhulu, the Place of the Great Chief, to pay homage to the Bloodline. For it was here in this shady, fertile basin, surrounded by a rampart of hills and fed by a spring on the Tonjaneni Heights, that Zulu and his clan originally settled and prospered and grew. And it is here that the nation's Kings are buried – Zulu, Phunga, Mageba, Ndaba, Jama and Senzangakhona, in that order.

Each royal grave is marked by a euphorbia tree and the men

visit each one in turn, where praise-singers wait to regale them with tales of the King buried there.

Finally, there's the Calling of the King, when Shaka at last emerges from his seclusion. After the cheers subside, he announces which of his amabutho he'll allow to take wives after the First Fruits. These men may now wear the isicoco, the head ring.

More cheers and cries of 'Bayede, Nkosi!' *Hail to the King!*

Then he names the new regiments to be formed by the age-sets whose turn it now is to be conscripted, and they're shown the shields by which they'll be identified.

While the cheers wash over Shaka, a line of warriors forms up in front of him. These are men of the Dhlamini clan, renowned for their fleetness of foot.

At a signal from Mbopa, they move forward, each carrying two small reeds: the umtshingo and invenge.

This is the moment the nation has been waiting for.

And Shaka announces that these special messengers may now go forth, playing their reed flutes so that all might know the nation has his permission to partake of the First Fruits . . .

★

Shaka's decree that the final rituals of the Umkhosi would now be enacted by the King, and only the King, didn't worry her. She can see how this new ruling would consolidate his power, which was (is?) also her power. What did trouble her, though, was the fact that he hadn't discussed the decision with her first.

He valued her counsel, for her pragmatism counterbalanced Mbopa's cynicism, and she could also call on Ndlela's expertise when precedents were needed, or when the matter involved interpreting (or circumventing) some tradition or other.

Yet, despite that, Shaka hadn't said anything to her of his plans.

Was it because of the White Men? Had he already decided to invite them to attend the climax of the First Fruits? For *that* was a move she would have certainly opposed fiercely.

He knew her views about them. Her *pragmatic* views. It's pointless to wish them away – or kill them – for they are here now, and even if they vanish more will take their place. But they must be held at arm's length. Commanding them to attend something as important as the Umkhosi is allowing them to get too close.

Even if they didn't understand what was going on, or the ceremony's true importance, they would still be there, adding something and thus affecting the rituals.

The thing is . . .

★

The thing is, she believes the two things are connected: Shaka's decree about the Umkhosi and his inviting the savages from King Jorgi to attend the climax of the harvest festival.

Everyone had been trying hard to forget the madness that erupted after Nandi's death. But Mnkabayi's not sure Shaka's properly recovered.

To her the King is like a screaming man who's suddenly fallen silent. The killing had stopped, yes, but this is a mere cessation signalling the beginning of a new kind of madness, with unfettered rage becoming cold cunning.

And Shaka had invited the White Men to the First Fruits, because he intended to use the Night Muthi to divine their secrets.

And what he had seen . . .

★

What he has seen has . . .

What?

Terrified him? Unsettled him? Puzzled him? Disturbed him?

It's hard to think of the Bull Elephant as being any of these things. But isn't that why these are such dark days?

She had warned him!

She had warned him to be wary of these savages who dwell in the house of the sun.

★

*Shaka! Bull Elephant! King of Kings. Spear Red to the Haft! Sitting Thunder! Defiler and Defyer!*

*I wanted you to come. I welcomed you. Your brothers' eyes were dim but in yours I saw the light of ubukhosi: the strength, the power, the wisdom that would see us elevated.*

*I myself willed him into being, but now his day is done — so I must see to it that he is made to set like the sun.*

# 14
# A Chat With Jakot

JAKOT [*yawning*]: How much longer?

DINGANE [*gazing up at the sliver of moon*]: Not much longer.

JAKOT: Really?

DINGANE: No, but then the moon becomes like a snail when one is obliged to watch it.

★

The two are standing guard. Each man has a wildebeest cloak draped over his shoulders, and each carries an iklwa. Nearby, a longer hunting spear has been thrust into the ground beneath the canopy of a tree. It tilts at a slight angle and, if you stand at the spot where the spear leans away from you and look up at the moon, its proximity to the branch that was pointed out to you when the shifts were assigned shows you how much longer you have left to shiver here and try to stay awake. Once the moon touches that branch, it's time to wake up the next pair of sentries.

★

DINGANE [*after a few moments of silence*]: I have been thinking – about what you said.

JAKOT: Cha! I merely lost my temper with that hippo! I bear him no ill will. In fact he can be quite entertaining at times.

DINGANE: Nonetheless it's easy to forget what you've been through.

JAKOT: You mean the fact that I might actually know whereof I speak? And because some of the things I speak of are unpalatable, it's better to treat me as an object of derision.

DINGANE: Come now! You know you only have yourself to blame for these frequent lapses you notice in our appreciation of your brilliance.

JAKOT: You have me there, my prince. But all too often the truths I speak befoul my own mouth, and it is better to . . .

DINGANE: Play the trickster? But, as I said, I've been giving your words some thought. And it occurs to me we have hardly, if ever, spoken about your knowledge of the ways of the White Men . . .

JAKOT: The White Men interest you suddenly?

DINGANE: Is this not the great service you said you could offer my brother the King – a knowledge of their ways that enables you to look beyond their honeyed words and discern their true motives, and how they might react to this or that decision?

JAKOT: I tried, my prince.

DINGANE: Do you mean to say my brother the King should have dealt with them differently?

JAKOT: Hai! Far be it from me to criticise the King's policies!

DINGANE: You can speak freely this night, Xhosa.

JAKOT: Very well, then, I believe your King has chosen a wise strategy when it comes to the White Men dwelling at the place you call Thekwini.

DINGANE [chuckling]: Why should you be wary of proffering such a view?

JAKOT: Why shouldn't I? For, these days, it seems to even speak out *for* the King is to invite peril.

DINGANE [shaking his head, patting Jakot's shoulder]: And am I to be considered one of those who are likely to make your sudden loyalty perilous?

JAKOT: No, because to you I will say more.
DINGANE: I'm listening . . .

★

And so, keeping his voice low as they patrol the perimeters of the camp site, Jakot explains that while Shaka's policy of friendliness to Farewell, Fynn and company was a clever strategy, it was – is – also one demanding close and constant scrutiny of what's happening at Port Natal. The traders themselves are easy to deal with, for they simply want ivory and gold – but they'll be followed by others who want to acquire land. More and more land. And Jakot speaks from experience, he insists. Clashes between the Xhosas and nomadic white cattle farmers have seen the borders of the Cape Colony pushed ever eastward along the coast. The Crown will intervene to sign a peace treaty with the nearest Xhosa ruler, thereby establishing a new border along one of the many rivers that bisect the region. But it's not long before some pretext is found to break that treaty and push the Xhosas further east.

★

JAKOT: I have listened to your praise-singers, and I know how it was. You were threatened on all sides, but Shaka changed that. Now I say to you that you face an even bigger threat. These White Men are different, and you'll need more than a strong army.
DINGANE: We'll need a strong King.
JAKOT: A strong King, yes, not one who hides away in his hut. And one who is wily enough to understand the threat posed by these interlopers.
DINGANE: It's said my brother the King used the Night Muthi and the First Fruits to uncover their secrets . . .
JAKOT: He could have spared himself the trouble. These savages have no secrets, for their intent is plain. Do not judge all White

118

Men by those at Thekwini. Being outnumbered as they are, they will remain docile. And, as I've said, they want only things they can carry away easily.

DINGANE: And which have no value to us, anyway.

JAKOT: Yes, but beware, for others of their tribe will start to want more. We are to be lied to, then beaten, and soon made to follow their ways. That's how they see us.

DINGANE: But a strong King . . . a wise, wily King . . .

JAKOT: Would be a good start.

★

*A good start, yes*, thinks Jakot, as he settles down on his sleeping mat some time later. But, from what he's seen back in the Cape Colony and from what the scars on his back tell him, he reckons even a strong King won't be enough. But he'll never tell Dingane that. 'Speak freely,' the Needy One had said, but Jakot doubts he's ready for such truths, not least because they point to the ultimate futility of the prince's own ambitions.

# INTERLUDE
## Post-Coital Intercourse

*Thrown overboard into a stormy sea, the waves lifting him high and then dropping him down, down, down, Davy Jones calling out to him, stone walls rising up around him . . . then his head comes up with a start.*

*Not drowning.*

*More like drunk. Head spinning. Body numb. Limbs immobile.*

*He frowns.*

*This is something different.*

*He doesn't know how long he's been unconscious, can't tell whether it's day or night. He's back in the big hut and the torches are melting the copper walls, so that hasn't changed. But there's this . . .*

*He's sitting on some kind of high-backed chair — another artefact they've acquired from God knows where — and his arms are bound to the armrests . . .*

*. . . and, in realising that, he feels the burning across his shoulders, the ghost of that accursed pole, his muscles and tendons now screaming after their release . . .*

*Release?*

*Could it be his servitude is over?*

*Because this is different . . . Yes, they seem to have smeared that hideous potion over his privates, but he hasn't been thrown back onto the rack. (That's how it felt, at any rate: as if he was being stretched on some inquisitor's rack.) Instead he's sitting upright, and a kind of table has been pushed up to his stomach. And there's a silver bowl on it, filled with food. And the old witch is raising a gold goblet to his lips.*

*Bemused, bewildered, befuddled, he allows the liquid to trickle down his throat. It doesn't seem to be alcoholic, but it isn't too vile, has a vegetable taste . . .*

*But it must be alcoholic – why else would he feel so drunk?*

*And his ordeal has to be over, because, let's face it, his 'performance' has been waning. So let them find someone else . . . and let him go. Why not? He's done his share – a silent chuckle – oh, yes, he's done his share! And he's determined. He's no fool and he knows he won't be able to take all the treasure with him, but he's determined to take as much as he can carry – and he's also determined to survive. To make it to the coast, so that he can enjoy his riches.*

*Oh, yes, he's determined. He sniggers. Determined and drunk.*

*Very drunk.*

*Now a silver spoon is hovering near his mouth.*

*He squints. The old witch again, feeding him.*

*He opens his mouth.*

*Chews.*

*Some kind of stew . . . vegetables . . . and – he frowns – some kind of sliced-up sausage. That can't be right – surely these people don't know how to make sausage. No matter, though, for it's delicious.*

*And he's deliciously rich.*

*And deliciously drunk.*

*He opens his mouth to accept another spoonful from the crone.*

*And grins up at the queen, who stands in front of him, with her breasts bare, her only adornment a necklace that seems to be comprised of strips of leather.*

Way hey and up she rises!

*He tries to tell he knows a song about a drunken sailor, marching away from the fall, the rope on your shoulder, stamping to keep time –* way hey, and shave his balls with a rusty razor *– but the words don't come. And it's not because he remembers she won't be able to understand anything he says to her. It's this numbness, he feels: it brings with it a happy apathy.*

Farewell and adieu to you, ladies of Spain, *he thinks with a silly grin, and then greedily slurps up another mouthful of the stew.*

Is he ready? *asks the queen.*

As ready as he'll ever be, your Fertility.

*He watches this exchange with the same silly grin.*

*The queen steps forward.* You have reached the end of your reproductive efficacy, *she says.* You are no longer of use to us.

*He licks his lips.* 'Sorry, me old doxy, can't understand a blind word.'

As you've seen, we have kept our word . . .

*He juts his chin out towards the goblet.* 'Wouldn't mind another swig o' that,' *he says.*

We've kept our word, and have provided you with all the shiny baubles and trinkets you seem to value so much.

*'Put him in the bilge and make 'im drink it!'*

This is a mystery our elders have long grappled with: why people of yours and other tribes should risk their lives, and slaughter others, just to acquire this rubbish. *The queen taps the edge of the gold goblet.* Which can't even be fashioned into a strong blade!

*'Yes, yes,' he says, his eyes fixed on the goblet, 'some o' that!'*

Because none of us has been able to fathom the reason behind what seems suspiciously like pure madness, we have stockpiled and guarded the artefacts left behind by those who tried to subjugate our ancestors.

*At last the crone lets him have a drink.*

*'Thankee, Mistress Cackle!' he says.*

For who knows, *continues the queen,* they may yet deliver up their secrets, their power. But I doubt it!

*Another spoonful of stew. He smacks his lips.* 'Not a blind word,' *he says to the queen.* 'Me no savvy you talkee-talkee.'

I doubt it, because I see you and I wonder how all this rubbish has ever benefited you. Clearly you consider it valuable, but I cannot see how it's ever been of value. Has it brought you wisdom? Has it brought you strength? I don't think so. For just look at you! You are weak! Wrung dry!

*The old crone has moved to his side. He looks down – what's this? – can it be? She's cutting his bonds. It's really over! And he's going to take as much of that treasure with him as he can carry.*

*Then he frowns. The queen is now holding out her hand, the first finger raised.*

We value other things, *she's saying.* Things which bring us strength.

*Only vaguely aware that the old lady has moved behind him and is now cutting the bonds that hold his right arm to the armrest, he frowns, tilts his head, wondering why the tip of the queen's finger seems so swollen.*

We value things which allow us to grow and stretch, and then vanquish the puny Kings who surround us. And so that which is rightfully despised becomes a powerful talisman! Do you see?

*She thrusts her hand closer.*

*He stares.*

*. . . and stares.*

*The old woman steps away from him.*

*And he stares at the thing on the queen's finger.*

*Sees that the queen's finger has been in fact slipped inside the thing.*

*Then she levels the finger at him, and he sees the hole at the centre of the thing . . .*

*Sees that it's . . . well, he doesn't know the correct word for it, of course, and anyway, right now there's no word to express it, just a loud shriek – a loud shriek, then a gasp and a scream that goes on for ever.*

*Slipped over the tip of the queen's forefinger is the glans of his penis and, should he be of a mind to investigate further, he'll find the rest of his*

123

*prick chopped up sausage-like in the stew the old lady's been feeding him. But he's toppling backwards, the horror giving his legs strength, and his hands are pushing through the primitive anaesthetic potion to close over the bloody stump between his thighs.*

★

*When next he regains consciousness, he's dangling from the branch of a tree, with his wrists on fire. But even as the memories come crashing back, the first hyena grabs his left foot — and pulls.*

# 15
## Into The Darkness

He staggers off the path, finds a tree trunk to lean against, and sticks two fingers down his throat.

Dry heaves at first . . . then a geyser of vomit splattering against rotting leaves.

The Induna spits, but that does little to alleviate the burning in his throat, or the foul taste in his mouth.

He pushes himself away from the trunk, identifies the path again . . . shuts his eyes and raises his head toward the sun.

*Cold.*

His toes and fingers, especially, feel as if they've been encased in frost, and this . . . the sunlight, warming his face, his eyelids and his chest, feels good.

But only momentarily.

The ice is deep inside him, and he wants to clasp his shoulders to stop himself from shivering. By his reckoning, the sun is almost at its zenith; it's hot and he's sweating, yet freezing.

*Where are they now?* He hopes Njikiza and Dingane have set a good pace.

He sees again the udibi's anguished angry expression when the Induna insisted he would go after the old woman and her party by himself. Anguished, angry and outraged: why couldn't the udibi stay with him?

Njikiza and Dingane knew the truth, of course, for they saw it in his eyes, in the sweat on his brow, in his efforts to speak without slurring. They could see he had developed the trembling sickness, and that he wanted them to get away from him as soon as possible, for many believed it to be contagious. They also understood that if he – or they – told Mthunzi the truth, they wouldn't be able to persuade him to return to Bulawayo with them.

Even Jakot realised what had happened and had also tried to chivvy the udibi along, saying the pair of them should go ahead of Dingane and the others so as to fill their waterskins – and that was something Jakot couldn't do alone, carry all those full waterskins.

And the Induna had struggled to stand upright and wave to them as they left, because he also had not wanted to alarm Phepho, Namasu and Sola. The effort had cost him and then he'd dozed a while, after dropping to the ground and resting his back against a tree.

'Let us fetch the first sangoma or nyanga we find,' Dingane had hissed, after the udibi was finally led away by Jakot.

'Too far,' mumbled the Induna, meaning he would need a Zulu healer and they were still deep in unfriendly territory.

'I will carry you, then,' said Njikiza.

'No, and you know why!' They couldn't risk others becoming infected.

Reluctantly, his two friends had agreed the Induna was right. While Njikiza held him upright, Dingane had 'dressed' him, draping waterskins across his chest and making sure his bedroll was firmly in place.

Of course, he had no real intention of going after Duthlle, but he knew he had to get away from the compound. It was clear the slavers had been working closely with a local chief who, sooner or later, was certain to send some warriors to see what had happened to them – and to the men he had lent them. There was also the chance that, although he had instructed Mthunzi in no uncertain terms to return to Bulawayo – and on the way

Njikiza and Dingane would keep a close eye on him, especially when they stopped for the night – the udibi would disobey the Induna's orders and sneak away to come looking for him.

The fact that the Induna has ended up following the same path Duthlle and her people took is therefore pure coincidence. It was merely the first track he spotted as he staggered away from the compound.

★

Sick, very sick. His lower back aching. Spasms in his gut. Nausea in his chest. Dry mouth. Spinning head. Fell asleep last night feeling fine; woke up this morning feeling as if he'd been trampled by a herd of cattle.

And their hooves are still gouging into his back, pounding in his head.

Got to keep moving.

*(Why?)*

This foot, then that foot.

Sweating.

Hot and sweating. And also cold.

Lost his shield somewhere.

Still has his iklwa.

Mustn't lose his iklwa.

Can't hold it in his left hand because the fingers there are sore.

'I have heard . . .' he had begun, before running out of energy, and speaking became just too much effort.

And Dingane had instantly understood what he was trying to say. He too had heard of instances where those afflicted by the trembling sickness had fought it without any help from an inyanga, and had defeated it.

And he had heard how some inyangas treated the disease by forcing you to keep moving and thus keep sweating . . .

127

Why are those fingers sore? He tries to flex them, and winces as a pain sharper than the others taunting his body forces him to cry out.

★

Stop.

Sunlight in a clearing.

Rest.

Raising his head, he looks around. He really should move further away from the path – for safety's sake, because you never know who might come along.

He grunts, feeling satisfied that at least he's still thinking of things like that.

Not that he's about to move, though.

Not just yet.

But he will.

Soon.

Because he's got to keep moving.

Because he can't die.

He promised Shaka . . .

★

*Night. It was night, with Kani preparing his supper, and he and the udibi were due to depart at first light for Thekwini . . . night and then Pampata was there, trembling.*

*'The King . . .' she'd begun.*

*'What about the King?' the Induna had interrupted, feeling his heart miss a beat.*

*'He wants to see us!' she replied.*

★

Mnkabayi's thinking about the White Men, those savages from across the Great Waters.

She's thinking of the conversations she had with Shaka, while trying to persuade him not to invite them to the First Fruits.

She's thinking of how she tried to describe to him what her spies had witnessed.

The fact that the izilwane were (and still are) offering succour to those fleeing his wrath had already angered the King. These creatures might have been cowards and criminals, but they were still his subjects, and the White Men seemed to be trying to recruit them into their own tribe, to have them reject Shaka and swear allegiance to King Jorgi.

Mnkabayi's spies had told her of how they were made to line up every morning while the White Men addressed them . . . and then a piece of cloth was made to climb a pole. At sunset, everyone stopped their chores to line up before the pole once more, while the cloth was lowered and folded with great ceremony.

Eventually, Shaka had gone incognito to see this observance for himself. The fact that he didn't know he was witnessing the raising and lowering of the Union flag was immaterial. It was all too clear to him he was seeing what amounted to a King's ministers holding court. That their audience couldn't understand what they were saying was also immaterial. Repeated over and over, the savages' incantations would work their magic and steal away Shaka's children.

He was right to be angry because of the White Men ignoring his warnings to stop offering runaways their protection, Mnkabayi had said. But he was also missing the deeper significance of their ritual.

Why, for one thing, she asked, did the savages choose this particular ritual as a way of inspiring awe in those they protected?

She wishes she had grabbed Shaka and shaken him, and told him to think. Just think! How could he not see they were saluting the sun's arrival, then honouring its setting? How could he not see this as further proof they were of the sun, these savages whose pelts had been bleached by its rays?

★

*Filled with trepidation, they had approached the royal hut. Pampata had even briefly squeezed his hand before ducking inside the indlu. When he followed her, it was as if he was being swallowed up by the hut. There was a fire burning but Shaka was a shadow among shadows, all but invisible. His voice had sounded tired and frayed, the words emerging as slowly as the Induna's sickly footsteps on this day, but there was still a firmness there that brooked no argument, demanded instant compliance. And Shaka had told them how it was likely to be. And then, despite Pampata's protestations, he extracted a promise from the Induna, his most loyal warrior, that he would do his best to ensure it would not be so.*

★

On his knees.

Dry heaves wrenched out of an aching chest.

Something wrong with his left hand. Moving his fingers inflames the pain, and the swollen stiffness now extends down to his wrist.

His head is filled with mist.

A terrible thirst.

He pats his right side where his waterskin hangs – or should hang, except it's no longer there.

Vague memory of emptying it in a vain attempt to douse the drought in his throat, then tossing it aside.

Where's his shield?

Ah, right – lost it some time ago.

His spear!

He's still got his iklwa. At least he's still got his iklwa.

Hunched on his knees as the cramps reawaken.

★

Mnkabayi's again thinking of the White Men, and how strenuously she tried to warn Shaka.

'You have to be careful,' she'd hissed anxiously, 'for they are of the sun, we are of the moon.'

See how the sun has burnt away more than their humanity, she'd told him. Because all is revealed by the sun's glare – or so they believe – they have grown arrogant and feel no need to consult with their ancestors, or to appease them! They are truly izilwane, wild beasts, who have learnt to imitate the ways of the Abantu – Human Beings – by walking upright and carrying weapons, building shelters and taming the iron.

But their reverence for the sun and fear of the moon-darkness that governs our lives – this gives them away.

She's thinking of these things when she finally acknowledges its presence. It entered her hut some time ago and has been standing over her, arms folded, a patient smile playing across its lips, like the shadow across the hut's wall – and it is dread.

*Dread.*

Something has happened to him – is happening to him still. Her sweet, sweet weakness, the only one who has any power over her, is in trouble.

She slips her fist into her mouth to stop herself from crying out.

★

Pampata, too, has a premonition. Or perhaps it's more of a presentiment.

Why had Shaka extracted such a promise from the Induna?

Why would he want to? Why would he feel the need?

What does he know?

What has he seen while peering into the shadows that surround him?

★

The Induna raises his head. Cold night has fallen, but . . .

He sniffs. A smell of burning wood? There's a campfire nearby. He rises.

Moving out of the trees, he staggers down a slight slope, heading diagonally away from where he believes the fire should be.

Just as he's about to reorientate himself, he stumbles into a donga, a dried-out watercourse.

He lands on something soft yet firm, like large waterskins filled to capacity.

The stench exploding around him makes him think: *Dead animals!* Then his right hand finds a face and – moving further along – an arm. And underneath him he can feel a ribcage and a pelvis. And when he tugs on the arm, to try and pull himself forward, the arm comes free, the shoulder flipping over to touch his wrist.

His left hand all but useless now, it's slow progress trying to worm his way over the dismembered bodies, using his one good hand to grip and hold, while kicking himself along with his feet.

Slippery wetness. Then a bloated torso expelling noxious gases as soon as the Induna puts his weight on it. A foot. Another arm, this time hacked off at the elbow. A head, quickly brushed aside.

Then, digging his feet into the earthy slope, he's finally out of the donga. And slithering forward over the dew-damp grass.

Can't die. Mustn't die. Gave the King his word.

Slithering like a snake. A putrid-fetid stench invading his eyes, his mouth, his throat. His left hand frozen into a claw. His legs weaker than a calf's.

Got to keep going.

Fortunately the reek of death doesn't quite obliterate the smell of burning wood.

*The fire . . .*

Must make it to the fire.

A campfire means people. The dangers of being so far from Zulu territory mean little now. He'll take his chances.

*The fire . . .*

He manages to clamber to his feet . . . and blunders into a clearing beneath a large tree.

The fire is a pile of embers within a circle of stones.

Right now, the fact that no one seems to be around doesn't bother him. He drops down beside the warmth.

Opens his eyes.

Must have drifted off.

Rustling.

A rustling in the grass.

That's what pulled him back to consciousness.

Without moving the rest of his body, he turns his head so he's looking away from the embers' glow and into the darkness.

The grass is alive.

The dead men are coming for him and the grass is alive, seething with legs and arms. Arms pulling torsos along, feet kicking heads forward, legs easing through the grass in a sinuous sidewinder motion, fingers digging into the dirt and then darting ahead.

Before he knows it, they're onto him. A clicking of teeth and the wet slap of rotting flesh, and fingers are clawing at his eyes, feet are kicking him, and a disembowelled torso tries to slide over his face.

He twists his shoulders this way and that, punching and kicking, but every time he knocks a hand away, there's another to take its place and teeth bite into his thighs, his arms, while a leg bends as it tries to crush his throat . . . and he bucks and pulls and twists.

Then, suddenly, there're only two hands, one resting on each of his shoulders, and a voice whispering, 'Easy, easy . . .'

# PART TWO

# *Over The Hills & Far Away*

We all shall lead more happy lives
By getting rid of brats and wives
That scold and bawl both night and day –
Over the hills and far away.
Over the hills and o'er the Main,
To Flanders, Portugal and Spain,
The queen commands and we'll obey
Over the hills and far away.

From George Farquhar's version of
the traditional English song,
'Over The Hills And Far Away'

Lieutenant Dub, who felt that the awful concoction was going to his head, knocked with his finger on the table and addressing Captain Ságner said out of the blue:

'The district hejtman and I always used to say: "Patriotism, fidelity to duty, victory over oneself, these are the weapons that matter in warfare." I am reminded of that especially today when our troops will in foreseeable time be crossing the frontier.'

Last lines from *The Good Soldier Švejk*
*And His Fortunes In The World War,*
dictated by Jaroslav Hašek shortly before his death on
January 3, 1933 (translated by Cecil Parrott)

*Voices . . .*

I wanted him to come. *How many times has Mnkabayi told him that?* I wanted him to come – or someone like him. *Confiding in him, her one-time lover, now an old friend and loyal induna:* And, when he came, it was as if I had willed him into existence . . .

*In a strange way that was true. As soon as she heard the brave young warrior in Dingiswayo's service was in fact Senzangakhona's first-born, who had disappeared with his mother so long ago, she began to think – to consider and wonder. And when her brother, on his deathbed, had broken the promise he made to Dingiswayo to acknowledge Shaka as his heir and had chosen dim-witted Sigujana instead, Mnkabayi had disappeared for a while, along with her hand-maidens who could be expected to defend her as fiercely as any man.*

*Later she told Ndlela she hadn't included him in her plans simply out of concern for his safety. So he doesn't know exactly where she went but, judging by the cordiality of their later meetings, he suspects she had gone to visit Nandi. There to plot. And negotiate.*

*But I saw it too. For, on that day, Shaka had met Dingane – another episode that had been the result of Mnkabayi's 'planning' – and addressed the nation for the first time as King, Ndlela had witnessed for himself the young monarch's nobility, the power in him waiting to be unleashed.*

*When Shaka spoke of the great things that awaited the nation, he didn't appear as a ruler seeking to awe his subjects with grandiose boasts. Instead he was a storyteller telling of great deeds that had already taken place – if only in his head. And he had the power to make those things* real. And when Shaka began to rebuild the Zulu army, Ndlela was happy.

Aiee, Shaka, your army, your mighty army – your loyal, disciplined amabutho – that would be your greatest achievement, for from that army flowed all else. Your greatest achievement, Father – but also your greatest evil, and the reason why we are where we are today . . .

*Inviting defeated clans to join the nation as Zulus was another smart move. As was promoting brave officers, thus enabling commoners to join the Zulu nobility.*

I wanted him to come . . .

*And now Mnkabayi wants to see Shaka put down like a rabid dog.*

*'He no longer cares,' she says. 'Whatever's wrong with him . . . well, he remains obdurate, won't listen to his advisors. He is endangering them all. Endangering the nation.'*

*Mnkabayi's right, even if those she has recruited simply see a chance for advancement, a way of increasing their influence and their wealth.*

*The problem is she believes Ndlela thinks she's wrong. That's not true. She's confusing two issues here. Allowing Mhlangana and the sangoma Kholisa to play dangerous games – that has nothing to do with Shaka himself. Raising a zombie has indeed set into motion a terrible train of events, but it's not the cause of Shaka's strange behaviour or why he must now be made to set like the sun.*

*No, the madness initiated by Mhlangana and Kholisa means that nothing they can now do will change the horrors that await the nation. From now on, as Ndlela has told Mnkabayi, nothing will ever be as it might have been or should have been.*

*But Ndlela has resolved to remain quiet, because making Shaka pay for the great evil he has visited on the nation might just gain them the forgiveness of the ancestors, and even strengthen them so that the amadlozi will be better able to help the Sky People in the hard years ahead.*

*Besides, only Ndlela knows the real reason. Only he knows why Shaka must be removed.*

*All else is lies . . .*

# The Adventure Of The Haunted Lake

I live.

Their belief has given me life. Their fear nourishes me.

I live – but these are dark days, and they have grown lax in their observances.

These are dark days and they crawl before Shaka, this bastard son named after a stomach beetle.

He who would usurp the ancestors and disregard the old ways.

He who has abolished the Initiation.

Let warfare be the rite of passage that proves manhood, he's decreed.

But a man is not a man without the Initiation, and who would go into battle with beardless boys?

Not I . . . and am I not a warrior revered for his bravery? Have I not walked with Zulu, the father of the nation? My exploits have made the praise-singers grow hoarse.

Now they sing only of Shaka.

Now they would serve only Shaka.

Herd boys trespass on this sacred haven by coming here to swim in the hot afternoon. They have been forbidden to approach the lake, but they follow the example of their King in mocking the old ways.

They foul this, my resting place, with their laughter and their disrespect, but they have not yet found *The Place*, the secret place, surrounded by reeds and hidden from view, where I go and strip and lie in the shallows, and become the warrior.

I live.

But someone saw me.

The warm mud on the bank. And my manhood hard. My manhood hard in the warm mud.

And she tittered.

And I looked up.

And there she was, peering through reeds that rose taller than herself.

And she laughed.

And I went after her.

And I caught her on the path.

And when she turned round and saw the rock in my hand, she screamed.

Then she was down on the ground, and I was on top of her.

And her face was soon porridge.

Red porridge.

I stopped pounding her, tossed the rock aside, and leant back to inhale the sky.

Ngadla!

I had eaten.

I smeared that porridge over my face, chewed the gristle. Her warm flesh.

I bent forward, biting at her lips, her tongue, her chin, her throat.

I reached into her shattered face and wrenched free a handful of wetness.

Warm wetness.

Sticky.

Slipping my fingers into my mouth I caught the stone.

Pulled it out and examined it.

Not a stone.

A tooth.

One of her teeth.

Dropping it into my pouch, I stood up again and returned to the lake, and lay in the shallows and let the water caress me – until I heard the screams that meant someone had found the girl.

Buya was next on the scene. Buya, that grinning fool with the twisted arm, who can never be a man because he can never be a soldier, and because Shaka has forbidden the Initiation. Buya came upon the old woman shrieking and hiding behind her hands, and he went to the village to summon the men.

There was anger and consternation. They searched everywhere, trying to sniff out strangers. But no one, I noted, came near the lake.

It was too late, though. I no longer needed them.

This porridge, this flesh was more potent.

When I felt hungry again, I fell upon a woman who had gone to fetch water from the stream that flows into the lake.

I was more cunning this time and went armed with an iwisa. I had my hand over her mouth before she even knew I was there. And twisted her neck.

I scratched and clawed, and then her stomach was open. I pushed handfuls of her insides into the water pot, which she had placed to one side while she pissed in the long grass. I beat her face with the iwisa until I could remove another tooth. Then I lifted up the pot and returned to the lake.

When I was full, I threw the remaining flesh into the water, broke the pot, buried the shards and hid the club.

She was the wife of an induna.

Fires burnt the rest of that night, and for the five nights that followed.

People spoke of a curse.

Buya pointed to the lake, said it was the warrior in the lake.

But no one would listen to him, because he was only a man-boy with a twisted arm.

I heard, though, and was pleased.

Sangomas were summoned. They danced and mixed potions and, just to show them what I thought of their magic, I took one of them next.

And when I had stolen his tooth, I pissed and shat on his robes, emptying his bag of bones and charms into the hole I'd left in his stomach.

Female flesh is tastier, more tender, but this had to be done.

Next, Shaka sent one of his indunas: a wise, brave warrior, I've heard it said. He arrived only with his udibi, and I laughed to see such arrogance. But even if he had brought with him a thousand men, he wouldn't have been able to defeat me.

I would have taken another woman then, just to remind the induna who was the true sovereign here, but everyone was afraid. No one ventured beyond the stockade – and if they needed to, they were accompanied by armed men.

And the induna moved among the people, asking questions, always asking questions. And his boy aped him by moving among the herd boys, asking them questions.

He it was who first spoke to Buya, who told him about the lake.

And about the warrior. The brave warrior whose spirit guards the lake.

'He is angry,' claimed Buya.

And the boy listened, and then he told the induna.

Who spoke to the chief.

'Cha!' said the chief. 'He has the mind of a dull ox, that one,' he said, not even caring that Buya could hear him.

And I was enraged.

'Buya,' sneered the chief, 'show him your war necklace . . . You see, Nduna? This one would be a warrior . . .'

I was enraged to see such an insult go unchallenged.

But Buya, the fool, just grinned and said, 'He is angry!'

And I made the sky turn grey. I made lightning whip the ground. And, in the battlefield roar of the storm, I found a spear and cut my way into a hut, seeking the blood of the chief's youngest daughter. Just seven summers old, she opened her mouth to scream, but tasted the blade of my spear instead.

I had to stand on her body to free the blade. Then I removed a tooth and slipped out into the rain.

When the body was found, the induna – this Shadow of Shaka – silenced the uproar and commanded all those who had come running, in answer to the second wife's cries, to gather outside the chief's hut.

The rest, the induna shouted, were to remain inside their own dwellings, and he appointed two of the chief's advisors to keep watch and see that his command was obeyed.

As soon as the storm passed – and it didn't last long – the induna summoned all of the men to the cattlefold in the centre of the umuzi. Then he moved up and down the lines, checking each man's hair and clothing for signs of moisture.

Or blood.

A futile gesture, since all those who had not initially come running at the uproar to see what was happening were completely dry, having sought shelter in their huts as soon as the storm broke. Or else they had good reasons and witnesses to explain why their hair and clothing was wet.

I would show him, I thought.

I would take the boy next, his apprentice.

'What is going on?' I asked him.

'Why aren't you out there with the rest of the men?'

Ignoring the boy's impudence, I grabbed his arm. 'Come, there is something I must show you!'

He twisted away. 'No, my master will be angry. You must join the others!'

'This is important!'

'Cha! What is more important than my master's command? You must come now.'

'No, *you* must come with *me*!'

'You must join the others!'

I grabbed his arm, my grip tighter this time. 'The other *men*, you mean?'

'Yes!'

'But, Boy, can't you see? I am not a man.'

'You are wet, Buya. Why are you wet?'

And he kicked me in the shin. And he slammed his forehead against my mouth. And then he was free, taking my necklace with him.

'Nduna! Nduna! Come quick! I am being attacked!'

But I was out of the hut, slipping around the side, before he had attracted his master's attention.

And the bushes were like spears rattling against shields to honour my passage.

And the water was warm as I lay back in it.

And the sky became brown as the water covered my face . . .

★

'We can't find him, Nduna!'

'You fools, the lake! He'll have gone to the lake!'

'Listen to him,' bellows the chief.

After the men have moved off, he turns to the Induna: 'This spirit, this warrior of the lake, it has possessed him?'

'That may be,' murmurs the Induna.

'Aiee! Who would have thought!'

'The crippled hyena must learn cunning.'

'This is so. But let me join my men now. My assegai would taste this monster's blood!'

'Good hunting, Numzane!'

The Induna turns to the boy. Is he well, or not well?

'Buya is the one who bears the bruises, Master.'

'I do not doubt that, Boy!'

'I have this . . .' The boy holds out the necklace.

It consists of an assortment of pebbles interspersed with bits of folded leather.

'His war necklace,' muses the Induna. 'The dream of a man-boy.'

'It is as the Numzane says, Master. He is possessed.'

'I do not doubt that, Boy, but not by any spirit! He is his own demon.'

'I do not understand, Master.'

'Look here . . .'

The Induna drapes the necklace over the palm of his right hand. 'Is it not our way that a warrior may take a relic from the battlefield as a reminder of his courage?'

'Yes, Master.'

With his left forefinger, the Induna points at one of the stones, a smooth, rounded pebble. 'You will find stones such as this by the shores of the lake.'

Seeing the boy hasn't understood the import of this, the warrior adds: 'Where the first body was found!'

The boy's eyebrows arch in comprehension.

'And this one? The shard of a pot. Was not one woman murdered while fetching water?'

'Yes, Master! It is so.' And that, adds the boy, is that not a bone from the paw of a lion, such as a sangoma might use for divination?

'You are right.'

The Induna holds the necklace up, twisting it from side to side.

The storm clouds have departed and the sky is aflame as the sun sets.

'Look here,' he says, taking one of the leather folds between his fingers and prising it open.

The boy shakes his head in disbelief.

The battlefield relics on the Induna's necklace are interspersed with lion's teeth – which are a sign of rank. However, hidden inside each of *these* leather folds is a human tooth.

Shortly after nightfall, the chief and his men return, crestfallen and angry, having been unable to find any trace of Buya.

The following morning they set about tearing down the entire village, intent on moving to more salubrious surroundings.

And the lake is thenceforth avoided as an evil place. Even thirsty travellers, strangers to the region who have not heard the stories, feel themselves overcome by a sense of unease, when they approach the reeds. And without quite knowing why, trying to laugh at their own foolishness, they seek another path, one that takes them away from those deep, dark, icy waters . . .

They will listen obediently to whatever he has to say, and will probably enjoy the tales he has to tell. But, they agree on their way to the meeting place, there's much they'd also like to ask him — much they will ask him if they can muster the courage (for old generals can be fiercer than cornered leopards).

Questions like: Is it true Shaka could barely speak Zulu when he took the throne?

Is it true he spoke with a lisp and was ugly; so ugly, in fact, that he told one of his advisors the man need never fear being murdered by the King, because everyone would then say Shaka had been jealous of the man's handsome features?

Is it true that he wasn't even a Zulu? That he wasn't Senzangakhona's son but the spawn of one of Nandi's other lovers?

And is it true Shaka himself had a hand in the murder of Sigujana, the son who succeeded Senzangakhona? Is it true he wielded the spear himself? Because that would mean he forfeited his right to claim the throne, for under Zulu law an heir may not murder his father or another heir.

Did he come to the People of the Sky as Dingiswayo's man, thus expected to obey his mentor and do what was good for the Mthethwas, rather than for those who were to be his children?

Or did he instead rebel? Did he betray Dingiswayo to Zwide?

But how, then, could such a cunning ruler let himself be fooled by the White Men who have since proven themselves so deceitful and malicious time and time again?

Or is it true that he foresaw this: that his dying words were a prophecy — and that, with his last breath, he told how White Men would invade the land like locusts?

*Why did he let Mzilikazi escape? Or did his former favourite simply outwit him? But how could that be possible?*

*Mzilikazi? That brings them to the marrow of the bone, all else being merely mindless chewing. These and the myriad other questions they'd like to ask about those long-ago days fade into nothingness when it comes to the one question – the only question if it comes to that – they'd like to ask the greybeard.*

*Is it true what some suggest . . .*

*. . . claim . . .*

*. . . mutter . . .*

*. . . whisper?*

*Is it true that Shaka survived the second assassination attempt?*

*Is it?*

*Is it true he was spirited away by Pampata and a group of warriors still loyal to him?*

*Is it?*

*Is it true he survived the assassins' blades and, having grown tired of the capriciousness of his children, he travelled north where he joined Mzilikazi, took another name, and acted as one of his favourite's advisors until he – the mighty Shaka – passed away peacefully in his sleep . . . ?*

*Is it true?*

*Is it?*

# The Adventure Of The
## Young Officers & The Old General

It's early December 1878, Cetshwayo is King and war with Britain looms.

They don't know it, of course, but the People of the Sky have a clash between the ideologies of the guardians of British imperialism, local insubordination and the Russians to thank for this sorry state of affairs.

The Reform Act of 1867 had effectively doubled the number of (male) voters in England and Wales, and some saw this as a little too much democracy. With an electorate to bear in mind, politicians might no longer have the ruthlessness required if Britain were to retain all those pink areas on the map.

For one thing, others had entered the lists. Germany was flexing her Prussian muscles, while the French remained . . . well, if God had really intended Britain and the Frogs to get along, He wouldn't have created the English Channel.

Then there were the damn Yanks.

In October 1866, Sir Bartle Frere, then governor of Bombay, woke up one morning to find the USS *Shenandoah* riding at anchor there. Since Britain had built cruisers for the Confederacy, the 1,397-ton screw sloop could just as easily have been there to bombard the city with its rifled and smoothbore howitzers and its 7,500-kilogram Parrott rifle which had a range of seven kilometres – and, as a horrified Frere observed, the much-vaunted Royal Navy had nothing afloat within a thousand kilometres to take her on.

Strong, resolute leadership was called for. Instead, as Sir Garnet

Wolseley would later put it, while there was 'no decline in the manly powers' of the Empire's soldiers and sailors, 'the quality of our rulers, the fibre of our ministers' had 'undergone a change for the worse: they have conformed to the democratic system of the day.'

The thinkers and strategists in Britain's military establishment began to believe that, to protect the Empire, they were entitled – nay, duty bound – to take matters into their own hands should it become necessary.

In 1875 Governor Andrew Clarke disobeyed his instructions and entrenched British 'influence' over the Malay states by siding with the Chinese. Interpreting his brief in his own way, Lord Lytton started the Second Afghan War in 1878 and, in Disraeli's words, 'only secured insult and failure'. George Colley did likewise at Majuba in 1881, while General Gordon refused to evacuate the Sudan in 1883.

This kind of insubordination also led to the Anglo-Zulu War of 1879. British High Commissioner Sir Bartle Frere ignored repeated warnings and could have stopped the war – 'but chose to go ahead, even though he knew that it was a step too far and beyond any acceptable discretion he could expect to wield,' notes historian Damian O'Connor.

Why did he do it? Bearing in mind that during his career he'd freed slaves, founded universities, initiated irrigation schemes and was hailed by Florence Nightingale as 'the best of men' when his sanitary reforms gave Bombay a lower death rate than London, why then did Frere disobey orders and issue Cetshwayo with an impossible ultimatum that could only lead to war?

This is where Russia enters the picture.

★

They follow the rustling, silver-flecked stream and, rounding a curve, arrive at a place where the ravine widens to allow a broad strip of grass and trees on either side of the brook. Twenty men armed with spears and shields, they have four bulls and two cows with them. This must be the spot, they decide – a kloof whose entrance is all but invisible, as its walls curve this way and that like a wildebeest's horn, so from afar it doesn't seem as if there's a break in the scarp.

While some of his companions look around and wonder *What now?* and others drop into the long grass to rest, Zamo crosses the stream. The water is cold and it soothes his tired, aching feet.

These men are all junior officers in Cetshwayo's amabutho, and they are still getting used to their ranks. Which means they're still at that stage where they revel in giving orders, after having had to obey them for so long, and therefore bringing them together like this is a recipe for chaos – and also, as Zamo believes, a test. He reckons this expedition is about more than listening to some stories, no matter how enlightening and instructive those tales might be, for their initiative, ingenuity and, yes, their leadership abilities are also being evaluated.

Whatever the case, a band of young officers gathered together, with no troops around upon whom they can exercise their new authority, is unlikely to get anything much done. But, as in any group, one or two individuals are likely to emerge as leaders. Zamo is one of those, not least because he's amongst the oldest.

This side of the stream stretches wider than the other. Climbing the slight incline, he notices that huts have stood here at one time. The floors remain resilient and only here and there have tufts of grass managed to force their way through the hard-packed dirt, while creepers have trailed across from the surrounding foliage.

But something – a disquiet that slips across the borderlands of his consciousness – tells him it wouldn't be a good idea to camp here.

Returning to the other bank, he quietly takes Fanele aside. Wiry, with long legs, Fanele is known as Cheetah because he's fleet of foot; a few summers younger than Zamo, they've been rivals for a while, and he's the one most likely to object should Zamo start issuing orders to the group on his own initiative.

Zamo knows how to handle him, however. After pointing out they have to get themselves organised as quickly as possible, he suggests that both of them take charge, decide on a list of tasks and apportion them. Cheetah nods; he's been thinking the same thing, he says. Good, says Zamo, let them get started. He suggests the first thing they do is put a lookout on those rocks up there. Because the ravine curves and the slopes drop away, the man should be able to see the whole plain . . .

★

By the 1870s the Great Game had resumed, with Russia increasing its influence in Afghanistan and eyeing India's north-west frontier once more. Then, in the Balkans, the Bulgarians revolted against their Turkish overlords. With their eyes on Constantinople, the Russians threatened to intervene. If they captured Constantinople, their navy could threaten Britain's lifeline between London and India, which passed through the eastern Mediterranean and the Suez Canal.

Furthermore, although privateering had been outlawed by the Treaty of Paris in 1856, Russia had established a 'volunteer navy' to do just that – to raid ports, destroy shipping and coal stocks, and even send marines ashore to rob the banks, before disappearing over the horizon again.

The Cape of Good Hope suddenly became of extreme strategic importance. If Suez was closed to British shipping, the Cape would be on the only secure route to India, and so had to be protected from Russian raiders.

That such an attack was possible had been demonstrated by the sudden appearance of the USS *Shenandoah* at Bombay in 1866. And three years earlier, the Confederate States' *Alabama* had visited Simon's Town, situated on the shores of False Bay, on the eastern side of the Cape Peninsula.

However, the colony's defences were virtually non-existent and its guns obsolete. The garrison had also been greatly reduced.

To remedy this state of affairs the colonial secretary, Lord Carnarvon, had chosen Sir Bartle Frere. There wasn't a better candidate, from Carnarvon's point of view. Frere had the necessary experience and he was a good man in a crisis, as he had shown while governor of Sind during the Indian Mutiny of 1857. He was the ideal 'man on the spot', capable of operating without guidance – or interference – from Whitehall.

On the other hand, he was also close to retirement and the governorship of the Cape was hardly a post of suitable distinction for an imperial administrator of his stature.

But Carnarvon dangled the carrot of 'confederation' in front of him. The colonial secretary had introduced the bill for the confederation of Canada in 1867, and for a long while had wanted to achieve something similar in South Africa – with the Boers presumably taking the role of the cantankerous Québécois. If successful, this would see Frere become South Africa's first governor-general, with the possibility of a peerage. His salary would also increase and, as Saul David puts it, 'it was all too much for a man of Frere's vanity, ambition and impecunity to resist'.

When this man Lord Salisbury had once called 'quarrelsome and mutinous' arrived at the Cape in April 1877, he set about improving the colony's defences.

It didn't help that the telegraph cable from London extended only as far as St Vincent in the Cape Verde Islands. From there messages had to be carried to Cape Town by steamer, so if things deteriorated between Russia and Britain, the colony wouldn't get advance warning of possible raids.

But the point is, writes O'Connor: 'Frere was sent out to South Africa not to tame the Zulus but to get ready to fight the Russians.'

And, three weeks after he arrived in Cape Town, Russia duly declared war on Turkey and sent its army into the Balkans.

★

By early afternoon, an idladla, or temporary hut, has been constructed for their guest of honour, under a marula tree. A collection of branches, thatch grass and reeds has been used, but the structure is neat enough. The young officers decide not to build any temporary huts for themselves; instead they'll sleep under the stars.

A large, flat-topped boulder, found further upstream, has been carried to the hut and placed a few metres in front of the entrance close to the fire circle.

The men will sit in curving rows on the other side of the circle while the old-timer addresses them, so more boulders are fetched to enable those seated at the back to see over the heads of their comrades closer in.

Another group has finished constructing a temporary kraal for the cattle several paces along from the idladla.

While helping to build the hut, Zamo had found some poles that had been eaten by ants, which suggested a cattle byre had been in this spot previously.

But that's not the only thing he finds.

While the others settle down to wait for the hunting party to return, Zamo again crosses the stream, skirting the raised area, and wades through the long grass on the other side. He's right opposite the vague roundel where the third hut in the row had been, when his foot kicks something.

Bending down, he picks up a skull. A human skull.

He continues on his way, staring at the skull he now holds, when it suddenly feels as if he's treading on dried branches. He looks down again, then leaps sideways, on to the higher ground where the huts once were located. Bones are littered amid the grass, and there's also an old spear. Gently placing the skull on the ground and carefully making his way between the femurs, ribs and tibias, Zamo retrieves the weapon.

Like the wooden posts he found, the haft has been eaten down by ants to about a third of its length, but the broad blade tells him this must be an old-style iklwa. Aiee, armed with such weapons Shaka's impis had roamed far and wide, proving victorious wherever they trod.

*Will we be able to honour their name, their courage, their loyalty? Although, in our case, we do not seek conquest, merely to protect our homeland*, thinks Zamo. He wonders what those old warriors would think of that, and of how their tribal ambitions have shrunk in these dark days.

*For once more we find ourselves hemmed in, jostled by arrogant nations who think the Zulus are there merely to be swept aside or set to work on their farms and in their towns.*

His discovery also vindicates the unease he felt earlier.

He gazes up at the blue sky, at the aloes and mother-in-law's tongues scattered about the slopes of the ravine, at the shimmering stream. Something bad happened here. The spirits of the dead are at rest, but the horror lingers.

★

On arriving at the Cape in April 1877, Frere was told that Sir Theophilus Shepstone, the governor of Natal, had taken it upon himself to annex the Transvaal. This set the precedent for Frere's tour of duty, which saw him constantly being forced to react rather than take control of the situation.

And Shepstone's action was especially serious. The Voortrekkers had left the Cape Colony in order to retain a certain way of life; to escape the world, in effect, and to be left to their own devices. And it had taken a lot of 'shooting into the brown' to secure this territory. On their way to becoming Boers, the Voortrekkers had had to fight off Mzilikazi's Matabele and other tribes; then there was also the ongoing border dispute with the Zulus to the south. So the Boers weren't going to take this annexation without demur – but they got clever.

The British had been quietly supporting the Zulus in this border dispute to stop the Boers from forging a land corridor to the sea. Were the Boers to resort to arms, they thus faced a war on two fronts: against the British and against the Zulus. However, now they realised that, with the Transvaal having become British, the border dispute had become Shepstone's problem. They could bide their time, keep their resentment in check, and play up the Zulu threat. With that out of the way they could then deal with the British (which they duly did in the First Anglo–Boer War of 1880–1881).

Shepstone toured the disputed area and then met with Cetshwayo's prime minister, Mnyamana of the Buthelezis, on

October 18, 1877. Angry and feeling betrayed, Mnyamana named the Buffalo River – as far as the Drakensberg – and the Drakensberg itself as far north as the sources of the Vaal River as the borders of the Zulu nation.

Shepstone rejected this in favour of the Blood River and the Lynspruit up to its source.

Cetshwayo later modified his demands but, facing growing dissent among the Boers, Shepstone claimed still more Zulu land for the Transvaal.

Eventually, Sir Henry Bulwer, the lieutenant-governor of Natal, and one of the saner minds on the scene, suggested an independent Boundary Commission be set up to investigate the claims of both sides. As Saul and other historians have pointed out, he did not believe that the Zulus were intent on war. Neither did he believe they were a 'rope of sand' – to use Shepstone's description – of discontented tribes that would easily disintegrate if attacked.

Cetshwayo was happy to accept the suggestion. So was Frere, since it gave him more time to build up the British forces needed for the coming conflict. Faced with the possibility of having to cope with a Zulu war, a Boer revolt and a Russian naval attack all at the same time, he had resolved to follow the advice Shepstone had proffered in January 1878 that 'no permanent peace can be hoped for until the Zulu power has been broken'.

Cetshwayo was 'the secret hope' of every petty independent King who felt that 'his colour should prevail', opined Shepstone.

★

Night has fallen. The men have made two fires, and then feasted on a buck the hunting party brought back. The first shift of sentries has been posted at the mouth of the ravine, and the others are sitting around the flames discussing the campaign to come, and the glory that awaits them.

Zamo lies on his back, on the slope behind them, watching the stars sprinkled across the sky and listening to the chatter of his companions.

*We have regularly frightened the Boers up north, so why should the Redcoats be any different? Aiee, the praise-singers and beauties across the kingdom had better prepare themselves, for they will be kept busy once Cetshwayo's lions have stamped on Somtsewu's red ants!*

Zamo has expressed the same sentiments when in his cups, but more and more often of late he's been bothered by the fact that the others can't see there's a difference between guerrilla raids against isolated Boer farms and warfare that involves massed regiments, men on horseback, cannon and firepower. A few amabutho armed with antiquated muskets cannot hope to match the hail of lead they'll face, should they come upon a well-defended position. Hai, see how the outnumbered Voortrekkers broke the Zulu army on their laager at Blood River in 1838, the women loading the muskets while the men fired, and thereby enabling them to keep up a continuous fusillade!

*But*, he thinks to himself with a sigh, *we have drunk the King's milk and soon we will wash our spears in blood, and we will go wherever the generals' axes point . . .*

★

In order to discipline the Zulus, Frere needed reinforcements. He duly sent his request through to the Colonial Office in London, where Sir Michael Hicks-Beach had replaced Lord Carnarvon as Colonial Secretary. Prime Minister Disraeli and the Cabinet denied Frere's request on October 12, 1878.

Although the Berlin Congress of July 1878 had ended the Balkan crisis, Russia remained within striking distance of Constantinople. (And, as O'Connor reminds us, it's important to remember the Russian army was within a day's march of

Constantinople throughout the period of the Anglo-Zulu war, only withdrawing in August 1879.)

In addition, in September, a Russian diplomatic mission had arrived in Afghanistan to pay court to Sher Ali, the country's emir.

Facing the possibility of war on two fronts – in the Balkans and in India – Disraeli was doubtful as to the wisdom of diverting troops to one of those colonies he had once described as 'millstones around our neck'.

With war against Afghanistan looming, he said: 'If anything annoys me more than another, it is our Cape affairs, where every day brings forth another blunder . . .'

The Cabinet would later reverse its decision and send troops, but Frere was ordered not to attack the Zulus.

But what did Whitehall know? Frere was 'the man on the spot' and, writes O'Connor, he confidently expected war with Russia would begin in April or May 1879 when the Balkan passes opened; so that left him a very tight time frame in which to bring the Zulus to battle before he would need to be back on the vital ground that was the Cape; which meant he had to fight soon or he could not fight at all.

So, on December 11, 1878, an ultimatum was presented to a King who had no intention of going to war against Britain anyway. Cetshwayo was to disband his army or the British army would come and do it for him. The fact that the time frame decided upon meant this ultimatum would be impossible to meet wasn't Frere's problem.

★

Where is this old-timer? It's sekupakati kwemini – midday – and there's still no sign of him. One of the young officers suggests that perhaps the journey has proved too much for him, and he's gone on to that greater journey. The others snigger. It's certainly a possibility, but Zamo suspects it's another test.

Midday becomes selima tambana, or early afternoon; which becomes seku ntambana, afternoon proper, and the man still hasn't appeared.

'Do you really think he's testing us?' asks Klebe, whose name means 'Hawk', as the hunting party sets off, heading past them.

Zamo shrugs. 'Perhaps we are all being tested in various ways,' he says, because they aren't the only group of young officers sent out to rendezvous with an old-timer who served during Shaka's time, so that the youngsters can be reminded of how things were and how they can be again.

The fact is, it's only since Cetshwayo's come to the throne that their nation has begun to regain some of its former glory.

The People Of The Sky have gone through some humiliating times, days that brought defeat after defeat. But now Cetshwayo has set about changing that. Here is a King who can square things with the ancestors and restore the great days of Shaka – which is exactly why the White Men fear him.

Afternoon slides into the tranquil time of seliba ntubahle – when all people look beautiful. It doesn't seem as if the old general will be arriving today.

Clutching an armful of firewood, his head down so that his chin can secure some of the twigs, one of the young officers staggers up to the fire circle and drops his load. Then, rubbing his hands, wiping dust and bark off his chest, he finally looks up.

And sees an old man standing in front of the temporary hut.

The youngster gapes. The old man smiles at him. Turning his head over his shoulder, the youngster shouts, 'Madoda!', summoning the others.

Zamo and Hawk are first on the scene, the former instantly recognising the old-timer as the one they've come to meet by the long scar stretching diagonally across his stomach, from above his belly button to where it disappears under his isinene.

'But how . . . ?' begins Zamo.

The old general smiles. 'A wise nduna once taught me that when one is tracking prey, one would do well to stop and look behind one from time to time.' He rubs his hands together. 'Now let us get started.'

★

And he will tell them of great deeds and fierce battles, this old general, who once served as an udibi to one of Shaka's greatest indunas, a man whose deeds are still celebrated by the praise-singers. But he'll also tell of how Shaka brought justice to the nation. He'll tell of the baby and the python. Of the Vanishing Man and the Man Who Was Bewitched. Of the Stockman and the Misplaced Kraal. Of the man who knew too little and said too much. He'll tell how he and Pampata beat the cannibals, and of the day he inadvertently caught a crocodile. Tales of how the Induna helped Shaka to trick Zwide and how Dingane, Njikiza, Radebe and the Induna thwarted the Thembus. There are some things he won't mention, such as the zombie that haunted the First Fruits, or how the Thembus attacked and massacred a village; and he still can't talk of Mgobozi's death, during a senseless skirmish with the Pondoes, without his voice starting to crack.

But he will not spare his young charges by feeding them only the amasi of the past. If they are to be reminded of – and emboldened by – the legacy that runs through their veins, and guides their spears, they must also be told of grimmer times, because these tales speak of perseverance and determination. And if they are to hear of acts of valour on old battlefields, he will also tell them of the hollow fear that precedes the command to attack, when all are still whole and the sky is blue and the dust has yet to rise. And of the howling madness that awaits them when the axe is at last waved and pointed, setting free Cetshwayo's lions, who are also Shaka's lions, for in knowing these things, knowing they are not alone in feeling these things, they'll remain true to their regiments, their comrades, and will let terror become their ally, feeding their muscles and guiding their spears, so that they might just survive the tempest.

And so he will speak of great deeds and fierce battles, and the exploits of big Njikiza, the Watcher of the Ford, who once held back a whole army; of Mgobozi who loathed sangomas, and drove Shaka crazy in his ceaseless quest to be where the action was thickest in order to escape the nagging of his many wives; of Pampata who could wield an iklwa as well as any man . . .

Tales both true and tall.

*Voices . . .*

*Sounds and voices.*

*Dim and distant voices speaking to him from the other side of the sky.*
*A dark shape sitting in darkness, reminding him of his obligation, of the*
*promise thrust upon him. A whisper snaking out through the haze: 'You*
*gave your word, now you must keep it.' A woman hugging him, asking*
*him, telling him, pleading with him to keep safe. A young man, vaguely*
*familiar, saying, 'Let me stay, let me stay.'*

*Then one voice rises out of all those sounds that threaten him: the slith-*
*ering of dismembered legs through blood-drenched grass; the scraping of*
*long nails digging into dirt, coming closer; entrails like pythons coiling*
*around his neck, his waist . . .*

*One voice saying, 'Easy, easy.' An old woman, old yet strong enough*
*to banish those sounds, the broken bodies, and to hold him down.*

*A sagging . . . then the flood of pain. In his stomach. In his back. In*
*his head. Now she leaves him alone.*

*Darkness . . .*

*Voices. It's morning and she's no longer alone, for there are other voices,*
*young female voices. But she is still all he can see. His cracked lips part:*
*'I . . . I know you.' A nod, a gentle instruction: 'Drink this.' Branches*
*and leaves fragment the sky above him. Then the cramps return. Time*
*stretched like snot, then breaking, bringing darkness.*

*Breasts brush his head. A woman holds his head in her lap, so that*
*Duthlle can feed him the muthi. Duthlle! That's her name! He tries to*
*tell her he recognises her, but she's not looking at him. Instead she's*
*addressing the other woman, speaking words he can't understand.*

*Women? He has the sense of being surrounded by women. Are some* carrying shields and spears, like warriors? Or is he imagining it?

Sometime later, a man's voice wakes him up . . . a man's voice rising into a scream. The Induna tries to lift his head, but it's as heavy as a boulder. The scream ends in a truncated gurgle, and he's killed enough men to know what that means.

He wakes up again in the sunshine. Someone's carried him outside here. Duthlle is crouching beside him. 'Well, Zulu,' she says, 'it seems as if we have a problem.'

While she tells him that he clearly doesn't have the Trembling Sickness, his eyes drift past her to where five men sit back-to-back in two rows of three; except for where there's a single gap in one row. One of the women, who carries a shield and spear like a warrior, and who is in fact a warrior, he realises, stands guard over the men. That empty space at the end — he remembers the man who screamed.

Pain draws his attention back to Duthlle, who's examining his left arm, which is so stiff and swollen he can barely move it. Clicking her tongue, she says she's been a fool. 'Does this hurt?' she asks squeezing his forearm above the elbow. His wince is answer enough. 'It is not too late,' she murmurs, gently squeezing at his forearm along its length until she reaches his wrist.

He writhes, cries out, and a command from Duthlle brings two young girls to hold him down. 'I am sorry,' she tells him, 'but this must be done if we are to save you.' Gently raising his fingers with her right palm, she adds: 'But, don't worry, these things are predictable.'

More pain as she examines each finger in turn. Then a smile. 'It is here,' says Duthlle, meaning his middle finger. 'I told you these things are predictable.' If he could raise his head, twist his arm round, he'd see two tiny bite marks in the folds of skin covering the knuckle.

'You have been bitten by a spider, Zulu,' she says, as he lies panting in the grasp of the other women. The men are now forgotten; he is only happy the pain of her examination has ceased. 'And you are lucky, because we can still stop the flesh from rotting, and save you!'

The new muthi she mixes for him quells the stomach cramps, eases the ache in his back, and in his head. The potion she smears over his right hand helps the swelling go down, takes away the stiffness. Soon he can even flex his fingers.

Gradually he becomes more aware of his surroundings. One morning he awakes to note that additional female warriors have arrived, and the double row now comprises twelve men, six on either side. Roused by a scream later in the day, he sees two of the female warriors hauling one of the prisoners away.

'A certain amount of culling is necessary right from the start,' observes Duthlle.

He wasn't aware she was there. 'Culling?' he murmurs.

'Culling,' she repeats. 'But Zulus don't have to worry.'

Culling . . . he remembers the bodies in the pit. Was that the result of more culling? Were they the same men Duthlle and her companion had been captured with? Hai, but what made them so afraid that they were unwilling to speak after the Zulus had rescued them?

He drifts off.

The next day Duthlle wakes him up to feed him. He is getting stronger.

'You saved me,' he murmurs.

'Yes, I did,' says Duthlle. 'But don't be too grateful, Zulu, for you may yet live to rue that.'

# The Adventure Of The Philandering Prince

Ukuhlobonga, he said. It was just ukuhlobonga: the Pleasure of the Road. A mere dalliance. A hard cock pressed up against clenched thighs. And if penetration occurred, a fine of a few cattle paid to the girl's father would suffice. And she would still be regarded as a virgin.

'Did you complain when I singled you out?' he asked. 'No!'

'Did I wrench your thighs open?' asked Mhlangana, and once more answered his own question: 'No!'

No, you groaned and you sighed. You held me tighter and offered me your lips. You whispered endearments, as well as throatier imprecations to thrust harder – and deeper. *Deeper.*

Running the back of his hand over his lips: oh, yes, she enjoyed it. Giving voice to the thought: 'You enjoyed it! Don't lie!' A mocking sneer: 'It's only now that you complain. And you come to me with a squalling brat and demand marriage? Marriage!'

The impertinence! He is a prince, she a mere dalliance. How dare she!

Did she think she was Nandi?

Well, that was just it. That was why he couldn't chase her from his kraal like a feral dog.

Turning away from her, he calls for Bamba.

'Master?'

'Take her . . .' Glaring at the woman, her defiance undimmed by his rage: 'Take this one away. Get her out of my sight, for I must think.'

He grabbed the woman's elbow. 'I must think, pretty one,' he hissed, 'of reasons not to have you thrashed, or worse.'

Looking past her, at Bamba: 'Here, take it!' His hand comes up in the gesture of one who has just dropped something unpleasant. 'And return to me immediately!'

'As you wish, Master.'

He swung round, showing her his back. He meant thereby to indicate his disdain, but he also wanted to free himself from those eyes – her eyes – so knowing.

And she did! She did know what he was thinking.

*Nandi!* That's how she wanted to be seen – as a second Nandi, impregnated by a Zulu prince and then spurned.

Because how would Shaka react when he heard one of his brothers had treated – or was about to treat – a maiden as Nandi had been treated so many years ago, time having done nothing to soothe the King's anger and stop the memories from rankling?

What would he do?

And Mhlangana was sure the girl would see to it that word of her treatment at his hands reached the Bull Elephant's ears.

Any other King and it would have been something to laugh about. How naive this girl was! Who was to say how many others she had opened her thighs for? Who was to say the baby was really his?

'Master?' Bamba had returned.

'You heard what was said?'

Bamba nodded.

'Does she have the brat with her?'

'No, Master.'

'No, that would have been too easy!'

'Master?'

'A mother and child on the road, travelling alone? Aiee, who knows what might befall them some dark night on a perilous path.'

168

Bamba coughed. A polite interruption. 'There is the sister, Master . . .'

'Ah yes,' said Mhlangana, only vaguely remembering the presence of a second, younger girl while he had been doing his wooing. Or, rather, the gruff monosyllables giving way to the sudden lunge which passed for wooing in his case. He was nowhere near as adept in the art as his brother Dingane. Nor as proficient in making good on the promises of pleasure hidden within his honeyed words.

'Doubtless the brat is with the sister.'

'She indicated as much to me, Master.'

'Speak to her, did you, Bamba?'

'Merely to warn her.'

'Good, good. How dare she! How dare they! Because I tell you, Bamba, this is something they cooked up together, her and her sister. For one alone would surely see the folly of threatening a prince into marriage! Preposterous! But two together – hai, the one encourages the other, like naughty children.'

Mhlangana scratched his chin, then nodded. 'Doubtless the pair of them think they're being very clever, but we'll show them what true cunning is.'

Bamba will leave tomorrow, with an escort of, say, six warriors. He'll take the maiden back to her home kraal.

'You will tell her you are my representative, and you are there to negotiate the lobolo to be paid.'

'And then, Master?'

The prince grinned. 'And then nothing, Bamba! The rest will be up to the ancestors!'

★

A shimmer slicing through the night, slipping between the sounds, the barks and coughs, the chirruping and rustling. Like a whisper or a fleeting thought. Easing past the sentries and the dozing huts like a breeze. Not even the dogs notice him.

Which is as it should be.

For is he not a prodigy, the child who spoke while still in the womb, saying: 'Mother, I am ready. Give birth to me!' Is he not the one who thwarted the cannibals? Is he not the night? That special, potent night of the dead moon, called isifile, and ngolu mnyama namhla – the dark day thereafter – when human beings are especially vulnerable to evil.

But not him, of course, for he is one of the creatures that make the time of the dead moon and the dark day so dangerous.

And so he slices through the night, a momentary frown, a vague presentiment.

★

A clicking sound.

Mhlangana's eyes snap open. He had drifted off despite himself, for he was expecting this visitation, but now he is instantly awake, his eyes probing the darkness inside his hut . . .

. . . which is too dark . . .

The prince raises his head slightly. Cha! The weasel has doused the embers he had carefully cultivated before tiredness and the boredom of waiting had caused his eyes to droop.

'You are awake, my prince.'

A statement, not a question, and even further cause for irritation. First the clicking of the tongue, summoning him the way a master would a lackey, then this sardonic stating of the obvious.

'Such perspicacity,' says Mhlangana, sitting up.

As usual he's surprised by its voice. *His* voice. It's slightly hoarse and grating, but it's able to adopt the refinements used by men – the amabeshu growl, the feigned politeness that covers sinister motives, like the isinene, the hauteur of the leopard skin, the boastfulness of plumes. And it's unnatural because you'd expect one such as this to speak as a snake might, with a threatening hiss; or perhaps the inane snigger of the vervet monkey.

'I came as soon as I saw the smoke,' says the voice in the darkness. (Where is he? Why do his words seem to be coming from somewhere near the domed roof of the hut?)

'But I am perplexed,' continues the voice. (Had he – it? – been clinging to the thatch directly above Mhlangana? But surely he would have heard the scuffle of nails, when the weasel changed position, because the source of the voice definitely seems to have moved to a spot near the hut's entrance.)

'Perplexed?' asks Mhlangana, his eyes aching with the effort of trying to penetrate the blackness.

'Yes,' says the voice, shifting to the prince's right, 'for I cannot understand why it took you two sleeps before you sought out General Hlakanyana's assistance.'

(Hanging against the wall in that section of the hut are some hollowed-out tree trunks, wherein the prince's more precious head-plumes, those made from ostrich and black finch feathers, are stored. Why hasn't he heard wood scraping against thatch, some kind of rustling, or any other sounds one would expect from a creature moving along the hut's curving wall?)

Mhlangana rises to his feet, resolved not to strain his eyes any further. The effort is too distracting – which is doubtless the weasel's intention. It also hampers his strategy of adopting a casual air in his dealings with the creature. (Because, with this one, even revealing distaste will be considered a victory. For he will – probably quite rightly – see one's disgust as a sign of weakness to be exploited.)

'What's that you say?' asks Mhlangana, stifling a yawn.

'Two sleeps, my prince, and with this being such a serious matter?'

That he – it? – should have heard of Mhlangana's predicament doesn't surprise Shaka's brother. Hlakanyana has his ways of finding out even the most carefully guarded secrets.

'Think you so?' asks the prince, feigning indifference.

'Indeed. The more so as you are not quite ready to, shall we say, capture the King's attention. Not just yet.'

'Watch your tongue!'

'Cha! We are alone. Your sentries are elsewhere, as you intended.'

'Nonetheless.'

'Nonetheless,' the other echoes.

Aiee, that voice! He will never cease to be unnerved by it. Although the fact that this creature can actually speak is alarming in itself. Yes, when it opens its mouth you'd be forgiven for expecting gurgles and howls and other such baby sounds. Or a sound not of this world. But not *words*.

'Besides, yours was not the only path before me,' murmurs the prince.

*Now* there's a soft thump . . .

. . . which after a second's consideration isn't all that reassuring. It's a sign the weasel has decided to stop acting like a baboon, but it also means the prince wasn't mistaken and that this creature had somehow been scurrying across the walls of his hut.

'Hai,' says the creature, speaking now from somewhere within the isililo sesifazana, the female section of the hut, 'here there is only one path. And it's mine! For am I not a prodigy? Am I not the one who told his own mother when he was ready to leave her womb? Did I not cut my own umbilical cord? Did I not tame the leopard? The night?'

General Hlakanyana, he boasts, is the only one who can make this toothache go away . . .

General Hlakanyana is the only one who can make this woman and her child and her sister vanish like the morning mist.

General . . .

Yes, yes, he gets the picture, mutters the prince.

But does he also understand that every night that passes endangers him even more? Because, adds Hlakanyana, Mhlangana surely doesn't want word of his transgression to reach Shaka's ears – and the chances of that happening increase the more they delay.

What's more, sending Bamba off to initiate lobolo negotiations could have the opposite effect. Such a holding action might yet turn this event into a rout, because the fact that the prince is now showing a willingness to wed the wench is good reason for her to broadcast her happiness to the world at large. Still, it's something that they can turn to their advantage.

'What do you mean?' asks the prince.

'Well, I won't have to go looking for her. I'll know where to find her.' And her sister and the baby won't be far away, either.

★

They speak some more, then he – it – departs before the prince realises he's gone and Mhlangana ducks out of his hut to stand seething in the cool night air.

The way Hlakanyana had the effrontery to remind him that, even if he did marry the girl, Shaka's gaze would remain firmly fixed on him! And, as the creature had hinted, Mhlangana can't afford that; he can't afford such close and sustained scrutiny. Not if he wants to see his brother overthrown.

*Overthrown?* No, there will be no usurping. When that day dawns, he'll merely be taking the throne back from the Beetle. Retrieving what is rightfully his.

★

To make matters worse, a gale has blown up. It whistles between the huts, mocking even the tightest thatch and threatening to rip it off, toss it aside as though it were a flimsy mat. It moans and groans. It flattens the grass and tears off leaves and even branches from the trees. Only those who need to will venture out, and meanwhile the herd boys shelter among their cattle as they guide the animals home a good few hours earlier than usual.

And Mhlangana always finds his mood changed on windy days – flattened like the grass, you might say. It's harder for him to concentrate and his temper is that much more brittle.

And he needs to concentrate, right here and now. He needs to watch and listen.

Why is the Induna here? Has Shaka somehow heard of his brother's problem with the maiden – and sent the Induna to investigate?

If that's the case, thinks Mhlangana grimly, he couldn't have arrived at a worse time!

But that's just it: the timing is wrong. Things have happened too quickly. Shaka might well have heard of his indiscretion . . . but could an emissary have got here so quickly?

It's about a week later, and even though Mhlangana had vacillated for a few days after the unpleasant encounter with the girl, it's still unlikely that even the Induna could have covered the distance from Bulawayo to here in that time.

That's assuming the girl hadn't boasted of her accomplishment even before coming to find the prince and therefore, the story having already reached Shaka's ears, the Induna was on his way even as the girl drew in sight of Mhlangana's kraal.

'No,' thinks the prince, pulling his wildebeest cloak tighter around his shoulders and shuffling further away from the hut's entrance. 'Bury that thought.' Anyway, the reason the Induna has given for his presence here is believable. And it contains a nugget of information that might yet prove valuable.

For why has Shaka sent the Induna to reconnoitre the border with the Ndwandwes? Is it true, as some whisper, that the Beetle has a spy in Zwide's court? Could it be that the Induna was sent to meet with this spy? And isn't that a sign Shaka is preparing a second campaign against the Ndwandwes?

But these are musings to be put aside for now. What matters is that the Induna is here.

Things had been going well, and this affair had almost been resolved, now this.

Mhlangana peers out of the hut's entrance. He can't see much – just hard-packed dirt and part of the indlu across the way – but the haze is there. A fine spray of sand and dust staining the sky.

Movement . . . then the Induna himself is squatting in the hut's low opening.

'Come in, come in,' says the prince.

Bamba takes the warrior's place as the latter shuffles into the gloom of the indlu. The prince tells him to keep watch.

'As you wish, Master,' says Bamba, standing with his head turned away from the gale's jagged teeth.

A Zulu hut has a door of sorts: a square wickerwork screen that can be slid into position between poles planted on either side of the ikotamo, or door-arch. The prince asks the Induna to pull this to after them. It should provide them with a little more shelter from the wind, while the gaps between the intertwined leaves that make up the isivalo will still allow some light through.

'You have spoken to the woman?' asks Mhlangana, as the Induna turns back to him.

'Yes, Master.'

'So everything is ready?'

'Yes, Master.'

'Are we doing the right thing, Nduna? I could not forgive myself were harm to befall the infant.' After all, there's still the possibility that this woman they seek had killed her sister.

They've been through this before, and the Induna has to bite down on his impatience. He needs to return to Bulawayo, where Shaka awaits him; but, of course, Mhlangana is a prince who must be humoured.

'You are right, Master,' says the Induna. 'We can't be certain. But I don't think this was the work of a woman.' The body had been too battered: broken bones had pushed up the skin in some places; her eyes were all but invisible, sunk deep into swollen tissue; and there were what looked like bite marks on her throat, shoulders and hands.

'And, on hearing of the killing, the sister fled,' muses the prince. 'Because she knew who was responsible and was afraid for her own safety.' Too true! And the reason why his own situation has become so hazardous.

Yes, says the Induna, that's very likely, because why else would she have made arrangements with a neighbour – the woman he and Bamba have just been to see – to look after her child? And these arrangements had been made before the murder, so the sisters had obviously known they were in danger.

'And you haven't been able to discover what this danger was?'

'No, Master.' And this suggests to the Induna that death for one or both of the women had not been a foregone conclusion. With a baby to take care of, they would not have willingly placed themselves in jeopardy. No, there had to have been the possibility of some gain; of something to make the risk worth taking.

'But they were wrong,' says the prince, 'and now one is dead and the other is hiding who knows where.'

She's out there somewhere, and she may be frightened, but she also knows who was behind her sister's murder, and Mhlangana can't have that. Even if she's unable to muster proof, she'll still have the King's ear. Mhlangana won't be able to shrug off her accusations, because there'll still be the grim fact of the baby itself – and the girl's other claims. But the Induna thinks he has found a way of luring this troublesome female out into the open.

The neighbour taking care of the child has told him how devoted the mother was to the infant. Inevitably she'll come for him, and the story they've put about – that Mhlangana will be taking the infant with him when he returns to his home kraal – will only cause her to hurry. Then, reunited with her child, she can make good her escape.

Yes, thinks Mhlangana, and then head straight to the Beetle at Bulawayo . . .

★

Muttering the Zulu equivalent of 'Fuck this', Bamba moves around the curved wall of the hut until, dropping to his haunches and resting his back against the thatch, he finds himself a modicum of respite from the wind.

As one of the few who know about Hlakanyana's existence, Bamba wasn't surprised when he received word from the thing's slave that Mhlangana had ordered Hlakanyana to intervene in this affair. He'd even wondered why the prince hadn't sent Hlakanyana in the first place, not that he would ever have dared to suggest that. He's allowed to know of the creature's existence, but never permitted to mention it in the prince's presence. Only Mhlangana can introduce the monster as a solution to a problem.

And when Bamba came to realise why the prince hadn't simply despatched Hlakanyana to deal with the conniving maiden (and her sister) in the first place, his disgust only intensified.

Bamba was to draw out the prey, which, in effect, made Bamba a servant of the creature's, just like the poor slave who had sought him out two days ago. A warrior can serve a prince as selfish and spiteful as Mhlangana, and still see his own kraal filling with cattle – but to be a creature's creature, that is too much!

And that his prince seems happy for him to act in such a capacity . . . well, that needs some thought. That's a development that needs to be chewed on, with one eye on the hills, and on the path you'd take were you to set off for KwaBulawayo.

Worse still, Mhlangana doesn't seem too perturbed by the possibility that Bamba might be blamed for the girl's death. He is, after all, known to have had an 'interest' in her! Is this how it will be one day? When Mhlangana feels Bamba has served his usefulness, will he simply sacrifice his induna – and in such a way that Bamba is unable to betray any secrets?

A wry grin. Aiee, but she had tricked them in the end! Saying she understood his master's need to be discreet, she had arranged to meet Bamba by the river after nightfall. It would be their second meeting, and the one where Hlakanyana was to intervene.

Had the girl herself suspected something? Or was it her sister who urged caution?

Bamba reckons it's the latter. Though he met the sister only once, she had immediately revealed herself to be the more forceful of the two.

But, however it happened, it had been the sister who turned up to continue the lobolo negotiations with Bamba, only to find Hlakanyana waiting for her instead.

And now the other one has vanished. And the Induna is here.

★

It's 1819 and it is indeed happenstance that's led the Induna, his udibi and two soldiers of the Fasimba regiment to this umuzi. He's told Mhlangana they're returning from undertaking a reconnoitre of the Ndwandwe frontier, but in fact it's as the prince surmised. Shaka has a spy called the Honey Man, who is close to Zwide, and the Induna was sent to meet with one of his messengers. The meetings occur whenever the moon is isilucezu – in the first quarter.

And it was merely coincidence that he and his party arrived here yesterday morning, shortly after the girl's body was discovered. The news from the Honey Man isn't urgent – Zwide is still rebuilding his legions after the thrashing they received at Gqokli Hill – but Shaka is waiting and the Induna needs to get back to KwaBulawayo as soon as possible.

At the same time, as a representative of the King, the Induna couldn't spurn the village headman's pleas for help, and he had agreed to oversee things until Mhlangana arrived. The umuzi lay within in his district – in fact, one of his indunas had been courting the dead female's sister; and this man had gone to fetch his master as soon as the body was discovered.

'Nduna, I must ask you this yet again, for it is something else I need your reassurance about. Are you sure Bamba . . .'

The wind bumps against the hut, then staggers off with a low moan. Look up towards the smoke hole in the apex of the roof, and you can see swirling dust caught in the weak rays of sunlight, as the haze outside tries to invade the indlu.

Mhlangana tries again: 'Are you sure Bamba didn't have anything to do with this?'

And again the wind attacks the thatch, and again there's the groan like that of a dying man.

The prince should know what his own man is capable of, but the Induna doesn't point this out. Instead he says he doesn't think so. Bamba arrived here and announced his intention of courting the maiden to the headman, who was the girls' guardian since their parents were dead, their father having fallen at Gqokli Hill and their mother succumbing to illness a few months later. Then Bamba met with the girl. When she didn't arrive for their second meeting, he'd said he waited a while before rejoining the warriors who had accompanied him to the village. The sister's body was found the following morning.

'He could have slipped away while the beer flowed, but I think you are right, Nduna,' says the prince.

Bamba had no reason to harm either of the girls, adds the Induna. Considering which, that's one of the elements which puzzles him the most. Why had the *sister* gone to meet Bamba? 'This is why we must find the other maiden, Master,' he suggests.

'Oh, I agree, Nduna, I agree!' Mhlangana pauses a moment, marshalling his guile, for this next manoeuvre requires caution.

But, he explains, it might take a few days before the girl becomes desperate enough to come for her baby, even though she knows he'll be leaving soon and taking the infant with him.

'And I know you are anxious to get back to Bulawayo.' The prince holds up a hand. 'Cha, do not say otherwise, for I know you are on an errand for my brother. And I know that, as much as you want to assist me here, that errand must take precedence over all else. So go, Nduna, make ready for an early departure tomorrow morning, when, hopefully, this infernal wind has left us. Continue on your journey, and my men and I will wait here for this maiden, to see what she has to say.'

The Induna hesitates but a moment, then says: 'I thank you, Master, for understanding my predicament.'

'Think nothing of it. Clearly my brother sent you to the Ndwandwes for a good reason. Now you must finish your assignment.'

'I will do as you say, and leave on the morrow, Master,' says the Induna. Secretly, he's loath to leave the matter unresolved, but he really has no choice.

★

She comes for her child the following night. The risk is great, but the herd boy, who is infatuated with her, and who has been bringing food and drink to her hiding place, has told her the prince will be leaving the next day and taking the baby with him. Quite why Mhlangana should want to do this, after having denied paternity, is beyond her, but it means she has to act now, tonight.

Hiding behind a low storage hut, she hears her baby cry, then sees Malinde leave the hut. At least she assumes it's Malinde, the older woman with whom she left her child. And she doesn't stop to consider where Malinde might be going at such a late hour. *Her baby!* Getting her baby and leaving this place, that's all that matters right now.

She darts forward, and ducks inside the hut.

There's her infant, wrapped in a cowskin. She can just make out the tiny form in the glow of the embers in the fireplace.

She shuffles towards the baby on her hands and knees, tears of joy and relief in her eyes. How she's missed him.

'What nonsense is this?' her sister had wanted to know, and that's why she herself insisted on going to meet that fool Bamba the second time. Did the prince really think he could fob her off on to one of his indunas? Or perhaps it was all a ploy to seize possession of the child. 'No, better let me go this time,' the sister had said, 'I'll put him right!'

Her poor, brave sister. She'll avenge her, never you fear, but first she must get her precious son to safety.

And she's about to scoop the baby up, when the cowskin parts and the assegai blade is thrust into her throat, stilling her scream of horror before it even has time to form.

And then he seems to suffer a relapse of sorts. A fuzziness fills his head, and his limbs feel limp. He can barely move, and needs help when he has to piss or shit, with his arms draped around the shoulders of two of the female warriors who, from the tone of their exchanges, resent having to help him. Once, when a disturbance breaks out over where the men are secured, he's left to drag himself back to his sleeping mat by the fire.

What's wrong? He can't ask because Duthlle has gone off somewhere, and none of the other women speaks his language.

He's worried – afraid, even – because he thought he was getting better.

'But you are! Have no fear about that.'

The Induna opens his eyes. It's the time of isifile, the dead moon, but he has no trouble making out Mgobozi's features.

'G–General?' he whispers.

'Hai, do not assume you have set like the sun and embarked on the Great Journey.' Mgobozi looks around. 'Although I'd say you face a tramp of comparable duration.'

'What . . . what is wrong with me?'

'They have healed you, but now they've changed the muthi and seek to keep you docile.'

'Why?'

'Oh, come now, Nduna, you can't be that docile! They clearly mean to keep you with them, and this is the easiest way. It also leaves the others free to guard the rest of the captives.'

'Captives?'

'Yes, and you are one too – the one they most fear.'

'The old woman . . . ?'

Mgobozi shrugs. 'I don't know where she's gone but, if you were to ask me, I'd say she's off rounding up the remainder of her little herd, so that they can be on their way.'

'But to where? And why?'

'I cannot tell you that. I can only see what you see, and hear what you hear, Nduna.'

The Induna tries to nod, but it's as if he's floating in mud. It's all he can do to keep his eyes on Mgobozi.

'I . . . I am sorry, General.'

'Sorry? Why?'

'Sorry I wasn't there . . . wasn't there that day . . .'

'Cha! It was my own foolishness that led to my demise. And if you had been there, Nduna . . . well, perhaps more of those Pondo worms would have died. But then again, there might have been two dead Zulus instead of one!'

And doesn't the Induna remember the conversation they had had around a campfire beneath a purple sky, one night? The one about puddles and lakes?

Indeed he does.

'Some men, like our Father, have minds like lakes: wide and deep, which is to say capable of deep thoughts and with an understanding as wide as the sky,' Mgobozi had said that night.' But as for me, my mind is like a puddle! Just as any good soldier's should be,' he had added to the amusement of the Induna and Radebe, who was also there.

'A puddle, General?' asked Radebe.

'A puddle, Radebe,' repeated Mgobozi. 'There is no need for depth, or width. Show him the enemy and that is all he needs. That and the cattle his King rewards him with.'

He had meant every word, he told the Induna later, while they were taking a piss. 'And there lies true contentment for me, in the ebb and flow, crash and clatter of battle, where forward, forward, ever forward is the only way to go,' he'd explained.

However, there were those like the Induna who were something else altogether. 'It is so,' he said. For as long as great deeds are praised, Shaka's name would be remembered. 'But,' he continued, 'it is your muscles and sinews, and the muscles and sinews of those like you, who will bind this land together, give it its strength and ensure there are future generations to discuss great deeds and to praise Shaka's name.'

'So be patient,' says Mgobozi now. 'They'll have to stop feeding you the muthi when it's time to depart. And, as I said, I think you have a long slog ahead of you. It will be arduous, but use that time to recover. To help others.' There's a frightened youngster among the captives, who can't be older than sixteen summers; the Induna should attach himself to the boy, aid him when he falters. In doing so, the Induna will be able to rest too. It's an old recruit's trick – stopping to help a fallen comrade during a punishing drill, so you yourself can rest – and something the general always watched out for.

'Me, too,' murmurs the Induna.

'Do that, then. Bide your time. Watch and wait.'

'I – I am sorry,' says the Induna, 'sorry I wasn't there that day . . .'

'Cha! While taking care of my wives and children – a man couldn't ask for more. So do not fret, Nduna! For I am in your debt.'

The Induna's fingers twitch as he tries to raise his hand, for Mgobozi now seems to be seeping away into the darkness.

'But are you listening to me?' asks the general. 'You will do as we have discussed?'

'Y-yes,' says the Induna. 'Yes . . .' he murmurs again, his eyelids growing heavy.

'For seeing what you see, and hearing what you hear,' says Mgobozi as he fades from sight, 'I'd have to say you're in a certain amount of shit here.'

# The Adventure Of The Persistent Suitor

The persistent suitor has dropped a burning torch into the cavern. Peering through the opening in its roof, he can clearly see his beloved's face gazing up at him. She's giggled a bit, pretended to be afraid, chided him for not following her down there, but pulling up the rope instead. She's become annoyed with him, telling him this might have been funny a short while ago, but now he must help her. Annoyance has turned to anger – what does he think he's doing? Anger has given way to spitting rage, like the impotent flailing of a younger, weaker sibling. Just wait, just wait until she gets out! Rage became weeping, finally, pleading. Why is he doing this? 'Because I love you. I love you the way thirst loves water. You must see that. Why must you look away? Am I not enough? What more can I do?' So says the persistent suitor.

'But it can never be!' says the reluctant object of his affections. 'Can't you see that? Please, you must see that! Help me to get out of here, and we'll forget this, say it was just a game. I hid, you found me, and we'll forget this. Please!'

The suitor laughs. 'The time for games is over, my love. You *will* be mine!'

★

A chief's daughter has gone missing, and he was on the point of sending to KwaBulawayo for help. Then he heard that the Induna and some of Shaka's elite Fasimba impi were nearby, so he immediately despatched a messenger to find the King's representative.

Aside from the Induna and the boy, there are eight warriors

in the party, and their journey takes them over the rolling hills of the high country. It is a landscape of changing textures, with temperate, longhair grassland on the moist, south-facing slopes, and shorter, stubbier sourveld grass on the other slopes. The shades of brown and green are interspersed with the pink of proteas, the red-and-yellow cone-shaped flowers of red-hot pokers. Gnarled ouhout trees, bent like arthritic old men, announce the presence of streams; some have eland browsing on their shoots. Shadows in the sandstone ridges are caves and overhangs, where the strange markings of the Old Ones can still be seen.

Ignoring paths, the men travel in the straightest line possible, leaping dongas and streams, causing springbok to imitate them as the animals bound away. Spear grass has sharp pointed seeds, but the warriors' bare feet have been toughened against such hazards.

★

'Beloved,' whispers the suitor, 'you know the story. Do you not know the story? You know it . . .'

And he tells her the story of the young girl who refused all suitors. She did not care for the young men of this region, she told her parents. But if one came from far off, she would marry him. Because she imagined elsewhere would be better. Then, one day, a handsome young man swaggered into the village. He had ivory bracelets on his arms and copper bangles, and at his waist was a Ma-Iti dagger, a relic of those who once tried to enslave us, and which these days, as you know, is a potent talisman. And he had a lion-skin cloak – which isn't surprising because he *was* a lion. A lion in human form.

And no one suspected anything – except the maiden's little brother, but he was told to shut up and mind his manners as soon as he tried to voice his suspicions. And the lion married the maiden. There was much feasting, with the mother proud of her daughter's handsome husband, and the father smiling over the bride price the young man had paid. It was more than he had ever hoped for – since his daughter had long ago acquired a reputation for being hard to please, and suitors had stopped paying court. The next day they waved goodbye to the couple, for the husband was taking his new wife off to meet his family.

After a long journey, they came upon an old hut standing alone and forlorn in the veld . . .

*'Much as you have often left me forlorn,' whispers the persistent suitor.*

. . . The husband told his wife not to be afraid. She was to wait there while he went on ahead to his village, which wasn't far, to warn them to make ready for their new arrival. He left her and was gone a long, long time.

Night fell and the girl grew ever more afraid. Then the lions came for her – for her husband had changed back into his true form – and they feasted on her, praising the lion-man. Such tender virgin flesh!

★

While the others seek out the quarters allocated to them, then begin preparing a meal, the Induna and the boy are ushered into the unumzane's hut. With him are his eldest son, his two senior wives and the clan's sangoma. Anxious faces – streaked orange and black in the flickering flames of the fire burning in the centre of the hut – greet the Induna and the udibi. Faces creased with worry and concern.

Truly, the unumzane is at a loss to account for what happened. Early one afternoon his daughter Sibongile went to fetch water. On the way to the stream she encountered her brother Zodwa and, according to him, she seemed her usual self. 'She was always cheerful, always laughing,' adds the chief, at which point one of the wives, clearly the girl's mother, starts sobbing softly.

After talking to her brother for a few moments, Sibongile continued on her way. That was the last Zodwa – or any of them – saw of her. 'I'll show you the path tomorrow,' he says.

'Was no one else fetching water?' asks the Induna.

'Not at that time,' says the unumzane.

★

'You deny me, ever on the lookout for someone better. But this is to be your fate: the one you choose will be a lion and he'll tear you apart. For all men are ravenous lions in these matters. Except me! And you already know that, because you know me! You know I'll never harm you. Why must you make things so hard? Haven't I suffered enough?

'I bring you food and water and sweet treats. I bring you my devotion, and would give you my life. Yet still you spurn me. Why do you make me suffer so?'

So says the persistent suitor.

★

Sibongile has been missing for four days now. Men were sent downstream, but could find no trace of her. 'Besides,' adds the chief, 'the water is safe. There are no crocodiles this high up.'

'That is so,' agrees Zodwa. He himself has roamed the hills, visiting every place he can think of. 'For as children together we would range far and wide. But in none of our secret places have I found any trace of her.'

'Just the pot,' murmurs the Induna.

'Left by the stream,' adds the chief.

'And unbroken?'

The chief nods.

'Are you sure of this?'

'Yes, Shadow of Shaka, it was only later that I broke it. Out of frustration! Where is she? Who could have done such a thing?'

Giving the father time to recover his emotions, the Induna turns to the sangoma: 'What about interlopers? Wayfarers? Strangers?'

'There have been some of those, Nduna, but none whose whereabouts cannot be ascertained.'

'You have done that?'

'Yes,' says Zodwa. 'I myself despatched the men.'

'Numzane,' says the Induna, addressing the chief once more, 'what of those who would wish your family or your clan ill?'

'Hai, Nduna, you know yourself those days are long gone . . .'

'But men and their envy endure!'

'Yes, but we have incurred no one's wrath. There have been no disputes.'

The Induna turns to the village shaman: 'You have thrown the bones?'

'More than once, Shadow of Shaka.'

'What do they say?'

The sangoma sneaks a wary glance at the chief. 'That she is somewhere nearby.'

'But how can that be?' asks the unumzane. 'We have looked everywhere!'

'Perhaps my warriors, being strangers to this area, will see what familiarity has made you overlook.'

'So we hope, Nduna.'

'Never fear,' says the Induna. 'Ngiyindoda ebekezelayo.' *I am a patient man.* They will begin the search at first light, and they will find Sibongile, no matter how long it takes.

★

'But that is not how the story ends!' she says.

'What do you mean?'

'Her brother . . . the bride's brother follows them on their journey. He waits until the lion-man has left, and then approaches the hut. Surprised to see him, his sister still refuses to believe his suspicions about her new husband. So he starts cutting down trees and sets about strengthening the hut. She laughs at him, calls him a fool, but he persists. And, by the time darkness falls, he's covered the thatch in thorny branches and built a sturdy gate to barricade the entrance. And when the lions come, they find they cannot get into the hut, where the boy and his sister cower in fear. Growing enraged, they turn instead on the lion-man and eat him!'

The torch is spluttering, almost burnt out. Her face, peering up at him, seems to be floating in the darkness.

'Don't you see?' she says. 'She is saved!'

The persistent suitor smiles gently, indulgently. 'As I would save *you*, my beloved.'

★

The Induna takes his leave of the chief but, outside the hut, he grabs the boy's arm and pulls him aside. After a few moments they see the sangoma come out. They follow him and, when they are some distance away from the chief's domicile, the Induna calls him softly.

The sangoma swings round. 'Nduna! You startled me.'

191

'I have a few more questions to ask you.'

'I am at your service.'

But, no, the shaman knows of no one in the village who would want to do Sibongile harm.

What about a shunned suitor, perhaps?

'Hai! This is perhaps why Sibongile is so well-liked, Nduna. She is fourteen summers, it is true, but she is still . . . well, a girl, Nduna. She has yet to discover the coquettish wiles of her sex.'

'That might yet inflame some.'

'This is true, Nduna. But in this village I know of no such man.'

'He might be able to hide himself as well as he has hidden her.'

'A frightening thought, Nduna.'

'One you must have contemplated, though, because the bones . . .'

'They do not lie.'

'And they say she is somewhere nearby?'

'Yes,' sighs the sangoma.

'We shall see,' says the Induna.

★

'Scream! Scream all you want, but no one will hear you. If this is how you choose to repay my kindness, do not let me stop you. Here . . . I will scream too. Let us both scream together!'

★

And the pot, he asks the boy later, as they prepare to bed down for the night – what does he make of the pot?

'The pot, Master?'

'The *unbroken* pot.'

'I – I do not know, Master.'

'Come now. She goes to collect water – she vanishes – all that's left is the unbroken pot.'

'She . . . she must have put it down, Master.'

'Indeed, she must have put it down. For it was not broken. What does that tell us?'

The Induna watches the boy's forehead furrow in a frown of concentration – then he supplies the answer to his own question.

'It tells us she knew whoever she encountered, because there was no struggle.'

★

'I am here. There's no need to be afraid. I am here.'

'Please . . . whatever I . . .'

'I can't hear you. Yesterday's screaming has clearly made you hoarse. But don't worry, I have brought you water. And food, of course.'

'Please . . . whatever I have done to you . . .'

'Whatever . . . whatever you have done *to me*? Do you mock me now?'

'No!'

'Do you mock me, feigning ignorance?'

'No! Please. This is madness . . .'

'Yes, it is. But you can end it. You have only to say the word. Say the word and I will take you away and show you the wonders of elsewhere. And with me you will be safe.'

'That cannot be. You know that! The shame!'

'Shame? Cha! It is too late for that! Even if they slay me and snatch you away from me, do you think you can go back there? You will lie and weep and beguile them, but behind your back – ha! Wherever you go, you'll think you hear whispering, but you'll never be sure. But I tell you this, you will be right. They will gossip and wonder and ask each other what really happened up here . . .'

'No!'

'Yes! Do you not see – in a way we are already betrothed! In a way our lives are already entwined, and it will always be so. For they, ignorant fools that they are, will have stumbled on the truth you refuse to acknowledge. That we are meant to be together!'

★

The next day, the Induna and his men split up into groups of two and set out to explore the surrounding countryside. The udibi is sent out with the herd boys, with instructions to keep his eyes and ears open.

The udibi soon learns all the herd boys adore Sibongile, and are concerned at her vanishing. Some whisper of wizards but, from the Induna's conversation with the sangoma, the boy knows to dismiss these as rumours.

'Yes,' he says, thrilled at his own cunning, 'but what if there are no wizards? What if some man has taken her?'

*What? In this village?* An indignant response. *Never! Not in this village!*

The Induna and the other men, meanwhile, spend a fruitless day. They follow paths, inspect caves, climb rocks, but are unable to find any trace of the missing girl.

★

'Can you hear them? Can you hear them calling? No? A pity . . . because then you'd know the pain you've caused! Hai! The pain you *continue* to cause! How can one so lovely be so selfish?'

★

Finally, on the evening of the third day, the unumzane summons the Induna. 'You have done all any man can,' he says sadly. 'I will be forever in Shaka's debt! But—'

'No!' interrupts Zodwa. 'Father, you can't . . .'

'It is time, my son. We . . . we have to acknowledge that fact.'

Zodwa stands up. 'No! Not me! You can, but I won't! I'll find her!'

He storms out of the hut.

The unumzane shrugs, tears in his eyes. 'It is time, Nduna. Time we began the funeral preparations.'

'I do not think that will be necessary,' says the Induna.

★

'Sibongile? Beloved?' Lying on his stomach, the persistent suitor shakes his head. What is this? Is she playing childish games now? He cares for her, brings her food and water, visits her every day – at great personal risk to himself – and now she plays games . . .

He calls her name once . . . twice . . .

Again: 'Sibongile?'

And again: 'Sibongile! Answer me! Talk to me!'

Frowning, he lifts himself up. On his hands and knees, he peers into the opening.

'Stop this! You're being childish!' He squints into the darkness below, then shuffles sideways around the opening. 'Sibongile? Did you hear what I said? They're preparing for your funeral. You'll be dead in a few hours. Is that what you want? Is that what you choose, even though I offer myself?'

He leans further forward: '*Sibongile!*'

Hands leap out of the darkness, grabbing his ears, and he's jerked down into the cavern.

★

Two of the warriors let down a rope and haul Njikiza and the Induna out.

'He's dead?' asks the chief.

The Induna nods. The fall has broken Zodwa's neck.

★

Later, on their way back to KwaBulawayo, enjoying the fact that for once he's doing the asking, the Induna will inquire how the udibi came know that Zodwa had kidnapped his own sister.

It is the heat of the day and they can afford to rest for a few hours.

'I was with the herd boys, as you commanded,' explains the udibi, 'and while we were talking, one of them pointed and said: See? There goes Zodwa, to look for his sister!'

He'd done this every day since her disappearance, said someone else. The boys hailed him, and Zodwa stopped on the path and turned in their direction. They wished him good luck and, raising a hand in acknowledgement, Zodwa continued on his way.

'And?' prompts the Induna.

'Master, they had already told me he went out every day and returned home only when it was getting dark. But' – the boy indicates the sleeping mat, the two gourds of water, the food satchel neatly stacked next to him in the shade of the flat-topped aloe – 'it seemed to me he was carrying as much baggage as I do when we have to travel many days . . .'

Why, for instance, was he carrying two gourds? Surely one who knew the area as well as Zodwa would know where to find water to quench his thirst?

What the boy doesn't tell the Induna is that it had taken him quite a few minutes to put all of this together. Zodwa had walked on and the herd boys had resumed their chatter, leaving the Induna's udibi distracted with the knowledge that he had become aware of something significant tugging at him. And when it all fell into place, he had to run like a cheetah to catch up with Zodwa.

Of course, Zodwa was aware someone might follow him, especially since the Induna's arrival, and the boy had realised this too . . .

'Hai! This little one's blade is sharp!' interjects Njikiza.

'This is so,' agrees the Induna. 'But let him finish his story, for soon we must be on our way . . .'

Noting how Zodwa doubled back on occasion to make sure he wasn't being tailed – surely another sign of guilt – the boy kept his distance and only followed him a short way. 'Then I hid,' he explains, 'and let him go on.'

The next day, he returned to this same spot and waited for Zodwa. He was surprised, at first, when the chief's son came from a different direction, but this seemed to further confirm his suspicions.

'Yet you didn't tell me any of this,' observes the Induna.

'I couldn't be sure,' says the boy. That day, the second day, he lay in wait and then started following Zodwa again. Clearly the chief's son believed that he was safe once he had reached that spot, and so he no longer made any effort to double back to make sure he wasn't being followed. Instead, he quickened his pace and led the other boy to a ravine: a narrow gash in a cliff face that enabled one to reach the summit with relative ease. Again the udibi hid himself, and stayed long enough only to make sure Zodwa entered the ravine and started climbing to the top.

Making his own way back to the village, the boy realised Zodwa's travails had taken them in a wide loop, and that the ravine was a lot closer to the umuzi than he'd realised. Indeed, you could see those same cliffs from the village.

The next day, the boy set out early. He returned to the ravine and was already hidden at the top when Zodwa began his ascent over the boulders.

The vegetation was sparse on the flat-topped escarpment, but he wasn't going to have to look for hiding places. There was no need to tail the chief's son any further, because the boy could now see exactly where he went. After Zodwa had left, the boy ran to the same spot – and found the girl in the cavern.

'Then I came to fetch you, Master,' he says.

★

'Her own brother . . .'

'She did not invite such . . . ministrations,' says the Induna. 'Never forget that.'

The Induna and his men rescued Sibongile that very night, and she remained hidden in her mother's hut while the sangoma tended to her. The Induna, meanwhile, reported to the chief and, after Zodwa had gone storming off, was able to tell him what had transpired.

Now they are standing on the rocks encircling the opening. 'He lured her here,' explains the Induna. The cavern had been a normal cave until a rock-fall closed the entrance, leaving only this hole in the ceiling. Zodwa had told his sister he had explored the cavern, and found some of the strange markings left behind by the Old Ones. He then persuaded her to come with him and had lowered her down inside first with no intention of following her.

'My men will close this,' says the unumzane. 'He was my flesh and blood, but he was no son of mine.'

'No,' says the Induna.

Surprise arches the chief's eyebrows. 'No, Nduna? What do you mean?'

The Induna points to the huts visible in the distance. 'You cannot have this reminder peering down on you. You cannot have your people looking over this way and knowing what lies here! This will not heal the wound.'

'But to let him rot – is that not a fit punishment?'

'Yes, but not here. Take him away, far away. Let only you yourself and a few trusted ones know where you have left him. In this way, people might more easily forget.'

The chief nods. 'You are truly the Shadow of Shaka!'

'Know this also, though. That is the easiest part.'

'What do you mean?'

'Your daughter, too, you will have to send away . . .'

'But I have just found her!'

'People speak with serpents' tongues in such matters. Some will begin to wonder what she did to encourage her brother.'

'But, Nduna, you yourself said . . .'

'I know – and you know – that she is not at fault here.'

'Then I will punish those who say otherwise.'

'And fuel the suspicions of others, Numzane?'

The chief sighs, seeming to sag under a weight.

'You are right, Shadow of Shaka,' he says after a while.

'Send her and her mother to live with her mother's clan. There she will be healed. As for this one . . .' The Induna indicates the opening in the rocks at their feet. 'Throw him far, far away, and let the ancestors see to him.'

★

'Hai,' chuckles the Induna, as they resume their journey home, 'but this took you some days – following then waiting, waiting then following!'

The boy grins. 'That's because I, too, am a patient man,' he says proudly.

The Induna pats his shoulder. 'That you are: both patient and a man.'

They carry on walking, the boy beaming to hear such praise.

*He was young, so young . . .*

*They were all so young.*

*Sometimes he finds himself wishing it's possible to herd all the good memories into one kraal, like cattle, so one can walk among them, enjoying them like one does with cattle. How much easier would it then be to weather the agonies of bad times and old age! How much better than the way things actually are, with everything jumbled, and with that quiet contemplation of a long-ago afternoon — when you and her were finally alone, and she was happy and wore flowers in her hair — suddenly giving way to screaming faces and iklwas striking like snakes.*

*Hai! But, then again, sentimentality can also trap one in a present that seems unfriendly, uncouth and unpleasant. And sentiment, who is sentimentality's quiet brother, also needs watching.*

*Did Shaka ever come to regret the way he had dealt with Soshangane, for instance? The man's bravery was certainly worthy of respect, as were his resourcefulness and perseverance in the face of the barren lands Shaka had left for him. And Shaka had duly permitted Soshangane — sentiment! sentiment! — to go free after the general had broken his spear over his own knee.*

*And off Soshangane went, only to later, however unwittingly, play a crucial role in Shaka's downfall.*

*Better to stick, for now, to what happened before . . .*

*And so the old general goes on to tell the young officers how Soshangane and his legions attacked after the harvest had been brought in. He had worked hard to retrain the Ndwandwe army, utilising some of Shaka's methods, but Zwide had been impatient for his day of reckoning. He also had his mother Ntombazi on his back, accusing him of cowardice. And*

Soshangane's legions had been sent into Zulu territory before they were ready and with few provisions, believing they could live off the crops taken from the villages they attacked.

However, Shaka had ordered his people to gather together all the food they could find, and then fade into the forests of his kingdom. An extensive hunt, undertaken before the invasion occurred, also saw to it that game was scarce.

Shaka's regiments then shadowed the Ndwandwes, watching as they became more and more hungry, desperate and dispirited. In retaliation Soshangane burnt all the umuzis he came across and destroyed the fields.

When he deemed the time was right, Shaka allowed his amabutho to fall upon the starving Ndwandwes, while Mgobozi and another regiment were sent on to Zwide's capital.

It proved a great victory for Shaka, who then allowed brave Soshangane to go free.

★

Later, after they've eaten supper and the warm African night enfolds them, the general tells them of Shaka's shongololo, the testudo he created to storm the plateau where Ntombazi had sought refuge — she who collected the skulls of all the chiefs her son had vanquished. Zwide might have eluded him, but Shaka had prepared a particularly apt ending for the old crone.

And to this day people say her screams can still be heard up on those heights . . .

# The Adventure Of The Purloined Heirloom

But the land and the nation need to recover from the depredations wrought by Soshangane. Villages must be rebuilt and fields reclaimed. To make matters worse, certain areas are undergoing a severe dry spell.

'See here,' says Nkululeko KaDingwa, allowing the dirt to dribble through his fingers. He's an induna yesigodi, or district head, whose umuzi is situated near a tributary of the White Umfolozi.

The soil is itshetshe, light and dead, almost like dust, while in other places it's isigagadu, rock hard.

The Induna nods.

His hands on his hips, Nkululeko surveys the field. It's now Umanulo, the August–September moon, which is the time of the first rains. By now the new grass should already be covering the land, but the sky remains obdurate. Men and women from the village have been scouring the surrounding hills, removing any sticks or sharp stones that point skyward, for sometimes the sky will see these things as spears threatening it and will retreat, withholding the rain the grass needs in order to grow.

The younger warriors, meanwhile, have gone searching for large boulders, which they dislodge and roll down the hills, for these become so hot that sometimes you can't even put your hand on them – and this heat shows the anger of the earth, and this could also be a reason for the sky withdrawing, for it assumes the earth is angry with it. Wherever possible, these big stones are rolled into the shade, or even into streams, so that they might cool down and the sky be reassured there is no enmity.

But that hasn't seemed to work either, says Nkululeko, wiping his brow.

And all have listened and listened, he adds, but none have heard — or even seen — the insingizi whose cry heralds the coming of the wet season.

So he's chosen to consult an inyanga yezulu, or rain-doctor.

But, in doing so, the induna yesigodi has to be circumspect. For obvious reasons, being a rain-doctor can be a perilous profession. Should a drought persist, the rain-doctor's 'clients' will invariably seek to try and pacify the sky by sacrificing the rain-doctor himself. Making their existence even more hazardous is the fact that Zulu Kings are ambivalent about them. After all, the King is the Father of the Sky; he should be the one to harangue it and command it to rain. Shaka has been a little more wise, however, realising how this puts the King in the same position as the inyanga yezulu, should the drought persist. In fact, it would be a worse position, as the King can't be seen to fail in any undertaking.

All the same, Nkululeko feels it would be better if the King doesn't know he'll be consulting an inyanga yezulu. Shaka will be concerned that the dry spell will spread to engulf the whole kingdom, like the great drought of 1802. And he might therefore be furious with Nkululeko for not having done something to end it earlier.

★

In order to summon rain, the inyanga yezulu needs to borrow the supplicant's most precious possession. In Nkululeko's case this is the clan's Umkhontho Wamadlozi, its Spear of the Spirits.

Every family owns one. It's used to slaughter animals and the blade is never cleaned; for to remove the nsila, or gore, is one of the worst forms of desecration known to the People of the Sky.

But this Umkhontho is even more special. Nkululeko's clan is famous throughout the kingdom because of it, and also the village as being the home of the spear. With a haft made from a wood unknown to the region and a long, slender blade more finely formed, stronger and easier to sharpen than any Zulu equivalent, it's said to be a Ma-Iti assegai, a relic from the days of the Phoenicians. Whether that's true or not is irrelevant, but Nkululeko's Umkhontho Wamadlozi is deemed extremely valuable because of its age, because of what it is – a thing of fine craftsmanship from another world – and because it's the potential source of much magic.

Unfortunately, Nandi has summoned Nkululeko to Bulawayo, saying she has a task for him, and you don't tell the Queen Mother you have something more important to do before you can attend to her needs. This is why he's asking for the Induna's help.

'Never fear, old friend,' says the warrior, 'my men and I are here.' They will see to it that the precious relic is safely conveyed to the rain-doctor's kraal three sleeps away. 'And we will see that it's brought back safely,' he adds.

'I thank you, old friend,' says Nkululeko, 'but I think getting it back will be the easy part.' He sighs. 'There's something else you need to know . . .' He casts a glance in the direction of udibi, but the Induna reassures him that he can speak freely in front of the boy.

'I was thinking of his safety,' says Nkululeko with a wry smile.

'He has me to look after him,' says the Induna. Noting the

udibi's outraged expression, he adds, 'And he can also look after himself.'

Nkululeko chuckles. 'I can see that. Aiee, that is truly a fierce expression, little one.'

'And this something else I need to hear?' asks the Induna.

Many sangomas and bandits would kill to get their hands on the Umkhontho, which is bad enough, complains Nkululeko. But now he's heard whispers from reliable sources that one of the princes has his eye on the relic.

That *is* worrying. Should one of the King's brothers send an army to snatch the spear from its rightful owner, he will feel the full weight of Shaka's wrath.

However, if the prince sends confederates, who can't be traced back to him, to steal the spear, and they're successful, Nkululeko will be the one to feel Shaka's anger should he dare to suggest the real culprit is one of the King's brothers. After all, what proof will he be able to produce? At the very least Nkululeko can expect to be stripped of his rank and forced to hand over a substantial part of his herd of cattle, as a fine.

None of this would signify that the King didn't secretly believe Nkululeko – quite the contrary. His judgment and the resulting punishment would merely be a 'public response'. Given the fact that Nkululeko has always served him loyally, Shaka will know he has to give some credence to what the induna yesigodi had to say. Privately, he'll wonder why his brother had wanted to acquire that specific artefact, and discuss ways to pre-empt any plans the prince might have in mind. He'll also see to it that he is watched even more closely than usual.

But for Nkululeko the damage will already have been done, and therefore the Induna knows they'll have to meet stealth with stealth. Especially since an out-and-out battle with men later found to belong to the prince's regiment also has to be avoided. That could be (re)interpreted as an attack on the prince himself.

'And this prince whereof we speak . . . now that the spear is to be conveyed beyond the safety of your village, would I be correct in assuming he has assembled his forces and stands ready to come to grips with this treasure?' asks the Induna.

Nkululeko chuckles and nods. His friend has asked him if the prince involved is Mhlangana, whose name can mean 'to come to grips with'. It's a conclusion that required little deduction on the Induna's part. There are only two princes who it could be, and the Induna already knows Dingane isn't interested in ancient spears. Grasping and venal, wanting what others have just to deprive them, stealing this clan's Umkhontho Wamadlozi is just the kind of thing Mhlangana would contemplate. And not necessarily because he plans to pass it on to a pet sangoma so it can be used in some ritual or other, intended to strengthen him or harm Shaka. He'd just want to possess it.

★

Back in Nkululeko's hut, with the udibi standing guard outside, the district head shows the Induna two scabbards. A few fingers wider than a man's hand, each is made of two iklwa hafts cut down and each lashed to a shorter crossbar at one end. Zebra skin has then been folded over this framework. At the end lacking a crossbar, the shafts are loose and can move inward, but this flexibility changes when the Umkhontho is inserted haft first. The width of the blade now acts as a second crossbar, keeping the rods apart at the open end and making the framework firmer and the skin covering tighter.

'Knowing how our situation grows worse every day, and therefore expecting my men to set off with the spear soon, his spies are even now watching us from the hills,' says Nkululeko. 'He probably knows that I have been summoned to Bulawayo, and that you'll be the one taking the spear to the rain-doctor.'

'Let us hope so,' says the Induna.

Nkululeko's nephew Alusi will be given one of the scabbards. Accompanied by a bodyguard of fifty men commanded by one of Nkululeko's brothers, he'll travel to the kraal of the inyanga yezulu, following the main and most obvious route.

'And the prince's spies will laugh themselves silly,' observes the Induna.

'Indeed,' says Nkululeko. 'Look at this fool, they'll say – meaning me. Does he think we're stupid? Why would he summon Shaka's most courageous nduna and then entrust the precious spear to a mere nephew!'

Nkululeko takes a mouthful of beer, and then hands the gourd to the Induna. 'Although, I'll tell you this, that boy is wise for his age!' says the district head. Alusi might just be seventeen summers old, but he's already shown an interest in the running of the village and the district, and has accompanied his uncle to Bulawayo many times, where he seems to have made quite an impression on Nandi.

'I do not mean to boast,' continues Nkululeko, 'but with so many of my sons being such layabouts . . .'

'It's good to see yourself reflected in at least one of your relatives.'

Nkululeko nods. And he is confident Alusi will be perfectly capable of dealing with the rain-doctor.

'Then, a day later, we ourselves will be on our way,' says the

Induna. Apart from Njikiza and the udibi, his party will include six warriors from the elite Fasimba regiment. He'll have the other scabbard and, moving faster, they'll take a lesser known but shorter route to the rain-doctor's kraal.

They will be the ones Mhlangana's men will follow and seek to ambush, because it's so obvious! A ruse so insultingly inept that it alone is a good enough reason to relieve Nkululeko of the Umkhontho; one so stupid doesn't deserve to have possession of such a precious relic.

Alusi and his men will leave the following day, as will Nkululeko. 'I am sorry I won't be here to see you off, old friend,' he says. 'But you can't keep the Queen Mother waiting.'

'This is so, but you need not worry. We will deliver the spear . . .'

Nkululeko nods. 'Then hopefully the rains will come.'

★

*When he deems the time is right, he orders his eldest sons to slaughter the cow, and then retreats into his hut to commune with the Great Spirit. Night is near and the boys work quickly and quietly. Silence is important, because it is coolness that draws the sky closer, whereas loud talk creates heat that pushes the sky away. Whenever they have to communicate, the youngsters speak in whispers.*

★

'I'm still not sure I understand,' says Bamba with all the deference he can muster.

Mhlangana and twenty of his men have moved close to Nkululeko's umuzi, so the prince can better conduct operations. Because they cannot afford to have their presence detected, they haven't been able to build temporary huts or even hunt for food – and sleeping rough for the past few nights and subsisting on porridge haven't improved the prince's temper.

'It's really very simple,' growls Mhlangana. 'Nkululeko has chosen his nephew Alusi to take the spear to the rain-doctor, because he himself has been summoned to Bulawayo by Nandi.'

Mhlangana smiles to himself. That's one of the most impor-tant pieces of information they've received – the fact that Nandi has sent for Nkululeko. There, *right there*, is further proof of the necessity of this undertaking. Not that Mhlangana mentions any of this to Bamba, of course.

Instead he asks what might be inferred from this, bearing in mind that the Induna and some of his men have arrived at Nkululeko's kraal.

That the nephew and the larger group will be the decoy, says Bamba. The Induna and his men will be carrying the real Umkhontho.

'Yes . . .' says Mhlangana.

Bamba smiles, relieved to have got something right.

' . . . and no,' continues the prince.

Bamba's smile vanishes. 'Master?'

'You are right to assume some form of deception is being planned,' continues Mhlangana.

Bamba nods.

'But you are wrong because you're assuming what they want you to assume.'

'What they . . .'

'Yes, what *they* want you to assume.'

Bamba squares his shoulders and tries to look as if he under-stands what the prince is getting at.

'They want you to assume that the Nduna will be taking the spear,' says Mhlangana.

'So the nephew will have the real spear?'

'No! Oh, no!'

'N-no, Master?'

'No, you're still assuming what they want you to assume. You see, it's like this. To confound anyone who might be thinking of stealing the spear, Nkululeko selects a mere nephew to carry it to the rain-doctor, and summons the Nduna to his kraal. Aha, think the thieves, this is clearly a trick! Obviously it'll be the Nduna who carries the real spear. And this is what Nkululeko and the Nduna *want* the thieves to think. But they haven't reckoned on Mhlangana. Oh no! You see, he knows that Nkululeko and the Nduna also expect these thieves to think again . . .'

'If I might interrupt, Master?'

'Yes, what is it?'

'Who are these thieves?'

'Who are . . . ? Are you trying to be funny, Bamba?'

'No, Master!'

'Who are these thieves?' mutters Mhlangana. 'The spear is valuable, Bamba, and Nkululeko would be a fool if he didn't think someone might consider stealing the spear, should it ever leave the village where it's closely guarded night and day. Not so?'

'It is indeed guarded night and day, Master,' says Bamba eagerly grasping at something he does know for certain.

Mhlangana's chin touches his chest as he lowers his head. To control his anger, he drags his nails through his hair, as if gouging his skull.

'That was not what I was referring to,' he tells a petrified Bamba. 'I meant isn't it obvious Nkululeko will assume someone – some thief or thieves – might want to steal his spear? And by thieves, I mean . . . well, thieves. Anyone but us.'

'Have you changed your mind, then, Master? Do you no longer intend to steal—'

'Shut up, Bamba.'

Mhlangana slaps at a mosquito, then he sighs, listening to the cicadas for a while. Finally, slapping at another mosquito, he says: 'Nkululeko and the Nduna expect these thieves to think that the Nduna will be carrying the real spear, while the nephew acts as a decoy. But then . . . *then*, Bamba, they expect these thieves to think again. To think *again*, Bamba.'

The prince regards his induna for a moment, waiting for his words to sink in. That's hard to tell, since Bamba is standing stiffly to attention and looking straight ahead.

They – Nkululeko and the Induna – expect any bandits who might have their eye on the Umkhontho to think *Hang on! Isn't this a little too obvious?* explains Mhlangana. Aren't they *expected* to think the Induna will be carrying the real spear?

'And so, Bamba, they – these thieves – will decide that, in fact, it's the nephew who will be carrying the real spear, while they are meant to go off after the Nduna and his men. But, as I said, they haven't counted on Mhlangana. Oh no! He has seen through their ploy, Bamba! They can't fool *him*! You see, I know, Bamba – I *know* that it will in fact be the Nduna who is carrying the real spear.'

And therefore it's on the Induna's path that they will prepare their trap.

Now Bamba must go and brief his men, for they are to leave tomorrow.

Bamba bows his head, says 'Yes, Master,' and strides away, thinking: 'So the Induna will be the one carrying the spear? Fuck me, that's what I said in the first place!'

★

'For one whose mind is so unsound, your reasoning in this instance is remarkably sound,' says a voice from behind him.

Mhlangana, who's been sitting watching night swallow up the trees and bushes while waiting for this visitation, doesn't bother to turn round.

'You're lucky I have need of your services,' he says.

'So are you.'

'Meaning?'

'Come now! You undid the knot of who will have the real spear, so this one shouldn't give you too much trouble.'

'Your impertinence bores me.'

'Well, look at it this way, I have served other masters and their henchmen before you, yet currently you and Bamba are the only ones who know I exist.'

'Cha! Begone, monster! You have heard what is to be done, and you have work to do.'

★

*Once the animal has been slaughtered, the eldest son approaches his father's hut. Quietness being so important, he sinks down on to his haunches in front of the entrance – and waits for his father to notice him. The inyanga yezulu has meanwhile told the Great Spirit of his intentions, and emerges from his hut wearing only a loincloth. The cow's gallbladder has been removed and, while his sons continue to skin the animal, he rubs part of the gall itself over his chest and shoulders. Then he accepts the umcakulo from one of his younger sons. It contains some of the bile and, raising the bowl to his lips, he drinks the dark liquid. A stick is dipped into the rest of the bile and then fixed to the fence surrounding the kraal where calves are kept. When the skin is ready, it's smeared with fat and carefully rolled up. Balancing it on his right shoulder, the father leaves the homestead.*

★

The Induna and the udibi are among those who are there to see off Alusi and his bodyguard of fifty men the following morning. The truth is, the Induna doesn't share his friend's assessment of Alusi. Certainly the boy is advanced for his age, but in all the wrong ways, reckons the Induna. He's noticed a tendency towards swaggering and arrogance whenever Alusi believes he isn't being watched by his elders; his uncle's favouritism has clearly gone to his head.

The Induna also suspects Alusi has sought to court his uncle's favour, or indeed the goodwill of anyone who might be able to further his ambitions. On these occasions he hides his fawning behind a good-natured smile and an eagerness to do whatever's asked of him (tasks he'll probably palm off on to his younger siblings). He also seems to have mastered the art of agreeing with everything his uncle says, without appearing too obsequious. When his opinion is sought, for example, he might ask some intelligent-sounding questions, requesting clarification about certain points, before allowing sudden understanding to blossom on his countenance and then nodding his agreement like one who has been persuaded.

And this morning the Induna notices the look of peevishness that flits across Alusi's face when Nkululeko takes the scabbard away from him and hands it to his own brother, who'll accompany the boy. The older man will retain possession of the Umkhontho until they reach the rain-doctor. After recovering his aplomb, the boy nods obediently, but the Induna notes the dark look he gives Nkululeko and his other uncle, as the two move away to make sure everything is as it should be with the men.

The Induna won't mention his misgivings to Nkululeko, for that would simply add to the burden he already carries. Also, kinship can blind an uncle to a nephew's faults, and have him turn on those who try to point these out, even if they're close friends.

After Alusi and his bodyguards have departed, it's Nkululeko's turn. He'll be travelling to Bulawayo with another one of his brothers. The Induna wishes him a safe journey, and reassures him yet again that all will be well with the Umkhontho.

★

*When he reaches his Special Place – which no one else will dare go near – he removes two horns from a cleft in the cliff face, where they are kept cool. Each has been hollowed out and contains muthi. Many of the ingredients come from the Great Waters, and include seaweed and izikhukhukhu, or sea urchins. Both are regarded as essential components; without them the muthi will be useless. And he makes regular trips to the ocean to collect these, as well as pieces of vegetation washed up by the waves. His Special Place is situated in a kloof, where a slender waterfall sends a stream through a deep pool, before it becomes shallow enough to wade through. Having retrieved the horns, he crosses over to a large flat black rock in the centre of the stream. Wrapping the skin around himself, he lies down, with the two horns next to him. He'll remain here for the rest of the night.*

★

The girl comes screaming down the path. The Induna's men immediately fan out on either side of him, two of them turning to watch the rear. But she doesn't seem to notice this. The girl has a baby strapped to her back, and is shrieking something about her grandfather. The Induna grips her shoulders and holds her firmly until she's able to compose herself.

At last he works out that her grandfather has fallen into a river. Whereupon the girl sent her little brother off to summon other members of their family, while she ran in the opposite direction, hoping to encounter some wayfarers.

Now they must please help her!

The river's easy to spot, due to the tangle of greenery follow-ing its course. The Induna, who's carrying the scabbard rolled up in his sleeping mat, instructs three of the men to follow the bank downstream. Chances are, they'll be looking for a drowned man now. They are to return when the sun touches the moun-tains they can see to the north. The udibi will look after the woman. The other two soldiers – Phepho and Radebe – will remain with the Induna. They find a trail taking them to a stream that flows into the river. Judging by the footprints, this is where these people customarily fetch their water.

On hearing the udibi calling for him, the Induna leads Phepho and Radebe to a fork in the path, where the udibi is waiting.

The woman's name is Lombi, he reports. She and her younger brother and their grandfather live in a collection of huts a little way further up there. The grandfather's name is . . .

The Induna stops the boy here. 'There is no grandfather.'

'Master?' asks the udibi, giving voice to the startled expres-sions of Phepho and Radebe.

'And I doubt there is a little brother,' adds the Induna.

Well, he did think that was strange, confesses the boy.

'How so?'

'She – Lombi – said their relatives live some distance away, and will only get here tomorrow. I mean, Master, there must have been other ways to try and save the grandfather.'

'Other than letting him hang on to a branch all night, you mean?'

'Yes, Master.'

'Has she killed him then, Master?' asks Radebe.

The Induna chuckles, checking the sky. The others will be

rejoining them soon – when he'll explain to them that their search was merely for form's sake.

'No,' he says. 'We knew to expect a trap and I believe this is it.'

★

*Sometime during the night, a whisker on the surface of the water, Umonya approaches the rock where the inyanga yezulu lies unmoving. Slithering on to the rock, the snake licks the fat off the skin that covers the rain-doctor. Then it lies across the two horns containing the muthi. This is to cool them down even further, to make the medicine as cool as it in fact is. When this is done, Umonya returns to the pool.*

★

The hut is like any other: a framework of saplings covered with thatch, and a floor made of a mixture of crushed ant-heap and clay covered with cow-dung and well shined. In the centre there's the isiko, or fireplace. To the right of the hut is the isililo samadoda, the male side; to the left there's the female side, the isililo sesifazana. In the rear is the umsamo, the place of the ancestors, who divide their time between here and the cattle kraal. Sleeping mats, clothing, gourds and skins containing water, medicine or beer hang from the wall.

The Induna carefully places the spear, safe in its zebra-skin scabbard, in the umsamo amid the lion skull, the bronze amulets and other items deemed precious by the owner as well as the pots and calabashes which are also stored there.

Leaving the udibi to watch over the Umkhontho, the Induna goes to check on the men. The seven will surround the hut; one will sleep and will be woken up when it's his turn to stand guard, while the soldier next to him will rest and so forth.

The Induna then moves around the indlu, checking that the thatch remains tight and there's no sign of any disguised holes.

Satisfied, he calls the udibi and, with Radebe guarding the rear of the hut, the men prepare and eat their evening meal. Lombi has offered to cook for them, but they've politely refused. Better to make their own meal using their own rations; if this is really a trap any food prepared by other hands might be drugged.

The Induna watches Lombi closely as she enters the hut to light the fire, with the baby still strapped to her back. She smiles at him as she exits the indlu; he returns the smile, using it as an excuse for studying her closely to make sure she isn't carrying something she shouldn't be.

After the meal, which is simply porridge, the Induna and the udibi roll out their sleeping mats within the isililo samadoda, the hut's male side. They talk for a while in low tones, discussing tomorrow's journey, deciding where they'll have to be when the sun reaches its zenith, if they're to make the village by night-fall.

Then there's silence as the two lie back, and the chirping-click-ing-cracking night sounds take over.

And he waits, with the cowhide loops biting into his armpits. He clenches and unclenches his tiny fists for the umpteenth time, to stop them from going numb. His feet are hanging loose; an arrangement that seemed okay at the time, but now he wishes he has something to rest his feet on.

Night sounds. And the passage of his breath through his nostrils, as loud as a herd of stampeding cattle. And the soft rustling whenever he tries to readjust his position the tiniest bit – that's the sound of a waterfall.

Still, he manages to hear it: a soft snore.

A smile in the cramped darkness.

No matter how soft it might be, a snore is still a snore, and when two men have to sleep side by side, and the one starts to snore, sooner or later, his companion will nudge him, just to get him to shift position and shut up. That's if the companion is still awake. If he's asleep the snoring will continue unabated and he may even add his own rasp to it.

And Hlakanyana waits. But there's none of the growling and grumbling that occur when a snoring man is elbowed close to the brink of consciousness. It seems as if both are asleep.

Carefully, he straightens his right arm, the fist emerging out of the upper end of the rolled-up mat. By moving to the left, he slips out of the right hoop that keeps him suspended within the mat, then immediately brings his hand down to grip the hoop.

And waits, listening.

Nothing to be worried about (he hopes).

He repeats the manoeuvre with his left arm, so he's left hanging from both the hoops, his feet protruding out of the bottom of the rolled-up mat and touching the floor.

He releases the hoops and, squirming his shoulders, eases first his right arm and then his left downwards so that his arms are pressed against his sides.

And waits, listening. And giving his muscles time to stop screaming and adapt themselves to his new position.

There is, however, little chance of his legs being seen; only a close examination with a flaming firebrand will reveal them. They're in the shadow of the wall, half concealed behind a low pile of skins. Between the rolled-up mat and the umsamo, stands a large pot.

When he feels he's able to move stealthily enough, he sinks to his knees and brings his head and shoulders out of the rolled-up mat. And then he lies prone behind the skins, his head facing the pot and the umsamo. He's next about to worm his way forward, when—

The boy is up and striding toward the indlu's entrance.

Hlakanyana presses his face into the floor, cursing himself. Didn't even hear him stir, never mind get up.

When Hlakanyana looks up again, the boy has left the hut. For a moment he considers darting forward and grabbing the spear. He could be back here, hidden, before the boy returns. But, no, in his haste he's likely to kick over something in the dark.

And it's just as well he hasn't made a move for the Umkhontho. When the udibi returns from taking a piss, he checks to make sure the spear is still in its place in the umsamo, before lying down on his sleeping mat.

And Hlakanyana lies sweating in the dark, waiting for the boy to fall asleep again.

★

*A cavern in the cliff face, close to where he keeps the hollowed-out horns containing his muthi. A quiet place. The crackle of the waterfall and the birdsong that announces the coming of dawn are part of that quietness, like beads woven into the pattern of things. Laying the cow-skin aside, he reaches for one of the two fire-making sticks that are kept here. It's the female stick, the one that lies horizontally when fire is being made. One of the horns contains male medicine; the other contains female muthi. Carefully, he pours a small amount of muthi from the male horn into the hole in the female stick. The other stick, the male stick now held between his hands vertically, he dips into the horn containing the female muthi. 'Nsondo,' he whispers, using one of the praise names for Nkulunkulu, the Great Spirit, 'these are your medicines. See how I am using your medicines. Please look kindly on my appeal!'*

★

Lombi has just finished reviving the fire outside the hut, when the Induna emerges early the following morning. He's clutching the zebra skin scabbard used to protect the Umkhontho. Lombi rises and greets him. She has her baby strapped to her back, as before, and he returns her greeting and asks her how the little one is. She bows her head and says he is well.

She will now fetch water, she adds. The Induna nods and has to step aside as the udibi emerges from the hut. He heads straight to the fire to warm his hands, greeting Lombi as he passes her. She returns his greeting and asks the Induna if she may enter the hut, as her largest water pot is kept in there.

The Induna tells her to go ahead.

Inside the hut, Lombi moves over to the female side. As Hlakanyana slips out of the rolled-up mat, she removes the water-skins she used to pad out the bundle strapped on her back. Then she removes her body wrap, squats, and lets Hlakanyana leap on to her back. Straightening up, she reties the imbeleko, making sure a cursory glance will simply reveal a tiny head, hands and feet.

Finally, she picks up the water pot. Stepping out of the hut, she balances the pot on her head and moves past the warriors still gathered around the fire.

Once she's out of sight, further down the path that runs to the river, she clasps the pot under her right arm, and breaks into a run, ignoring Hlakanyana's curses as he's bounced about.

Bamba and two warriors are waiting at the stream, standing in the water so as not to leave any footprints. Untying her imbeleko, Lombi allows Hlakanyana to slip down on to the ground. He raises his right hand to show Bamba he has the Umkhontho.

Lombi takes her baby from one of the warriors, while Bamba helps Hlakanyana up on to the other soldier's shoulders. The foursome then move away, wading upstream.

When Lombi returns to the hut, with the full pot balanced atop her head, the Induna and his men are getting ready to depart. She breathes a sigh of relief, because clearly they haven't yet realised the Umkhontho has been swapped for a valueless spear.

After checking that Lombi is certain her little brother will return later in the day with some relatives, to look for her grandfather's body, the Induna orders his men to be on their way.

★

*The male stick goes into the hole in the horizontal female stick. He begins to rub his palms together, causing the male stick to revolve, in a rapid, steady motion. Then a low murmur, as he names the Zulu Kings who have joined the ancestors: 'Zulu! Gumede! Phunga! Mageba! Ndaba! Jama! Senzangakhona! Help your children!' A rustling sound as his palms spin the vertical stick. 'Nsondo,' he says raising his voice slightly, 'Nkulunkulu, Great Spirit, give those I speak for rain. Give them rain so that they can till the earth. Do not let them die, Nsondo, Lord of the Sky. Why do you withhold this thing? Who has made you angry? Do not be angry, for they have come seeking your forgiveness and mercy. They are humbled. Let the rain fall!'*

★

They arrive at the umuzi closest to the inyanga yezulu's homestead late the following afternoon. With more than a hundred inhabitants, not counting any regiments who might happen to be stationed there, it's the largest village in the district and is spread over a shallow slope. The unumzane is expecting them, and traditional greetings are exchanged. Then one of his sons conducts the Induna's men to the huts that have been assigned to them.

The Induna and the udibi, meanwhile, make their way to the rain-doctor's kraal, which is about a kilometre away. Reached by a steep path, the cluster of huts is perched atop a spur overlooking the valley where the village is situated. Those seeking the inyanga yezulu's assistance are expected to wait at the spot where the path branches off from the main track.

Alusi and his uncle are already here, the former agitated and pacing up and down, while the latter sits placidly atop a rock, the zebra-skin scabbard resting on his lap.

As soon as Alusi sees the Induna, he comes storming over. 'Where have you been?' he demands. 'What took you so long?'

Then, remembering who he's speaking to, he stops, holding up his hands palms outward. 'I'm sorry, Shadow of Shaka! I am merely' – *overwrought*, thinks the Induna – 'anxious to see this matter concluded.' A sickly grin. 'After all, our fields . . . well, you have seen them, you know how desperately we need rain.'

'I trust your journey was uneventful,' says the Induna.

Alusi nods. The uncle has joined them by now. 'You are well?' asks the Induna, his raised eyebrows and half-grin letting the uncle see he's aware the man has probably had a wearisome day having to endure Alusi's fretfulness and impatience.

Then he hands Alusi the scabbard. The youngster bends over, struggling to extract the spear. When he straightens up, clutching the assegai by its blade, he's wide-eyed with astonishment.

'B-b-but,' he splutters, 'this isn't it.'

'Neither is it the one we set out with,' says the Induna.

'What do you mean?' asks Alusi. Even his uncle appears perplexed.

Ignoring the question, the Induna turns and points down along the track they've had to follow to reach this place.

'Shadow of Shaka, I don't understand,' says Alusi, handing the spear to his uncle and moving forward to stand beside the Induna.

'Be still and look,' says the Induna.

Alusi glances around, eyeing the sky with its orange-tinged clouds. Turning back towards the Induna, it's clear he's about to remind the older man it's getting late, and the rain-doctor will see no one after sunset. But the Induna puts a finger to his lips and points down the path.

And there comes a figure, growing from the size of a fist to that of a boulder, and details begin to form. A shield. Broad shoulders. A club resting against his left shoulder. A big man growing ever bigger. It's Njikiza, the Watcher of the Ford.

When he reaches them, he exchanges greetings, then tilts his shield face-down toward Alusi. Three spears are attached to the isihlangu. One is a long hunting spear, the other is an iklwa and the third is . . . It takes Alusi a few seconds before he recognises the Umkhontho.

He turns to the Induna. 'What is this? How . . . Why . . . ?'

'Never you mind,' says the Induna. 'Just take it. It's almost sunset and you must hurry.'

★

After Alusi has left, the Induna asks the Watcher of the Ford if his trip was uneventful.

'As a stroll,' replies the big man. 'And you, Nduna, how did you fare?'

The warrior grins. 'We had an interesting time,' he replies, and goes on to tell Njikiza and the uncle about their encounter with the woman called Lombi.

'So it was as my brother suspected,' says the uncle. 'An attempt was made to steal our spear.'

'An attempt which succeeded,' adds the Induna.

'When did you find out the spear had been replaced, Master?' asks Njikiza.

'I suspected something had happened, but waited until we were far, far distant from that strange place before I checked.'

That was a day ago, muses Njikiza, and that could mean Mhlangana already has the spear in his possession and has realised it's not the Umkhontho.

'Does that mean our return journey will be just as fraught?' asks the uncle.

'I don't think so,' says the Induna. Mhlangana will see, in the fact that the spear his men have brought him isn't the real Umkhontho, a subtle warning that Nkululeko and the Induna know that *he* is behind the theft, and not merely some bandit. This should deter him from trying again.

The two men nod their agreement; then Njikiza asks if the Induna knows how the spear he was carrying got swapped.

The Induna shakes his head. However it was done, it was masterful. But he does know this: the day will come when he's able to share his appreciation with the perpetrator of the feat.

★

The sun has set, leaving behind a purple sky, when Alusi rejoins the others – without the Umkhontho. Concerned, Alusi's uncle asks his nephew what's happened. All is well, says Alusi. He and his uncle had already delivered the cow to the rain-doctor and he now said Alusi could return mid-morning tomorrow to retrieve the Umkhontho.

The following morning, with the sun halfway to its zenith, Alusi insists on going alone to fetch the Umkhontho. But that's out of the question, says the Induna. 'I will accompany you,' he adds, and Njikiza and the udibi will go with him.

Alusi's face hardens and the udibi can see he's on the verge of arguing with his master, but the youngster manages to swallow his indignation and adopt a sulk instead, striding out ahead of the other three as they set off for the inyanga yezulu's kraal.

They've been waiting for him for a little while when suddenly there's a shriek and Alusi comes racing down the path from the rain-doctor's kraal, flapping his arms like a hadeda about to take off.

Njikiza and the Induna move to intercept him.

'The spear,' he's saying. 'The spear!'

Njikiza drags Alusi over to a nearby rock and sits him down.

'What about the spear?' asks the Induna.

'The rain-doctor . . .' gasps Alusi.

'What did he do?' asks the Induna.

And it comes spilling out – how the inyanga yezulu had said he didn't have the Umkhontho.

'He . . . he asked me what I was talking about,' says Alusi. 'He s-said I'd n-never been there and had n-never given him the spear.'

★

A few minutes later, the Induna and Njikiza are halfway up the path that leads to the inyanga yezulu kraal.

The rain-doctor – short, wiry, bald – leaps on top of a rock just a few metres away from them.

'Aiee,' whispers Njikiza, 'he looks like a bald baboon.'

'What do you want, Shaka's Shadow?'

'So you know who I am,' replies the Induna.

'Hai, why shouldn't I? I am not a turd-brain, unlike some I'm looking at right now.'

'Turd-brain?' growls Njikiza.

'Hush!' whispers the Induna. Raising his voice, he asks if the one called Alusi was here yesterday.

'And this morning, rhino-breath,' says the rain-doctor.

'Yes, to retrieve a certain spear,' says the Induna.

'Ha!' barks the rain-doctor and, looking very like a naked baboon, he leaps on to another rock. 'So you are the one he went crying to! You and that big hippo over there!'

'There'll be more than crying when this hippo catches him,' mutters Njikiza.

'Well, there is the matter of the spear,' says the Induna.

'What spear, dung beetle?'

'Yes, there is that too.'

'Aiee, do all of Shaka's Shadows speak in riddles?'

'I meant that is precisely the same question you asked the youngster, when he came to fetch it this morning.'

'And are you as deaf as he is? Again I say: what spear?'

The rain-doctor had insisted that, if he was to make the rains come, Nkululeko KaDingwa had to lend him his – or the village's – most precious possession, had he not?

Folding his arms, the rain-doctor nods.

And, in this instance, that meant an especially valuable Umkhontho Wamadlozi.

'So I was led to expect,' says the rain-doctor.

'Expect?' asks the Induna.

'Yes, expect; for this valuable weapon never materialised.'

'It was delivered to you yesterday.'

'No it wasn't,' says the rain-doctor.

'*Liar!*'

Njikiza and the Induna both turn. With the udibi following haplessly behind him, Alusi is heading up the path toward them.

'*He's lying!*' he shouts. '*Lying!*'

Two strides, and big Njikiza has dropped his club and grabbed hold of Alusi. 'Be still,' he orders.

'Does he speak the truth?' the Induna asks the inyanga yezulu.

The rain-doctor shrugs, scratches his left armpit. 'Does he? You tell me what you think, O Gloom of Shaka.'

It doesn't make sense. Why would the rain-doctor take the spear? And in such a foolish way – one that would see him imme-diately suspected. Granted, the Umkhontho is extremely valuable, but an inyanga yezulu regards his own powers as beyond value. They are hereditary, too, and not just anyone can claim to be a rain-doctor. The related dangers aside, it's a position that accords great status upon one, and it relieves one of the many mundane obligations expected of other folk living in a district. For one thing, a rain-doctor doesn't have to keep his own fields if he doesn't want to; the nearest umuzi will supply the family with food (partly as a form of 'commission' for the custom his pres-ence brings to the village's cattlemen).

It doesn't make sense, decides the Induna, regarding the rain-doctor's cocked head and his folded arms. The inyanga yezulu has the air of one watching a dim child groping for comp-rehension.

He wheels round. 'Is he?' he asks Alusi. 'Is he lying?'

'What?' says the youngster, trying to pull away from Njikiza, his voice high-pitched with shock.

'You heard me!' says the Induna.

'You heard him!' calls the inyanga yezulu.

'How . . . how can you believe *him*?' demands Alusi.

'Because I can't believe he'd be that stupid.'

'Certainly not as beef-witted and feeble-minded as those who are bothering him right now,' adds the rain-doctor.

The Induna spins his spear and rams the haft into Alusi's chest. 'Where is it? Where did you hide it?'

There are other questions to be answered, such as who persuaded him to try and steal the spear, and why he chose such a silly way to do so, but they can wait.

The haft of the Induna's iklwa jabs Alusi's chest again. 'Where is it?' he demands.

★

Bamba lays the zebra-skin scabbard across the prince's palm. His hands trembling imperceptibly, Mhlangana stares at the covering so intently, it's as if he's trying to count every single tiny hair that makes up its black and white pattern. The one within him – the other Mhlangana, who doesn't have to worry about masks and hiding his true feelings, or his madness – has a hard-on that could break rock and is licking his lips while his eyes gleam so brightly that it's daylight inside the hut.

Shifting his position on the pile of mats, and squirming because the other Mhlangana's erection has pushed into his own cock, stiffening it, the prince looks up at his senior induna.

'Am I to assume that neither you nor that . . . that creature have . . . ?' His covetous gaze drops to the zebra skin once more.

'Opened it?' murmurs Bamba. 'No, Master.'

If there's lust in Mhlangana's fumbling fingers, there's also glee, decides Bamba, watching the prince trying to pinch the tip of the blade so he can pull the spear free of the scabbard. He's put one over not just *her*, but Nkululeko and the Induna too.

Finally the prince manages to draw the spear from the scabbard.

'Such artistry,' he says, tilting his head. Another time, another place he'd have a jeweller's loupe screwed into his right eye.

Bamba gapes. He hasn't ever seen this fabled Umkhontho Wamadlozi before, and isn't aware if the prince has. What he does know, however, is that both of them have seen an ordinary iklwa – and that's what he's looking at right now. And he doesn't think the Umkhontho is just your standard iklwa with a short-ened haft. After all, isn't part of its value due to it being so old, maybe even dating from the Ma-Iti?

He's wondering whether to say something, when the prince pauses in his appreciation of the spear.

'This . . .' he hisses, looking up at Bamba. 'This is . . . This is not . . .' He stands up, lets the spear drop as if it's suddenly become too hot to hold. 'What have you done?'

'Master, I—'

'No,' interrupts the prince, 'not you! You wouldn't dare! Where is that little monster?'

'He left us half a day away from your umuzi, Master.'

'Left? Or fled?'

'I – I couldn't say, Master.' Bamba swallows. 'I had the scab-bard in my possession all the time!'

Stroking his chin with his thumb and first finger, Mhlangana turns away from Bamba. 'Then they tricked us! Nkululeko and that lizard who serves my brother so loyally – they have tricked us!'

'Then we must retaliate, Master.'

Mhlangana turns back to his induna. 'Oh, we will, have no fear about that! But we must bide our time. This matter,' he adds, indicating the iklwa lying on the hut's floor, 'is over.' He narrows his eyes. 'We can only hope that old bitch fared no better.'

★

*Sparks are husbanded, then they grow and spread to the kindling. When the fire has caught, the inyanga yezulu adds green branches. This creates black smoke. He adds more green branches and leaves, and the smoke billows out of the cavern. Billows and rises up into the sky. If the Great Spirit has been appeased, this smoke will become the clouds that bring the rain down upon the thirsty earth.*

★

As eager as she is to hear the maiden's news, she first sees that the girl is given something to drink and settled on a pile of mats, for she has come a long way, very fast.

'I'm sorry, Ma,' says the girl.

The older woman lays a hand on her shoulder. 'Calm down and tell me what happened.' To give her more time to restrain her tears, she adds: 'Start with the journey there. Was it uneventful?'

'Oh, yes,' nods the girl, managing a smile. 'For I met big Njikiza on the road and we travelled together.'

'Good, good,' murmurs the older woman. Njikiza's company might have made the maiden feel happy and safer; but for herself it's the exact opposite.

'He looked after you?' she asks.

The maiden nods after a sip of water.

'But you didn't . . .'

'Hai no, Ma! I told him I was going to visit relatives.'

'Good.' She wouldn't have chosen this girl if she thought she was that stupid, but she has to make sure. It's bad enough that the colouring of her skirt would have identified the maiden as one of her girls.

Sitting off to one side, Mnkabayi lowers her head to hide a smile. Njikiza? If Njikiza was around, that meant the Induna was somewhere nearby. If she'd known Nkululeko had involved him, she would have told Nandi to forget about it. No matter how well laid they might have been, her plans wouldn't have stood a chance!

Not that Nandi would have listened. Despite her son's many victories, and the land he has acquired for the nation, she's still obsessed with helping Shaka to find his Ubulawu, his talisman.

Senzangakhona's Ubulawu had been destroyed on his death, and Sigujana hadn't had time to find his before Shaka had him assassinated.

Shaka, meanwhile, has professed disdain for the tradition. 'Let my mighty army be my Ubulawu,' he's said.

But that hasn't stopped Nandi from nagging him, and trying to assist him in finding his Ubulawu.

Thinking it possible that Nkululeko's famous Umkhontho Wamadlozi could be the talisman, she had used her wiles – not to mention promises of rapid advancement – to persuade Alusi to steal the spear.

And now he's failed.

Nandi dismisses the maiden and turns to Mnkabayi. 'What say you? Has Mhlangana succeeded where I've failed?'

Mnkabayi is intrigued by the stories Nandi has heard about Mhlangana also seeking to steal the spear. Perhaps this devious nephew has some potential, if properly guided. She especially enjoys the very distinct possibility that Mhlangana was moved to attempt stealing the spear only because he knew of Nandi's interest in the artefact. (For why else would he be interested in the Umkhontho?)

But Nandi has asked her a question, and Mnkabayi shakes her head. 'Hai, I think not! Not if the Nduna and Njikiza were involved.'

Nandi considers this a moment, then nods.

'And when this Alusi talks, as he most definitely will, what will you do then?' asks Mnkabayi.

'What can they do? They would not dare risk my son's wrath,' says Nandi.

'This is so,' agrees Mnkabayi.

★

Nandi is right.

Nkululeko is waiting for them, having arrived back at the umuzi a few days before. But his complaints about the rather nebulous reason Nandi gave for wanting to see him die on his lips when he sees his favourite nephew trussed up and being marched along in the midst of the contingent of warriors.

The Induna leads the stunned district head back to the latter's hut. He first tells of the girl and the missing grandfather, and how the spear he was carrying disappeared during the night they spent at her homestead.

'And it was just like that,' he adds ruefully. 'It was as if the spear was spirited away. I still cannot tell how it was done . . .'

But Nkululeko's mind is still on Alusi. 'And then what happened?' he asks.

The Induna tells him of the clumsy manner in which Alusi tried to steal the real Umkhontho. It was a performance that pleased the rain-doctor so much that he said he no longer had to borrow the spear to prepare himself for the ritual, as he now had enough of a feeling for this clan's nature.

'So that is one thing at least,' says the Induna, trying to calm his friend. 'The ritual has been performed.'

Nkululeko nods distractedly, the plight of his people momentarily forgotten, and bellows for Alusi to be brought to him.

While the Induna and Njikiza look on, Nkululeko and two of his brothers proceed to interrogate the youngster. Only a few whacks with an iwisa are needed before Alusi tells how he had panicked when he realised he wouldn't be allowed to travel to the rain-doctor's homestead alone and how he had hidden the precious spear on his way down the slope the first evening, hoping he'd be able to retrieve it the following day.

And who had inveigled him into stealing the Umkhontho in the first place?

'The Queen Mother,' mutters Alusi through broken teeth.

And Nandi was right: the only thing they can do is look at each other in alarm, and let the matter drop.

'Aiee, I don't know which is worse,' growls Nkululeko after Alusi's been dragged away, 'that one's stupidity or his treachery.'

'He doubtless overestimated how far Nandi's protection could reach. Although . . .'

'What?' asks Nkululeko, as a smile plays across the Induna's lips.

He has just remembered, says the Induna, and tells how Njikiza had met one of Nandi's maidens on the road. She was also going to the village closest to where the rain-doctor lived; although she had told him she was going to visit relatives.

'So all Alusi had to do was get the spear into her hands,' muses Nkululeko. And anyone who dared touch one of Nandi's maidens would feel the wrath of Shaka himself.

It also explains Mhlangana's sudden interest in the Umkhontho, continues the Induna, for doubtless he had heard of Nandi's plans . . .

'The Ubulawu!' interrupts Nkululeko.

'Precisely!' says the Induna. 'And this is good news.'

'How so?'

Nandi will see in her failure to secure the spear a sign that the ancestors don't favour the undertaking, and therefore the

Umkhontho can't be Shaka's Ubulawu. So she won't try again, which means neither will Mhlangana – as he merely wanted to steal the spear because Nandi wanted it.

★

Later that night the clouds begin to stack up over the village. And the following morning, the sky melts and it begins to rain.

# PART THREE

# *The Wild Cat People*

For more than a year, numerous and strange reports had at intervals reached us, some indeed of such a character as induced us to treat them as the reveries of a madman. It was said that a mighty woman, of the name of Mantatee [Mantatisi, queen of the Wild Cat People], was at the head of an invincible army, numerous as locusts, marching onward among the interior nations, carrying devastation and ruin wherever she went; that she nourished the army with her own milk, sent out hornets before it, and . . . was laying the world desolate.

Revd Robert Moffat, who was based at the
Kuruman mission on the fringe of the Kalahari desert
in the 1820s (cited by Peter Becker in *Path of Blood*)

When I buy a bull, I always start by looking at the 'business end'. I want to see large testicles and a well-shaped scrotum. That's the most important part of a bull. No matter how good he is otherwise, if he can't sire calves, he's no good to me.

Anon, quoted by P. Massmann in 'Scrotum: An important factor in bull selection', *2008 Simmentaler Journal*

When Zwide of the Ndwandwes sent his men to go and kill Shaka, in the campaign that would end on the slopes of Gqokli Hill, rainfall up-country meant the White Umfolozi could only be crossed in three places. Nomahlanjana, who was commanding the Ndwandwes, decided not to split his force, but instead sent his men through the first ford he came upon.

It was lightly guarded by Zulu soldiers instructed to delay the Ndwandwes for as long as possible. Rapids lay below the narrow crossing and the water reached shoulder height close to the opposite bank. The Ndwandwe soldiers waded into the river in files proceeding four abreast, each man holding his shield and spears high in one hand, while gripping the shoulder of the man in front of him with the other.

The current was fierce, rock gave way to mud, and suddenly the Zulu force guarding the ford didn't seem so insignificant. In fact, a company of fewer than two hundred was able to hold off an army numbering eight thousand, until the level of the river began dropping.

Njikiza was there that day. A giant of a man, almost two metres tall with a chest like a mountain range, he'd swapped his assegai for a huge spiked club. The Ndwandwes fell like reeds beneath that mighty weapon, and he was forever afterwards known as Nohlola Mazibuko – The Watcher of the Ford.

And how different was that day! A lot hung in the balance – for Shaka's regiments were still, by and large, untested – but there was a sense of victory in the air. The sense, inspired by Shaka, that they were on the brink of something great, something momentous. It ignited their muscles, filled their nostrils, straightened their backs.

And now look at them, rulers of all they can see!

'Look at us!' Njikiza had told the Induna, the day before they left.

*Hunched shoulders, shifty eyes, shuffling feet. A royal hut mired in gloom, sunk in gloom, swallowed by gloom, and a King trapped within its obsidian interior.*

*Treacherous thoughts.*

*Why hasn't the King ordered a withdrawal?*

*Why hasn't he called his men back?*

*Wise Nqoboka, who is commanding the regiments in Mozambique, has offered the King a way of doing this that won't attract criticism. By having his messengers mention the slavers, he's all but begging Shaka to order him to 'redirect' the army, and have them go after these creatures.*

*This will take them to healthier environs.*

*It's highly unlikely Shaka will have missed the import of this seemingly irrelevant addendum to a tale of suffering — so why hasn't he seized the opportunity?*

*Why isn't Shaka trying to save his own men?*

★

*Thoughts to distract him from the torture of merely putting one foot in front of the other; to distract him and enable him to keep on keeping on, even though he feels permanently light-headed and a part of him is urging him to drop out of line and invite the nearest female warrior to finish him off.*

*Thoughts that give him energy because they are so disturbing, give life to the part of him that wants to survive, so that he might punish his captors before setting off to destroy those who threaten the King.*

Hai! But what will you do . . . ? What will you do, brave Induna, if those who threaten the King are in the right? What will you do if Shaka's lassitude, his willingness to see half his army destroyed, is really killing the nation, and those who conspire against him are following the old ways, seeking only to do things in the way laid down by the ancestors?

*What will he do?*

Will you even have a right to interfere, brave Induna? And, if you do, does that mean you too are putting your own interests before the welfare of the tribe? In this instance, those interests have to do with honour and loyalty, and not personal gain, but it doesn't matter. For it's still the tribe that will suffer.

*What will he do?*

★

*First things first, though. He must find a way of freeing himself, before he can help anyone else. And before he can do that he must recover his strength. Fortunately, it seems Duthlle, the old woman, would like to see this too. And, although they keep his hands tied together and he's guided by a leash affixed to a leather strap around his throat, much like the stock that redcoats used to wear, the pace isn't too arduous.*

# 1
## Something New

The domed roof of the big hut is lost in flickering darkness. Torches line the walls and are attached to the pillars, so that these columns resemble an ever-shifting forest. There's a sickeningly sweet smell in the air, as if a million flowers have been crushed into near nothingness and their scent let loose like a swarm of flies. The reddish-brown floor gleams like jasper; it could even be made from that black-veined gemstone. Anything's possible in a structure like this, where the wall is lined with copper that's become molten liquid in the torchlight.

Four flabby, toad-shouldered, toad-jowled men, with stomachs that hide their loincloths and bald pates that shine like the floor, lead the Induna up two steps and on to a low stone platform, where two posts are sunk into the floor. With long, delicate toad fingers, they wrap leather cords around his wrists and fasten him to the posts so that he's caught between them, his arms held rigid by the pole tied across his shoulders. Then one pulls his loin covering down to his ankles, while another, with much feigned delicacy and sniggering, pinches the tip of his penis sheath and suddenly yanks it off, as though trying to frighten the organ erect.

Pots of warm water are produced and all four begin to wash him.

'Hai,' says Duthlle, coming through the arched doorway directly opposite the Induna just as he aims a kick at one of the eunuchs, 'they are trying to help you. Don't you want to be clean and sweet-smelling?'

The Induna says nothing, merely watches her approach him. She's wearing a grey cuirass with rubies set into it, and is carrying a staff with an ornate rounded head comprised of rubies set into gold.

'Come, come, Zulu,' she says, peering up at him. 'Let that scowl go away and sit in the shade a while, for it must be exhausted. And you'll probably need it for later.'

Despite himself, he has an erection. Prodding his cock with the tip of her stick, she says: 'And I'm sure a scowl is the last thing on the minds of Zulu maidens confronted by this beast.'

She switches to her own language, presumably translating this last observation for the eunuchs, who giggle – and lower their guard enough to enable the Induna to bounce his foot off one's chin.

A burst of gibberish from Duthlle sees attempts at retaliation confined to handling his cock roughly while soaping it, and then she shakes her head at the Induna.

'*Do not try to turn round or acknowledge me in any way,*' said the elderly man who led him here after the Induna's arms had been tied to the heavy wooden pole that was laid across his shoulders to create a kind of yoke.

'*I am a Mthethwa, Zulu, and my name is Mkahi,*' said the man who carried a short stiff whip made of rhino hide, and who guided his captive by pulling on one of the strips of leather attached to each end of the pole.

'*What is this place?*'

'*What is this place?*' muttered the old man. '*This is where madness comes to be suckled.*'

'*Where are the men?*' Approaching the city, they had been led past fields and vegetable patches and grazing cattle. Those out hoeing and weed-ing were men; elderly men mostly, wearing crumpled, grubby loincloths. They were watched over by tall, bare-breasted women carrying long spears and wearing skirts comprising weighted tassels made from zebra and red hartebeest tails.

*A snort. 'The only men here are servants. Dogs like me. Keep on walking straight.'*

'Where are the men?' asks the Induna.

'Is that the first question that flits across your mind? Typical.' Duthlle makes a loud sniffing sound. 'I think you are fragrant enough now, Zulu.' She claps her hands. The eunuchs bow to her and leave the hut.

'Those are not men,' hisses the Induna, as the old woman turns back to him.

'I never said they were. They have their uses but they are not men, for men are good only for breeding.'

Standing to the side of the Induna, she uses her stick to raise his prick so she can examine his testicles. 'Yes, for breeding,' she sighs, 'and often not even for that.'

She lets his prick drop and steps away from him, smiling. 'Come, come, Zulu, you may not have realised it, but it's the way of the world – the way things are meant to be.'

*They passed three women. Two of them were plump and rounded and each was swathed in a scarlet toga-like garment; they immediately turned their backs to the men. Tall, flat-chested and manly, the third woman glared at them, daring them to give her a chance to use her spear. The Induna had noticed similar behaviour as they were led through the settlement upon their arrival – some women hiding their faces in their hands, while others, who were clearly warriors, silently glared at them.*

*'Did you see the animosity in her eyes?' hissed Mkahi, a few footsteps later. 'Males are seen as a curse here. They are strangled at birth. Do you hear me, strangled! They don't even bother to wash the birth-blood off them.'*

*'But a mother . . . the bond she has with the child growing in her belly?'*

*'Weren't you listening, Zulu? Yes, some try to save their male chil-*

dren, and for doing so they are banished. At least that's what the others are told. But I know better —they are killed along with their children. And they are only a few, because males are considered a curse! They are deformed creatures, human but not quite human, which only makes them more diabolical as far as these harridans are concerned. For them even a miscarriage is better than coughing out a male.'

'Men are good only for breeding, and often not even that. But women, Zulu . . . women are for companionship and, yes, love – the tongue being so much more supple and entertaining than the cock.'

The Induna makes to speak, but Duthlle holds up a hand. 'Let us pretend you've already spewed forth your indignation, so if you must say something, say something sensible.'

The Induna grins. He wasn't about to give her the satisfaction of parrying threats and profanities. 'Sensible?' he says. 'I see nothing *sensible* here.'

'And yet, while we must capture some, as we did with you, there are many more who come willingly.' Duthlle smiles. 'Many more. But that shouldn't be surprising since we are, after all, dealing with men, who know only one master.' She raises her staff. 'That,' she says, pointing at the Induna's penis. 'The snake that just has to stir for there to be trouble. And watch out when it bites.'

*'Where are you taking me?'*

*'The queen wants to see you.'*

*The Induna didn't like the sound of that. 'Why . . . ?'*

*'Why you?' interjected Mkahi, and he chuckled. 'Because you are a Zulu warrior, and I don't think she has seen one of Shaka's lions before.' Refugees and criminals fleeing the Bull Elephant's displeasure, yes, but not one of his amabhubesi, his lions. 'You will be something new for her, Zulu.'*

'Does the queen often single out a prisoner for special attention?'

Another chuckle. 'Not often, but occasionally, when she wants a taste before the Selection.'

'Selection?' echoed the Induna, for Mkahi had used the same term Zulu stockmen employed when speaking of selecting bulls for breeding purposes.

'Hai! Haven't you guessed why you are here? Do you really think the likes of Duthlle will waste their time travelling far and wide merely to seek servants?'

Mkahi pulls on the right rein, thus turning the Induna in that direction. 'Come, come, Zulu! Has the journey here worn you out so badly you can't think straight? I hope not, for tomorrow you will need all your wits about you, because there will be a Selection. Last time, Duthlle found the queen a White Man and it was deemed there would be no Selection, but his seed proved unsatisfactory and the queen's sister was angered, and now she plots against the queen, it's said . . . although that's nothing new, for she's always plotting against her.'

'But first there must be a selection,' observes the Induna.

'Ah! I see I was right to order that Mkahi be the one who brought you here. The old fool has been talking his head off – which will indeed be removed. But I think we'll keep him with you until the Selection is done. And, of course, there must be a selection, for only the best bull will suffice.'

'And the rest are . . . what? Culled?'

Duthlle shrugs and says it's part of the process, part of the Selection, since those who fail can't be left to pollute other tribes. Other women might not be as enlightened as the Cat People, but that doesn't mean they – and their wombs – shouldn't be protected as far as possible.

'And some men still come willingly?'

Well, there is an additional enticement, says the old woman.

'We offer them their heart's desire,' she adds, noting the Induna's quizzical expression. 'For you, I assume, that would be all the cattle you can herd.'

The most recent incumbent received gold and diamonds, all the treasures the tribe had accumulated over the years, artefacts from forgotten dynasties.

'And if I refuse to participate?' asks the Induna.

'Then the others will kill you.'

'And if I kill *them*, and still refuse?'

'That won't be possible.'

Before the Induna can ponder further her strange choice of words, Duthlle turns. 'Behold our queen,' she says, with an expansive gesture in the direction of the doorway opposite.

# 2
## Favourable Traits

She is naked. Rolls of fat of decreasing diameters wobble above her waist, with the lowest sagging over her genitals, while the highest are elongated by two heavy breasts. Thighs, almost as wide as a man's arm is long, taper down to grey knees resembling giant knuckles, swollen calves, slender ankles and small, plump feet with toes spaced far apart like stones a child has pressed into mud. Her face is a full moon rising out of a series of pendulous chins.

After bowing to the queen, Duthlle climbs the steps of the platform, to stand behind the Induna.

*So*, says the queen, giving the Induna a slow once-over, *this is one of them?*

*Yes, Your Fertility, this is a Zulu.*

Moving closer: *Ho! See the defiance in this one's face.*

*Yes*, says Duthlle, *such is their nature. They are very warlike, Majesty. A desirable trait.*

*Yes, yes, I know — you have told me so many times! His teeth?*

'Show Her Majesty your teeth, Zulu.' Bending closer to the Induna's left ear: 'And don't waste your time resisting us. This is not a battle worth fighting.'

*He baulks?*

Duthlle straightens. *No, Majesty.*

The Induna opens his mouth.

The queen leans forward, peering, then tilts her head. Nods. *No foul odours, Your Fertility?*

Her eyes now focused on the Zulu's genitals, the queen shakes her head in an absent-minded way.

The tip of Duthlle's staff touches the Induna's left hand. *If your Fertility were of a mind to check, she would see he has chaffed knuckles. The guards at the pen say he killed two men who tried to bother him while he sought a resting place. Now he is no longer bothered, although he does not waste his energy by seeking to establish himself as the leader of the pen.* Adaptability to environment is another desirable trait, concludes Duthlle.

Moving to the front of the platform, she runs the tip of her staff up and down the Induna's torso. *And, as your Fertility can see, there's nothing wrong with his frame. Firm muscles. Broad shoulders. Strong thighs. All highly desirable.*

*And you say this is what is needed,* says the queen looking up at the older woman.

*Well,* says Duthlle, *given their King's triumphs along the coast, one would presume these Zulus are of superior stock.*

*For men,* adds the queen.

Duthlle inclines her head.

*We certainly have exhausted the potential of those around us.*

*That is so, Majesty.*

*Even the White Man . . .* Is the queen's tone accusatory? Does she blame Duthlle for the failure of that experiment? Clasping her staff in two hands, the old woman keeps her face placid, and fixes her gaze a few centimetres above the queen's head.

*He was what was needed too, not so?*

'You yourself told me to find you one,' Duthlle tells herself, 'and deemed the colour of his skin the trait that made up for all other deficiencies – the lack of teeth, the skinny hunched frame, the overall weakness that meant it was just as well a Selection wasn't held.'

*But instead, he was exactly what my sister needed to further the discontent she claims my rule has sown. I am not happy, Duthlle. Not happy at all.*

*This will change that, Majesty.*
*You seem certain.*
*Well, he is a Zulu, Majesty.*

★

After the queen has left, Duthlle tells the Induna he's done well, and summons the eunuchs. This time there are only two of them. Moving on to the stone platform, one unties the Induna from the posts, while the other looks on from a safe distance, levelling a long spear. There's some bumping of wood against wood, but the first eunuch is finally able to manoeuvre the Zulu away from the posts and down the steps.

'What now?' asks the Induna, addressing Duthlle.

She chuckles, as if it should be obvious. 'You'll be joining the queen.'

'Joining?'

'With.'

The Induna stiffens, then relaxes as the eunuch begins to smear some kind of scented oil over his back.

'But what of this selection you seem to set so much store by?' he asks.

'It is what it is, Zulu. There is no determining beforehand as to who will be left standing. That is one of the method's strengths.'

'But?' prompts the Induna as the eunuch's hands skate over his buttocks.

'There are certain bulls the queen has deemed a little more fitting than the others.'

'The queen? Cha! You mean yourself, don't you?'

Duthlle inclines her head modestly. 'I am known to have a good eye,' she concedes.

'And so your queen gets first taste.'

'Of what one of Shaka's lions has to offer? Yes. Because who

250

knows who will be left alive after tomorrow?' Indeed, a split-second of carelessness might see the Induna eating dirt before the day's half done. 'And that would be a waste, since I really do believe our queen will benefit from your seed.' She holds up a hand. 'Do not see that as a compliment, Zulu. It's merely a matter of ensuring you fulfil the only function that makes the existence of any man vaguely tolerable for everyone else.'

'What about this?' asks the Induna, as the eunuch gingerly begins to oil his chest.

'What about what?'

'This,' he says, bending to the left and then to the right, to indicate he's referring to the pole strapped across his shoulders.

The eunuch steps back to admire his handiwork.

'It stays put,' says Duthlle.

Fair enough, says the Induna and twists his upper body, swinging the yoke in an arc of 180 degrees and knocking out one of the eunuch's teeth en route.

A petulant action, perhaps – and one that earns him a thwack across the shoulder blades from Duthlle's staff, the rubies biting into his skin – but worth it for all that.

★

'So, Zulu?' asks Mkahi, as he marches the Induna back the way they came. 'You were gone a long while. A very long while. Did you enjoy your audience with the queen? Could you manage to function, with that weight atop you and your arms pinioned like this? Do you know why your arms are kept raised so?'

When the Induna doesn't respond, the Mthethwa cackles. 'Because men may sow the seed, but they are not permitted to touch the sacred soil.'

'Tell me more about this place.'

'You find yourself in a tribe of women, Zulu. What more do you need to know?'

'Infant boys are strangled, but what happens to the girls?'

'They are raised by their mother until the time of *their* selection. That is, of course, a gentler process than the one you face on the morrow.'

'What happens?'

'They are examined by the older women, led by Duthlle, who decide whether each girl will become a Mother or a Warrior.'

The Induna must surely have noticed that there are two distinct 'types' here: the thinner, more manly females, and the plumper, more womanly females who wear red coverings. The former are the Warriors and the latter are the Mothers. Warriors devote their time and energy only to becoming proficient in waging war, while the Mothers rear children, make pots, weave sleeping mats, cook meals, and so forth. Some are even responsible for making spears and shields.

Anything menial . . . well, as the term suggests, that's men's work.

'Do they have enemies?' asks the Induna.

Not for a while now, says Mkahi, but recently Mzilikazi and his Matabele have come sniffing around. Currently, though, the most serious threat to the queen comes from within her own family.

The Induna grunts. Clearly some things never change, no matter what's to be found between the legs of those who rule.

'The queen's sister has been claiming the queen is cursed, therefore unfit to rule, for she has had three boy children in a row now, whereas the sister has only ever produced one. And, with the Matabele somewhere nearby, she can point to that as further proof of being right.'

Mkahi chuckles. 'Perhaps this is why you were singled out for special attention, Zulu.'

Certainly he suspects that Duthlle went off to specifically find the queen a Zulu.

'New blood, you understand,' continues the Mthethwa. 'Find one of Shaka's lions whose semen can be expected to produce the lioness who will prove the sister and her followers wrong.'

# 3
## The Herd

A cold morning that scoured the bones and kicked you in the kidneys has turned into a blazing hot day that drenches you in sweat and sears the sand.

The Induna lets the milling, muttering mass push him to its fringes – push *them*, in fact, because the youth Mgobozi pointed out has attached himself to the Zulu. And the Induna's not going to waste any energy by shooing the boy away. He now tugs at the lad's arm to attract his attention, drops to his haunches and indicates the youngster should do the same.

The boy squats next to the Induna, bowing his head as though that will make all of this vanish.

The Induna, meanwhile, surveys their surroundings. As he'd noticed yesterday, the fence surrounding the corral isn't very sturdy. But it doesn't have to be, since it's there to separate the pens encircling the large arena. Someone attempting to escape won't get far, as warriors armed with spears and shields have moved in to provide a second, more formidable palisade beyond the fences to the rear.

The Induna spots old Mkahi and the other servants gathered in the space between the warriors and the fence; squatting on their heels they appear to be awaiting instructions. The warriors are dressed for the occasion: white feathers rise from their head-dresses and, in addition to a tasselled skirt, each woman wears a cuirass made from small plates of hardened leather laced together in parallel rows. A few of them sport black feathers and grey cuirasses, possibly made from dried rhino or elephant hide. The Induna assumes these women are officers.

As Mkahi has explained, two sets of corrals have been built at regular intervals around the arena, with space for spectators (and more warriors) between each adjoining pair. There are twelve such enclosures and, when the gate of one corral is opened, the men from inside it will be expected to fight those pouring out of the pen on the opposite side of the arena.

The Induna shifts his attention to the other bulls within the kraal. Some, he notes, seem eager for the contest that awaits them. These are the bigger men, many of whom are doubtless here voluntarily. They strut and preen and try to intimidate those less enthusiastic about the forthcoming contest. Muscles are flexed, sneers are sneered and fists are slammed into palms. Occasionally there'll even be a deliberate bump, usually targeting someone deemed too puny to retaliate. A bump and a snarl, causing the smaller man to cringe away; then the bigger one will look around, with eyes narrowed, daring anyone else to intervene.

The Induna shifts his attention to the arena itself, a large oval expanse of dirt that's a shade lighter than an oribi's hide. Composed of powdery dust atop a harder sub-surface, it seems swept and pristine, unsullied by a single hoof- or footprint.

Wiping the sweat from his face, he swallows. Conserving his energy is all very well, but he's going to need some water sooner or later. There's a trough fashioned out of a hollowed half-log on either side of the rear gate of their pen. Last night, one of them contained a brown-coloured mess intended as feed. The other trough contained water. Both are empty now.

A cheer, picked up by the warriors behind them, passes around the arena. The herd surges forward to the front gate for a better view. The boy wants to rise, but the Induna restrains him. He will know what they face soon enough, and there's no need for the youngster to upset himself prematurely.

Moments later the first screams can be heard, and now most of those who went to have a look-see are forcing their way back towards the centre of the pen.

Screams, shrieks, shouts . . . each one greeted by a cheer.

★

Then it's their turn, and as the Induna suspected, some of their fellow captives start fighting as soon as the gate is opened. But they're driven forward by the others, as are those loath to enter the arena. Try to turn back and you're immediately putting yourself at a disadvantage. And some of the men leave the pen in a sprawl, and are either trampled or pounced upon by those who seem to think they'll be safe, for a while at least, if they're seen to be grappling with an opponent. It's only the men to the very rear who have any control over the way they enter the arena, who can choose to leap over those cowering in the dust, or attack those who have already fallen upon the fallen. And the Induna marks these men who've had more or less the same idea as he did. They're clearly the ones to watch.

But they're still eager, and impatience finally sends them surging forward on the heels of the main body, using it as a shield as it collides with the group from the opposite pen.

The Induna and the youth are the last out. Having had to restrain the youngster when the rush started for the gate, he now grabs him by the elbow again and leads him away from the bodies, away from the lifeless limbs and staring eyes, from the blood seeping into the sand. A man staggers toward them, his eyes empty red sockets, his hands helplessly groping the air; the Induna raises his foot to shove him backwards. Another, with his legs lifeless, his right arm twisted unnaturally, is trying to pull himself back to the safety of a pen. A third man lies on his back, choking, with his larynx crushed.

There had been pauses between each previous bout, and the Induna reckoned this was while the bodies belonging to the previous herd of contestants were being removed. He sees he was right, for only the blood now remains – large swathes of black-ish-red. It's as if the earth itself has been wounded.

He halts the trembling youth just a few metres away from the front of the third pen along. This one still has to be opened, and the dirt hereabouts is clean.

The Induna pulls the youngster down beside him, ignoring his anxious, questioning look. And, ignoring the mêlée a few metres away, he notes that the fence circles the entire arena except for the upper quarter. On a low dais occupying the centre of this sector are the queen and others of her inner circle, shaded by thatch umbrellas held aloft by serving girls. On either side are rows of cheering women, the front ranks sitting on the ground, the rear ranks apparently standing on some kind of platform.

Some of the enclosures seem empty. No, wait . . . Over there, and there, he can see men. Clearly the winners are returned to the pens they came from; now they're standing at the gates to watch the next bout.

★

He turns his attention back to the scrimmage in the centre of the arena, watching how four men together bring down a fifth. But they scarcely have time to savour their victory when each of them is attacked by a stronger warrior. One is thrown through the air, to crash into a pile of bodies. Aiee! Such a foolish waste of energy on the part of the thrower. See! There he tries to hoist another man into the air, but this time takes a little longer about it. And see! He throws the man but, before he can turn, he's hit in the back by another. A scrawny, wiry fellow, who's on to the bigger man like a fungus the moment he hits the dirt; gripping the bigger man's ears, he begins pounding his head against the ground.

A warrior who has mud rubbed into his hair and across his chest, and is wearing a red loincloth, waits until the man on the ground goes limp before attacking the assailant, catching the scrawny man while he's still clutching the other man's ears.

The herd is gradually being thinned. Aiee! Such a cooperative herd! It even takes care of its own culling!

But the Induna knows he himself will have to enter the fray soon. As he considers who to choose, though, there's sudden movement to his left — a lunge spotted from the corner of his eye.

The Induna throws himself to the right.

Somehow the youth has managed to smuggle in a warthog tusk with a sharpened tip — and he's just attempted to gouge the Induna with it. If it hadn't become caught up in his loincloth, as he tried to remove it, chances are the youngster would have ripped open the Induna's flank. As it is, although the Induna was already moving sideways, the tip of the tusk has left a deep cut in the side of his upper thigh.

Coming up on to his knees, the Induna stares down at the wound, then up at the boy.

Who looks almost sheepish. Or perhaps it's merely the disappointment, and dread, of one who saw his chance, seized it — and failed.

The Induna takes another look at the wound, then punches the youth in the face.

Retrieving the tusk and gripping it in his left hand so that it protrudes between his first and second fingers, he gets to his feet. Rivulets of blood and sweat run down his left leg. He bends, scoops up a handful of sand and pats it into the wound.

*Well, this is a good start*, he thinks.

# 4
## Worm Man & Gorilla

He watches two men finish off a third. Aside from himself, they're the only ones still upright. They move apart and begin to eye each other. One of them is the tall man covered in mud – and the Induna sees now that his hair is braided and smeared with ochre pigments, so it seems as if clay worms are oozing out of his skull. The other is thickset and resembles a gorilla, with sloping shoulders that end in long arms. He steps to his left, Worm Man moves to his right, and both go into a crouch, ready to strike. Then Gorilla spots the Induna.

Straightening, he points past Worm Man. *Look over there, behind you!*

His opponent's not falling for that old trick, though. He makes as if to lunge forward, and Gorilla backs away further than he has to, and points again. It's as if he's saying you can look behind you now, because I'm too far away to reach you in the time it'll take to turn your head.

All the same, Worm Man backs away, putting even more space between them, before turning.

He sees the Induna. He had thought they were almost done, but here's one more. He scans the fallen bodies, this thicket of broken limbs and unseeing eyes, of writhing and groaning men. Crippled, blinded, these are as good as dead, so the Zulu is definitely the last of the herd still able to fight, decides Worm Man. Aside from the two of them, of course.

He half turns to Gorilla, tilts his head in the Induna's direction. The latter nods. They will work together again for now.

And as Gorilla begins to move toward the Induna, Worm Man

grins. Things couldn't be working out any better; let Gorilla and Induna tire themselves out.

There's about fifty metres separating them, and the Zulu waits until the short man has covered about half that distance, and is running at full tilt, before he himself starts racing forward.

A cheer from the crowd urges them on, these two men charging towards each other like a couple of rhino battling for supremacy.

Just before impact, the Induna veers slightly to the left and extends his right arm, earning himself a long-drawn-out hiss of disappointment and disapproval from the crowd.

Both men wheel amid the settling dust, the Induna in a crouch, his eyes fixed on Gorilla, Gorilla staring at the Induna, frowning . . . confused.

Then he looks down and sees his intestines come slithering out of the gash the Induna gouged in his side as he passed him.

Another frown, then he topples backwards, whereupon the Induna shifts his attention to the dirt. The warthog tusk was knocked out of his hand as it caught against the man's hipbone. Where is it?

*There!*

He's reaching for it just as the sound of running snags his attention. The Induna turns to his left, and catches Worm Man's shoulder in his solar plexus. He's sent sliding across the dirt and then the man's on top of him, his knees crashing on to the Induna's thighs, his hands finding the Zulu's throat.

Big hands, strong fingers, closing tight, the thumbs crushing the Induna's windpipe.

He forgot about the other adversary in his eagerness to regain the tusk, now he's paying for that mistake. The Induna can't breathe, has had the wind knocked out of him, and now he's being choked. Wide eyes, clenched teeth directly above him, urging him to die, die, *die*.

His legs are trapped, and the man's sitting too far down for the Zulu to throw him off.

The Induna's fingers find the man's thumbs, and become claws pulling against them. Dark spots fill his vision. His tongue is a giant slug in his mouth.

Can't.

Breathe.

Then an arm curls around the other man's neck.

And is withdrawn, trailing an arc of blood.

And Worm Man's grip goes limp, his fingers slipping away from the Zulu's burning throat.

With almost the last burst of energy he can muster, the Induna's palms come up to stop Worm Man from toppling forward on to him, trapping him further.

Gulping in mouthfuls of dust, he pushes the man off him . . . and finds himself staring up at the youth, who's retrieved the tusk and cut Worm Man's throat.

Before either can do anything, Mkahi and the other servants are there, too.

Hissing 'Hurry! Hurry!', the old Mthethwa helps the Induna to his feet. His hands on Mkahi's shoulders, his chest heaving as he fights to recover his breath, the Induna watches as the youth is led away.

Noticing the warrior's quizzical expression, Mkahi explains that two are allowed to survive this round.

He guides the Induna back to the enclosure. Gripping the Induna's wrists, he lowers the warrior on to the ground. Then he disappears and returns with amanzi, *water!*

The Induna drinks greedily, seeking to assuage his thirst and soothe his throat. He can still feel ghost-like fingers squeezing his windpipe.

The water, he reflects – listening to the cheers and ululations that announce the beginning of another mêlée – it's not an act of mercy but merely a way of prolonging their entertainment.

'What's next?' he asks, his voice a rasp.

With his finger, Mkahi stabs four dots into the sand next to the Induna. Four will fight, he explains. He draws a line between the first pair, then one between the second. Four will fight, but each pair will be tied together at the throat, he adds.

At the throat, thinks the Induna grimly – aiee! He's been half strangled once already.

And with the cut in his thigh . . .

Seeing the Induna examine the sticky sand clinging to his wound, Mkahi whispers that there's nothing he can do about that.

'Then we'll say nothing more about it,' says the Induna, reaching for a second waterskin.

# 5
## The Four

The first two come out of their pen ready for action, ready to inflict damage! The plaited leather cord linking the men together is just under three metres long, and therefore it's fairly easy to coordinate one's own movements. There's almost no need to jerk or pull one's partner into line and, with a little care, one can avoid being brought up short accidentally.

The Induna emerges from his pen, carrying his partner over his right shoulder.

Without considering the logistics such a move would later entail, the man had attacked the Induna while they were still waiting for the guards to open the gate.

Isithutha! *Idiot!* What was he thinking? Not that that's really important right now.

While the other two look on in disbelief, the Induna strides over to a piece of sand where there's no blood, and drops the corpse. The cord attached to the leather stock fastened around his throat is long enough for him to stand over the dead man with a foot firmly planted on either side of the body.

His two opponents are clearly from the same tribe. Both have long hair and both wear kilts of a light brown colour that end just above their knees. Their skin is also lighter, closer to caramel than the Induna's chocolate-brown. The battles that got them here are visible in the form of scratches and cuts across both their chests.

The Induna opens his arms wide in a gesture that says *What are you waiting for?*

The two look at each other, and charge, but they haven't got further than four paces when the man on the left moves too far to one side.

The leather snaps taut and pulls the two back together. Their shoulders collide, each tries to grab the other to retain his balance, then both are in the dust.

Laughter and jeers from the crowd.

The men pick themselves up. For a moment it seems as if they're going to turn on each other. Then one holds up his hand and gestures towards the Induna.

They retreat a few paces. After checking they're both ready, they charge again.

This time the manoeuvre is perfectly executed. As they reach the Induna the cord is stretched almost to its full width and seeking his throat. But the Zulu spoils everything by ducking under it at the last moment. And the men blunder past him, one of them on either side.

By the time they're able to stop themselves and turn around, the Induna has risen to his feet and wheeled to face them again.

Although they don't exactly paw the ground, they resemble bulls about to charge as they ready themselves for their second attack. Then they're off and running, their feet slapping against blood-sodden dirt.

They try to come in low, but the Induna drops into a crouch, placing his palms on the dead man's chest to steady himself . . . and the cord again sweeps over his head.

A drumming sound as the spectators stamp their feet and the female guards bang their spear hafts against their shields to show their displeasure.

Another pass, which the Induna again evades easily.

They barely tried, he realises – a sign, perhaps, that they have something else now in mind.

He stands and turns to face them, and sees they've wheeled already and are coming back at him.

He just has time to raise his hands in an effort to deflect the cord, then he's on his back, gasping for breath.

He tries to sit up, but can't, because the cord tying him to the dead man is now stretched to its fullest extent. He's going to have to shift sideways, closer to the body. He moves his legs, which are lying across the man's chest . . .

. . . then the other two come crashing down on top of him.

At first he thinks they're both attacking him, but it soon becomes apparent they're fighting each other.

★

A mound of bodies: the man on top strangling the man beneath him, shaking the other's head, as if he can knock the life out of him, pressing down with his knees and trying to crush the air out of the other man's stomach; and the other man trying to knock him off, heels digging into the dirt, seeking purchase, pelvis rising, hands clawing at his killer's face, yanking his hair, trying to press his thumbs into the man's eyes. But, like a shout becoming a whisper, this frantic activity lessens as the life begins to leave his body. First his hands drop away, then his legs stiffen, before going limp – and the other man tightens his grip, his teeth clenched, his fingers aching, *squeezing*. Then he straightens, arches his back and howls, his hands rising, curled into arthritic claws. It's a wild beast cry of triumph that's picked up by the spectators, so that the howl becomes a roar. But no one can see the grimace as he straightens his fingers. The pain! It feels as if they've been broken. Panting, he wipes his forehead in the crook of his elbow, and stares at the sky until breathing is easier and the whistle in his chest fades.

Then he peers down to make doubly sure the other man is

dead, and that's when a hand rises up, slipping under the dead man's right armpit to grab the leather cord that still ties the killer to his victim, and pulls hard, bouncing the killer's forehead off the dead man's face – then allows the man some slack, enough for him to straighten, before pulling down hard again – and yet again the man is allowed to lift his head, before the Induna pulls on the cord. This time the man stays down, collapsed on top of the body of the man he strangled – which is lying on top of the Induna himself.

# 6
## Isidlakathi!

'See anyone else you can beat, Zulu?'

As the Induna turns away from the gate, one of the eunuchs accompanying the old woman pushes the tip of his staff against his chest, to ensure the Induna keeps his distance.

'I was merely watching,' says the Induna. And it's a good thing he found within him the energy to rise and move over to the gate, because what he's just seen has given him a modicum of hope.

'Some fall easier than others,' says Duthlle, glancing past the warrior to where servants are removing corpses. They drag them by the feet, leaving broad trails in the dirt, so it's as if large slugs have passed, spreading blood instead of mucus.

'This is so,' agrees the Induna.

'Yet I feel you may yet fight your way to triumph.'

'Is it important for you that I do?'

Duthlle shrugs. 'Well, you *are* one of mine. I found you.'

'So my honour will be yours?'

'In a way, not that I need it. But I will say this: if the way to triumph is now shorter for you, it's steep, very steep.'

In due course, when it's his turn to enter the arena again, he sees what she meant.

His opponent – and there's only one this time – is not quite a giant, or isidlakathi, and the ground doesn't tremble with every ponderous step he takes, but that's scant consolation. Here is a colossus whose feet are almost as big as an elephant's, whose head seems to brush the sky, his grey hair even looking exactly like the frost one finds in higher altitudes.

And his girth matches his height – a family of baboons could shelter under his gut – and his arms are tree trunks, his fists the size of boulders.

The Induna looks around desperately, like an actor who's read the script, but is still hoping for the best.

The arena has shrunk in size – and that's not an optical illusion brought on by the human menhir standing yonder. With the weaker animals having been culled, and combat now a matter of one-on-one bouts, warriors have gathered in front of the pens situated in the lower arc of the oval. There are rows and rows of them, with their spears and narrow rectangular shields and white ostrich plumes, reducing the area of the battleground and in effect forcing the combatants to fight for their lives closer to the queen's dais.

The Induna returns his attention to the Dlakathi (and he can't help but think of him as that). At least there's no chance of the giant sneaking up on him, or attempting a sudden rush – but, once again, that's scant consolation.

Just to do something, the Induna takes a step to his right.

His opponent takes a step forward.

A second step to the right is met by another step forward, the Dlakathi's shadow surging forward, too.

Wanting to see what will happen if he reverses the process, the Induna takes two steps to his left.

Unperturbed, the big fellow takes two steps forward – and it doesn't escape the Induna's attention that, while he himself is more or less back where he started, the Dlakathi has moved more than a little closer.

He takes two steps back, and the Dlakathi lunges forward.

But while that avalanche of fat, muscle, bone and aggression might bring to mind a charging elephant, he's nowhere near as fast as an elephant. But still the Induna's not taking any chances. He waits a few heartbeats – to make sure the Dlakathi is locked on course, his momentum making any veering to the right or left a little more difficult – then he sets off running to the right, following an arc that takes him further away from his opponent and delivers him also to the Dlakathi's rear.

Not bothering to follow him, knowing that would be a waste of energy, the big man slows to a shuffle and gets himself turned around.

There's the inevitable drumming and booing from the crowd. They want to see the big man tear the Zulu apart. Nothing less will do.

As the noise dies down, there's a shout from the dais. It's from one of the eunuchs. Standing next to the queen, he's obviously passing on her instructions. The peevish, high-pitched pronouncement sees one of the warriors behind the Dlakathi break ranks and run towards him. When she gets close to him, she raises her arm and throws her spear. It embeds itself in the dirt next to the Dlakathi.

After a moment filled with bellowing from the crowd, he finally looks down at the spear.

Then, after another moment, he twists his torso round to examine the woman. Mountain ranges rise and fall across his massive forehead as he frowns, seeking to connect the two – the spear and the woman.

She jabs her finger toward the assegai, points at him, indicates the spear again, then makes a throwing motion with her right arm. The crowd comes to her aid, calling on the big fellow to pick up the spear.

The Induna glances at the rows of warriors arrayed behind him, but no one's about to come forward with a weapon for him.

Clearly it's been decided the Dlakathi needs something to make up for his lack of speed, while the Zulu can fend for himself.

No, wait . . . something *is* happening on this side. After some more chirruping from the eunuch, the warriors behind the Induna move forward, thereby ensuring he has less space to manoeuvre in.

And here comes the Dlakathi. He's finally figured out what's expected of him and holds the spear above his right shoulder, the tip of the blade sniffing out the Induna.

Who retreats several paces until movement glimpsed from the periphery of his vision causes him to snatch a glance over his shoulder. The female warriors in the first rank have lowered their spears between their shields, so he won't be able to retreat much further.

He faces the big man again: this slope of muscle, fat, bone and just plain meanness. It's there in his eyes, that meanness, in those tiny, tiny coal-black eyes pressed deep into his face.

The spear looks little more than a twig in the Dlakathi's huge hand.

Then he throws it.

The Induna leans sideways, putting his weight on his left leg and watching as the assegai flies past him with a slight wobble.

A hiss from the crowd, followed by a gasp. The spear has hit one of the guards lined up behind the Induna. She now sags forward, the haft protruding from between her breasts.

Easing his way between the lowered assegais, the Induna reaches for the haft, pulls the blade free and backs away again, the spear now in his left hand.

Out of reach of the warriors, he snaps the shaft over his knee, so he's left with a weapon more like an iklwa. Then he goes after the Dlakathi.

Who looks around anxiously, clearly expecting someone to throw him another spear.

When it's clear none is forthcoming, he takes off in another elephant-like charge. Only this time he's heading, not for the Induna, but toward the nearest wall of shields. When the warriors there realise he's not about to stop, they lower their spears and, very like an elephant, the big man impales himself on a multitude of blades. Shouting and swinging his fists, he breaks through the first rank, and it's only the spears of the second and third rows that eventually bring him to a halt.

# 7
## The Other One

'Brother,' hisses Makhi, shaking the Induna out of his stupor. 'Brother, listen to me!'

The Induna sits up, wiping his eyes. 'Must I fight another one?'

Makhi nods. The Induna makes a move to stand, but the old servant restrains him. 'Listen to me, Brother,' he says, handing the warrior a waterskin.

'What is it?'

'Do you know how Zulus and Mthethwas regard twins as a curse?'

The Induna swallows a mouthful of amanzi and nods.

'Well, in some cultures this is not the case. There are even those who revere twins.'

'Yes, and . . . ?'

'Well . . .'

Makhi moves to one side, so that the Induna can see the gate at the far end of the pen, the one leading to the arena.

'I'm sorry,' he whispers.

'Fuck,' says the Induna.

'Nonetheless . . .' says Makhi, inclining his head toward the gate.

'I don't believe it,' mutters the Induna, climbing to his feet.

Warily he begins to make his way to the gate, where the Dlakathi's twin brother awaits him, vengeance glinting in his eyes.

When the Induna pauses, the twin curls a finger, as if beckoning the Zulu closer.

Well, that's not going to happen.

The Brother rattles the gate. The Induna stays where he is. Let the guards come for him; because, right now, he prefers his chances against them than trying to get through that gate and fight off the giant at the same time. He has a vision of the isid-lakathi grabbing his ears and pulling him through the poles it's constructed of.

However, when feathered troops do appear, they also are inside the arena. Using their long spears as prods, they push the Brother back toward the centre. Clearly the big man was only allowed here as a way of whetting his anger; the fight itself must take place closer to the queen's dais.

Makhi then darts forward to push open the gate. The Induna waits until the Brother is a sufficient distance away – and there're enough spearmen between the two of them – before entering the arena.

Yet more warriors have been brought in, and the space thus reduced even further. But the Induna's aching muscles, the fact that the gash on his upper thigh has started bleeding again, means the second isidlakathi still seems to be standing far away; a long journey to be undertaken, with all these watchful eyes on him eager to see broken bones.

The Induna wipes the sweat from his eyes.

*Concentrate!* See how the Dlakathi has quietly begun to drift your way. He knows that you're tired, and that the thoughts of tired men wander. He would use your inattention to get closer.

And the crowd is on the giant's side. They hold back their hisses of displeasure, lest these force the Zulu out of his lethargy; instead, they watch the two men sizing each other up in silence, connoisseurs who know that the final clash, when it comes, will be worth the wait.

And, of course, they can still enjoy the Dlakathi's cunning.

Just as heavy, with a gut as big as his brother's, he certainly seems to be smarter than his twin. And it's not only those tiny steps forward which he hopes the Induna won't notice – it's more the fact that he refuses to be driven by his thirst for vengeance. He's going to take his time, do this right, and not risk making himself vulnerable with an incensed onslaught.

*Thirst* . . . The Induna has drunk as much as he could before being forced to enter the arena yet again, but now, moments later, his mouth is already dry.

So how is this same dry heat affecting the bigger man?

Hard to tell, for he continues to look much too pleased with himself.

And the longer he hesitates, realises the Induna, the harder it will be to cajole his muscles into action, and the thirstier he'll be.

He suddenly darts forward. When the Dlakathi refuses to be drawn, but remains standing still, the Zulu veers off to the right. And now there're jeers and hisses from the spectators. But the Induna doesn't stop. He continues in an arc that takes him beyond and behind the big fellow.

He waits for the Dlakathi to wheel round to face him, then heads to his right again, in a second arc that takes him behind the giant once more.

Again the jeers, and again the Dlakathi turns to face the Induna. Neither he nor the crowd seem to have realised how much closer the Zulu has approached.

The Induna moves to his right once more, and this time the Dlakathi turns to *his* right.

It's what the Induna's been waiting for. He changes direction and rushes forward, hitting the Dlakathi once, twice, three times in the lower back. Then, ducking under the big man's right arm, he shoots to his left, out of hitting or grabbing range.

He isn't aware that it's the big man's kidneys he's pummelling; he just knows that the lower back is an especially vulnerable area, so he repeats the process several times – getting closer in short arcs until he can reach the Dlakathi's back, deliver three punches in rapid succession, before retreating.

The trouble is, while the Induna's knuckles are becoming swollen, the Brother shows little sign of damage. In fact, he seems quite unaffected. Twice he catches the Induna a glancing blow with one of his massive fists, and it's only because he's lighter, more nimble, that the Zulu's able to scurry out of his way.

With his left eye swollen shut, his head throbbing, the Induna retreats a few paces to reconsider his options.

But there's not really much more he can do. The big man has to be feeling tired, but that won't help you if you get caught between those massive arms, or have that body drop on top of you.

The Induna darts forward yet again, feints to the right, moves left and is able to deliver two punches to the creature's kidneys.

And so it goes on, with the Induna keeping to his hit-and-run tactics, and the spectators booing every punch he throws.

That the Brother might be tiring is seen now in how slowly he turns to face the Induna. But the Induna is also fatigued, and suddenly the Dlakathi swings round as the Zulu comes in to punch him, throws his reserves into a lunge and grab – and the Induna finds himself caught.

His head lowered, his arms around the Zulu's waist, the Brother makes to pick up the Induna. But he's slow, and the Zulu is able to send his left foot backward and pivot it to keep his balance.

Then, twisting his hips to the left, he brings his right elbow down on to the Dlakathi's neck.

The huge hands loosen and the Induna's able to move away.

The Dlakathi's on his knees, but the Zulu's unable to press home whatever advantage he might have. His legs are trembling, his hands are swollen and throbbing, and now his right arm is numb from elbow to fist.

He moves behind the big man, waits for the latter to begin climbing to his feet, then moves in again. But the Dlakathi's used those few moments to marshal a little more energy. And the Induna feels the tree-trunk arms close around his waist, feels himself lifted . . .

Then he's thrown.

But this brief spurt of energy sees the Dlakathi throw him too high and he's able to land on his feet, a few paces in front of the monster.

As the latter lumbers forward, the Induna drops into a crouch and, just as the mountain of sweat and fat, muscle and bone hits him, he sends himself forward, head-butting the Dlakathi in the groin.

There follows the sense of a weight moving, then falling away from him. He's on his hands and knees and when he looks up he sees his opponent lying flat on his back.

The Induna clambers to his feet and staggers away, expecting Makhi to approach him with some water. Instead, spears are levelled and he's made to halt. Obviously he's not going be allowed any rest before what has to be the final bout begins. Turning away from the spears, he watches as a large group of servants drags the big man away.

Then he's prodded forward, and soon the open area has shrunk to a U-shaped space in front of the queen's dais.

And there's the old woman materialising out of the fog of his fatigue, at first flickering like the light from a firebrand, then solidifying as his breath becomes less ragged . . .

Standing in a prizefighter's slouch, with his legs apart, his fists clenched but kept down below his waist, the Induna looks around. Feathers and shields, and spears, those in the front rows lowered, those to the rear prodding the sky. Duthlle is probably waiting for the ranks surrounding the pair of them to fill up, or for him to claw his way closer to consciousness. His eyes, sunken within engorged pouches, find her again. Her smile spreads, becomes a beatific glow. Or so it seems from behind the slits in his swollen face.

His tongue finds the sharp ridge of a broken tooth. Swallowing is something that requires care, thanks both to the thirst and to the pounding his throat has received. He dare not twist to the right, because pain as sharp as an assegai blade lies in that direction; he dare not lean too far forward, because the weight in his skull will cause him to topple over; he dare not unclench his fists because it feels as if it is only in doing so that he prevents his hands from blowing up like huge ticks.

A commotion in the crowd and Duthlle turns, barks some commands. The Induna makes an effort to stand up straighter. He even manages a smile for the old woman as she approaches him.

'I see the wind wasn't lying when it brought tales of the strength of Shaka's lions,' she says. 'And it seems to me it's true what they say – that you can't just kill a Zulu, you have to push him over or else he'll continue fighting.'

She eyes the Induna for a few moments. 'Ho! I am tempted to ask if it has been raining bruises today, for you are drenched in them. What say you? Do you think you'll be able to best this one last foe?'

'It's as good as done!'

Laughing, Duthlle claps her hands and turns, so that she's looking in the same direction as the Induna. At her command, two of the shields part, and the Induna's next – and final – opponent is pushed into the arena.

Duthlle raises her arms and moves away from the Induna. *Sisters*, she shouts in that angular language favoured by these people, which is all clicks and consonants. *The Selection is almost over. And see what fine breeders we are left with. Truly, our gods have favoured us this season, and those whose time it is are truly fortunate!*

She goes on in this vein, and the Induna examines the dais, where the queen sits along with members of her family and inner circle. (That one sitting at the end has to be the jealous sister Makhi told him about.)

The queen is over to the Induna's right. She's seated on a throne with a vast semicircle of copper rising behind it. Strange symbols have been etched along the perimeter, and a fan of white ostrich feathers creates a smaller semicircle within the larger one, and this serves as a headrest. However, she sits forward now, leaning over her rolls of fat. An array of different-coloured feathers – red, purple, blue, black – have been slipped into her hair. A beadwork chest piece tries to cover her pendulous breasts and there are rumours of a skirt somewhere amid the folds bunched around her waist.

The one the Induna presumes is the sister sits on the very opposite side of the dais, about as far away from her sister as she can get while still remaining on the same platform. Her throne is similar to the queen's, only the copper back is much smaller. In fact, it's so low she has nowhere solid to rest her head should she lean back. She is as heavy as her sister and wears only a blue feather and a green one in her hair. While the queen is listening to Duthlle's oration, and occasionally eyeing the Induna, the sister seems more interested in watching her royal sibling, her chin all but vanishing as her lips ease open in a pout. An older woman sits on a low stool immediately next to her.

The Induna's eyes move past the other women lining the platform to find—

Yes, there's a similar stool next to the queen, and that's clearly Duthlle's place. So, each of the women has an old-timer to advise her.

A cheer engulfs the conclusion of Duthlle's peroration and the Induna's eyes locate the sister again in time to see her and her old woman exchange a glance – and an almost imperceptible shake of the head. Possibly Duthlle has praised the queen. Whatever the case, the look that passes between them, the way each shakes her head, tells the Induna that here are two women resolved not to put up with this situation much longer.

He remembers Makhi's words: *The queen's sister has been saying the queen is cursed, unfit to rule* . . .

But Duthlle's stopped speaking. It's time to turn his attention to his opponent . . .

# 8
# And Then There Were Two

The Induna can barely stand upright. His ribs and back ache. His hands are grotesquely swollen. The gash in his upper thigh is still bleeding. Therefore he's relieved to see his opponent is also battling a similar range of . . . infirmities. There are the bruises, swollen ovals, some a shade lighter, others a darker shade than the rest of his skin. There's the sluggish gait of a drunkard trying to walk in more or less a straight line. There's that pattern of cuts and scratches across his chest.

The two men eye each other warily.

Then, after a certain amount of circling, they engage in a lethargic grapple barely worthy of the name.

'Eshé, ndoda,' says the Induna.

'Eshé, ndoda,' replies Mzilikazi.

'Long time no see, old friend.'

'If I remember correctly the last time we met it was I who saved your hide.'

'This is so,' agrees the Induna. 'And now I would like to return the favour.'

'Hai, *this* I'd like to see.'

'And so you shall, old friend, for as soon as I spied you breaking heads, I knew how we might extricate ourselves from this madness.'

But first, continues the Induna, let them fight a little lest their hosts begin to get suspicious.

Good idea, grunts Mzilikazi. He twists to the right, preparatory to grabbing the Induna's wrists and throwing him over his shoulder.

'Easy!' hisses the Induna. His ribs . . .

'Sorry.'

They move apart. The Induna throws a punch. Mzilikazi turns his head just before the fist clips his chin. He staggers backwards, his arms windmilling, and then drops on to the ground.

The Induna follows him down, grimacing, and straddles Mzilikazi. Who brings his hands up a moment too late to prevent the Induna from clutching his throat.

'How come you to be here?' asks the Induna.

'Stupidity.'

'Stupidity?'

'My own.'

'You will now throw me to the side.'

'Are you ready?'

The Induna nods. He falls sideways as Mzilikazi twists his torso.

Moments later, it's Mzilikazi who's trying to strangle the Induna.

He and some men had come to reconnoitre, explains Mzilikazi.

'You mean you were planning to attack these savages?'

'Indeed. And I still do. Now, more than ever, I'd like to see them vanish in the same way Shaka has made his foes vanish.'

'Yet here you are.'

'We were taken by surprise. It was, as I said, sheer stupidity.'

'My turn,' says the Induna.

Mzilikazi nods. Lets the Induna throw him off. Both men clamber to their feet. There's some circling, a few feints, then they're back into the grapple.

'What happened to your men?' asks the Induna.

'We were separated, and they too were set to fight, but clearly success has eluded them.'

'I'm sure they acquitted themselves well.'

The two men move backwards and forwards.

'How is Shaka?'

'He is well,' says the Induna.

'And the White Men?'

'Docile.'

A series of hisses snakes around the spectators. The warriors start banging on their shields.

'Our hosts grow restive,' observes Mzilikazi.

'Indeed, it is time to end this.'

'And how do you propose to do that, old friend?'

'Listen . . .'

# 9
## Departure

But these bulls are tired bulls! See how slowly they move! See how they fight, then pause and lean together, their heads almost touching! Then the one punches and the other falls, and one could milk a cow in the time the fist takes to travel to the chin or chest, then milk another one in the time it takes for the man to fall and the other to follow through, and fling himself on to him. And then . . . and then it's as if he's simply sitting on the other and holding his hands against his throat. Tired, tired bulls. A strange kind of dance, the men leaning together and turning, turning . . .

And then suddenly they're right beside the dais. And the Induna is leaping on to the platform, while Mzilikazi moves to the right – has snatched a spear from one of the astounded guards, broken the haft over his knee to shorten it and thrown the weapon to the Induna, before anyone can react. The Induna's heaved the queen to her feet; standing behind her, he catches the spear, pushes his other arm through her chins to encircle her neck and presses the tip of the blade against her cheek. And there's Mzilikazi bounding past them to grab Duthlle. He too has a spear, which he presses against her waist, as he shuffles closer to the Induna.

'Tell them to let us through if they want their queen to live,' says the Induna.

'Clearly you have been hit hard once too often today, Zulu.'

'Tell them!'

With a shrug, Duthlle switches to her own language. But her words seem to have no effect. All the women seem mired in shock. Even the ranks forming the outer rim of the arena remain where they are.

'She needs some encouragement,' the Induna urges.

Nodding, Mzilikazi increases the pressure on the blade so that the tip penetrates the skin just below Duthlle's ribs.

'Tell them again,' he growls.

Again Duthlle speaks and this time there's a shifting. The women on the platform begin to slowly ease away from the men and their captives, while the warriors move forward.

'Tell them . . .' says the Induna.

'I know, I know,' says Duthlle, a ruby of blood glistening on her side, around the blade's point.

She orders the warriors to halt two paces from the dais. The Induna looks around, noticing there are stairs to the rear of the stage. He turns, with the queen in his grasp, and waits for Mzilikazi to get into position. Then, with Mzilikazi walking backwards behind the Induna, they move down the steps and along the path that skirts the rear of the pens. Women surround them, parting to let them through then closing ranks once they've passed. It's no good ordering Duthlle to tell them to keep further back. The road between the huts and the pens is too narrow; the women can barely move themselves aside to let the men through.

'Where do you think you're taking us, Zulu?'

'Do not worry yourself about that,' says the Induna, wondering if it's his imagination or is the queen really walking more slowly, holding back, in effect, so that he has to bump her forward – an action which almost always seems to involve, unwittingly, pressing his penis against her buttocks.

*There!* She's done it again, ensured he slips between her buttocks. As he stiffens involuntarily, the queen giggles.

'Just make sure none attempt to rescue their queen. And keep reminding yourself that your survival depends on our survival,' the Induna tells Duthlle.

The old woman calls out another series of commands. But if the staring, snarling crowd suddenly seems to fall behind them, it's because they've now reached the edge of the village. And the Induna has to order Duthlle to tell her people not to try and outflank them.

A path branches off the road and continues up a gentle slope, towards a ridge of flat stones sitting there like teeth in a jawbone. After telling Mzilikazi what he's about to do, the Induna pushes the queen on to this path, using his chest this time.

'Wait, old friend,' calls Mzilikazi.

The Induna gets the queen turned around in time to see a disturbance progressing through the crowd. Shouts and curses ricochet between the warriors and other women, eventually to erupt into the space between the men and their pursuers.

It's the queen's sister and her elderly advisor, accompanied by a few warriors and some officers. They wear headdresses adorned with plumes of a different colour to the other soldiers, suggesting that they're members of the royal sister's personal guard.

Mzilikazi feels Duthlle stiffen. 'What is it?' he asks.

'This is not good.'

The sister starts to speak and, for the first time in their brief journey together, the Induna has to struggle to keep the queen still.

'What's she saying?' he asks, meaning the sister.

'This is not good!' repeats Duthlle, as the sister continues to harangue the crowd, pointing in their direction every now and again.

The queen twists and turns, so the Induna has to tighten his grip around her neck. He pushes her forward till he's standing next to Mzilikazi.

'Do not try my patience, crone,' he says.

Duthlle turns to stare at him. 'She is claiming she is now queen.'

'What?'

'Let me go, fool. It doesn't matter any more!'

At a nod from the Induna, Mzilikazi releases the old woman, while the Induna still keeps hold of the queen.

'She says how can they ask for a surer sign of the gods' displeasure? She is saying look how weak the queen is — see how easily she has allowed herself to be captured. This one can be queen no longer. *She* is now queen — and her first command is for them to kill all of us.'

The Induna and Mzilikazi exchange glances.

'Fuck,' says Mzilikazi.

'My sentiments exactly.'

'What do we do now?'

The Induna shrugs. 'Run.'

Both shove their captives forward, turn and race off through the grass, aiming for the ridge. After a few paces they're joined by a third man. 'Well, why not?' Makhi manages to pant. Behind them they can hear Duthlle shouting loudly, doubtless trying to counter the sister's claims.

'Look!' gasps Makhi, stopping so suddenly that the Induna is five, six paces past him before he sees how the old Mthethwa is pointing to where men — Mzilikazi's Matabeles — are pouring over the ridge.

Later they'll learn that, after the capture of their chief, Mzilikazi's indunas had placed spies in the hills watching the comings and goings in the city of the Cat People, and had kept a regiment in constant readiness, should Mzilikazi need them.

They were, of course, also making plans to attack the city itself. In fact, having at last identified the place where their chief was being kept prisoner – so a contingent could be despatched there directly – they were going to fall on the Cat people in two nights' time, after the moon had vanished.

For now, though, the Induna and Mzilikazi and Mkahi are just happy to heave a sigh of relief as the Matabeles form a skirmishing line between them and the armed women, and they're able to continue on their way at a more sedate pace.

# PART FOUR

# *Shaka's Lions*

I, Inguos Shaka, King of the Zulus and of the country of Natal, as well as the whole of the land from Natal to Delagoa Bay, which I have inherited from my father, for myself and heirs, do hereby . . . in the presence of my chiefs and of my own free will, and in consideration of divers goods received – grant, make over and sell unto F. G. Farewell and Company, the entire and full possession in perpetuity to themselves, heirs and executors, of the Port or Harbour of Natal . . . together with the Islands therein and surrounding country, as herein described . . .

> From the land grant signed by Shaka,
> cited by Henry Fynn in his *Diary*

And 'mid this tumult Kubla heard from far
Ancestral voices prophesying war!

> From 'Kubla Khan'
> by Samuel Taylor Coleridge

Just how much of a threat did Cetshwayo KaMpande represent to British interests?

Zululand was supposed to be independent. Yet the British government seemed intent on interfering in the country's affairs, the designation 'king' to them clearly meaning zamindar, merely a noble landowner. First there was Shepstone, who was then Secretary for Native Affairs in Natal, sanctioning Cetshwayo's right to the throne on behalf of the British government as early as 1861, then there was the coronation itself.

Described as tall and handsome, with a muscular build, Cetshwayo was in his mid-forties when his father Mpande KaSenzangakhona died in October 1872. His coronation was held in a large marquee erected by the British. Shepstone started by laying down the law – literally. Britain would support the Zulus so long as there was no indiscriminate bloodshed in Zululand and no one was condemned to death without a trial or by the King's consent. The man the Zulus called Somtsewu then placed a scarlet mantle on Cetshwayo's shoulders and a crown better suited to a pantomime on the King's head.

Cetshwayo, however, had already been crowned by his izikhulo, the great chiefs who made up his council of state. Attended by various white dignitaries, Zulu abanumzane and smart amabutho, this other coronation was a farce held solely for the sake of the British.

In short, Cetshwayo was indulging in a bit of realpolitik. For at that time the British were valuable allies, as they supported the Zulus in the border dispute with the Transvaal to the north. When Shepstone subsequently annexed the Transvaal Republic, Cetshwayo couldn't be blamed for hoping matters would now be resolved in the Zulus' favour, or for feeling betrayed when Shepstone demanded even more land on behalf of the Transvaal.

But by then Shepstone had realised Cetshwayo wasn't going to prove as pliable as Mpande had been. In his later years, the last of Senzangakhona's sons had grown so fat that he had to be pushed about in a cart by two servants; yet Cetshwayo was gradually emerging as the 'immovable one', who possessed all the qualities of the man he most admired – his uncle, the mighty Shaka.

As Shaka had done, he began reorganising the Zulu army, which would eventually come to number forty thousand men, according to Shepstone's estimate.

As Shaka had done, he trained his men well, instilling in them a sense of discipline – and a desire to let their assegais feast.

And as it was in Shaka's time, so it was now. The kingdom was once again surrounded by formidable neighbours. But, unlike Shaka, this new warrior King had to play the political game. Going forth and seizing territory was no longer an option.

But Shepstone (and others) saw in this army a bunch of young hotheads eager for blood. Could Cetshwayo really control them? As a series of border 'violations' in 1878 seemed to demonstrate, he even had trouble controlling his own chiefs.

Although he vehemently denied this criticism, the King would have had something different to say in private. He'd thought his acceptance of Shepstone's 'coronation laws' would bring his more 'independent' chiefs to heel, since these laws asserted the King's status as the nation's sole ruler. This didn't happen, however, and Cetshwayo constantly found himself having to defend the actions of wayward abanumzane who refused to understand his wider strategy.

★

In July 1878, two wives of chief Sihayo of the Qungebe clan, based near Rorke's Drift, fled into Natal with their lovers. Sihayo's eldest son Mehlokazulu, with two of his brothers, an uncle and thirty mounted men all carrying firearms, went after them. They were accompanied by a large *impi* on foot, armed with spears and shields. The wives were seized and dragged back to Zululand, where both were executed. No one else was harmed, but the white settlers in the region, who claimed to live in constant fear of a Zulu attack, were horrified. The timing was bad, too, as relations with the British were tense. But Cetshwayo pointed out that a similar incident had occurred two years previously, with no fuss being made, and that the Natal police often made arrests in Zulu territory without asking for his permission.

Another incident was a little more serious, as it involved White Men. In late September, two surveyors from the Colonial Engineers Department were apprehended by a group of Zulu warriors as they inspected a drift across the Thukela. The regiments were keeping a constant watch on the nation's borders and the two men were suspected of seeking places where wagons and artillery could cross. They were interrogated for a few hours, then released. One of the men thought the incident insignificant and wasn't going to report it; the other, however, had his pipe stolen and went straight to the authorities.

For Frere the theft of that pipe became the equivalent of 'Jenkins' Ear'. (When his brig the Rebecca had been boarded by members of Spain's coastguard, and he was accused of piracy, the master of the ship, named Robert Jenkins, had protested and allegedly had his ear cut off by the Spanish commander, Julio León Fandiño. This small incident was one of those which had led to war with Spain in 1739.) Although Bulwer pointed out that the Zulus had every reason to feel a little annoyed, as by that time British forces were pouring into Natal, Frere insisted to Hicks-Beach back in London that the 'roughing up' of the men and the taking of the pipe was further proof of 'Zulu aggression'.

Then, in early October, Mbilini KaMswati and his men attacked a group of Swazi refugees within the disputed territory. This Cetshwayo could have done without, and he summoned Mbilini to the royal capital at Ulundi – the High Place – for a dressing down.

But, when it came to provoking the British, Cetshwayo himself wasn't guiltless. In September he gave orders for a great hunt extending from the Ncome River down the Thukela to the sea. The hunt was actually a pretext to step up surveillance of British movements along the other side of the Thukela River, and Cetshwayo also used the opportunity to summon three amabutho, which practised various manoeuvres as well as their musketry.

Elements of these regiments then made their appearance close to the border, armed with guns, spears and shields, and with udibis carrying their supplies. Cetshwayo later claimed that, because game was growing scarcer, the annual hunt had to cover a larger area than normal. However, as Laband points out, the British rightly saw this as a show of force.

But such activity was surely understandable, given that Britain's own military build-up in Natal seemed to point to an imminent invasion of Zululand.

At the end of September, Cetshwayo ordered the amabutho to stand down, persuaded by those of his councillors who wanted to maintain – or restore – good relations with Britain. Not wanting to be caught off guard by the British, he ordered the regiments to reassemble in a fortnight's time. Again this was understandable because, on October 19, British troops had begun moving into the disputed territory around the Boer settlement of Luneburg.

At the same time, though, a rift was opening up in Cetshwayo's council of state, between the younger leaders of the regiments who were eager to prove themselves in war and the older councillors who wanted peace. Unfortunately for the latter, those among the British, like Bulwer, who also wanted peace weren't nearly as influential.

★

There is therefore no reason to doubt the sincerity of Cetshwayo's words to Bulwer (cited by David): 'I hear of troops arriving in Natal,

that they are coming to attack the Zulus and to seize me,' said
the King. 'The English are my fathers, I do not wish to quar-
rel with them, but to live as I have always done, at peace with
them.'

# The Adventure Of
# The Man Who Wanted Mushrooms

In *The Glamour and Tragedy of the Zulu War*, W. H. Clements recounts an anecdote that began doing the rounds in Pietermaritzburg, the capital of the Natal colony, shortly after Sir Bartle Frere arrived there in September 1878.

It seems Frere and his son went hunting in a forest near Zanzibar, and got lost. After wandering about for several hours in the heat, they came upon a hut. The woman living there welcomed them with typical African hospitality. She produced some eggs and a skillet, and soon the hungry men were making an omelette. Glancing around the hut, Frere spotted a string of dried mushrooms hanging from the central rafter.

These, he decided, would make a tasty addition to their omelette. Over the woman's vehement protestations, he reached up to pull down the string of dried mushrooms, and added them to the pan.

Later, after Frere and his son had consumed the omelette (and mushrooms) with great relish, the husband arrived. He made to greet the White Men, but his wife interrupted. Gesturing to the rafter, she told him what Frere had done.

The husband flew into a rage, telling Frere and his son that they had eaten all his war trophies – namely, the ears of the enemies he had killed in battle.

The story is probably apocryphal. At the same time, though, it has the aspect of a parable in the way it underlines many of the character traits that saw Frere start a war with the Zulus. As we'll see, the fact that the story takes place in Zanzibar is also ironic.

Frere and Lieutenant General Frederic Thesiger were in Pietermaritzburg to inspect the build-up of forces, and the streets of the capital at this time 'presented a lively and picturesque scene, consequent on the manifold styles and colours of the uniforms worn by the Imperial and Irregular Forces', Clements tells us.

There was the 'soldier of the line in his scarlet tunic'; the 'stalwart artilleryman in his neat blue tunic'; the 'swaggering Natal Mounted Policeman' in his 'sombre-coloured shell jacket, jaunty forage cap, "Officers Jacks" and jingling spurs'; the Frontier Light Horse trooper in 'his rough and ready cord uniform with a red pugaree carelessly twisted round his wide-awake'; the 'dashing Natal carbineer in his neat blue uniform with white or silver facings'.

Frere had been distraught on hearing of Lord Carnarvon's resignation, since his softcock replacement, Hicks-Beach, couldn't be counted upon to do the 'right thing'. But in the fifty-year-old Thesiger he found another ally. Thesiger, who had arrived in South Africa earlier in the year – and who would become the 2nd Baron Chelmsford in October – had already had a jolly time putting down a Xhosa uprising in little more than two months. Now he was ready to take on the Zulus, who he believed would be as easy to defeat.

Frere was relieved because if he was going to get away with his insubordination – or doing what was necessary to protect Britain's interests, as he would have put it – a quick campaign was what he needed.

★

*Is it true, they ask, building up to the one question they want answered, is it true, General, that Shaka cut open the bellies of nine pregnant women so he could see how the baby developed?*

'Nonsense!' says the old general. That was a lie cooked up by the King's enemies, and swallowed by the White Men in the way children slurp up amasi, the White Men being gullible about such things.

Consider how easily they were fooled – and horrified – by Shaka's habit of interrupting a conversation to point to a man who was then put to death on the spot. Hai, Fynn and the others never realised that these were criminals already sentenced to death, who Shaka made stand among the crowds who always gathered in those early days when a visit by the white savages was still a novelty. They were accompanied by two guards who became the men to obey Shaka's sudden command.

So . . . no, this story about the pregnant women is a slander not to be believed. (In fact, only the belly of one heavily pregnant woman had been cut open, at Shaka's behest – and that had been to see if her baby lay the same way in the womb as would a calf; but the general's not about to mention that.)

*Is it true, numzane, they ask, that Shaka mocked the White Men for wearing shoes?*

'Yes,' says the general, 'for the King deemed this a waste of cattle hides.' Why hadn't their ancestors given them tougher feet, so that they could use leather for making more practical articles, such as shields?

*Is it true Shaka was so strong he could lift the biggest bull by its hindquarters?*

The general chuckles. 'That depended on how drunk the onlookers were,' he replies.

★

Paul Kruger was also in Pietermaritzburg, having stopped there specifically to speak to Frere. Although, at the time, he had no official position in the government, Kruger was a popular figure who the Boers said represented Transvaal interests. He was returning from his second visit to London, and met with Frere and Thesiger ostensibly to update them on the progress of the former republic's talks with the British government. But he used the opportunity to again play up the Zulu threat.

In truth, though, he was preaching to the converted. Frere had told Hicks-Beach he had sent Thesiger to Natal 'just in case', to marshal the troops there already and ensure the colony could defend itself against a Zulu invasion (there were all these ominous signs, you see). Instead, as Bulwer suspected, he was 'fully determined' on war with the Zulus. And that was partly why Frere himself was visiting the colony – to set Bulwer right. The governor, complained Thesiger, kept hampering his efforts because they might be misunderstood by Cetshwayo.

There was another problem, too. In an unseemly expression of the English concept of 'fair play', the Boundary Commission appointed by Bulwer had ruled mostly in favour of the Zulus!

But even this, Frere realised after some reflection, could be used to their advantage. Announce the findings of the Commission first, then, while they were still grinning, hit them with the ultimatum. That was the way.

★

*Tell us, they ask, about Shaka's house, numzane!*

It's an oft-told tale from childhood, but it bears repeating (especially by one who was there).

'And so it was,' says the old general, 'that Shaka asked Fynn to build him a White Man's house . . .'

Fynn went to Port Natal and returned with Ogle, who was the best carpenter among them. Ogle duly laid out his tools on a buckskin mat. He had brought with him a saw, a hammer, a gimlet, an adze and some nails. Shaka recognised the hammer, because a version of this tool was used by those who crafted assegai blades. What were the other implements?

Ogle showed him how the saw was used, and how the adze – with its blade set at right angles to the shaft – was employed to smooth or carve rough-cut wood. Then he demonstrated the gimlet, a hand tool twisted like a corkscrew, for drilling holes in wood, thus making hammering in the nails much easier.

Frederick, one of Fynn's servants, was interpreting at the time, and Shaka instructed him to tell his masters the King now understood how these tools were used. Leaving Frederick to translate his words, Shaka turned, winked at the Induna and the others of his inner circle. He then whispered something to the Induna's udibi, who instantly raced off.

'Let it be known,' said Shaka addressing Frederick once more, 'that I am in awe of the ingenuity of these devices, and am even more desirous of becoming the proud owner of a residence such as the ones they've told me their people live in.'

By the time Frederick had finished translating Shaka's words, and Fynn's response, which was just as flowery, the udibi had returned, carrying a piece of wood.

It was a species of ironwood Shaka had acquired especially for the occasion.

Fynn had told him White Men built their houses out of wood, he said. Very well, then, this was the kind of wood he wanted used in the construction of his White Man's house.

Did Ogle examine the piece of ironwood with a leery expression? Did he try and warn Fynn who, immersed in the gravitas of the moment, urged him on without listening? Did he even give Shaka a knowing grin?

Whatever the case, the gimlet broke after only two twists. Shaka held up a hand, silencing the sniggers of his izilomo. Give the man a chance, suggested the gesture. He then indicated the hammer.

Ogle duly started trying to hammer in the nails. He gave up after four of them had been bent before entering even a quarter of the way into the ironwood.

When Shaka and the other Zulus had finished laughing, he observed that these houses Fynn spoke of were clearly best built in the White Men's land, where the wood was softer.

In fact, said Shaka, he would be happy to send six men to build a house for King Jorgi in the Zulu style. For although he had been told that King's houses were much bigger than his, they can't have been as strong or as neatly constructed.

★

On September 30, Frere again wrote to Hicks-Beach, requesting reinforcements and warning that Natal was 'slumbering on a volcano'. Hicks-Beach asked Disraeli to put the matter before the Cabinet again, adding that he was 'by no means satisfied' that a war with Zululand was inevitable. And if war did break out, the six thousand troops already in South Africa could manage things.

Frere's request was again denied, as matters in Eastern Europe and India were growing more and more serious.

But in late November the Cabinet changed its mind and agreed to send Frere two battalions, on the condition that he use 'all proper means to keep out of war'.

And, in a second letter to Frere, Hicks-Beach wrote that Britain was 'most anxious not to have a Zulu War on our hands right now'.

Meanwhile, back in South Africa, the ultimatum had been drawn up. Some five thousand words long, it asked for the surrender of those involved in the border crossings perpetrated by Sihayo's son and Mbilini's men, and a fine of one hundred cattle for the mistreatment of the surveyors.

Then it really got down to business. The Zulu army was to be disbanded and could not be re-formed without the permission of the British who would henceforth oversee the running of the country.

Cetshwayo had thirty days to comply with these and with the other demands.

★

*Let us speak now, says the general, of the battle of IzinDolwane. He's well aware of where the young officers are trying to lead him, but it's a question he's not ready to answer — and he doesn't believe it's an answer they're ready to hear yet.*

Farewell and Fynn would later claim that Shaka coerced them into accompanying the Zulu regiments, but it's more likely they went along to curry favour and show off their firearms, even though, as Fynn notes in his *Diary*, powder was scarce and their weapons 'out of repair'.

Whatever the case, Farewell, Fynn and several 'native servants' trained in the use of muskets met the Zulu regiments at Nobamba. Jakot was with them, too, but unarmed. When he asked for a gun, Farewell refused to give him one, but Shaka snatched a Brown Bess from one of the 'servants' and handed it to the Swimmer.

En route, Farewell was injured. He was left in care of the headman of the umuzi where they had been staying, then the army continued on their march, the amabutho spread out in a single line across the plain, driving before them rhino and buck.

They were now in the high country, and moved in easy stages to cope with the altitude. Fires were more difficult to make and every morning several men were found frozen to death. Whenever entering a forest, they rested for two days while Shaka sent spies out. Contingents were also sent to forage for food.

When the spies returned, they told the King that Sikhunyana and his army were waiting for them in the wooded country of a mountainside in the IzinDolwane hills. There they had formed a protective circle around their women and children and cattle.

Clearly the Ndwandwes were expecting a second Gqokli Hill, thinking this time they would be the ones in a position of strength, suggested Mdlaka. Shaka responded with a grunt. He seemed tired, his generals would later report. Lethargic. Uninterested.

After what seemed like forever, Shaka announced that the regiments were to move into position early the next morning and proceed to surround the hill.

★

Frere and his cohorts erred somewhat in choosing to deliver the ultimatum at the beginning of December. The First Fruits would be approaching its conclusion at the end of the same month, meaning all the Zulu regiments would be at Ulundi, ready to be deployed where necessary.

But, as far as Frere was concerned, that was neither here nor there. Neither did he believe he was actively disobeying his orders. He wasn't starting a war. Far from it – he had given the Zulus an opportunity to toe the line. If they shunned that chance – failed to meet the ultimatum – it wasn't Frere's fault. And Whitehall had to know that any hesitation to carry out their threat would be seen as weakness by the Zulus — and could lead to greater problems further down the line.

★

*What about the White Men and their izibamu, their guns? ask the young officers.*

'They were there,' says the general, 'amid the regiments.' Except for Fynn, who had climbed a nearby hill so he could watch the battle.

Shaka, of course, would be directing his forces from another hill, and had instructed the udibi to join him. 'After all,' he said, 'we are both nursing wounds acquired at the same time, so let us stand together today.'

The boy had felt sure he was ready to take a more active part in proceedings, but the cold they had encountered on the march had caused his wound to begin aching, and so he was secretly relieved by Shaka's order.

Jakot, meanwhile, had persuaded Fynn's servants Michael and Frederick to join the Fasimbas, who had been ordered to move around to the rear of the mountain. They were to watch the Ndwandwes gathered on the slopes, but also to guard against a second force sneaking up to take the Zulu amabutho by surprise. Leaving his companions to lurk in the rear, Jakot joined the Induna and Njikiza in the front rank. He greeted them and, ignoring their surprised glances, immediately turned his attention to the Ndwandwes.

Shaka sent off his runners, and the Zulus advanced to within twenty metres of Sikhunyana's men. Insults began to fly, but the Ndwandwes remained in place. And Shaka wanted them to come to him, instead of having his regiments forced to charge uphill.

The Induna later told the boy what happened next on the opposite side of the hill. A few minutes after they moved into position, and with the Ndwandwes showing no inclination to obey Shaka's wishes, Jakot calmly raised his Brown Bess and fired. The shot went high, and the Ndwandwes hissed in derision. The Induna stared at him. *What was that for?* Jakot ignored him, reloaded his musket and fired again. Again the ball went high. Again a hiss of derision.

Now, while Jakot reloaded his musket, a man moved out from the Ndwandwe ranks. Judging by his plumes and feathers, he was a nobleman of some sort. Dropping his spear and shield, he began to move from side to side, his legs apart, his knees bent, his arms akimbo. Clearly, he was daring Jakot to shoot again.

The Xhosa raised his Brown Bess for a third time. The Induna thought he was shaking, because of the way the barrel wavered from side to side, but in fact Jakot was taking aim. And, while the Ndwandwes bellowed with laughter, he fired and planted a ball in the centre of the dancing man's forehead.

Enraged now, the Ndwandwes charged, forcing their comrades on the other slopes to do the same. A clash of shields. The first Zulu rank took the impact, while the men behind them, armed with longer spears, crouched so as to thrust them between the legs of the warriors. Cries of *Ngadla!* of pain. Three minutes or so later, the armies separated, like a giant crocodile opening its jaws.

Both sides had taken heavy casualties and now Shaka ordered his army forward. The Ndwandwes were caught before they could re-form. More shrieks. More blood. And this time the Ndwandwes got the worst of it, and retreated again, while the Zulus stood their ground.

When the King had his men charge a third time, the Ndwandwe ranks were shattered. While some of his regiments chased the fleeing soldiers, others set about slaughtering the women and children.

★

More pragmatically, Frere knew the poor line of communication that existed with Britain would work in his favour.

Lord Chelmsford had promised him a quick victory. The war would be over, he claimed, before Whitehall knew what was happening – and who then would dare censure an official who had removed (what he believed to be) a very real threat from the borders of one of the Empire's colonies?

This is why the fact that the anecdote related by Clements is set in Zanzibar is so ironic, because Frere had pulled a similar stunt there. When the local sultan refused to halt the slave trade, Frere informed him the Royal Navy would send a squadron to intercept the slavers. He had no authority to make such a threat, but it had the desired effect. The slave trade in Zanzibar was ended – and Frere escaped criticism.

So, a quick campaign and he'd be fêted as having brought South Africa closer to confederation and created the stability needed to deal with Russian raiders, should these appear.

Needless to say, Isandlwana fucked that up, and a war Frere believed would last one month extended into six.

At the same time, though, Isandlwana was very much a pyrrhic victory for the Zulus, as it saw an unwanted war that could have been cut short with a negotiated peace become a crusade to restore Britain's national pride, and one which led to the eventual ruin of the kingdom the mighty Shaka had established.

'I had been in the Induna's service for about two seasons when the events I am about to relate took place,' recounts the general. 'So I was but a small boy, nonetheless I was still able to appreciate the great skill my master showed.

'It was on the fringes of the mighty Nkandla forest near the Black Mfolozi that there lived a Blade Man . . .'

His listeners know how important metal workers were in Shaka's time, for they were the ones who produced the thirty-centimetre-long tapering *ukudla* for the *iklwa*, as well as blades for the various other spears the Zulus used. And, although the crude smelting process they employed meant the metal they produced was actually a flawed form of steel, the blades they crafted were strong and remained sharp for a long period.

'His name was Mbaxa,' continues the general, 'and his homestead was built on a slope in a clearing among the trees.'

Six huts were each set on a step dug into the incline so that the floor would be level. Mbaxa and his wife Nkezi lived in the first hut on the left as one approached the kraal from the fringes of the forest; it was the biggest hut, as befitted Mbaxa's status as the head of the family. In the next hut along there lived Mbaxa's cousin, Hlanya. As the *inyanga yoku pisela*, who fitted the blade on to the *uti*, or haft, he too, being regarded as a craftsman, enjoyed a certain amount of status, and took his meals with Mbaxa and Hlanya in their hut. In the third hut along lived an old uncle who looked after the cattle and tended to the vegetable garden.

In the first *indlu* on the opposite side there lived Mbaxa's father. He was old but still spry, and he had passed on the secret of the ore to his eldest son, as was the custom in those days, and would still occasionally visit the forge to proffer advice. Next door lived Mbaxa's three younger brothers. They helped him at the forge, as apprentices who would one day strike out on their own. Finally, there was Mbaxa's sister, who cooked for all the menfolk, except Mbaxa and Hlanya, although she cleaned his hut along with the others, as Nkezi had refused to do so, saying she had enough to do looking after her husband's needs.

Beyond the uncle's indlu on the right-hand side row was a large storage hut almost the size of Mbaxa's. It was here that finished spears were kept as well as the wood for the hafts. Opposite was a small cattle byre, and beyond that lay a vegetable garden.

The path that ran between the two rows of huts, where it momentarily lost its purpose and became the open area in front of the dwellings, re-formed itself and swung left, passing the storage hut, byre and vegetable garden, and continued along a low cliff of grey rock that was darkened by moss. Several metres from the homestead, as the yellowwood, red beech and tamboti trees and their retinues of undergrowth began to close in, you first came upon Hlanya's ishabu, or workplace. This resembled a hut with half its roof missing, and the arc of wall that should have been supporting that half was about waist-high. Hlanya could work here in the sunlight, then store his tools and finished spears under cover, behind a curtain of cowhides stitched together.

Several metres further along, hidden from sight by a bend in the path, was Mbaxa's forge. From here on the path lost itself in the depths of the forest.

'Now Nkezi was from Bulawayo,' says the general, 'and Mbaxa had met her after delivering a consignment of assegais to the capital. He was instantly smitten and began lobolo negotiations right away. Nkezi's father was amenable, as Blade Men were considered even more important than the princes of the house of Zulu. As for Nkezi's feelings . . . who knew?'

*What is certain is she soon became bored living at the homestead. To safeguard the secrets of their craft, all metalworkers built their kraals far from other settlements; here the nearest village was a two-day walk away. Nkezi was no longer surrounded by friends, no longer had anything exciting to do or to look forward to, and she felt robbed, cheated even. What was the point of marrying a man of Mbaxa's rank if you couldn't show him off to your friends and — more importantly — your enemies?*

*'But less than a day's walk away was another homestead, and this belonged to Yisa, who was a Wood Man. About twice a month he and a group of ten or twelve boys — various sons and nephews — would follow the path that led through the kraal and past Hlanya's working place and Mbaxa's forge. They collected the wood to be used for the hafts.' While his boys went on ahead, Yisa would discuss how much wood was needed with Mbaxa and Hlanya, as Mbaxa also required a supply of a special hot-burning kind to fuel his forge. Yisa and his wives would also visit the homestead from time to time, and Hlanya, Mbaxa and Nkezi would visit his kraal.*

*No one could say when Yisa began to notice Nkezi. No one noticed the looks and smiles he used in order to make his interest known to the bored young bride. As for Nkezi herself, it's possible the first positive sign she gave Yisa that she too was interested was when she started bringing bowls of milk to the men whenever the Wood Man visited. If Mbaxa thought anything about this change in behaviour, this sudden attempt at hospitality, it was pride — and perhaps relief that his young wife seemed to be settling down at last.*

*No one noticed that the moment Yisa's boys returned with their loads of wood and began stacking them in the storage hut, Nkezi set out to find some herbs with which to enliven her husband's meal. And no one noticed how Yisa hurried on after speaking to Mbaxa and Hlanya, leaving his boys to find their own way home.*

# The Adventure Of The Adulterous Wife

'Shadow of Shaka, this is truly a great tragedy, but I cannot see how I can add to your knowledge of what happened.'

'Neither can Mbaxa.'

'It is said he has no memory of the event.'

'See? You know more than you think you know. What else have you heard?'

'Not much, Nduna. I am as stunned as everyone else.'

'Where were you when you heard the cries?'

'I was working.'

'Your place of work is down that path, is it not? And Mbaxa's forge is some paces further along . . .'

'Yes, Nduna.'

'His brothers help him. But you work alone?'

'That is so, Nduna. You, who have marched with the King's regiments, will know how a man's life may depend on my work. So, in fitting the blades myself, I can be sure I've done the best possible job.'

'Have you seen Nkezi since the murder?'

'No, Nduna.'

'Did she have other lovers?'

'I did not even know she had Yisa for a lover.'

'The dead man.'

'Yes, *him*.'

'Do you think Mbaxa capable of murder?'

'Ha! Do not think you will hear me betraying my cousin! Besides, that is why you are here, as the Shadow of Shaka. That is for you to discover! A man with Mbaxa's talents, his expertise, is not one the King wants to see sent to the impalers without good reason.'

★

This is true. The Zulu smith is a very important man and the secret of taming the iron is kept in a single family and passed on to generation after generation. What might be called his workshop is usually situated some distance from the homestead, in a place sheltered from the wind by reeds or trees.

The furnace consists of a hole scooped out of sandstone, as this rock can handle high temperatures. The ore is placed in here along with a large quantity of charcoal. The fire is kept whitehot by blowing air through an eland's horns into a pair of leather bellows whose outlet is a clay tube thrust into the fire. Often two sets of bellows are used.

Lumps of heated iron are then removed by an apprentice and placed on a flat stone, where they're beaten into shape by using large rocks. Pieces of iron are used as hammers for the finer work of finishing off the blade.

There are two ways of fixing an assegai blade to its wooden haft, meanwhile. A piece of skin may be used to bind the blade to the haft. Or the blade may be glued on to the haft with an adhesive made from the root of the ingcino plant and strengthened on the outside by means of fibre from the inntana plant.

★

'Hai, do not for a moment think the King will stay his hand if it transpires that things are as they seem and that Mbaxa killed Yisa.'

'I understand that, Nduna. But could I ask why you think things might not be as they seem?'

'You are not the only one who can say he knows little, Hlanya. After all, there were no witnesses to the attack – Nkezi was still

311

in her hut, presumably waiting for Yisa — and your cousin has said he was so angry he can't remember what happened after he grabbed hold of Yisa. Besides, I always believe that nothing is as it seems until I have seen for myself.'

'A good strategy, Nduna, if I may say so.'

'All the same, it's a story that makes sense. A man learns his wife is betraying him, loses his temper and attacks and kills her lover.'

'Is it not a story that also calls for a modicum of mercy? Who can claim they wouldn't behave in the same way, if they found themselves in a similar predicament?'

'Is . . . was she a dutiful wife?'

'Nkezi? Yes.'

'How was she with you?'

'We never quarrelled, if that's what you're getting at. As to what she thinks of me, you'll have to ask her.'

'But her charms, her beauty — these weren't lost on you?'

'She was my cousin's wife, Nduna!'

'You would take your meals with Mbaxa, and so you would have been served by her. On these and other occasions, did you notice if anything appeared amiss between your cousin and his wife?'

'No, Nduna.'

'Hai! Beware of trying to protect him!'

'I understand the consequences of that, Shadow of Shaka, but I'm not lying.'

'Then, truly, this is a unique man and wife! To have no disagreements, no sulking — aiee! A makoti must obey her husband, but she has her ways of getting him to change his mind. Yet you say this marriage was as a swathe of sand upon which there were no footprints!'

'Things like that . . . ? Yes, there were things like that, Nduna. I did not mention them only because I believe they have no bearing on this tragedy . . .'

'A frown and a hesitation. You have remembered something. Speak!'

'These past few days . . .'

'Yes? Out with it, Hlanya.'

'Mbaxa may have been ignoring Nkezi.'

'May have? What do you mean?'

'Seemed to be, then. He *seemed* to be ignoring her.'

'Another important piece of information you didn't realise you possessed!'

'Please, Shadow of Shaka, I can't say for certain he was being cold to her. I will not lie to protect Mbaxa, but neither do I want to see him condemned because I've misinterpreted something.'

'It was one of your assegais that killed the lover.'

'Come now, Nduna, I merely fit the blades Mbaxa forges. I do not use them!'

'Mbaxa must pass your place of work to reach his forge, am I right?'

'Yes.'

'So that is a time when the two of you can talk in private. Did he never mention any suspicions he might have had about Nkezi?'

'No, Nduna.'

'Did he tell you he knew she had a lover?'

'No, Nduna.'

'But these are things he would have told you?'

'But he didn't, Nduna!'

'That's not what I asked. My question is: would he have confided in you? I mean, out of all the people he knew, would he have chosen you to share his secrets with?'

'I . . . I suppose so.'

'And every morning he would pass your place of work on the way to his forge.'

'Yes.'

'And since you are close, are more than merely family, he would stop and talk.'

'Yes.'

'Every morning?'

'Yes.'

'The two of you talking . . . sharing snuff, as is our way?'

'Yes.'

'And he never told you that he suspected his wife had taken a lover?'

'You have asked me that already, Nduna, and the answer is still no.'

'So you did not know your cousin – and friend – was a cuckold?'

'*No!* And there you have it, Shadow of Shaka. As I said before, I do not know how I can help you, because I know precious little. And, yes, I feel a fool to have had these things going on around me without noticing anything.'

'Well, consider how long it took Mbaxa to realise what was going on.'

'That's true.'

'And like you, he must have felt a fool. Only, with him, it would have been far worse. Yet you tell me . . . you tell me, Hlanya, that this man who is both your cousin and your friend, never came to you to share his shock and anger.'

'Perhaps he felt shamed by his wife's behaviour. Or perhaps he meant to speak to me but events overtook him.'

'Yes . . . You were working that day?'

'Of course, Nduna.'

'And Yisa came by with a batch of wood for you?'

'Yes.'

'He came from the opposite direction, meaning he had first passed Mbaxa's forge.'

'I suppose so.'

'Cha! That is how the path runs! And that is Yisa's usual route!'

'Yes.'

'You know this.'

'Yes, Nduna.'

'What happened then?'

'I . . .'

'You don't know? Well then, let us suppose.'

'I'm not sure I understand what you want of me, Nduna.'

'You know Mbaxa well, so perhaps you can confirm my suppositions.'

'I . . . very well, then.'

'Very well, then, let us say something happened. He'd either begun to suspect Yisa was fucking his wife, or he knew it for certain. And this something had happened recently, or else he would have confronted Yisa on his previous visit. Does that make sense to you?'

'Yes, Nduna. Although I knew nothing of these things.'

'Yes, that is strange . . . It is strange that, on finding out about Yisa and his wife, he didn't come straight to you! For you could be counted upon to sympathise and share his anger. I can understand him not yet confronting his wife, but to not turn to his best friend . . . that is, as I say, exceedingly strange. Nonetheless that is what happened.'

'Yes, Nduna. And, now that you point it out, I also find it strange.'

'Be that as it may, let us return to that day. Mbaxa knows something is going on between Yisa and his wife. Then here comes Yisa and his boys, heading past the forge. Because they're all carrying wood there's no time for them to stop and chat. Yisa merely greets Mbaxa in passing. Now let us make sure we under-stand the effect this has on your cousin. There he is, angry and brooding – and the boys who assist him say he was especially ill-tempered that day – and then there comes along the very cause of his anger. A man who, oblivious to the fact that Mbaxa knows he's tupping his wife, must seem very smug to your cousin. Superior, even! Maybe he's even secretly laughing at him. And how the pair must mock him when they're together – Nkezi and this Yisa. See how blind Mbaxa is! See how stupid he is! What say you, Hlanya?'

'It's plausible, Nduna. Certainly my cousin is someone given to brooding about things . . . especially if he believes he's been wronged.'

'Ah! *Another* valuable bit of information you didn't know you knew. But back to your cousin . . . He continues tending his fire for a while, but all the time he's seething. Growing more and more enraged. Finally, he thinks, *No! This is too much!* He'll have it out with them. Maybe he'll even catch them together. But he won't be made a fool of any longer! And when next his brothers look up, he's stormed off. And when he reaches the homestead, Yisa's already told his boys to go and amuse them-selves and is clearly about to enter Nkezi's hut. Coming up behind him, Mbaxa grabs him and drags him off to the side, between the huts. There's a brief struggle and Yisa is left dead in the dirt. Stabbed.'

'That's what they say happened, Nduna.'

'Yes, *they*. We have to rely on what *they* found, because there were no witnesses, and Mbaxa says he can't remember what happened after he grabbed Yisa. But his sister and father and uncle found him standing over Yisa's body – and drew the obvious conclusions.'

'He is my cousin, yes, and I would like to see him exonerated, but even I can't see what other interpretation there could be.'

'Where were you at the time?'

'I have already told you, Nduna, I was at my place of work.'

'Then you would have seen Mbaxa come past. You would have seen how angry he was. Did you not try to stop him? Ask him what was wrong?'

'I . . . I called after him.'

'Is that all?'

'I was busy, Nduna. And don't think I don't regret not trying to stop him! Aiee, I wish I had. I will forever rue letting him go.'

'Then where were you?'

'Nduna?'

'You heard me. Where were you?'

'I told you, I was working.'

'And yet . . . Well, you see, Mbaxa's brothers, having had to face your cousin's wrath all morning, continued with their labours after he left, and two of them delivered a batch of blades to your workplace, and they say you weren't there.'

'. . .'

'I can't see what other explanation there could be than the obvious one. You *did* go after him, didn't you?'

'. . .'

'Silence will avail you little now, Hlanya. Indeed, it might even lead me to think you are unafraid of trying my patience.'

'All right, yes! He came by and I stopped him, asked what was wrong.'

'And that was when he told you why he was so angry?'

'Yes.'

'That was when he told you Nkezi was parting her legs for Yisa?'

'Yes!'

'And then you went with him to find Yisa?'

'Yes!'

'Why didn't you try to restrain him? You must have seen where this would end.'

'He was angry, Nduna, and he had the strength of ten bulls. I tried, but he threw me off.'

'And then he threw himself on Yisa?'

'Yes.'

'And they struggled?'

'Yes!'

'This was a another chance for you to intervene, while they were still fighting like herd boys.'

'That's easy to say now, Shadow of Shaka. I panicked. Things got . . . They got out of control so fast.'

'This is what Mbaxa says. Things got out of control, *he* got out of control and the next thing he knew was that others were there, and he was standing over Yisa's body.'

'Well, yes . . .'

'And you were there, too, Hlanya.'

'Yes, Nduna.'

'Why?'

'What do you mean, Nduna?'

'Why did you decide not to tell me that you had followed your cousin, and you were there when he attacked Yisa?'

'I . . . I don't know. Perhaps I was trying to protect Mbaxa, but not by lying. By just . . .'

'Not telling me everything.'

'I . . .'

'I wonder what else you aren't telling me. Let us see. You saw Mbaxa go past. That you didn't tell me. You went after him. That you didn't tell me, either. You saw him confront Yisa, who was clearly on his way to Nkezi's hut. And you saw him attack Yisa. These are also things you didn't tell me straight away. And here's something else you haven't mentioned: it was you who stabbed and killed Yisa.'

'Nduna, I—'

'Come now! Yisa was stabbed with an iklwa! In his rage Mbaxa would have picked up one of his own blades. You were the one who possessed the finished spears. *You!* And why would you intervene in such a manner and kill Yisa?'

'. . .'

'It was her.'

'Yes, Nduna.'

'You are enamoured of her.'

'Yes.'

'And you were genuinely surprised she had taken a lover. As surprised and angry as was Mbaxa.'

'The bitch!'

'Because why couldn't it be you?'

'Well, why not, Nduna? I was there, available, and she had to know . . . to know what she meant to me . . . how I felt about her.'

'When did you find out?'

'That day. Mbaxa had been acting strangely for a while and I kept on asking him what was wrong.'

'Because you began to suspect it had something to do with your beloved.'

'Yes, Nduna. It was evident in the way he'd begun to treat her. But I never thought it was because she was with that lizard Yisa!'

'No, doubtless you were wondering how you yourself could use this rift to further things with Nkezi. Aiee! The thought of being the one who comforted her! How your loins must have squirmed in anticipation! But there was one reason, one cause, where your comfort would not have been needed.'

'Yes.'

'And you only found out about it that same day, when Mbaxa stopped by your place of work and told you what was the matter, told you – see that Yisa, who's just come by? Well, here's what he's doing! And he didn't even need to ask you to go with him. You were only too eager to accompany him, and you took an iklwa along with you.'

'Yes.'

'And suddenly you saw your chance. You could get rid of both the husband and the lover, then Nkezi would be yours. For, despite her betrayal . . . and you felt even more betrayed than did your cousin . . .'

'Because if she was unhappy, why didn't she turn to me? Why not me?'

'But your feelings for her were so strong that you were willing to forgive her that transgression.'

'My feelings, Nduna? My feelings! Where do you think these feelings come from, Shadow of Shaka? Yes, I stand guilty of murder, Nduna! And yes, I was willing to let an innocent man pay for my crime, a man who moreover is my cousin and friend. But I did not act alone, Nduna! Oh no, I did not act alone! She must go to the King's impalers too! For she has bewitched me, bewitched all of us – Yisa, Mbaxa and me! She must be made to pay! She must also be punished!'

Unable to sleep, the old general joins Zamo by the fire. The young officer is in charge of the sentries tonight. It's summer but the nights still carry
a chill up here, and both men stand warming their hands. The general
has his back to the slope and Zamo notes how he's looking across the stream
to where the huts once stood.

'There was a kraal here once?' he asks, seeking to sidestep his embar-
rassment as the general's gaze shifts and he realises the young officer is
watching him.

The general nods.

'Did you know the people who lived here?' asks Zamo.

'Yes.'

The crackling of the branches being consumed by the flames, echoed by
the rustle of the stream. Cicadas and frogs. The squeaking wagon-wheel
croaking of the river frogs; the complacent burp of guttural toads. The
stridulation of wings being rubbed together. Then the hoot of an owl.
Fortunately, it's far away, for it's an animal favoured by abathakathi and
therefore when you hear one very close to your hut it's a foreboding of
death.

The general chuckles, breaking the momentary awkwardness occasioned
by his earlier uncharacteristic curtness.

'Would you share your thoughts, Zamo?' he asks.

'I was thinking of the last story you told us tonight: the one of the man
who knew too little, but said too much.'

The young officer sighs. 'I don't mean to sound defeatist, General,' he
continues, his eyes fixed on the old man's face, seeking to monitor his reaction to his words, for that is exactly how a defeatist would preface pessimistic
comments, 'but I was thinking how like poor Yisa we are. If Hlanya

*hadn't killed him, Mbaxa surely would have done. So it is with us: if it's not Somsetwu and his masters, it's the Boers.'*

*'Meaning if one doesn't attack us, the other will.'*

*'Yes,' says Zamo. 'And better the Boers, for they are few in number and spread far apart. But that is not to be.'*

*'No,' sighs the general, his eyes now on the flames, 'and we have much to settle with those savages.' Looking up to address Zamo: 'And you are merely expressing a truth, you aren't being defeatist. But neither is your name Zamo, is it?'*

*He laughs as the younger man gapes, thereby instantly giving himself away.*

*'No,' he continues, 'I knew your grandfather, Namasu, the Resourceful, and I see him in you. You are Olwayo KaImpama, whose bravery is already being praised by his numzane, Mbilini KaMswati.'*

*'And who now must hide,' adds Olwayo bitterly. He is one of those who Frere's ultimatum insists be handed over along with his chief Mbilini.*

*'Now let us return to Yisa, for this may reveal yet another truth to us.'*

*Assuming 'this' refers to his true identity and the fact it must remain hidden, an intrigued Zamo asks what truth this might be.*

*'It is this,' says the general. 'Yisa was no innocent, for he was tupping Mbaxa's wife.'*

*A smile spreads across Zamo's face as understanding dawns. 'Are you asking if we have somehow brought this trouble upon ourselves?'*

*'Let us rather say I'm wondering how far the parallels you discerned in this tale extend.'*

*Very well, then, says Zamo, let them consider the incident involving him that is mentioned in the ultimatum. First of all, the poor unarmed Swazi 'refugees' they attacked on the Ntombe River, near the Boer umuzi of Luneberg, were in fact camped in the long-disputed territory claimed by the Zulus. Secondly, no white LongNoses were harmed. And, finally, the* poor Swazi refugees, whose fate so disturbed the British, were a roving band of cattle thieves who, when they believed they could make it to the coast without attracting attention, occasionally abducted Zulu women and children they'd sell to the slavers who continue to operate in Mozambique.

Why shouldn't Mbilini move against them? And why should the British have made no attempt to investigate the incident more fully?

'All they did was look at the bodies and then condemn us.'

The general nods.

'Yisa was committing a crime. But what crime did we commit? Hai! And if there is any doubt, as in the matter of who killed Yisa, why can't they seek out the truth, as your Nduna did!'

The general nods again. He is one of the elders who believe Cetshwayo should have kept his chiefs in check, protecting them from themselves, in effect. When there are leopards or lions in the area, the precious cattle are kept closer to home. With things as they have been ever since the British annexed the Transvaal, Cetshwayo should have followed the same principle, for they are dealing with an especially dangerous lion here.

But the general won't pursue the matter with Zamo; it is anyway too late – for this lion is already on the move.

As are Cetshwayo's lions, who are of course Shaka's lions, reflects the general, as Zamo says he must check on the sentries and moves off into the darkness.

# The Adventure Of The Missing Traders

I'm of a mind to begin this story at the end (*says the old general*). For it will be easier told that way. Oh yes, indeed. So! To begin at the end . . .

It was a hot day, the sun as loud as a mother-in-law. The heat seethed and sizzled, turning us into wet mud. And the path was steep.

The cattle added to our suffering. The track wasn't very wide and we had to keep the three bulls and four cows in a specific formation. You'll see why, soon enough.

The three bulls proceeded abreast in front, and the road was just wide enough to allow this. Then, walking behind the bull in the middle, was the Induna. On either side of him were two of the cows; behind them came the other two. I brought up the rear, and had to make sure the cows didn't try and crowd together in the middle of the track. I was carrying water sacks and the usual baggage, which made the incline seem even steeper. The Induna carried a long hunting spear, which was the only weapon we had.

My thighs were burning and sweat stung my eyes. But the Induna must have been struggling with the slope as well, while battling to keep the bulls more or less in line and moving forward. For he seemed as surprised as I was when a tall, scarred man suddenly stepped out of the shade.

The bulls were now close to the top of the slope, and the Induna had to click his tongue and tug on their tails to bring them to a standstill, as the man took up position in the centre of the path, with his hands on his hips. He was wearing an umutsha, but also the kind of covering White Men favoured on his upper body – a tattered old shirt, in other words.

'Aiee,' said the man, 'such fine-looking cattle!'

The Induna wiped the sweat off his brow and nodded.

'Do they belong to you, these fine beasts?' asked the stranger.

When the Induna said yes, he shook his head. 'No they don't,' he replied.

At this point a second man rose out of the bushes to our left. With the butt of the musket pressed against his right shoulder, he was aiming the weapon straight at the Induna.

Instinct made me glance back down the path.

'Don't think of running, Boy,' warned the scarred man, and I watched as a third bandit stepped out of the bushes close to the foot of the incline, a musket resting in the crook of his arm.

'Come now.' The scarred man took a step back and gestured to his left, where there was a gap in the trees and bushes. 'Deliver the cattle to our kraal.'

Clicking his tongue again, and prodding the beasts with the haft of his spear, the Induna guided the bulls the rest of the way up the slope, then got them to turn left into a tunnel composed of branches and creepers.

I made sure the cows followed and then, as the last cow on that side drew parallel with the man holding the musket, I slipped under it, the udder brushing across my back . . .

. . . I still remember that (*says the old general with a faraway grin*) – the way the udder and teats brushed my back . . .

I slipped under the cow, and charged the musket man. My shoulder hit his waist, winding him, knocking him backward into the bushes. The gun went off, blocking my ears and giving me a lungful of smoke. Coughing violently, I snatched the weapon away from him and smashed the butt into his face.

Meanwhile, as the cattle passed on through the tunnel, the Induna had dropped his spear and leapt for a branch extending over the path, then used it to swing himself over one of the cows to land right in front of the scarred one. The man wheeled round, ready to flee, but Phepho and Namasu were already there. They were panting, and drenched in sweat from their sprint up the path on the other side of the hill, but there was no way the bandit was going to get past their spears and shields.

There were three other men in the clearing, but the cattle had spread out, hampering their movement. And Sola and another warrior, coming through the narrow trail that entered the opposite side of the clearing, were able to deal with them easily.

The Induna called to me, asking if I was well.

Rising, I said yes. The bandit at my feet wasn't, though.

I looked down the slope again, where Njikiza stood over the dead man. His club resting against his shoulder, there was no way the big man was going to climb up and join us. He had already been up and down this accursed mountain enough times, he had declared.

★

'So all the bandits were made to eat dust,' says one of the officers.

The general nods. 'Except for the leader, the scarred man. He was taken to Shaka and sent to the impalers, but not before he was made to tell us where all the dead men were buried, so that their spirits could be returned home.'

This is done by the head of the family taking the branch of a buffalo-thorn to the burial site. The ancestors are called upon, and the spirit of the one who has died far from home enters the branch. This is then carried home and placed in the sacred area at the back of the hut, where the spirit can rest in peace.

'General, you say you were about to join your regiment,' chips in another of the officers.

'Yes?'

'Only, in the previous tale you seemed . . . younger.'

'Yes. Do you find this confusing?'

The officer shakes his head. 'No, General, just . . .'

'Confusing?'

The others laugh and the general holds up a hand for silence. 'One story leads to another, regardless of which comes first. This is the way of these things, so does it matter?' He waves his hand dismissively. Besides, this then that, followed by this other thing, then that other event – chronology, in other words – is for dullards.

'For do we always move forward in a straight line? How many times have we made plans to go here, only to find ourselves over there? If the echoes of the past affect our deeds and decisions today, who's to say that whatever is to come doesn't do the same? If you have an unpleasant task to perform tomorrow, doesn't that affect your mood today? Make you do things you might not otherwise have done?'

★

How are we to know, continues the general, how are we to know that a man doesn't begin his life being formed and shaped by the earth? Then he is pulled from the ground by his sons and carried to a hut, where he opens his eyes to find himself floating on a lake of pain, of unbearable agony. But an inyanga ministers to him, and gradually he finds the pain draining out of him, until one day he's able to leave his sleeping mat, supported by a relative on either side. He's left out in the sun, but this is good, too, for he feels himself growing ever stronger. Soon he can get around with an iwisa, a walking stick. At this time, perhaps, he and his sons, who are a little younger now, retrieve his first wife from the comfort of the earth, and carry her to a hut, and let the inyanga feed her the muthis that absorb the pain.

Meanwhile, he finds he no longer needs a walking stick. His gait is still slow, but he feels flaccid muscles growing firmer, joints becoming more supple, the grey disappearing from his hair. There are times when he gets sick, weakens until he must lie down to let the fever decrease. The seasons pass, and pass again. One day, his body torn and bleeding, he goes into battle with his comrades, causing corpses to rise up. And then he emerges whole and refreshed, missing a few scars. And the seasons pass, and pass again, until one day he's told to lay down his shield and spear, these weapons of war, and is set to tending the cattle who feed us and clothe us. Long lazy days in the veld with his friends, and all that went before forgotten. Such bliss!

Then, younger, smaller, he is dragged crying to the village and told not to wander too far from his mother's side. He soon sees this is even better than herding the cattle. He has few responsibilities and his friends from the veld have joined him and there are still adventures to be had, and all that went before is forgotten. But he is growing ever smaller and weaker. Soon he can't walk anymore and he spends a lot of time screaming, because he's afraid. However, suckling his mother's nipple and being carried on her back calm him. Then comes the terrible day when, howling, he is forced into his mother, forced right inside her. But soon he experiences a comfort the like of which he's never

329

experienced before. And contentment fills him as he becomes smaller and smaller, nourishing his mother, becoming a part of her, until the last of him, that vital spark, is taken up into his father's loins.

'Who's to say this is not the way things really are?' asks the general.

★

Placidly he surveys the confused, bewildered faces before him.

Only Zamo meets his gaze, a half smile playing across his lips, which doesn't surprise the general. He's a wise one, and the old man hopes he'll survive the madness to come because, after the bodies have been planted, the nation will need those like him.

Then the general returns his attention to the dazed looks of perplexity on the other faces. 'Who's to say ... Cha! The past sires the future and the present is merely the pain of birth,' he mutters. Then he shrugs, scowls and waves a dismissive hand, as if to say *I'm old. Deal with it.*

A white cattle egret swoops low, going to catch flies amid the beasts in the temporary kraal. The general's eyes drop to a group of mother-in-law's tongues, with their long pointed leaves – like a tirade ending in a sharp rebuke. And over there is a millipede, with its armoured segments ... Has he told them yet of Shaka's shongololo? Those days remain aglow in his memory, even though he sometimes struggles to remember what happened yesterday. The curse of the aged? Hai, he believes it to be more of a gift – because the older you get, the less pleasant yesterday seems. At the very least it's a harbinger of today's aches and pains, not to mention the slights some old-timers experience at the hands of resentful relatives. And today ... well, let us say, it promises nothing good for the morrow. No, better to live in the distant past.

330

'Cha,' he says. 'Let us return to our tale . . .'
' . . . and end at the beginning,' says Zamo mischievously.
'Indeed,' chuckles the general.

★

Pointing at Hawk, he beckons him forward and picks up a stick. Following the general's instructions, the warrior draws a series of lines: some of them curving, some of them straight, and then two Xs on opposite sides of one of the straighter lines. Hawk then hands the stick to the general and returns to his place, while the men in the rear rows stand up so they can see the map properly.

★

To end at the beginning (*says the old general with a grin*), it all began with a trader and his four sons. Carrying about eight tusks, they spent the night at this umuzi (*he points at the X closest to him*). The father had a sack of beads and he was looking to acquire more ivory.

Now (*continues the general, pointing at the furthest X*) to reach this umuzi by nightfall they had to leave very early in the morning. As you can see, the first umuzi is next to a river, and the road they were due to take ran along the river then curved inland to climb a high promontory. (*The general straightens up.*) On the other side, as you can see, the road moves away from the river and runs through the veld until it reaches the second village. Notice there's another split in the road here, with a branch skirting the umuzi.

About five months pass, then the father's brother arrives at the first village, looking for his brother and four nephews. The unumzane says yes, he vaguely remembers the wayfarers. They stayed at his village and then left for the next one. But, when the brother and his companions arrive at the other village, the

331

unumzane says the brother and his sons hadn't been there. And if the father was after ivory, he would surely have spoken to him. Besides, he pointed out, there is the other path, the one which skirts the village.

The men were back two days later. The headman at the next village along the same path hadn't seen the traders either. They were accompanied by the village's unumzane, because a party that had left that place a few weeks previously had also not returned.

This gave rise to a series of consultations and, once the dust had settled, it was realised that for a long while people had been disappearing along this road. And so emissaries were sent to Bulawayo to ask Shaka for help. He, in turn, sent the Induna, and with him came Njikiza, Phepho, Sola, Namusu (*looking at Zamo*) – and me, of course. We spoke to the unumzane of the first village, and set off the following day.

As soon as the hill came in sight, the Induna halted. We were on a slight rise and the road dipped before climbing the hill, and he stood still as if he had spotted something. I tried to work out what he was looking at, but couldn't.

Then, without a word, the Induna set off again. At the top of the hill, while we sought the shade and our waterskins, he paused again and looked back the way we had come. Then he strode over to view the road we had yet to descend; next he was back studying the way we had come. I took him some water and, after a few mouthfuls, he told Phepho to jog down the slope a way and stop as soon as he whistled. Next went Namusu, who would stop wherever he was when the Induna whistled a second time. I was next, and as I set off, I heard Njikiza saying he wasn't made for climbing cliffs, and would therefore remain up here as a lookout, if my master didn't mind.

Once we were in position in a line stretching down the rise, the Induna himself joined us. Starting with the first man he'd sent down, which is to say Phepho, he began examining the bushes next to him. He did the same thing when he reached each of us in turn, ducking into the undergrowth and rustling about among the dead leaves and branches. Then he led us back to the top of the hill.

Once we were back alongside Njikiza, the Induna pointed down the road again and asked us what was wrong. 'What is wrong with this, madoda?' he asked. 'What is not right?' We squinted. We stared. We shaded our eyes and peered. Njikiza chuckled, which showed he understood, and which made us look all the harder. Finally, just as I was reluctantly going to admit I at least didn't see what the Induna was referring to, Namusu pre-empted me. 'Sorry, Master,' he said, 'but we can't see anything wrong with this path.'

'Hai,' said the Induna, 'when last have you seen such a *straight* path? Look! See!' he said. 'A path as straight as an iklwa haft! How often do you see that?' And, of course, he was right. As you yourselves know, madoda, our paths follow the exigencies of the land. Our people – as well as the animals that create the trails – go around lumps and bumps, boulders and thorn trees.

But here . . . Well, look, said the Induna – see the lighter lines of foliage to the side of the road, some at the places where he had made us stand – that was a sign of newer growth now covering where sections of the old path had once run. And he told us he had found stumps where trees had been cut down. Someone had worked hard to straighten this road. The fact that they had needed to work surreptitiously, without anyone noticing, doubtless made that work all the harder. But they knew the rewards would be there. Oh yes! And the same was true of the road running down the other side of the hill, which had been straightened as well. Why?

In a flash of inspiration (*chuckles the old general*) I saw the answer. It was really very simple. Those paths had been straightened so that anyone standing where we were, at the top of the prominence, could see wayfarers approaching from a long way off. And they could also see if they were worth robbing, or whether it was better to remain in hiding.

Speaking of which, their lair had to be somewhere very close.

There wasn't much space up there, and soon we found the spot where a tangle of dead branches hid a gap in the bushes. It was clever of the bandits to remove the leaves, because dead leaves would have made the . . . well, let's call it the gate . . . more noticeable.

Removing just enough undergrowth to allow us through, we entered a shady clearing, where we found a crude shelter and a fire circle. Because it was almost completely covered by the branches of the surrounding trees, there was very little grass, but a patch of dirt immediately caught the eye. It was as big as a war shield; perhaps a little longer and wider. And the sand here was fresher, a bright reddish-brown compared to the hard dark-brown dirt elsewhere. Someone had been digging there. We all looked at each other: had we found the traders?

The Induna handed his iklwa to me and unclipped a long hunting spear from his shield. Moving to the patch, he began to thrust the haft of the spear into the sand. It didn't take him long to find something solid. He tapped it once, twice. Definitely solid. We dropped on to our knees and started scooping out the soil with our hands.

Elephant tusks.

Namasu (*continues the general*) found the second path –

although it was more of an animal trail. It was on the opposite side of the clearing to the main entrance, and led through
the bushes covering the spine of the ridge, zigzagging here and
there until it reached a road that bypassed all the villages situated along the first road. This was clearly how the bandits came
and went.

But where would they be now, as the clearing showed signs
of having been deserted for a while?

★

'The beads,' says Zamo.

The old general raises his eyebrows, inviting the young officer to continue.

'The traders, General,' continues Zamo. 'The father had a
large amount of beads with him, which he intended to trade for
more ivory . . .'

'Ah, yes!' interrupts Cheetah, not to be outdone. 'The bandits
had taken the beads and were using them to acquire more tusks.'

'And because they had buried the tusks they had stolen, that
meant they would be coming back,' adds Zamo.

'This is true,' says the general, 'and remember, too, they had
worked hard to straighten those paths, so this was not a lair they
were going to abandon in a hurry.'

★

We couldn't come through the trail and take them from the
rear, because it was too narrow. We would have had to move
in single file, and there was too much chance of making a noise
that would alert them (*observes the general*). However, we could
keep watch at where the trail ended, and thus see when they
returned. 'Why not lie in wait and catch them then?' I hear
you ask. But as it turned out, only two of them used that trail,
and we had to assume the others reached the clearing via the

other road, the shortcut, probably to check if the entrance had been found.

We waited a day, then borrowed some cattle from the unumzane and set off to be robbed. And you know what happened next . . .

The People of the Sky hold cattle, izinkomo, to be very special. These animals give their all to Abantu, Human Beings: they provide meat and milk; their hides are used for shields and clothing, the horns for adornment and decoration; even the hooves are useful as treats for a man's dogs. A cow or bull is also required in various rituals, and cattle make up the lobolo, or bride price. It's not surprising, then, the isibaya, the cattle kraal, is regarded as a sacred place where the ancestors reside. In fact, so important is the byre that the word 'kraal' is used to describe the whole settlement or homestead. It's also not surprising that a man's wealth is measured in cattle.

So valuable are these beasts that it's said in Shaka's time, even when the King was revered, the various headmen made sure bullock horns were never among the gifts he received, as they believed any other person possessing these horns could kill off the rest of the giver's herd.

Many sangomas specialise in the treatment of cattle. A lot of different muthis are used and the shaman isn't paid if the cattle die. There's a herb, for example, which is said to make an inkomazi, a cow, give her milk more freely, and ways to force a cow who has lost a calf to accept another, allowing it to suck and so draw the milk.

The loss of one's herd is an economic tragedy on a par with a stock-market crash; indeed, 'cattle' and 'capital' derive from the same root word. As an added precaution, then, the ukusisa custom sees a man keeping some of his cattle at another's kraal, so if disease destroys his home herd, not all his izinkomo will be lost.

The cattle themselves are forerunners of the indigenous Nguni breed. They are medium-sized, with bulls weighing between 500kg and 700kg, and cows weighing about 390kg. Izinkunzi, bulls, have well developed, rounded muscular humps. The cattle are excellent foragers and will graze and browse on steep slopes and amid thick bush alike.

Aesthetically, they're beautiful creatures, with an incredible collection of colour combinations and impressive horns. And, in Shaka's day, favourites among the herd were given added 'ornamentations'. Their ears would be cut into various artistic shapes, and excrescences resembling buttons and tassels were fashioned on the head and neck by tying up segments of the skin. Even the horns were induced to grow in different shapes.

And the Zulus had a name for each of the various colour patterns displayed by their cattle.

# The Adventure Of The Misplaced Kraal

He came awake bewildered, the rime of sleep was still caught in his eyelashes, and his eyes were burning.

That smell: the stench of burnt hair mixed with the sweet smell of marijuana.

Where was he?

The faint glow of the embers remaining in a nearby circle of stones was enough to confirm that he wasn't in his own hut.

Whoever this hut belonged to, its walls were weighed down by skins and . . . were those animal skulls?

Ah, yes . . . He hoisted himself up onto his left elbow. He was in Namango's hut.

And the sangoma had induced him to smoke marijuana mixed with something else.

Yes, there lay the hollowed-out rhino horn with an opening bored into the tip.

*Something else* . . . It's those other ingredients that turned a pleasurable activity into a struggle not to vomit, with Namango urging him to keep it in . . . keep it in.

Then, after the struggle and the strain: a summit of sudden calm. A floating feeling.

Then . . .

*This.*

Coming awake, bewildered. Dust in his throat and wanting to cough, to gag.

The mixture he had smoked was supposed to make him see why the bones were against him; to discern the nature of the threat he faced. 'I can help you,' Namango had told him, 'but I can take you only so far. You will need to go the rest of the way on your own.'

He'd been afraid – who wouldn't be? – and Namango's reassurance that he would bring him back was of little comfort. It wasn't that he didn't trust the sangoma – far from it! – only that he was about to enter the realm of the ancestors.

But now?

Nothing.

He sat up.

And saw the bull's head filling the hut's entrance, the tips of its horns just touching the arch on either side.

But something was wrong.

The way the head was slightly tilted to the side . . . The way it seemed to be regarding him . . . The way the head was held . . . No bull he knew of had a neck that supple. No bull he knew could crouch in a hut's doorway like that.

So if not a bull, then . . . ?

A man-bull . . .

Even as the thought formed, he felt hands close around his ankles. And the head receded from the opening as he was dragged towards the doorway. And then he was staring up at the stars.

Clambering to his feet, he stumbled away, trying to escape the man-bull.

And found himself standing in a cattle byre.

And not just any isibaya, but the kraal he himself had erected especially for his precious cow.

*But that couldn't be!* The byre was at his homestead, three valleys away from the sangoma's kraal!

'Are you sure it was your kraal?'

Vakashi the Cow Man nods without hesitation. The Induna

has seen it for himself; truly there is none like it. 'This is so,' concedes the Induna.

Haunted by Namango's mutterings about some impending tragedy involving his prized cow, Vakashi had a special kraal constructed for her as her calving time drew near. The byre was situated just a few paces from his indlu, and had been built between neighbouring huts. In fact, one indlu was left inside the kraal and had been partially torn down to provide the cow with a place to shelter should the weather change.

That distinctive half-hut, swears Vakashi, had been there that night. It was one of the features that helped him identify the isibaya as his own, despite his confused state – which confusion had deepened when he realised how that couldn't be so. He couldn't – shouldn't – have been in his own kraal. Or else, if he was, that couldn't be the sangoma's hut behind him.

The fact that the Induna and Mbopa seem unmoved by the Cow Man's tale is of little consolation to the udibi. Seated on the ground next to his master, he has to fold his arms around his knees and hold on to them tight to stop himself from trembling.

★

Suddenly, Vakashi remembered the man-bull who had dragged him out of the sangoma's hut. He wheeled round, but the creature had vanished.

He looked down and saw the ground was muddy on this side of the thorn fence. He really was standing in his own cattle kraal.

And how had he got across, or through, the fence without any scratches?

Then a more pressing thought: if this was his isibaya, where was his cow?

He regarded the half-hut. She wasn't sheltering there.

He looked beyond the thatch, and that's when he saw the man, though he couldn't make out his face. Amashoba adorned the man's arms and legs, feathers curved out of his headdress, and he was carrying a big isihlangu, or shield, its curved rim partially obscuring the warrior's features . . .

He was carrying an assegai too: a long throwing spear used for hunting.

As Vakashi watched, the man's arm came forward, sending the isijula toward him.

Then Namango was shaking him. He was back in the sangoma's hut, and it was dawn.

Vakashi pushed the sangoma aside and blundered outside.

The cattle byre wasn't there. The sangoma's vaguely dilapidated homestead was exactly as it always was.

Then he looked down . . .

'I looked down, Nduna, and there was mud on my shins, and covering my feet.'

Bending, he scooped up some and raised his fingers to his nose. He could smell the dung!

Stifling a grin at the startled hiss escaping from his udibi's pursed lips, the Induna nods. 'And so it was almost as if you really had been in a kraal,' he says.

'Hai, not just any kraal, Nduna! The kraal I myself had built.'

Which was three valleys away!

'How can that be, Nduna?' Vakashi looks to Mbopa: 'How can that be, old friend?'

'What did the sangoma say?'

'He asked me what I had seen, and when I had told him, he said this was troubling. Things might be even worse than he expected!'

★

Following the sangoma's instructions, the Cow Man returned to his homestead. Here, the first thing he did was check on his cow. His concern, growing with every step he took, had vanquished his fatigue and strengthened his legs. The churning in his gut drove him on at a pace that a young man would envy. The way he saw it, if he really had somehow been transported to his isibaya the fact that his cow was nowhere to be seen there was ominous. And a feeling of dread had oiled his aching muscles.

For this was a most precious cow. Her progeny comprised strong heifers who would one day produce the sweetest milk in the kingdom, and bulls who would rule the herd and whose hardiness would be passed on to the sons they sired.

To Vakashi's relief, the cow seemed unaffected by the horrors that had befallen him.

But what was this?

Ignoring the anxious questions his wives and elder sons were throwing at him, he dropped to his haunches.

There, exactly where he had been standing the night before, were footprints.

He straightened. It couldn't be! It just couldn't be!

Gingerly, he placed his left foot in a matching indentation. It seemed to fit.

Namango had ordered him to get some rest, but that was easier said than done and sleep eluded him. He kept seeing the warrior with the shield and isijula. He kept seeing the figure's arm whip forward, and the spear flying straight at him. The soldier was so close he couldn't miss.

Yet somehow he had. Or maybe he hadn't. Perhaps that spear was misfortune travelling through the darkness of the world beyond this one, heading towards him, and there was nothing he could do about it – even with the sangoma's help.

Namango had warned him that it would happen like this. It would be like a cowskin being unrolled, he said. Each time Vakashi smoked the special muthi and ventured out of the gate between here and there, he'd see a little more. But he'd been hoping he'd only have to go through the ordeal once . . .

Then it was the next day and he had to return to the sangoma's settlement.

This time the mixture Namango gave him to smoke seemed even more vile.

This time there was no man-bull.

This time consciousness found him on his knees in the kraal. His kraal.

And there was his cow. Her calving time very near now, she stood under the covering afforded by the remains of the hut. He could just make out her markings in the deeper shadows pooled there.

He reached out a trembling hand, was about to call out to the animal, when he realised they weren't alone.

He looked up and there was the warrior, still faceless, towering over him.

'Who are you?' asked the Cow Man. And he raised his arms and twisted sideways as the spear struck home.

'And then it was morning and I was back in the sangoma's hut,' says Vakashi.

'What did he say?' asks Mbopa.

'He listened to my tale, then said this was very serious. But we had learnt something, he added.'

'What was that?' asks the Induna.

They now had a clearer idea of when the attack would take place, explains Vakashi. For he had seen his cow and it still had not calved.

'Ahh,' says Mbopa, while the Induna nods.

Vakashi swallows. His hands part, come together again. This is why he has come seeking the help of his old friend. Truly he had almost wept with joy when he heard Mbopa was visiting his home kraal! Because his cow is due to calve tonight, or tomorrow at the latest! He'll be seeing his last sunset shortly, if Mbopa and the Induna can't help him.

The Induna leans forward. 'What did the sangoma suggest?'

Vakashi's hands come up. 'Hai, something I cannot do,' he says.

★

Twice he had ventured away from the realm of Human Beings, and twice he had been attacked. But, as frightened as he was, he had stared at the sangoma in horror.

'It's the only way,' said Namango.

'No!' said the Cow Man, rolling away from where the sangoma crouched.

'No!' he hissed, as he stood.

He would not sacrifice the cow!

No, never!

But what if the man who came out of the darkness wasn't willing to stop at him? What if, after killing Vakashi, he turned his attention to the Cow Man's family? Would he see his whole bloodline wiped out?

'No,' said Vakashi, shaking his head, refusing to listen further to the sangoma.

'No,' he said, 'I will arm myself! I am no weakling! I will arm myself and protect my family and my possessions against this invader!'

Namango had gripped the Cow Man's elbows before the latter knew what was happening. 'What you saw,' he said, 'tells me

345

you are doomed! This man will kill you! And, worse, he may turn on your family. You won't sacrifice your cow, but who will protect her when you eat dust?'

Vakashi freed himself from the sangoma's grasp and ducked out of the hut. He paused a moment just past the threshold, because he had been half expecting to see the cattle kraal to his right, just as it had been the night before.

But, of course, it couldn't be! That isibaya was three valleys away!

'I am sorry,' whispered Namango, coming up behind him a few moments later, 'but I can only speak the truth! The Calling guides me in this matter, this is the only way we can change what will be!'

He laid a hand on the Cow Man's shoulder. Think about it, he whispered – could he identify his assailant?

No, said Vakashi, for the man's visage was hidden from him, blurred by the ripples of the inevitable.

Struck by a sudden thought, he turned to face the sangoma. 'You concede that we are dealing with a man here, do you not?'

'Well, yes,' said Namango, 'but I do not see why that matters.'

'It matters,' said Vakashi, 'because if we are dealing with a Human Being, and not a thing from wherever wizards get their creatures from, then that means things cannot be inevitable! And therefore I may yet best him! For is that not Shaka's way? Hasn't he showed us we need not cower any longer? That we can – and must – fight for what is rightfully ours?'

A wry smile. 'And now here we sit.'

Mbopa nods. 'Do not worry, old friend, you will live to see many sunsets yet!'

'Do you really think we can vanquish this creature?' asks Vakashi.

'Not a creature, a man,' interjects Mbopa.

'Which makes him even more dangerous! But your decision to face him down was the right one,' says the Induna.

'I had no choice, Nduna. Without that cow, we will be greatly impoverished.'

'Cha, you exaggerate now, Vakashi.'

'No, Mbopa, I have seen it happen. Let bad luck get a foothold in your kraal and it is as bad as any disease. Even worse! Because no amount of culling will help. I am done with scrabbling in the dirt with crops not fit to feed a baboon. I cannot go back to that life.'

'And you won't,' says Mbopa. 'Your torment will soon be over.'

★

'He wants this cow for himself, this greedy sangoma, and, having secured it, he will then leave here and seek his fortune elsewhere, perhaps among the Xhosas,' says Mbopa once Vakashi has taken the udibi to show him the cow.

'Hai! Why flee?' asks the Induna.

'Of course! The need to slaughter the animal will be the pretext he needs to take possession of it. But he'll slaughter another animal and no one will know the difference.'

And Vakashi's cow and its calves will be smuggled off to a relative in a faraway district, adds the Induna.

'But now Vakashi has refused to hand over the cow for a sacrifice . . .'

'Doubtless had your old friend acquiesced, no one would have been more surprised than this lizard. He could still have pretended to slaughter the cow. With Vakashi dead, though, the path becomes a little easier.'

'Yes,' says Mbopa. 'He should have no trouble persuading the widows to part with the cow — especially if he has them believing the family is cursed and the sacrifice is needed to appease the ancestors and so ensure others don't die.'

The prime minister scratches his chin. 'But how did he do it? How did he get Vakashi from there to here? How did he make it so that Vakashi leaves a sangoma's hut and finds himself at a cattle kraal three valleys away?'

'Cha!' says the Induna. 'Let us first rescue Vakashi and his cow, then we will beat the answer out of Namango.'

'Now *that* would be a pleasant way to spend an evening, Nduna!'

★

Later that morning, the Induna pays the sangoma a visit. Namango isn't at home, which doesn't surprise the warrior — the shaman is doubtless off somewhere preparing for the night's festivities. Instead, the Induna's attended to by a young woman, one of Namango's sisters who's part of the entourage that sangomas invariably attract. When she asks him what he wants, he tells her he's visiting relatives in the district and, having heard of Namango's reputation, has come seeking a love potion.

The woman nods, and shuffles off to fetch the muthi.

This gives the Induna time to examine the homestead.

Set on a gentle slope, it comprises an arc of four abodes and a cluster of smaller storage huts. The buffalo horns affixed above the doorway of the third indlu identify it as the sangoma's lair.

The Induna drifts closer, scratching his left shoulder, trying to look like one who is waiting and not spying.

The place is dilapidated. The huts have been battered by the elements and need rethatching. Long grass is creeping closer. Even the hard-packed dirt meant to keep dust away from the dwellings is fractured, and it vanishes almost totally just a few paces from the huts.

The Induna crosses over to one of the storage huts. Standing here, he can see further down the slope. There's an abandoned isibaya down there – the remains of a thorn fence, and a circular patch slowly being reclaimed by weeds. Then the gradient steepens to meet the series of bushes and twisted trees that announce the presence of a stream. Sandstone cliffs rise up on the opposite side.

The Induna turns at the approach of the woman, who is carrying a small gourd. The Induna listens as she tells him how he is to administer the potion to the one whose affections he wants to win. When she's finished, he reaches into the pouch at his waist and holds out his hand.

The woman examines the beads in his palm and picks out a few. When he reckons she's chosen enough to match the value of the muthi, he clenches his fist. She snatches her fingers away just in time. He meets her hiss with a grin, replaces the beads in his pouch, and holds out his hand again.

With poorly concealed ill grace, she hands over the gourd. The Induna thanks her, takes another look at the old cattle kraal a few metres away, then turns to leave this woe-begotten place.

★

The boy is waiting for him along the path that leads to Vakashi's homestead. He emerges from his hiding place as soon as he sees the Induna approach.

Is he well, not-well?

'Ngisaphila,' says the boy. *I am well.*

Has anyone come along the path?

The udibi shakes his head.

They walk on in silence for several paces, the Induna waiting for the boy to muster his courage.

'Master,' says the udibi at last. 'Was . . . was he there?' The path is wide enough for him to walk alongside the Induna.

'Hai, no, little one. And I said I would be surprised to find him sunning his carcass, remember?'

This is so, but the boy has been hoping the Induna would be proved wrong. The thought of the sangoma on the loose somewhere, doing who knows what, is not comforting.

'Be patient, Boy. We will meet him soon enough.'

The udibi nods. Another thought to fill him with dread.

'And do you know what you will see?' continues the Induna, glancing down at the boy. 'You will see a man, not a sangoma. You will see one who has never heard the Calling, but instead uses lies and fear to trap his prey!'

They reach a fork in the path. Without pausing, the Induna begins the ascent toward the ridge, the udibi falling in behind him.

They must get back to Vakashi's homestead as quickly as possible, so they can start making their preparations. However, at the summit, the Induna pauses to wait for the udibi, knowing the boy's been giving his words much thought and will have further questions.

'Master?' begins the udibi after offering the Induna the water sack he carries.

'Yes.'

'Vakashi . . . he . . . well, he says he's seen . . . many times he's seen proof of the sangoma's prowess . . .'

'This is so. But when a man loves a maiden he can't find fault in her. Indeed, he will ignore those who try and point out her shortcomings to him.' And if those trying to warn him are correct and the female is only after his wealth, it will take him a long while before he recognises that fact. It's unlikely their words alone will guide him, only his own experience of her perfidy will eventually change his opinion. And that process will often be painful.

This is why they have to ensure Vakashi sees for himself how that Namango has been tricking him. He must learn that the sangoma's plans were laid some time ago – perhaps it was even the Cow Man's renown that drew Namango to this district – and therefore Vakashi can trust nothing this crocodile has ever told him.

★

Midnight comes and goes, and the early morning hours bring with them a mist. It slips in between the huts almost unnoticed, and curls and clings, and settles. The ground vanishes and the smaller huts are gradually submerged.

Because of the makeshift kraal situated to the right of Vakashi's indlu, the man-bull has to approach the dwelling from the rear – through an opening in the perimeter fence made and then disguised a few nights ago.

The mist swallows all sounds and he's able to move swiftly. But when he reaches the rear curve of Vakashi's hut, he pauses. Places a hand against the thatch and listens.

All is still. Frozen. The muthi he swallowed before setting out has started to work, and it's as if he's separate from all this. Invisible. Protected.

He presses his palm more firmly against the thatch. Does Vakashi groan and roll on his sleeping mat inside, taunted by the memories of his visions? Or is he awake and staring into the darkness, wondering what he can do to protect himself?

Hai! Does he still not realise there's absolutely nothing he can do to save himself?

So it doesn't matter if he's asleep or awake . . .

A grin behind the bone mask – it really doesn't matter.

Tightening his grip on the spear, the man-bull creeps forward.

When he reaches the front of the indlu, he pauses again, just to make sure no one nearby has left their hut to take a piss.

That there are no sentries doesn't worry him: Vakashi has been warned not to tell anyone what he has seen in those visions, as this will only endanger them as well. When the attack comes, they too will fall.

Two, three steps and he's at the entrance. Now he sees there's a faint orange glow emanating from within. A fire has been allowed to become embers. He also sees that the screen serving as the door hasn't been pulled across the opening.

The man-bull crouches and moves under the low archway, gripping the left side with his free hand.

That's as far as he gets.

For, hovering on his knees, by the embers of the fire in the centre of the hut, is Mbopa.

Shaka's prime minister grins, waves, and says: 'Sawubona, Numzane Bull!' *Hello, Mister Bull!*

The intruder backs out of the doorway, and stands upright so quickly the muthi makes him dizzy. He hasn't recognised Mbopa, of course; all he knows is that whoever's in the hut it isn't Vakashi.

But, before he can swallow his surprise, the Induna drops down alongside him. He's been perched on top of the hut and warned Mbopa of the man-bull's approach by dropping a stone through the indlu's smoke hole.

He's armed with an iwisa, a solid stick with a knob on the end. He swings this, hitting the man-bull in the lower back. And hits him again, this time across the shoulder blades, as the intruder sags.

But, as the man crumples, Mbopa shouts a warning, and the Induna has to leap over the man-bull to confront the shriek charging out of the darkness.

It's the woman he encountered earlier today, clutching a long hunting spear.

The Induna leaps over the man-bull, and steps to one side. The blade just misses him and he grabs the haft before the old woman can change direction. Forcing the blade upwards, he lays the iwisa across her flank.

It takes another blow before she lets go of the spear. Tossing the isijula aside, the Induna steps forward and bounces the end of the iwisa off the top of the woman's skull.

'Nduna!' calls Mbopa.

Another confederate: this time a youngster who's probably one of the sangoma's students. He's carrying an iklwa, and drops into a crouch.

Bad move.

The Induna feints a sweeping blow at the youth's head, and as the latter lunges forward with a gleeful hiss, the older man changes direction. The head of the iwisa connects with the iklwa's blade, forcing the spear downward.

The hornless ox staggers past him and, catching the assegai Mbopa tosses to him, the Induna rams its blade into the youth's back. Lifting his right foot he pushes the dying boy off the blade and redirects his attention to the sangoma's sister.

She's lying on her side, hands pressed against shattered ribs, her lips glistening with blood. Her whimpers become a shriek as the Induna stabs her in the side.

'Ngadla!' he hisses. *I have eaten!*

He twists the blade, then withdraws it and tosses the spear aside.

By now Mbopa has removed the bull mask from the sangoma. Only . . .

'What's wrong, Master?' asks the Induna, as he notes the surprise on the prime minister's features.

'Look!' says Mbopa, indicating the groaning man with an upturned palm.

The Induna moves closer . . . looks . . . swallows an intake of breath . . . and looks again.

It's not Namango. The one wearing the mask isn't the sangoma, but yet another of his acolytes.

Mbopa and the Induna exchange a glance – and reach the same conclusion at the same time.

'Go!' says Mbopa, clambering to his feet. 'Go! I'll be right behind you.'

★

Vakashi rolls his head. Ahh, the exquisite pleasure of a good piss. Despite everything – and he still can't understand why he had to seek refuge at Mbopa's homestead – a good piss is still a good piss.

Finished urinating, Vakashi turns round to find himself facing Namango.

The sangoma wears the isinene and ibeshu that comprise the Zulu kilt – not for him a mask this night – and is holding an iklwa.

He laughs at Vakashi's surprise.

'Did you think you could fool me?' he asks. 'Cha! You are the fool! And those who serve the Beetle and would help you, they too are fools.'

The tip of the iklwa's broad blade presses against Vakashi's chest. 'Did you not think I would have spies watching you? Aiee!'

354

He doesn't need to do this, protests Vakashi, fighting to keep his voice steady. 'For all that you have done for me, I would gladly have given you a calf.'

A *calf?* It's the mother he wants; it's the mother who has the power.

'Do not insult me by now offering me the cow, for I know that, as soon as you have freed yourself from my blade, you'll go scurrying to Mbopa. No, you must die.'

But Namango's the one who buckles. Regaining his balance, he turns to face the udibi.

He touches his side, raises his hand and smears the blood across his own cheek.

'Hai! So weak! But dead children make strong muthi, and my pots await you.'

As he makes to move forward, though, Vakashi throws an arm around the man's neck and pulls him backward.

'In his stomach!' he shouts, pulling his arm tighter. 'Stab him in the stomach. Finish him.'

★

Vakashi intercedes on the udibi's behalf when the Induna arrives. It was his fault, he says, for he had told the boy he didn't need company just to take a piss. The Induna, however, is simply relieved neither have been injured. As is Mbopa, when he arrives panting some time later.

'So,' he says after a few mouthfuls of water, 'what say you?'

They are standing around the sangoma's body. 'You – and the Nduna here – were right, old friend,' says Vakashi. 'Maybe once this creature obeyed the Calling, but not any more. No, he told me so himself that he was only after my cow.'

'This is so,' murmurs Mbopa. But the look he exchanges with the Induna confirms they're both thinking the same thing. How long before Vakashi decides that, perhaps, in some way, the sangoma's warning had been true – even if he himself had turned out to be the one carrying the spear? How long before drought or a sick cow or a timid bull has him seeking out the services of another sangoma?

★

The old general, who was once the Induna's udibi, chuckles. 'Aiee,' he says, 'if this Namango really heard voices, they didn't belong to the ancestors.'

He extends his hand and the officer sitting nearest him hands him the gourd containing beer. He drinks, smacks his lips, and hands the gourd back to the warrior.

'And so,' he continues, 'we see yet again how Shaka, our Father, sought to protect his children from sangomas.'

The old general pauses – eyes those sitting closest to him – casts a concerned glance over the others seated behind them.

'What's wrong?' he asks, feigning innocence.

'General,' says the same warrior who handed him the beer, 'you are toying with us.'

'Yes, General,' says another officer. 'We would know *how*!'

'How?' asks the general, furrowing his brow.

'Yes, numzane,' says a warrior in the second row. 'You say Namango the sangoma was a liar and a thief, and we do not doubt you, but we would still like to know how he stole Vakashi from his hut and placed him in a kraal three valleys away.'

The general grins. 'You will be disappointed, my young lions.'

'Nonetheless, General,' says Zamo, 'we would know.'

'Very well, then' says the old general.

And he tells how, later that day, the Induna had taken them to Namango's homestead, which was by then deserted.

'Look! See!' he had said. Calling on the udibi to help him, he moved to the storage hut opposite Namango's indlu. Together they were easily able to lift the whole structure and shift it.

Next, the Induna stepped over to the large hut standing a few paces away. Gripping a section of thatch, he pulled it away so that they were left with a portion of the hut, just as was the case in Vakashi's makeshift cattle byre.

The Induna pointed to the ground: see how it was broken up here. Merely add some water and it would resemble the churned up earth of an isibaya.

It was spotting this on his visit to the kraal – broken ground where there should be hardpacked dirt – that had got him thinking, he added.

Sons and nephews from Vakashi's homestead, as well as those from the homesteads belonging to Mbopa and Vakashi's brother, had accompanied them to the sangoma's lair, for they were now to tear down the settlement, and the Induna instructed them to follow him.

He led them to where the cattle byre had once stood. After examining the remains of the thorn fence there, he laughed and showed the others what to do.

Soon, while Mbopa, Vakashi and the older men looked on, they were rearranging the fence between the huts. Namango had thrust long assegai hafts into the fence at intervals, enabling a few men to lift and move the fence without injuring themselves on the thorns.

Once they had finished terrorising the Cow Man, one of Namango's acolytes would have raced to Vakashi's kraal to replicate the footprints in the mud there – probably an unnecessary precaution, but one which would have added to Vakashi's unease.

'And that's what happened,' declared the general.

As for the inkomazi he'd seen, that had been a similarly pregnant animal daubed with mud to imitate the markings of Vakashi's own cow.

'Yes,' says the old general, after a moment's hesitation, 'the stunned way you look now, that was the way Mbopa and Vakashi looked that day. But, truly, there was no sorcery, merely cunning.'

And they must remember, he adds, the second kraal had merely to roughly resemble the first, for having smoked the muthi, Vakashi was in no state to examine it closely when he staggered out of Namango's hut.

Besides, he had other horrors to occupy his attention, like the man with the spear.

*What's left of the White Man is found lying under a Large-leaved Albizia,*
*which is known to the People of the Sky as the Umvangazi. His skin is*
*starting to turn a dirty opal; his eyes are open, staring at the canopy above*
*him. His mouth also gapes open, looking like a mole's burrow amid his*
*brown beard. His arms are outstretched, but bent at the elbows as if he*
*was trying to grab for the tree trunk behind him.*

*He's wearing a coat crudely fashioned from cowskin and, under that,*
*a much-mended light-blue shirt. The hems of both garments are torn.*

*And, except for a length of spine protruding like a tail from under-*
*neath his ribcage, that is that. The entire lower part of his body is*
*missing.*

*Fynn, whose time as a loblolly boy at a London hospital has inculcated*
*in him a fascination with medical matters and inured him to such sights,*
*is down on his hands and knees, trying to peer inside the torso.*

Fascinating, *he mutters as the Induna, the udibi and Jakot stand by*
*patiently.*

*'Indeed it is,' murmurs Jakot.*

*The Induna snorts. 'You agreeing with one of your masters? This is*
*truly a memorable day.'*

*'No man is my master,' responds Jakot.*

*'Nonetheless, what did he say?'*

*'Merely that this' – Jakot sweeps his arm, taking in Fynn, the body,*
*the tree – 'is fascinating.'*

*' He is not angry that one of his kind has perished?'*

Fascinating, *says Fynn again.* I think that's the heart, but all the
other organs are gone. Fascinating, *he whispers yet again, as he directs*
*his attention to the vertebral column.*

'This one . . .' says Jakot. 'Well, let us say, the lowliest tribe would be ashamed to acknowledge him as one of their kind.' Doubtless, Fynn will go through the motions, he adds, and will insist on a burial, but this man won't be missed by anyone back at Port Natal.

Resting back on his heels and regarding Zephaniah Bracegirdle's remains, Fynn is embarrassed to find himself faintly . . . well, relieved. As unchristian as it might seem, there's no getting round the fact the fellow has been a disruptive influence at Port Natal ever since he arrived about four months ago. Always complaining and conniving, trying to sow discord, and refusing to do his share of the work needed to improve the settlement.

Fynn had always felt the hairs on his neck rise whenever Bracegirdle made an appearance – because it almost always presaged a confrontation.

Thank heavens he was too lazy to make the trip to Bulawayo! Instead he preferred roaming from stream to stream, panning for gold.

And now he's dead.

With a sigh Fynn climbs to his feet. Turning to Jakot, he says: Ask our erstwhile friend over there what he thinks did this.

'Now there is a question I'd also like to hear answered,' says Jakot with a grin. 'What say you, Zulu – what caused this, do you think?'

'A hyena.'

'A hyena?' repeats Jakot with exaggerated incredulity.

What does he say? asks Fynn.

He says a hyena did this.

Ahh, says Fynn glancing at the ground immediately around him.

'Tell him not to bother looking for spoor—' begins the Induna.

'Because he has walked all over it, thereby obliterating any tracks? Or because this hyena of yours was a very special hyena?'

'What do you mean?'

Jakot shrugs. 'I mean what I say, Zulu.'

What are you talking about, Jacob? interrupts Fynn. What else is he saying, confound you?

Hai, majesty, he is merely remarking on the smell and the flies, and says although Shaka has ordered all Zulus to cater to our every whim, he hopes you do not expect him to help you convey the carcass to Port Natal. He will do so, if that is what you really wish, but . . . *Jakot shrugs, letting his words tail off.*

He has a point, *says Fynn.* Perhaps he will see his way clear to helping us bury the poor blighter somewhere around here.

I'm sure he will. *'What say you, Nduna?' continues Jakot turning to the Induna, and switching to Zulu.*

*'I say you are beginning to annoy me.'*

*'You are annoyed and I am puzzled. This is turning into an intriguing day. But you wound me, Zulu, for I have just saved you from some unpleasant toil.'*

*'What do you mean?'*

*'I have persuaded his madness over there not to insist you convey this smelly chunk of carrion back to Thekwini. Instead, he has merely asked that you bury it somewhere nearby.'*

*Before the Induna can reply, Jakot switches to English:* He says yes, he will be happy to oblige.

Good, good, *mutters Fynn who's on his knees again examining the torso.*

*'He looks for what's not there, but I find what is there more interesting,' observes Jakot.*

*The Induna keeps his gaze on the pair of bushbuck grazing over by a thicket of red bushwillows, far enough away from the men to feel safe. The antelope are dark brown, with white bands across the throat and chest, and white dots spattered across their flanks. Slightly bigger and heavier, the male has twisted horns.*

*Strange to see them out in the open during the day. Mind you . . . The Induna glances up. The sky is overcast, a bushbaby-grey overhead, becoming darker to the west over the mountain range there. Shy and solitary, bushbuck are mainly nocturnal, but they do venture out on such days.*

*The Induna's attention shifts to that blue-black headdress worn by the mountains. The colour suggests it's already raining over there, and a storm is likely to reach here before they know it.*

*Finally he meets Jakot's gaze. The interpreter has been waiting patiently for his response, the hint of a knowing smile curling the corners of his lips.*

*'And what is it that you find more interesting?'*

*'Come now, Zulu. See how the dead man lies?'*

*The Induna and the boy both look at the body of the bearded savage lying on his back; Fynn is in the way, gently tugging on the spinal column and watching Bracegirdle's head shift.*

*'Isn't he looking somewhat too placid for one savaged by hyenas?' contin-ues Jakot. 'He's been pulled at, tugged. Yet he appears to be asleep.'*

*'Placid,' says the Induna.*

*'Precisely.'*

*Another pause, with Jakot waiting while the Induna examines the darkness to the east. It isn't moving so much as* spreading *towards them.*

*This time Jakot breaks the silence. 'What say you, Zulu?'*

*Without waiting for an answer, Jakot moves closer to the corpse. The Induna and the udibi follow him. Standing up, brushing sand off his knees, Fynn assumes they're about to pick the body up.* Yes. Well. I'll look for a suitable spot, shall I? *he says, thinking it's the least he can do for the blighter.*

One near many stones, please, Master, *says Jakot.*

Er, right, will do.

*When Fynn's moved out of earshot, Jakot points to the man's arms. 'See how they lie?'*

*'A storm is coming, so let us not tarry here too long,' warns the Induna.*

*'Very well, then,' says Jakot. 'See how the man's arms lie?'* Could it be someone has looped a cord around the tree trunk — then tied one end of

*it around each of the man's wrists, wrapping the cord over the jacket cuffs so no marks will be left there?*

*'However, I am tempted to say there might indeed be a place where marks have been left,' says Jakot.*

*'Where?' asks the Induna.*

*Jakot steps forward and slaps the trunk. 'On the other side of this tree, gouged into the wood as the poor wretch twisted and turned, and the hyenas feasted. But I think anyone smart enough to have planned this wouldn't have been so stupid.'*

*For one thing, he adds, look at the bark of this tree. It is an old tree and the grey bark is breaking up, leaving convenient grooves everywhere. 'What say you, Zulu?'*

*The Induna shrugs, indicates he'll carry the end with the head.*

*Jakot is too engrossed in his own deductions to complain about that, although the udibi quickly picks up his master's shield and spears, just in case he's asked to help carry the end with that awful hollowness.*

*'Don't you think this is a most perplexing mystery?'*

*The Induna slips his hands under the man's armpits and lifts. 'So it is,' he agrees.*

*After examining the ragged wound a while, Jakot shrugs and picks up the torso by the spinal column. 'What?' he asks. 'Perplexing?'*

*'Or mysterious, but—'*

Over here, chaps, *calls out Fynn in English.*

*'But?' prompts Jakot as they begin to move sideways to where the White Man awaits them.*

*'But I also think some things are meant to remain mysterious and perplexing. What say you, Xhosa?'*

*Jakot's reply is a chuckle.*

*The spot Fynn has chosen is sandy on the surface, becoming more compacted a few centimetres down. Using flat stones, the three black men dig as deeply as they can go, which isn't far. The remains are lowered into* the hole, the sand is thrown back on, and rocks piled on top to keep predators away.

Then Fynn mumbles a prayer and they go their separate ways, the Induna and the boy returning to the Induna's home kraal, Jakot and Fynn heading back to Port Natal.

# The Adventure Of The Son,
# The Mother & The Mad Man

Some days in Africa, the sun blares out of the sky, turning man and beast into sluggards seeking only shade, although along the south-east coast the shade offers no respite from the humidity that accompanies and often overwhelms the heat, now like the remora, now like the shark itself. On other days in Africa, the sun is pale, blurred by dusty winds high up that presage a gale, thunder and lightning, a crop-drowning deluge. On days like today, though, the sun is a gentle caress, soothing, and reviving amid the cold shadows left behind by a frigid night.

The Induna lies stretched out on a large lichen-speckled slab of rock on the east-facing slope of a kloof. They are less than a day away from his home kraal – and from Kani, his wife – so there's time to enjoy the sun's beneficence for a while. Especially since last night saw them huddled together in their wildebeest skins, feeding the fire with numb hands until they ran out of wood and had to endure the icy pre-dawn hours with dying embers and chattering teeth.

Sleep had been in short supply, but the udibi hasn't sought out his own space on the warm rock. Instead he perches on the bottom edge of it, a little to the right of the Induna – where the latter can see him just by turning his head in that direction – and is swiping at the long grass with a stick. He enjoys the feel of the sun on his head, his shoulders, but his mind is on other things.

'Master,' he says at last.

'Yes?' murmurs the Induna, his face pressed into the crook of his left arm.

'It wasn't like that other time, when the maiden was murdered and you spotted the monkey snuff on the killer's leggings. It wasn't the flowers, was it, Master?'

The Induna grins. 'You mean petals, but you are right, little one.'

He doesn't have to look to see the boy's shoulders jerk in annoyance. And his grin only widens. One day, perhaps, the boy will realise that, while the others undoubtedly call him 'little one' to tease him, the Induna uses the term as a subtle goad to force the udibi to try and disprove the accuracy of that appellation by thinking deeper.

'What, then, was it, Master?' asks the boy. 'How did you know?'

'Cha!' The Induna lowers his arm and turns his head to gaze at the udibi's back. 'You have been with me long enough! You know the answer to that question, so you just have to find it. Think of Mgobozi and his shells: under which one is the pebble hiding?'

'Hai, Master,' says the boy, twisting round to face the Induna, 'that is . . .' He shrugs, not wanting to show a general disrespect.

'You are right,' says the Induna, 'it's a trick. But there was trickery here too!'

'With the petals, Master?'

Chuckling, the Induna slips the crook of his arm over his eyes once more, and says: 'Perhaps.'

The udibi furrows his brows and *thinks*.

The unumzane of the village had sent to KwaBulawayo for help, and in return Shaka had despatched the Induna and his udibi, because it wasn't just any old woman who had met her end in an unnatural manner. Her name was Dlali, because she had been born while her mother had been out working in a pasture, and she was the guardian of a sacred pool dedicated to Nomkhubula, the Princess of the Sky. As Umfumfu, the planting season, draws to a close, the women come here to bathe, drink beer and praise Nomkhubula. The following day they'll pick up their hoes and go and plant one more field of mealies. This one is for the Princess of the Sky. The crop there is never harvested, and pots of beer will be regularly left out for the princess to enjoy whenever she visits.

During the rest of the year, Dlali – as other guardians had done before her – kept watch over the isichibi, or pool, to ensure men from the village or, especially, strangers, didn't venture too close. Her status then was enough to warrant seeking the wisdom of Shaka – or at least one of his emissaries. But that first meeting at the ibandla tree hadn't exactly been fruitful. The unumzane had seemed anxious, ill-at-ease.

The udibi mentions this to the Induna, and asks why it was so. Surely the unumzane did not think he would be blamed for the death, but that's exactly how he was acting, in the boy's mind: like someone with something to hide.

'You are right about his discomfort,' says the Induna. But that had more to do with the fact the headman wasn't sure how to deal with the situation, and was peeved by this failure. Anyway this was ultimately women's business, but that was an excuse that couldn't quite quell his own feelings of guilt, and he was afraid he might be held responsible for not taking this 'women's business' more seriously and seeing that Dlali was properly protected. Especially since she claimed to have seen – and chased away – a White Man who had pushed his way through the rushes and seemed very interested in the pool.

Yes, there was that, remembers the boy.

And, it was clear the headman still only half believed Dlali's story.

'Was he trying to mislead us?' asks the boy.

'No,' says the Induna, 'he wouldn't have dared. But the presence of the White Man put him in a quandary.'

'How so, Master?' asks the boy, turning to the Induna.

The Induna lowers his arm once more, and lifts himself up on to his right elbow. That village had become wealthy through supplying the White Men at Thekwini with cattle and vegetables. Any trouble with the savages would jeopardise this trade. And there was no question of continuing it even clandestinely if Shaka – or the Induna acting as his emissary – decreed that it should be stopped. (This was, after all, one of the ways Shaka kept Farewell's men in check. Although they've started a few vegetable gardens, the settlement is dependent on the King for most of its food, so could be starved into submission should Shaka will it.)

The udibi resumes combing the long grass with his stick. It's trident grass, whose blades have fluffy heads.

They learnt far more by speaking to the unumzane's head wife. The Induna's rank, as Shaka's Shadow, meant he was one of the few males allowed to approach the pool and, as she led them there, she told them Dlali may have been old, and had to be carried up and down the steep path leading to the cavern where she resided, but there was nothing wrong with her eyes.

'If she said she saw a White Man lurking near the pool, then that's what she saw. And I will tell you something else,' she added, 'it wasn't the first time she saw him.'

That had earned a surprised *'What?'* from the Induna.

Indeed, continued the wife. Every month she visited Dlali during the time of itwese, when the new moon has just made its appearance, and again at isilibamuza, when the moon is about to disappear. On each occasion, both this month and the last, Dlali said she had seen a White Man.

He hadn't always been spotted near the pool. In fact, he'd seemed more interested in the stream above the pool, slowly making his way along the water's edge, where it was smooth and sandy. It had only been when he came close to the isichibi that Dlali had chased him away by calling out to the man; the other times she had merely watched him, while keeping her anger in check.

The wife had initially told only the other senior women in the umuzi about these 'visitations'. But, as soon as she heard the man had actually approached the isichibi, the wife had informed the unumzane, who, as the Induna could see, hadn't taken the matter seriously.

'Was it the same man?' asked the Induna.

The wife nodded without hesitation. She had asked Dlali the same question, and the old woman had been adamant.

Also there was someone else living up there on the ridge, and on two occasions he had seen the man as well.

'Someone else?' asked the Induna. Here was something the unumzane hadn't mentioned, but he soon realised why. He was an old man, this other person, and deemed a little ukuhlanya, mad, not quite right in the head, explains the wife. And, although they often ended up bickering like a married couple whenever they met, he supplemented the food brought to Dlali by women in the village with vegetables he managed to coax from the thin soil up there.

When they reached a fork in the path, the wife pointed to the cliff face that rose up before them. There – over there they could see the cavern where Dlali had lived. Pointing down the other path toward an impi of reeds, she explained that was where the pool was.

Aware of the need to be sensitive here, the Induna had suggested they first visit the cavern. They could see the pool well enough from up there – the elevation would, in fact, give them a better view. And, anyway, the old woman's body had been found in a depression among the rocks that formed the ridge. The implication, of course, was that this way he might not need to go anywhere near the sacred pool, although entitled to. The wife understood this and smiled gratefully.

They crossed the stream at a place where the fast-running water swirled around their ankles, and then tackled the trail leading up to the cavern. The wife hadn't been exaggerating when she had called it steep.

Now, a day later, the udibi's thighs and calves still feel a little stiff. Yes, he's used to walking long distances, but not at that gradient. He could see why the old lady had to be carried up and down the path, and he pitied those who had to do the carrying, no matter how frail and skinny the woman may have been.

Wood-framed panels created from woven reeds had been affixed in the opening of the cavern to protect its occupant from the elements. The dwelling was entered from the left, where there was a fire circle and some logs to sit on. While the udibi and the wife watched, the Induna went inside. The udibi could see gourds and pots hanging on the rear wall of the cavern. Keeping his head bowed, because the ceiling was low here, the Induna sniffed and reached into the pots and gourds in turn. It was from one of the pots that he withdrew a handful of white petals. Bringing his palm up to his nose, he smelt the petals, then dropped them back into the earthen ikhamba.

Stepping past the wife, the udibi could see even further into the abode. He watched the Induna lift the sleeping mat, which was now rolled up and standing upright. Then he peered into the large pot next to the mat, pulled out a few items of clothing, replaced them, and rejoined the wife and his udibi.

'Where was Dlali's body found?' he asked.

'I'll show you,' said the wife.

They followed her across sloping rock, fragments of stone breaking free under their feet, and through a break in the cliff, where there was a large donga surrounded by scree. Dlali had been found down there, lying on her back, impaled by a hunting spear.

Noting a quaver in the wife's voice, the Induna had said she could return to the village. He would report back to her later.

There was just one more thing, he said – where was this madman she had mentioned?

Over on the other side of the donga, said the wife. But they weren't to worry, because he'd find them soon enough.

The udibi stiffens as a lizard makes its appearance on a large chunk of rock about a metre away from him. It's a 25-centimetre-long Southern Rock Agama, its blue head fading to blend in with the grey stone. But to the boy watching its slow sinuous motion warily, its long, delicate toes seeming to bring it closer to the edge of the rock nearest to him, and with a thin dorsal crest running the length of its short, plump body, it's simply a miniature ingwenya – a small crocodile. And in common with other Zulus, the boy loathes crocodiles, and lizards.

371

Keeping his gaze upon the agama, the udibi lays his stick aside and bends sideways, his fingers scrabbling for pebbles lying at the base of the rock slab. When he has three or four, he transfers them to his left palm, selects one and throws it at the lizard. It bounces past the reptile's head and it flattens its body instantly. He throws a second stone aiming for just in front of the little ingwenya, in case it's thinking of charging at him. To his relief, the agama twists round and scurries in the opposite direction, its tail snaking behind it.

In Zulu, vicious criminals are called 'ingwenya'. And who but a vicious criminal would want to kill an old woman?

The son reckoned he knew, since he was pointing his arm and making a declaration almost before he had finished huffing and puffing his way up the path.

But first they met the madman. His dog preceded him, galloping over the crest of the donga to stand at the bottom, barking at them. When the boy made a stamping motion at the animal, the bark became a low growl. The Induna's hand came down on the udibi's shoulder. 'Do not taunt it,' he cautioned. 'Remain still.'

A short-coated blur of black and brown fur, medium-sized, well-muscled, almost stocky, being slightly longer than its height, the dog's of the grouping later to be known as Africanus – and it just wouldn't shut up.

Then there came a whistle and suddenly the inja, the dog, forgot about them; it turned, like that lizard just now, and trotted up the opposite slope of the donga to the crest, where a scrawny old man had made his appearance.

The Induna and the udibi watched in silence as the bow-legged old-timer came down the incline, the dog following sedately a few paces behind him.

'This was where I found her,' said the madman, without any preliminary greeting. He wore only a loincloth and a bead necklace.

'In the morning?' asked the Induna.

'Yes.'

'Why were you heading this way?'

'To bring her milk, of course,' said the man, not bothering to hide his irritation at what he considered a stupid question.

'This you did every morning?'

'Yes.' The word uttered curtly, almost as a snarl.

Then he seemed to relent, the memory softening his features, as he told them how he knew something was wrong when his dog came running back to him. Usually he would race ahead and wait for his master to catch up, for Dlali inevitably had a hand-ful of porridge ready for the animal.

The dog may seem vicious to them, but he only barks at – or attacks – strangers, added the madman. In fact . . .

'In fact?' asked the Induna.

'Ever since we saw the White Man . . . you know about him?'

The Induna nodded.

Well, ever since then, he'd taken to visiting her at dusk and leaving his dog with Dlali for protection. But that night the dog had stayed at home with him, because he had found jackal tracks earlier and had sat up with the dog to keep an eye on his cattle kraal, one of his cows having just given birth.

'Did you hear anything?'

No, said the madman, explaining that his homestead is too far away. And – indicating the ground as if Dlali still lay there – he added that it had been too far for her, too.

The Induna nodded, whereupon it took the udibi a while to realise both men were agreeing that Dlali had been fleeing her

373

attacker, and hurrying in the direction of the old-timer's home-stead.

'And no one knew the dog wouldn't be with her that evening?'
The madman shook his head. 'No one.'

'Aha! I see you have found the old crocodile!' The Induna and
the boy turned as the dog sped off in the direction of the
newcomer, barking excitedly.

The man stopped, raising his arms. He was wearing amashoba
and carrying an iwisa, and even the udibi had no trouble work-ing out that this was Dlali's son at last making his appearance.

'Get this animal away from me!' he demanded with a faintly
feminine shriek. 'Get it away,' he repeated, as the dog sank into
a hunter's crouch before him, growling.

The madman hesitated a moment as though giving the Induna
and the boy a little while longer to enjoy this sight of a tall man
wearing amashoba – which were meant to make the wearer more
imposing – quivering before a mere dog and not even able to
raise his iwisa in defence. Then the madman whistled twice, and
the dog returned to lie next to him.

'Bash that creature's brains out, then take his owner before
Shaka!' snarled the newcomer, pointing his iwisa at the madman.

'And you are . . . ?' inquired the Induna.

'The son whose mother that man murdered.'

'That man' responded by growling just like his dog, then hawk-ing a gobbet of spit to one side.

'He killed her!' insisted the son. 'He wouldn't leave her alone,
so she was always complaining about him – and when he got sick
of her spurning his advances he killed her!'

The Induna laid a hand on his shoulder in order to get him
turned around. 'You stay there,' he told the madman. Followed
by the udibi he led the son back towards the cavern.

'These are serious allegations,' he warned.

'And I stand by them,' said the son, squaring his shoulders. 'I stand by them.'

'How often did you visit your mother?'

The son frowned, puffed out his cheeks, exhaled before declaring that he visited her every second or third day on average.

'And she confided in you, and told you that this . . . ?'

'Murderous madman!'

'That he was bothering her?'

The son nodded vigorously. 'Indeed. They knew each other when she was much younger, and he's been infatuated with her ever since.'

'What about the White Man?'

'What White Man?' asked the son, drawing back imperceptibly.

'The one she saw lurking about the pool.'

A frown. She had never told him about any White Man. But that's not surprising, he added. She would more likely have reported anything like that to the unumzane's main wife.

The Induna nodded.

'But how can you even suspect anyone else, since it was him?' insisted the son, pointing past the Induna in the direction of the donga. 'He killed her, Shadow of Shaka! Ask anyone! He's mad, possessed. Why else do you think he lives all the way out here?'

Nonetheless, explained the Induna, they must consider all possibilities. One of these was that bandits may have decided that, since she was the guardian of Nomkhubula's pool, Dlali may have had valuable relics stored in her abode. Would the son mind stepping into the cavern? Since he visited his mother so often, he was likely to spot if anything was missing.

Mumbling that this was a waste of time, the son obeyed, the Induna following him in and moving to the side so as not to block any light coming through the entrance.

Less than a minute later, the son stepped out again, shaking his head. Nothing was missing, as far as he could tell.

'Very well, then,' said the Induna, 'let us go and confront the one who killed your mother.'

'Hai!' whispered the son. 'But be careful of that dog.'

Ignoring this, the Induna led the way back to where the madman and his inja waited, with the udibi following them behind the son.

The dog started barking again and the son quickened his pace so that he was almost tripping over the Induna's heels in his efforts to keep the warrior in front of him as a shield.

'Shut him up,' ordered the Induna.

The madman leant over his dog, muttered a few words, and the inja fell silent.

Looking to his right and seeing that the son was all but clinging to him, and even trying to hide behind him, the Induna gently pressed his palm against the son's ribcage and stepped away from him at the same time.

He then extended his left arm, twisted his wrist, unclenched his fist, and the udibi watched as a handful of white petals fluttered down into the long grass like dying moths. Then he noted the confusion on the son's face ... well, that wasn't surprising, as the udibi too was a little perplexed by the Induna's action. What *was* interesting was the shrewd look with which the madman was observing the Induna with his eyes narrowed and with what might be the beginnings of a smile teasing his lips.

'I found these here,' the Induna explained to the son. 'See

how dried up they are, unlike . . .' The son was still in mid-shrug as the Induna ducked down and plucked something off one of the tall man's leggings.

'Unlike this one, which is still fresh.'

Glancing down, then looking up at the Induna, the son shrugged again. 'I don't understand, Nduna.'

'These come from a tree which doesn't grow around here,' said the Induna. 'In fact, the only place you find these trees, and these petals, is along the river that runs past your homestead.'

'My . . . my kraal?' stammered the son.

'Your kraal.'

'How dare you!' said the son, channelling the force of his indignation into his hands and pushing the Induna aside. Then he turned abruptly and crashed straight into the udibi. Although taken by surprise, the boy threw his arms around whatever he could as the man tried to barge through him. As it was, he managed to cling to one of the son's long legs. It was enough to bring the man toppling down – and then the dog was leaping through the air.

It wasn't a pretty sight, decides the udibi, noting how the shadows across the way have retreated. They must leave now. He too can't wait to get home and see Kani. She'll make an agreeable fuss over him – for, along with Pampata, she's the only female he allows such a liberty. Not even the memory of the dog will deter him from enjoying Kani's treats.

Aiee! But it was terrible – the way the dog went for the back of the son's neck. Then, as the man rolled over trying to throw the animal off him, the dog was at his throat before he could do anything to resist. Blood squirting everywhere, the son tossed and turned, but the inja clung on, and it was as if the man had suddenly grown another physical appendage.

And neither the madman nor the Induna did anything to prevent this. And the udibi clambered up the side of the donga to get away from the blood.

It was only after the son had stopped struggling that the Induna told the madman to call off the dog. Which obeyed promptly as if, having brought down his prey, he had discovered the animal's meat was off.

The Induna poked the son with a foot. But even the udibi could see that there was a limpness about the body that confirmed the man was dead.

The madman was on his haunches, petting his dog. 'You saved him,' he said.

The boy stared at him, bewildered by this observation, then looked at the Induna, who was nodding.

'Because who knows what terrors he might have endured had he been turned over to the women.'

'This is true,' said the Induna.

The udibi stands, arches his back, stretches and yawns. Their baggage is packed and ready. But he must piss. Keeping an eye open for any other lizards, he moves a few metres away.

It was late afternoon and before the sun set the Induna had ascertained the son really did pass through the village every two or three days, and this habit had only started two months ago – about the time the White Man had first been spotted. Had he already been planning to murder his mother even then? Despite all he had witnessed while serving as the Induna's udibi, that thought made the boy shudder.

'But he couldn't arrive, show himself and leave, therefore he had to stay a while. So what did he do?' wondered the unumzane's head wife, when they reported back to her.

The Induna had chuckled. 'I think you know the answer to that.'

After a moment's thought, she nodded. And, with her help, the Induna soon tracked down the girl the son had visited whenever he came to the village.

As for the headman, he wore a look of bewilderment through all of this. And the udibi knew how he felt.

'Hai, if I had been there and that crocodile had told me how dutiful he was, by visiting his mother regularly, I would have known instantly he was lying. And then I would have wondered why. But you . . . how did you know he was the killer?' asked the wife, as they took their leave of her.

The Induna had merely shrugged and said the son had made it easy for him, by attempting to flee when accused of murdering his mother.

But that was — is — only a sip from the bowl of *How?*

As is the business with the petals. How did the Induna know to take a handful from the bowl in the old woman's dwelling and play that trick on her son?

And when the madman had shaken his head and said Dlali collected those flowers and dried their petals for their scent, and they were to be found everywhere, the Induna had merely smiled.

How did he know?

How!

'So, little one, have you solved the conundrum?' asks the Induna, when the boy returns. The warrior has roused himself and is busy gathering their baggage.

The boy's grin is now wider than the Thukela River where it meets the sea.

'Is that a yes?'

The udibi nods and calmly begins picking up the items he is to carry.

The Induna laughs. 'Aiee, truly, you have clearly learnt from Mgobozi how to tell a story! Come now, enough suspense! Speak up.'

'It was the dog,' says the boy, straightening.

The Induna's grin mirrors the udibi's. 'And why do you say that?'

The madman had told them the dog only barked at − and attacked − strangers. If the son really had been visiting his mother as often as he claimed he had, he wouldn't be a stranger to that dog. Yet the dog had barked at him when he arrived.

'Well done!' says the Induna as they set off. 'Of course, he could have then said he had been lying about visiting his mother because he didn't want the maiden's father to discover what he was doing to his daughter.'

'But instead he tried to flee.'

'And so turned suspicion into certainty.'

★

They had spent that night at the village; then, the following morning, had climbed up the steep path again to take their leave of the madman.

'I hope you are not too saddened by her passing,' the Induna had said, after quizzing the old-timer about the White Man's appearance, until he had a good idea of who that man was.

'Aiee!' replied the madman. 'You should have seen Dlali in her young days. I was merely one of many admirers, but one she favoured a little more than others. But my father couldn't afford the lobolo, so she married someone else.'

At least they had been able to make up for lost time during these past few seasons, noted the Induna.

'That is so. And she really was something special.' The madman sighed, then continued: 'But so was the guardian before her, and I am sure I'll be able to say the same of the one they send to replace her.'

The Induna had chuckled over that thought for the rest of the day.

'You are ready?' Mzilikazi asked him, on the night before his departure.

The Induna nodded. He had been with his old friend long enough for his wounds to start to heal and there was the promise he had made to Shaka; so he had to get back and see what was happening.

'I will not bother telling you that you're free to stay,' said Mzilikazi, 'for I have seen your eagerness to return growing day by day. But I will remind you that you'll always have a place with us. We could have great times side by side.'

'I thank you for the offer,' said the Induna.

'But you must now get back.'

The Induna nodded. Back to despondency and pessimism; to dismal, doleful days. But days when a bilious King needed loyal men, even if he himself didn't realise it, and instead seemed to find lassitude and ill-temper better allies.

And then there was the promise he had made to Shaka.

The two men said goodbye early the following morning. Husbanding his strength, but keeping up a brisk pace, it took the Induna four days to reach and then cross Ukhahlamba, the Barrier of Spears – the thousand-kilometre-long basalt and sandstone mountain range the Sothos called Maluti and which the White Men would name the Drakensberg. Moving from the freezing upper slopes, with their lichen-spotted rocks and cycads, to the silver proteas and bracken ferns of the lower sandstone regions where the Ancient Ones have left their spirits in hidden caves, he saw plumes of smoke in the distance.

The gradient was still steep, the paths treacherous, and he had to continually tell himself to stop trying to rush. But the call of those black columns, as straight as the trunks of giant tambotis, made your feet more

reckless, turned your heart into a beating drum. Then he was sprawl-
ing, suddenly launched forward, his arms out in front of him, his spear
clattering away. He had chosen not to carry a shield, knowing that
climbing would be involved, and even the bedroll tied diagonally across
his body – supplies and sleeping mat wrapped in a wildebeest cloak –
had proven a hindrance on occasion. But now it cushioned the impact of
the rugose stone slab that leapt up to scrape the skin off his palms and
knees.

Winded and surprised as he was, he immediately rolled on to his side,
expecting an attack from the rear. Because . . . because it was as if he had
been deliberately tripped. His left ankle was already starting to throb, and
he could feel the narrow ghost of a leather cord there. He sat up. To his
left were only bushes; to his right, a short steep slope of spear grass, and
then the precipice of an echoing gorge. He examined the path, the place
where he had seemed to trip, but saw nothing suspicious there.

As he stood, the flash of instinct had already passed and the pain was
beginning to make its presence felt. In his knees, his palms, even his chin.
Testing his teeth, feeling a bit woozy, he backed towards the bushes. A
rustle of leaves, the flaring of instinct once more, had him raising his hands
– but it was too late. The noose was already around his neck, and the
rustling increased as his assailant pulled backwards, tightening the loop.

Then a figure came crashing through the silver sugarbushes to his left
and swerved toward him. A child, not more than seven summers old, but
swinging an iwisa with all his might. As the rawhide cut into his throat,
the Induna raised his left hand and caught the round knob at the end of
the stick, receiving a loud thwack that stung his raw palm. What with
that and the loop constricting his larynx, he didn't notice a second assailant
coming at him from the right until it was too late. He tried to kick out,
but it was a weak attempt, ignored by the youth as he twisted his shoulders and buried first one, then the other fist into the Induna's solar plexus.

As the warrior folded forward, the man hidden in the bushes released *the loop, allowing the Induna to drop on to his knees. At which the child, having retrieved his iwisa, swung the stick with a mighty, teeth-pressed-into-his-lower-lip blow that hit the Induna on the side of the head, and knocked him sideways into unconsciousness.*

# The Adventure Of The Perturbed Prince

'I am sorely perturbed,' says Mhlangana.

Although the prince is trying to hide it, stroking the back of one of his bulls, the Induna can see he's more than just that. *Much* more.

The bull is impofu, or an 'eland', which is to say its dusty colouring and white legs resemble the markings of that breed of antelope.

Mhlangana disappears from the Induna's sight as he leans sideways to check something on the animal's hindquarters.

Straightening up, still keeping his eyes on the bull, he says: 'I know it's up to my brother—'

'The King,' interjects the Induna levelly.

'Yes, yes, the King,' snaps Mhlangana, unable to hide his irritation despite the fact he clearly wants to ask a favour of the Induna.

'I know the King,' continues the prince, 'is the one who . . .' His lips curl, his hands flail, as he searches for the right words. 'Who sends you out on these special errands.'

'He is the one who grants me the power to serve as his emissary, his Shadow who speaks and acts with his authority,' says the Induna, not liking Mhlangana's tone of voice, the way he has contrived to imply those errands are merely paltry tasks dreamed up by a lazy ruler with far too much time on his hands.

'Quite,' says Mhlangana with a rictus of a smile.

The bull snorts, flicks its tail at some flies.

'However, I am sure that, given what I'm about to tell you, he'll agree I'm in a situation that is extremely . . .'

Mhlangana strokes the bull's hide, as though seeking the right word there.

'Perturbing?'

Mhlangana looks up. 'I was going to say serious, Nduna.'

'Ah!'

'And,' continues the prince, like a man carefully picking his way past mounds of dung, 'therefore . . . therefore I think, were he not in retreat and I was able to discuss the facts of the matter directly with him, he'd suggest I seek your assistance, Nduna. Not least because he knows you'll agree with us – with me and the King, I mean – that this matter is most . . .' The words fade as Mhlangana takes a breath.

'Serious?' suggests the Induna.

'Perturbing,' counters the prince, allowing his true feelings to show for a moment as he suppresses a shudder. 'Most perturbing.'

The Induna waits for the prince to continue. But the latter just stands behind the bull, chewing the inside of his cheek as if the Induna has offered the beast for sale and Mhlangana is wondering whether the asking price is fair.

'I have consulted Mbopa,' he says at last.

Well, he would have had to if he wanted to get an audience with the King – not that Shaka has been seeing anyone at all these days.

'Without informing him of the details, of course. I think that, at this stage, given the uncertainty that blights the kingdom, the fewer individuals who know what's happened the better. But Mbopa indicated to me that he had no pressing, er . . .'

'Errands?' says the Induna.

'Yes, well, the point is he said I was . . . it was possible to ask you to . . .'

'Run an errand for you?'

'Hai, no, Nduna, this is something far more important. Far more . . .'

'Perturbing?'

'Serious! You see, Nduna, someone has tried to kill me.' The prince taps the bull's head and beckons to a herd boy to take the animal away.

'In fact,' he murmurs, moving closer to the Induna, 'one might say this, er, assassin has succeeded in a way.'

*

Every member of the Zulu nobility has a place of retreat, a dela innyoni, the King and the princes having more than one. It will be a small homestead comprising no more than five huts, kept habitable by a few servants, and a place where one can go, often accompanied by a sangoma, to meditate and commune with the ancestors. In truth, though, many are used for drunken parties.

The retreat Shaka possesses closest to KwaBulawayo is at KwaDukuza. The kraal where someone had attempted to take Mhlangana's life is even closer to the capital. Like the other princes, he has his own quarters at the capital. If Shaka were to fall ill or be threatened by elements within his own court, Mhlangana would want to be on the scene. If, on the other hand, things become a little too hot and Shaka starts hunting down those he believes are plotting against him, the retreat is a handy place to have as it enables Mhlangana to do just that. He can retreat, but not so far away he can't exploit a power vacuum, or some long-hoped-for calamity involving his brother.

But these are considerations to be mulled over and discussed with the udibi (who now is no longer his udibi) after they've gone to find out what's rattled Mhlangana so greatly.

Mthunzi has long ago recovered from the wound he'd received at the hands of the one who had tried to kill the King, and is still in the Induna's service, although far too old to still be an udibi. The return to their former footing had been ordered by Shaka himself at the time of that fateful First Fruits and this order has yet to be rescinded.

★

Mhlangana claims the murderer had been successful because, although he was at Bulawayo at the time, one of his servants, who had chosen to sleep in his master's hut, had been attacked instead. In other words, even though he had had no intention of visiting this dela innyoni in the foreseeable future, he felt it could just as easily have been he who was killed.

'It seems to me,' says the Induna as they make their way to the kraal, 'that either someone has something against this man, and therefore the prince need only concern himself about the discipline of his servants in future . . .'

'Or,' suggests the udibi, 'someone is issuing a warning to the prince, saying I can get at you anywhere.'

'And therefore the prince had better watch out.'

'And therefore has much to be seriously *perturbed* about.'

The Induna chuckles, for he has told Mthunzi all about his encounter with Mhlangana that same morning. Then he grows serious. 'Why do I think that the latter possibility is more likely?'

'Putting aside the prince's nature?' asks Mthunzi, for they are alone now and can speak freely.

The Induna nods.

'Well, there's the manner in which the warning was issued,' says the udibi. 'Aiee! A murdered man forced to wait for his murder to run its course . . . This is not something I am looking forward to.'

★

Oblivious to the expectant faces, the old general falls silent, remembering . . .

Remembering how relieved he had been to hear that he and the Induna had received an assignment that would take them away from Bulawayo for a few days. Of course, that was before he had heard the details, but even then . . .

He chuckles to himself. Even then, if given the choice, he'd have still gone with the Induna. Because the atmosphere at the capital had been as stifling as the smoke from a veld fire, with gossip flaring here, rumours leaping there. You knew how these things worked, for you had seen it many times before; and the Induna had told you often enough how you had to look beyond the words themselves for the story beneath the whispers and the gasps, the adjectives and adverbs – and how, often, there was nothing there. But, with Shaka skulking in his hut, these were times when anything could be possible. Anything could be true.

Yes, and see what then happened . . .

'General . . . ?' It's Hawk, tentatively trying to draw him out of his reverie.

His eyes return to the present and he looks expectantly at the young officer.

'You are teasing us, General,' says Hawk.

A chorus of voices concur with him, but it's Fanele, the Cheetah, who takes up the thread. 'What do you mean, General, when you speak of a murdered man who is still being murdered? A dead man who yet lives – aiee, that's a zombie!'

He is brave for even mentioning the word aloud, and knows it. And he will probably make a fine brutal officer, this one, sending his men in against impossible odds, obeying his orders as much to impress his superiors as because it's his duty. If promoted further, he'll probably make a fine brutal general, capable of coldly calculated strategies that will get the job done, no matter the cost in lives. That's if he gets that far and his own men don't kill him first . . .

Zamo laughs. Surely his rival is being far too melodramatic. It could be that the man had been severely wounded, he continues, ignoring Cheetah's scowl, and was still clinging to life.

The general holds up a hand. 'There was no zombie,' he tells Cheetah. 'And you are almost, but not quite, right,' he tells Zamo. 'As you will see, madoda, if you allow me to continue . . .'

★

'He is dead,' says the inyanga.

'Yet he lives,' replies the Induna.

'In a way.'

'You are not making sense.'

'I haven't seen the like before, Shadow of Shaka, and so I have sent for my father.'

'He has been murdered, yet he lives,' murmurs the Induna. Has the man been given a slow-acting poison, then?

'There's no poison.'

'You are certain?'

The inyanga nods. 'You will see what I mean,' he continues as he ushers the Induna and the boy into the hut.

The servant who chose to spend the night in his master's indlu has been left as he was found – lying on the prince's sleeping mat. A fire has been built in the centre of the hut, to better illuminate the interior. The man lies sweating, his head resting on an umcamelo, or wooden pillow. A maiden is on her knees beside him, mopping his brow with a strip of folded cloth, which she continually dips into a pot of water.

'His daughter,' whispers the inyanga in response to the Induna's questioning glance.

Hearing him, the girl turns. 'You must save him, Shadow of Shaka. You must!'

The Induna steps over to examine the man, the miasma of shit and piss around him growing thicker. The man is naked save for his penis sheath, and there's no sign of a wound. But more of the cloth the White Men have introduced to the Zulus has been placed between his legs.

'M-master . . .' says the man, breathing heavily. 'M-master, I meant no . . . no harm.' Panting like a tired dog, he seems to shrink, as if receding into his pain.

His daughter continues, anger obvious in her voice. 'He was doing his duty! He had seen someone . . .' glancing at her father, '*something* moving through the bushes . . .'

'Where?' interrupts the Induna.

'I know where,' says the inyanga. 'He told me about it, and I went with him to seek spoor.'

'When was this?'

Two days ago, says the inyanga, looking to the maiden for confirmation. She nods.

The inyanga is to show the Mthunzi the place where the servant thought he saw someone, then return here, says the Induna.

'He was only trying to protect the prince's hut,' continues the daughter after the other two have left. 'Trying to protect the prince himself!'

The Induna nods. The hut would have been cleansed after the prince's departure, both literally and with a ritual that involves burning a special kind of green wood that fills the hut with thick, fragrant smoke believed to remove remnants of the prince's spirit that have slipped away from him while he slept – which is a vulnerable time for any man. But, if he had enough time, an enemy sangoma might be able to find personal items, including bits of the prince's hair and other forms of 'body dirt' he can use in a muthi concocted to bring Mhlangana low.

But, if enough time was what he sought, why not simply throttle the servant while he slept; or direct one of his apprentices to kill the man?

Anyway, there were easier ways to acquire the kinds of 'sample' he'd need – and in greater quantities too.

And what exactly did he do to the servant?

As if in answer to this silent question, the interior of the hut darkens as an elderly man ducks through the entrance. As betokens his age, his umutsha reaches his knees and the front is decorated with a cataract of genet, blue wildebeest and zebra tails. A python skeleton, the vertebrae carefully strung together, hangs around his neck, amid a series of leather pouches of various sizes. Bronze amasondo are wrapped around his upper arms.

He bows his head in greeting. He is Bubele, the father, he explains. He has told his son, who was his apprentice until the last full moon and still lacks experience in these matters, to remain outside with the udibi. He hopes he hasn't been presumptuous. The Induna shakes his head; much time has passed since the intruder was spotted and two sets of eyes will be better than one when it comes to seeking any tracks that might still be there.

The older inyanga bows his head again. If the Induna will be so kind as to light a firebrand, he will examine the ailing man.

The Induna obeys, standing over the greybeard as he crouches next to the man's waist and carefully removes the bundle of cloth. It's dark blue, but darker patches are clearly visible. Bubele places the cloth aside and shuffles over to the man's feet, and raises a hand to indicate to the Induna that he must remain where he is.

'What is your name, Brother?' asks the inyanga, raising his voice.

The man's daughter answers for him: 'Eqa.'

'Eqa? Can you hear me?'

Eqa nods.

'The Shadow of Shaka here wishes to ask you some questions. Attend him well.'

Puzzled, the Induna looks at the inyanga, who tilts his chin in a brief gesture, indicating *Go on*.

'Were you woken up?' asks the Induna.

Eqa's fingers brush his daughter's arm and she leans forward as he mumbles something.

'He says yes,' she tells the Induna.

'Was he attacked? How did they stop him from struggling?'

The daughter leans forward again, then straightens. 'He was held fast and some kind of muthi was forced down his throat.'

'I don't suppose he recognised his assailants . . .'

'He has already told me he didn't recognise them, but knows he was held down by two women.'

'Women? Is he sure?'

Eqa touches his daughter's arm again and starts to murmur something. Then he screams, stiffens, and the daughter jerks away from him. Even the Induna gets a fright. Bubele has pulled the man's legs apart.

'What have you done?' shrieks the daughter, before trying to calm her sobbing father.

Bubele rises to his feet. 'It was better to take him by surprise and do it fast,' he murmurs to the Induna, who nods in understanding.

'And now let us see what we can see,' continues the inyanga, with a sigh. As the Induna leans over him with the torch, he drops on to his knees between Eqa's legs.

★

Although commonly used as a euphemism for the sex organs, the groin in fact consists of the two creases on either side of the pubic area. The aorta, the body's main artery, leaves the heart's left ventricle and rises towards the neck, where the carotid arteries branch off; then it goes downwards through the abdomen towards the groin. Here, it splits into a left and right femoral artery, each of which runs through its own side of the groin, then down into the thighs.

However, one need not know all of this to understand what has been done to Eqa. All one has to know is that a fast-flowing river runs through either side of the groin; a river always in flood. And interrupting the course of this river – offering it a chance to leave the body, say – will result in a tidal bore that will literally drain all the redness out of the body.

'Think of what happens when you cut someone's throat,' suggests Bubele.

'Then why not just do that – cut the man's throat and have done with it?'

The inyanga shrugs, says that's for the Induna to divine.

They have left the hut so the inyanga can deliver his diagnosis away from the daughter's ears.

'I believe Eqa knows more about this matter than he's told us,' murmurs the Induna.

'What makes you say that?'

'He is clearly in much pain, yet seems resigned to his fate.' He is not a man dying from a disease or some other natural cause; this isn't an expected end. He's been viciously attacked, but shows no anger, no desire to see the malefactors hunted down and caught.

'But you haven't finished telling me what was done to this man,' continues the Induna. 'You spoke of two rivers . . .' he prompts.

394

Two dangerous rivers, adds Bubele. And they're easily palpated, felt with the fingers, these fast-flowing dangerous rivers. And slender metal spikes, with flattened heads probably no longer than a man's first finger, have been pressed into the veins. He has counted two on each side of the groin, and there may be more, but it's not worth causing Eqa more pain to check. Bubele's seen all he needs to see.

The Induna still doesn't understand, though. Why not simply remove the spikes?

Bubele chuckles mirthlessly. 'The river, Nduna, the river — it will burst its banks just as when you cut a throat. This is why my son has spoken of a man who has been murdered, yet lives.'

Blood is oozing from under the heads; keep the spikes in and you'll merely prolong the man's agony. And he will die, make no mistake about that, whether from infection or gradual loss of blood.

'Remove one or all the spikes . . .' muses the Induna.

'The river will burst its banks and death will come quicker,' says the inyanga, adding that Eqa will literally feel the blood, the very life, draining out of him.

'So the killer has left it up to us to finish what he's started.'

'And this is not the first time I've seen this done.' It had been many seasons ago; just before Shaka became King, in fact. A wealthy man was the victim.

'Was the killer caught?' asks the Induna.

No, says the inyanga. It was as if everyone, his eldest sons and senior wives, his body servants and other members of his household, all had had their tongues stolen.

'I was called in merely to ascertain if the man could be saved, but I suspected they knew the answer to that question already.'

'Who removed the spikes?'

'I don't know, Shadow of Shaka, for I was sent away as soon as I had delivered my diagnosis. It was subsequently put about that the man had died of a disease. But this I can tell you, Nduna – few mourned his passing. He was known to be a vicious, heartless man, who was himself suspected of several murders.'

*And how many will mourn the passing of Mhlangana?* wonders the Induna. Aloud, he says: 'This was a warning, a threat.' He hesitates a moment, watching as Mthunzi and Bubele's son approach them. 'No,' he murmurs, 'it's more than that – it's a promise.'

The inyanga holds up his hands. 'I have told you all I know, Shadow of Shaka. And, given where we are, perhaps I have already said too much.'

Where they are is one of Mhlangana's retreats – and Mhlangana is a man you want to avoid.

The Induna asks Mthunzi if they found anything. The udibi shakes his head. Too much time has passed. Have they discovered what ails the man, he asks in turn.

They'll discuss it later, the Induna replies. Meanwhile, the boy is to help the younger inyanga to gather up his possessions and both are to help the daughter collect hers, and then wait for the Induna and Bubele on the road.

'Do not worry,' the Induna tells Bubele as they head back to the hut. 'You have not been here and this conversation hasn't taken place. Besides,' he adds at the indlu's entrance, 'you have an onerous enough task to perform without having to worry about a certain prince's spite.'

★

'It is time, my sister,' he says gently. 'You must say goodbye.'

'No!' says the daughter. 'You are the Shadow of Shaka, you must be able to do something.'

'Yes, I can,' says the Induna crouching next to her. 'I can see that his suffering is brought to an end.'

'No!' A wail, trembling lips, tear-stained cheeks.

'Listen . . . listen to him, little one,' whispers Eqa.

The Induna says he will give them a few moments alone together, then he leaves the hut.

Outside, Bubele has asked his son and the udibi to fill the biggest pot of water they can find before they leave.

Then he and the Induna squat on their haunches, resting their backs against one of the other huts.

The warrior waits until the pot of water has been filled and carried over to them before he stands up.

Holding her hand, he leads the daughter out of the hut and places her in the care of the youngsters.

When they have at last helped the weeping girl to collect her most precious possessions, and the three have left the settlement, the Induna motions Bubele to enter the hut with him again.

'Are you ready?' asks the Induna. He has relit the torch, and holds it over the servant so he can see Eqa's glistening face. 'I ask you this because I think there is something you still haven't told me.'

Eqa coughs, then manages to raise his left hand to beckon the Induna closer.

Handing the torch to Bubele, the warrior kneels beside the servant, but can't make out what the man is trying to tell him.

'What?' he asks, leaning forward so that his right ear is all but touching Eqa's lips.

'General . . .' whispers Eqa.

The Induna frowns, thinking the man is delirious and has forgotten his rank.

But then Eqa tries again: 'I. Know. Who. Did. This,' he says, his breath rancid in the Induna's ear. 'I know,' he repeats.

'Who?' asks the Induna. 'Who did this?'

'He's back.' Eqa coughs. 'Back.'

'Who?'

'General Hlakanyana! He's back!'

'Who is this general?'

'I think he's unconscious, Nduna,' interrupts Bubele.

The Induna straightens, stands. 'Did you hear any of that?'

'No, and I'm not sorry,' says Bubele, handing the torch to the Induna.

He can extinguish it and leave, because things will get messy now.

★

A short while later, the inyanga emerges from the hut, as bloody as a new-born calf.

'It is done?' asks the Induna.

'It is done.'

After he's washed himself as best he can, using the water in the pot, they leave the kraal. Let Mhlangana send his own men to bury Eqa, then collapse the hut and clean up the place if he so desires; but the Induna reckons the kraal should be left to nature and the scavengers.

After they've said goodbye to Bubele and his son, the Induna fills Mthunzi in on what the inyanga told him – and what Eqa had said.

'Hlakanyana? Like in the children's tale?' asks the udibi.

The Induna shrugs. He'll have to ask Mhlangana, although he doubts he'll get a straight answer from the prince – who can be counted upon to muddy the waters even when there's no reason to.

He never gets the chance, though. They come upon not one but two villages that have had cattle 'requisitioned' by Mhlangana's men. It's a practice the Induna knows Shaka disapproves of, as it's a sure way to encourage internal dissent. And, angrier than the boy's ever seen him, the Induna resolves to take up the matter with the regiment involved, who he realises would not have shown such flagrant disregard for Shaka's law without Mhlangana's tacit encouragement. Consequently, helping the prince track down this General Hlakanyana is the last thing on his mind.

Besides, when they return to KwaBulawayo, they learn some-one has tried to poison Mbopa, and the atmosphere has become even more stultifying in a world growing ever more awry, ever more giddy.

★

The old general falls silent, his thoughts lost in the past. Some of the others might be thinking *Is that it? A story with no ending?* but all of the young officers stay quiet; there is no fidgeting, no shifting of buttocks to seek a more comfortable position, no side-ways glance to see how one's neighbour is reacting to this. The general's introspection is palpable, like the wind pushing against one just as one nears the summit of a mountain. And even the dimmest of the young men there realise they are close to a reve-lation of sorts; the kind that comes when, after a long trek, one finally looks down upon a verdant valley one has heard about, but is only now seeing for oneself. The general's tales have created the trail, and now suddenly they're at the destination; or, at the very least, are at the gates of the city he's been leading them to. (Yes, just as the udibi and Njikiza and the others, worn out from travelling night and day to get there as soon as possible, once stood at the gates of Bulawayo – and saw what they saw and knew they were witnessing the end of a great era.)

Now they're afraid a wrong word, or even an ill-judged movement will shatter this moment, this arrival, as surely as elesifazane shatters the crops. (For, unlike elendula, when the sky plays, and the thunder is a comforting rumble and the rain is soft, elesifazane is thunder that cracks, with forked lightning, the tongue of an angry woman, who speaks without thinking.)

Zamo finds his gaze drifting across the stream to where huts once stood, and where he had found the bones. Then he sneaks a quick look at the general. What is it about this place that he asked them to meet him here? What happened—?

Oddly enough, it's one of the quieter of the young officers who breaks the silence.

'It is time, is it not, General?' He pauses, giving the old man time to fumble through the years and finally focus on his face, before he continues. 'It is time you told us what happened.'

A chorus of agreement, with Cheetah straightening, squaring his shoulders, getting ready to take control. But the other officer ignores him, speaking over his *Yes, General* . . .

'We have heard the stories, General,' he continues. 'We have heard the rumours. We have listened to the praise-singers. But we have never spoken to one who was there or, rather, one who was so close to events.'

'Did Shaka survive?' interrupts another youngster. 'Was he rescued by Pampata and the nduna you served?'

'And how?' asks Hawk. 'How did they do it?'

'I know our question will take us into dark days,' continues the first officer, as if the other two haven't spoken. 'But look where we are now! Are *these* not dark days? And have we not faced terrible times before?'

The general nods slowly. He'd known this question would come up sooner or later, and these men can't tarry here much longer. And that's just it: those who asked him to talk to the nation's young officers might not like him going into too much detail about that final year, those last days – but these are *men*! They may not have taken the head ring yet and so are, strictly speaking, still 'boys', but that doesn't mean they're children. They will be leading other men into battle to defend the nation – so at least answer their questions.

The old general, who once served as udibi to one of Shaka's most famous indunas, nods again and says, very well, he will tell them of those days and speak of things he knows, and of things he doesn't know.

# PART FIVE

# *How The Induna Came To Keep His Word*

The last barricade had standing there a girl of eighteen
 winters,
The virgin of Moscow, flower of the snow . . .
She aroused the admiration of the very soldiers who, weep-
 ing, killed her:
What killing! All the houses shuttered,
The windows with heavy eyelids of plank in order not to
 see! –
And the Kremlin itself has closed its gates – that it may not
 see.
The youth of Moscow is dead!

From *The Secret of the Night*
by Gaston Leroux

The voltigeur bundled Paradis out of the way and sank his
bayonet into the neck of a grey mare. Fat Louis chopped
the bayonet in half with his cleaver. Two soldiers as scrawny
and vicious as wolves grabbed him from behind, calling him
a stinking civvy. He lashed out and they started fighting.
Paradis ran and hid behind the mound of glassy-eyed horses.
The soldiers and ambulance men were throwing entrails in

one another's faces, while one sly devil cut himself off a
piece and sank his fangs into the meat.

From *The Battle* by Patrick Rambaud
(translated by Will Hobson)

Their meal over, Kani looks around to make sure they are alone.

'What is it, Sister?' asks Pampata.

'I have something to discuss with you,' says Kani, settling down next to her friend.

'And clearly it's important,' says Pampata.

'That it is.'

'Well, then, Sister . . .'

'I miss my husband, although, as you know, I believe he will return in due course.' This is true, for a part of Kani knows that her husband is well. Of course, there's still fear, doubt, a constant heaviness in her stomach, an unsettled feeling – but something tells her that, wherever he is, he is well.

'Of course,' murmurs Pampata. 'But what is it that you want to tell me?'

Nonhlakanipho sighs. 'I miss my husband, but my longing doesn't distract me so much I can't see how badly things have deteriorated here.' In fact, it's as if having to come to terms with the Induna's disappearance forced her to retreat a while, and now she has returned and is able to review the situation with fresh eyes. It's like not having seen a niece or a nephew for several seasons, and then visiting your kin and seeing how they have shot up in height.

'And what do you see here?' asks Pampata.

'I see' – get to the point; stop wasting time – 'that you are in danger, Sister!'

'Speak you now of my beloved's moods?'

'Hai, no! I speak of danger from others!'

'Then whenever have I not been in danger? But I have my own impi, and they will protect me – as will the King's men.'

'And you can still tell who the King's men are?'

That silences Pampata a moment. Then she shakes her head. 'Be that as it may, my duty is to remain as close to my beloved as possible.'

'You will not consider moving to a safer place, then?'

'Of course not! And you, my sister, should know better than anyone that I will never desert Shaka, no matter how much his feelings might change towards me!'

Kani rises and moves to the perimeter of the orange glow laid down by the flames.

'I am sorry if my tone hurts or offends you, Sister, but you know . . . more than anyone else, you know how much he means to me,' continues Pampata.

'It's not that,' says Kani, staring out into the darkness, while steeling herself for uttering the lie.

A deep breath (this has to be done!); then she turns to face her friend. 'What if that is what he wants?'

'What who wants?' frowns Pampata.

'Shaka.'

Now Pampata rises. 'Shaka? What do you mean?'

'He sent for me,' whispers Kani, looking away.

'What?' The word is a shriek, Pampata grabs Kani by the elbows and shakes her friend. 'What do you mean he sent for you? You have seen him?'

Kani nods.

'How was he? Has he been eating? Why did he send for you? Did he say anything about me?'

Glad for the last question, as it means less invention, Kani says: 'He sent for me so as to discuss you.'

Pampata lets go of Kani's elbows. 'Me?'

Get it over with! 'He wanted to speak to me about persuading you to leave Bulawayo.'

'Leave?'

'And if you refused to be persuaded, he said I was tell you he orders it.'

Speaking fast, to overwhelm Pampata's protestations, Kani explains how Shaka has suggested Pampata and her most trusted ladies-in-waiting are to make for Pampata's dela innyoni, her retreat. There they are to retrieve certain gifts the King has given Pampata, and which might be used against both of them. They are then to make for the Induna's kraal, where Kani will be waiting.

'I will go ahead and prepare things,' she adds.

'But why?' wails Pampata. 'Why doesn't he want me here?'

'It's to keep you safe.'

'Cha! I can look after myself. He knows that!'

Kani reaches for Pampata's hands, squeezing them. 'But, my Sister, haven't you considered how that, with you safe, our Father will have one less thing to worry about?'

# 1
## The Fleeing Man

**September 8, 1828**

The Induna's dangling beneath a stout branch carried by two males, the older one somewhere behind his head and the young boy in front, at the lighter end, where his feet are. And just then the binding that ties his wrists to the branch snaps. The Induna's shoulders hit the path, and he just manages to turn his head aside to dodge the branch, as the man behind him drops it. As it is, it thumps against the Induna's sternum, but he manages to bring his knee up to deflect it as the youngster lets go of his end, too. The leather rope has been wrapped tightly around his wrists, cutting off the circulation and leaving his hands numb, but he has to move fast.

He'd been caught by an old trick. A rawhide cord is threaded through a hollow stick to create a loop; the loose ends are tied to a length of strong wood such as the kind used to make spear hafts. The strongest member of the gang hides in some bushes alongside a path, and the narrower the trail the better. As the quarry passes, the loop is then dropped over his head. It doesn't matter if the hollow stick breaks during any ensuing struggle, as it's merely there to make it easier to position the loop. The man then pulls on the other, shorter, length of wood, thus tightening the noose, while his confederates emerge from their hiding places to help subdue the victim. Child victims are favoured, as then accomplices aren't needed; the noose is simply tightened and the child is yanked into the undergrowth.

Cannibals! What are they doing back here? Starting in Senzangakhona's time, they have been ruthlessly hunted down.

Shaka finished the job, leaving the few remaining survivors to flee up north along with the other refugees.

He hears vague snatches of conversation, arguing mostly: about who's going to carry him, and who's going to get the heavy side, and why can't they just butcher him here and now. He is aware of coming around, now dangling from the thick branch, with his wrists feeling as if they're about to be ripped off his arms . . . then trying to reach the branch or at least gouge his fingertips into the bark to relieve the strain . . . trying and failing, and sagging back into pain and semi-consciousness. Then the cord snapping . . .

Got to move fast.

The others in the group have left just these two behind. Now they're bickering: *Can't you tie a knot properly? I never tied it. Well, what about cutting him . . . just a little . . . for just a little warm blood . . . How does that sound?* That's the younger one.

The older boy pushes him away, saying the old man will be angry. And then they might end up with nothing. *Nothing! How about that?* Sneering, chuckling, he squats alongside the Induna, produces an iklwa blade fixed on a haft just big enough for a man's hand to grasp.

'Hey!' he says, turning as, out of sheer frustration, the boy aims a kick at him. The Induna seizes his chance, clapping hands that feel like flippers against the side of the older boy's head. His palms slip through the sweat running down the youngster's jaws, but he still manages to hook his fingertips over his captor's ears, pulling hard.

As the cannibal passes over him, the Induna frees his right hand, slaps his palm against the boy's stomach and pushes upward to flip him over. Then he sits up, grabs the pole and pushes it forward, through the loop binding his feet. Raising his knees, and using them as a pivot, he sweeps the branch against the younger one's skinny legs, knocking him over.

*Where's the blade? There!* The Induna reaches for it, starts sawing at the leather holding his ankles together.

He looks up briefly – realises the older boy's scream has brought the others running.

Freeing himself, the Induna stands, knocks the older boy away with a right hook to the chin, watches as he totters backwards, loses his footing . . . Then he has to deal with the young one, who's only about ten summers old and as skinny as a bulrush, but isn't about to let that stop him. The Induna brings the heel of the fist clutching the blade down onto the back of the boy's head, just as the child shoulder-charges him.

Stepping aside to allow the boy to crash into the long grass, he sees that the other youth is clinging to the edge of the precipice only by his elbows. At least that's one of them out of action.

The Induna turns to face the others. There are seven of them in all.

Two are big boulder-shaped creatures, grasping long spears in their huge fists. (More giants, thinks the Induna wryly.) A third looks like an unfinished version of the first two – big as them, but obese, with visceral fat sagging over his hips and a pot belly topped by a series of dugs. Two are just children – a girl and boy – and there's another boy of about sixteen seasons old. All three younger ones are armed, the girl carrying an assegai that's longer than she is tall. The final member, preceding the others and castigating them for their cowardice, is a gnarled old man. With his slightly crooked limbs, his skin seemingly as grey as his hair, he has the air of an emaciated baboon about him.

What are cannibals doing around here? What has happened to make them think it is safe for them to return and revert to their old ways?

The boy comes back at him from the side. The Induna swivels and stabs the child in the side of his neck.

A screech from the girl. Her spear lowered, she makes as if to charge him, too, but a curt command from the old-timer sees the older boy restrain her.

While the child writhes and shrieks somewhere to his right and behind him, the Induna tightens his grip on the blade. Perhaps if he can grab the old man – he's clearly their leader – maybe that would make them back off, and let him through.

Then one of the pair of boulders bellows something. The Induna has his eyes fixed on the old-timer, so he doesn't notice the alarm rippling through the group. But he does see how his prey bridles almost imperceptibly, then grins at him and, his eyes still on the Induna, takes a step back, says something to his pack, and they turn, and run down the path that follows the gorge.

The Induna straightens. A frown. A puzzled glance at his blade. A look to his right. A look to his left – where the older boy remains hooked on his elbows, his eyes pleading, his face shining with sweat. A final look at the cannibals disappearing down the path.

*Huh?*

Then the Induna wheels round.

Men have appeared on the ridge overlooking the path and the gorge beyond. But they are not Zulus – he can see that from the shape of their shields, which are rectangular – and more keep appearing even as he watches.

*Not Zulus.* So it's best he follows his former captors.

But first . . .

He picks up the abandoned branch and approaches the youngster clutching the edge of the precipice. Proffering the end of the branch, the Induna moves it up and down, indicating that the youth should try and grab for it. The latter has seen the warriors silhouetted against the skyline and knows they don't have much time. With a look of relief, the youth grabs the limb with first one hand, then the other.

The Induna raises his end of the branch and pushes it out into space. Leaving the older boy's screams to reverberate through the gorge, he sets off after the cannibals. Who shouldn't be here.

A quick glance over his shoulder: neither should *they*. While the main body lingers on the ridge, their leader has sent a detachment of thirty or so men after them. Jogging through the long grass, zigzagging to miss the rocks and cycads and tree ferns, they're following a diagonal course that takes them parallel to the path, while also gradually bringing them closer to it.

The Induna knows he's going to have to be careful – dead ground and shallow drops lie in wait to suddenly cut the distance between yourself and them. As it is, the soldiers are now close enough for the Induna to identify them as Soshangane's men. (*Soshangane?*) But none of this deters the warrior from seizing his chance to rid the world of one of these freaks ahead of him as he draws closer to the first of the cannibals.

It's the obese one, who's a sweaty mass of heaving adipose, now running for all he's worth, with his head down, his arms pumping. The Induna arcs around him and, when he judges himself far enough ahead of the wobbling man to give the latter a chance to halt his lumbering, but not dodge him, he wheels. His belly swaying from side to side, his arms flailing, the fat man is already slowing as the Induna drives his blade into his gut, then spins aside to allow all that corpulence to continue on its way.

He uses this opportunity to check the position of his — their — pursuers. The main party is moving directly down the slope, towards the path, while the other thirty or so are drawing ever nearer through the grassland.

The Induna turns and increases his pace, leaping over the wailing fat man. Fortunately, the path is as hard as rock, and also free of roots or clumps of grass.

First the cannibals, now this . . . What are Soshangane's men doing here anyway?

Like Mzilikazi's Matebele, those who followed the former Ndwandwe general into the north-east have, through intermarriage and conquest, begun to acquire the status of a tribe — known as the Shangaans. Which is why Shaka decided it was time to bloody their noses, stopping their move back southwards from the coastal plains of Mozambique. Now it seems they must have retreated, leaving their Zulu attackers to die in that swampy region, then moved inland to come at Shaka from the high country to the north.

Even if this lot is a mere reconnaissance in force, it's still not good news.

★

He keeps to the same path, even though the Shangaan soldiers are clearly trying to cut him — them — off. Right now there's no other option, though; and he's got to assume the cannibals aren't about to let themselves get trapped either. And, indeed, as he rounds a bend, he sees he's caught up with the main group.

One of the big men is carrying the old-timer over his shoulder, while the young ones are up ahead, with the teenager leading the pack.

The Induna sees how the path splits, and the younger ones take the higher branch, the teenager hanging back now to wait for those bringing up the rear. The trail they have chosen follows a parapet of sandstone rocks, with a steep slope to the left. Although there isn't much space on either side, and a misjudged step is likely to see one sliding down the slope with nothing to halt one's momentum, the Induna reckons they've chosen that route because they know it's easier to navigate. And since the parapet encircles a promontory, this path might provide the only way around it, meaning their pursuers will be forced to steepen the angle of their descent in order to make for this juncture, thereby enabling their quarry to put more distance between them.

The Induna chooses the other branch, however, the one that drops down into the gorge. As he already suspected, water oozing from the rock face feeds moss along the stony surface, making the going perilous. In fact the path is soon worn away altogether, but that's fine by him. The river that's created the gorge is wider here, with an inlet catching the dripping water, and he's now low enough down the precipice's face to make feasible a leap into the stream. The water's clear, too, showing him the depth is sufficient. Without a second glance he hurls himself into space, using the strength in his thighs to propel him as far out from the cliff face as possible.

★

He rises, amid a spray of droplets, to hear shouts coming from up above. A quick glance in that direction and he thrusts himself against the current, moving further up the gorge to where two spiked rock formations provide him with cover, and also enable him to see what's happening on the other path.

Either the leader of the Shangaans is a clever – and prescient – bastard, and had sent a second contingent the long way round to intercept their quarry, or more likely a scouting party was already coming along the path to link up with the main body. Whichever the case, they run into the cannibals just as the path turns a tight corner, and the screams the Induna has heard were those of the children. Now, as he watches, the teenager is trying to hold the Shangaans off, but the narrowness of the path avails him little. The first Shangaan charges at him, using his shield to crowd the youth while, hot on his heels, the second man thrusts a long spear into the youngster's flank.

A shout and a loud splash announce the arrival of the first detachment sent after the cannibals. Try to peer too far around the rocks, and the Induna is likely to be spotted. So it's only when a body floats past him that he recognises it as one of the big men. Looking up again, he sees how the other huge fellow – the one still carrying the oldster – is backed up against the wounded teenager. Both men are harried by their assailants, with the youth fading fast. Finally, with a weak thrust of his spear, he topples sideways, rolls through the grass, and is only prevented from dropping into the pool by a pair of cycads.

That's it, then, for the man-boulder and the old-timer.

As the Induna sinks onto his knees, so only the upper part of his face is visible, he hears the greybeard shouting at the big man to jump – jump – jump! But there's no splash and the Induna can only assume the other prefers to take his chances with the Shangaans.

The Induna moves closer to the wall of the gorge, pressing himself against the rock beneath a slight overhang. The Shangaans will want to search the surrounding area for any survivors still in hiding. Fortunately, of course, there's no easy way to reach the foot of the gorge.

He waits.

# 2
## The Watchers In The Dark

**August 11, 1828**

Shaka's beloved has risen up and has her iklwa ready, before she identifies the figure approaching her. It's the Induna's wife, Nonhlakanipho.

'What are you doing here, dadewethu?' hisses Pampata, shooting a nervous glance at the royal hut.

Kani explains how Thenjiwe, Shaka's chief body servant, had come to her and told her that Pampata had gone to 'watch over the King'. And see, she continues, she has brought extra skins so that they can stay warm, as well as some beer.

Placing her iklwa aside, Pampata helps Kani with the load she's carrying. She's glad of the company; as brave as they might be, she couldn't let any of her serving girls accompany her here – for the fewer who know about this the better.

The women get themselves settled, sitting on one of the wildebeest cloaks and drawing the other over their knees. Four bonfires burn in front of Shaka's hut. Yet although they do a good job of illuminating the compound and the fence beyond, they make the entrance to the hut seem darker, and blacker than a mamba's mouth.

Pampata's chosen a position in one corner of the fence. To their left, about a metre in from the opposite corner, is the entrance to the isigodlo. However, between there and here there's a sizeable pile of ivory tusks. This not only hides the women, but any intruder will have to take a few paces into the compound before they can see them. This is partly, of course, why Pampata has chosen this spot. She wants a chance to recognise the intruder in the light of the bonfires, before making her presence known and running the risk of that person fleeing.

Being in the corner means they're over to the side of Shaka's ilawu, or private hut; something which, alas, is also an important consideration, as it means the King is unlikely to spot them should he choose to leave the hut. Given the mood Shaka's been in lately, his seeing them there could elicit any response from pride at Pampata's courage to accusations of treachery – does she too now watch his hut waiting for her chance?

Pampata has to grit her teeth to hold back the tears. He wouldn't even care why she was there . . . She recalls the horrifying message old Thenjiwe had brought her: no time to ask why, just pick up a spear and shield and go and be there for him, for Shaka. But, given his mood – this deepening pit falling further and further away from her, and from the others who are loyal to him – there's every chance none of that would matter if he's of a mind to blame her too for whatever had thrust him into that pit.

★

'Shhh!' says Mhlangana.

'Shhh!' echoes Nolaka, the Leopard Man.

Several paces ahead of them, Bamba turns and thinks of hurrying them along, but, given their destination, he's not sure he wants to get there.

Like him, Leopard Man and Mhlangana each carry a shield and spear, but unlike Bamba both are so drunk neither can walk straight.

'Shhh!' hisses Mhlangana as Leopard Man almost lurches into a hut.

The prince still has his finger pressed to his lips, when he himself kicks over two pots, making a noise loud enough to rouse the hut's occupant.

'Who's there?'

'Be still!' says Nolaka, louder than necessary. 'And mind your own business.'

Sniggering, and holding up a hand to quiet his induna – then handing Leopard Man his shield – Mhlangana crouches by the isicaba.

'Hsst!' he says imperiously, leaning on his spear for support. 'You are but having a bad dream! A bad dream,' he repeats with a snigger, his shoulder hitting the wicker door. 'Slaughter your best bull tomorrow!'

Spluttering as if this is the funniest thing he's ever heard, Leopard Man peels away in an attempt to silence his laughter.

'This is what the ancestors decree!' intones Mhlangana, toppling backwards on to his arse.

'Who's there? What's going on?' comes a voice from a neighbouring hut.

Resting his shield against the nearest indlu, Bamba dashes forward and pulls the prince to his feet.

Using this as a chance to keep hold of Mhlangana, Bamba hustles him along, relying on Leopard Man to follow them.

★

'Why are we here?' whispers Kani. She leans forward to look down the length of the fence, then straightens up. Thenjiwe had merely told her how Pampata had gone to the isigodlo. 'Where are the sentries?'

'That's why *we're* here,' replies Pampata.

'*What?*' A hiss.

'Someone has withdrawn the King's guards.'

Mouthing the word *What?* again, Kani looks around her, and tightens her grip on the iklwa that Pampata's given her.

'How can that happen?' she asks.

Pampata shrugs. Each regiment takes it in turns to provide sentries to watch over the King; but she doubts there's been a breakdown in communications, with someone having forgotten to summon the next regiment on the roster. Tonight the royal guard has failed to materialise for some reason that has to be ominous.

Besides . . .

'Whose regiment was supposed to be here, anyway?'

'Guess,' murmurs Shaka's beloved.

'Aiee!' whispers Kani.

★

When he's judged that they're far enough away from the place where they'd caused the disturbance, Bamba steps in front of Mhlangana, placing a hand on his chest. 'Please, Master,' he hisses. 'Please reconsider what you're about to do.'

'About to do?' asks Mhlangana. He lowers his head to regard Bamba's hand on his chest. '*About* to do?' he asks again, as Bamba drops his arm. 'You mean what I *am* going to do. *Am*, Bamba. Am!'

Leopard Man narrowly avoids bumping into the prince, and he returns to him the latter's shield.

'And here we see the Spotted Coward,' says the prince, his spear pointing at Bamba. 'Spotted' refers to the fact the induna's skin has lighter blotches on it here and there. 'He cowers at night, hides by day!'

'And, try as he might, he can't fly,' adds Leopard, swaying back and forth.

'Because that would scare him too.' Mhlangana lowers his iklwa and punches Bamba in the sternum. 'Now are you with us?' Placing a hand on Bamba's shoulder and pulling him closer: 'Are you?' A gentle head-butt: 'Are you? Or would you prefer to have the praise-singers in generations to come tell the world of how you bravely tried to save your King?'

Drunkenness should not be part of one's armoury in a matter of such import is all he's really trying to point out, but Bamba nods.

'Good!' says the prince. He pushes Bamba away. 'Now go' – a hiccough – 'and rec-rec-reconnoitre.'

Turning to Leopard: 'And you?'

An unctuous grin. 'With you, as always, Master.'

'You once fetched me a leopard skin,' recalls Mhlangana. 'Now you'll have a chance to crush me a beetle.'

★

'Hai,' says Pampata, hoping to distract them from brooding on Mhlangana's perfidy. 'Your beloved will be back any day now.'

Kani shrugs. This thing is too big for such thoughts. The royal guard is missing – meaning Mhlangana's men are missing. Who else knows about this situation? Or who else is meant to know? Certainly not Pampata or Thenjiwe, but what about Mbopa? The prince himself? The King's other brothers? And what about Mnkabayi? It's said little happens that she doesn't know about . . .

Kani's gaze locates the King's hut. What is Shaka doing? What is he thinking? Does he lie awake, finding every breath an effort? Or does he roll about and kick, as Pampata has reported, unable to find respite even in sleep?

Then, a soldier on duty again, Kani scans the empty isigodlo.

Noticing the sudden intentness that's overcome her friend, Pampata follows her lead and allows her eyes to rove around the compound.

Anyone coming upon them behaving thus is likely to assume here are two women who believe their gaze and their determination alone will deter anyone intending to do Shaka harm.

★

Nolaka doesn't see them, however. Sent to check the isigodlo for any signs of life, he merely halts at the gate and goes no further. Dares not go any further, for one doesn't enter the isigodlo armed without the King's permission; instant death awaits those who do so. Such considerations are suddenly very important, and the fearless, ferocious Leopard Man is dismayed to find himself sobering up fast, the beer seeming to drain from his body quicker than he poured it in, as the enormity of what they're about to do suddenly strikes him. And speaking of 'strike', he's the one to do the 'striking', Mhlangana has decreed that it be so, by saying 'Crush me a beetle!' But it's not going to be as easy as that, is it? This is Shaka he now faces, and will he even be able to raise his spear against the man who is more than a man, who is King of Kings, Sorcerer of Sorcerers . . .

Slowly, unsure of what he's going to say to Mhlangana to dissuade him, without sounding like Bamba (who, if the truth be known, has sounded incredibly wise tonight and has thus risen in his estimation), and still too affected by having been so close to the King to come up with a simple lie like reporting that Shaka's body servants are guarding his hut, Nolaka backs away. He turns and jogs back to where he left the prince and Bamba.

And is at first alarmed, then relieved. For Mhlangana's spear and shield lie at his feet, and someone has the prince backed up against a storage hut. Instinct kicking in – his master is being threatened – he moves forward, but Bamba swings his shield arm out to restrain him. About to lay into the other induna, ask him what this is all about, Nolaka hears the prince's assailant speak.

'You fool,' Ndlela is saying, 'do you think killing a King is this easy? Do you think all it takes is some beer and a few spears? What about afterwards?'

The questions are rhetorical, since Ndlela has his forearm pressed hard against Mhlangana's throat.

'The kindling must be carefully placed, the seed sowed, effects and consequences must be planned for. They must be controlled. Think about it, fool. If you were to succeed tonight . . . And that's highly unlikely for, see, I am here and I am not alone! But, if you were to succeed, what would the army say? Are you assured of their support? How many will question your motives? How many will say you merely killed out of jealousy? How many will say you thrust the blade yourself? How soon before you yourself find your royal guard missing?'

Ndlela takes a step back, then tells Leopard Man and Bamba to take their master back to his hut. The prince is ill and he needs rest. An inyanga will be summoned tomorrow.

'Know this,' adds Ndlela. 'For your own safety, Prince, I will not inform your aunt of tonight's escapade.'

★

*That day I told you how I had been watching and thinking, and believed I had now spotted one among the royal herd who might be up to the task of deposing our mad King . . . I wish you could have seen your face.*

*But your surprise was perfectly understandable.*

*Dingane, Mhlangana, Bakuza, Mpande, Magwaza, Nzibe, Kolekile, Gowujana, Sigwebana, Gqugqu, Mfihlo, Nxojana. How often had we surveyed the herd? How often had we wondered who among the brothers had the courage to move against Shaka?*

*As you said so often, these are not bulls a man wants to build a herd with.*

*But you were wrong. We were wrong.*

★

Ndlela watches Leopard Man and Bamba guide Mhlangana away, reflecting that he is tainted, that one. Bad enough to begin with, his involvement with Kholisa and the zombie has made the prince worse.

'As you said so often, these are not bulls a man wants to build a herd with. But you were wrong. We were wrong.' Mnkabayi's words.

Scowling, he strides off into the dark. Seeking Mnkabayi, to tell her about the missing guards, Thenjiwe had found him instead. Pampata and Kani were now the only ones guarding Shaka, he had said. Ndlela had reassured Thenjiwe that he'd rectify the matter.

He whistles and six of his men emerge out of hiding.

They won't disturb Pampata and Kani; instead they'll watch the King's compound from here.

★

Pampata and Kani sit huddled together for warmth, the wildebeest skin pulled up almost to their chins. Kani's right hand is holding Pampata's left hand; fingers entwined, palms pressed together to capture a tiny bud of warmth. In their free hands, icy knuckles, flesh and wood seemingly fused together, each holds an iklwa.

# 3
## Guarding Shaka

'Drunk?'

Ndlela nods. It's the following day and they're walking among Mnkabayi's cattle.

Of course, he was going to tell her everything that happened last night; he had made his 'promise' to the prince only to help calm him down further, by reminding him that things hadn't yet gone so far that the incident couldn't be hushed up.

Mnkabayi raises her iwisa as if to ram the tip into the ground but, realising the futility of getting angry, she lowers it again, leaning on it instead.

'Drunk,' she sighs.

Doesn't the imbecile know this thing has to take the shape of a ritual, with all the preparation that such would involve?

Cha! It *has* to be a ritual, one where the main participants know their roles, and the correct responses, and where the rest – the ordinary people – know to remain silent and awestruck.

And, of course, there are those who will participate by dying – that being part of the reason why she has to put up with Mhlangana's suicidal shenanigans.

All involved must move like a well-drilled regiment so that anyone out of step, or attempting to break away, can be easily spotted.

'He seems to getting worse,' observes Mnkabayi.

Ndlela forbears from mentioning the reason for that, since she would simply give him her *Not again!* sigh if he tries to remind her why things are becoming more difficult than they should be.

Instead he shrugs and says: 'Impatience.'

Her eyes resting on the bafazibewela bull, so named because, with its brown upper markings and white belly and dewlap, it resembles a woman lifting her skirt as she wades in water, Mnkabayi ponders this remark a moment. 'He was impatient even as a child.'

'And, now that he's no longer a child, his impatience has outgrown and outpaced him, and become a dangerous weapon.'

'For all of us.'

'That is so, Ma.'

Mnkabayi moves closer to her induna. 'But we must wait, Ndlela. We are forced to wait!'

'And so we will, Ma. And we will also keep Mhlangana in check.'

'As long as we can.' Mnkabayi allows herself a wry smile. 'He may be my nephew but do not think I won't reconsider his involvement, should he cause us much more trouble.'

Ndlela bows his head in acknowledgement. 'If I might suggest something, Ma . . .'

'Go ahead.'

He explains how he had told the prince he wouldn't tell Mnkabayi about this shameful escapade. 'This puts him in my debt, then. Not that I think such niceties bother him – for he will do what he will. However, I believe if you let him think that I have honoured my promise, and therefore do not rebuke him, that may help curb his impatience for a while.'

'Lengthen his leash a little, you mean,' she says, using the Zulu word for the cord used to keep a cow from moving while one is milking it.

Ndlela nods. 'Bind a man too tightly and he'll begin to struggle even more fiercely.'

Mnkabayi calls for two udibis to hold the bull steady. Standing next to the beast's thigh, she leans forward and gently runs her hand down the neck of the scrotum to briefly – and just as gently – check the shape of the testicles.

This one is fine. He'll father many calves.

Nodding to the udibis, to indicate they can lead the bull away, she says: 'You make sense. I am anyway tired of chastising that one. So let him think he's had a lucky escape. But what of the other aspect of this sorry episode?' she asks. 'This insane order he issued his men?'

'My regiment now guards the King,' says Ndlela. 'He will not be abandoned again.'

★

Mhlangana lies fuming in his hut. The fact that last night's libations have left him with a thumping headache only adds to his anger.

'Do they expect me to be meek and afraid? Do they expect me to cower? Hai, they are the ones who must be meek and conciliatory. Who must cower at my feet,' he tells himself.

King or about to be King, it matters not; for not a breath can pass through those two things.

'And let them strut about. Let them crouch together and conspire. Let them accuse me of hateful deeds, of villainy. For soon they will understand the true depth of my villainy, of my hatefulness. They will see, then not see,' thinks Mhlangana.

'And when it comes to that bitch who is my aunt, I'll do the impaling myself. And it won't be through her arse.'

★

He has explained to Mbopa that his men will take over the guard duties at the isigodlo for the time being, as they are more reliable – an important consideration in these times. The prime

427

minister agreed, especially since Ndlela's veterans will be replacing Mhlangana's men. The regiments Shaka has 'given' to his brothers have been more to make the princes feel important (as well as to introduce spies into their kraals), and the soldiers in these amabutho aren't known for their discipline or, indeed, bravery – although Dingane's men are a little more dependable.

'I did not inform the prime minister about the gross dereliction of duty last night, but I'm sure he already knew,' continues Ndlela.

'Of course!' says Mnkabayi. 'But we can count on his discretion.' She adds, 'As long as it suits him.'

Mhlangana himself and the two indunas involved can also be counted upon to keep quiet, adds Ndlela. The one called Leopard had seemed terrified when Ndlela hauled him out of his hangover earlier this morning. 'He will remain loyal to the prince, of course, but he did not need my warning about keeping his mouth shut.'

As for Bamba, he too was apologetic. 'And I sense a growing disgruntlement in him towards your nephew, Ma, which means this one may yet be useful to us.'

'Hai! You know I share Shaka's distrust of traitors, no matter how valuable they may prove to be.'

'I meant only that this Bamba is a troubled man, Ma, and part of his . . . his disgust, let us say, comes from his loyalty to the prince and his inability to betray that loyalty.'

'Ah, I see now! You mean one who can be guided . . . persuaded?'

'Precisely, Ma.'

What of thenjiwe and the other servants? It was the old man who came to warn Pampata, was it not?

'Yes, and he will see their lips are sealed.'

'And woe betide anyone who disobeys his command!'

'This is so, Ma.' Ndlela chuckles.

'That leaves us with Pampata herself,' says Mnkabayi, her voice suddenly turning flat.

'And Kani,' adds Ndlela to himself. Aloud, he says: 'Yes, Ma, but she will not speak of—'

Mnkabayi cuts him short with a dismissive wave of her hand. Of course she won't talk; probably won't even tell Shaka, should she ever get to see him. But . . .

'She will have to be seen to when the time comes.'

Ndlela nods. The thought doesn't bother him: killing Pampata, preferably before she even hears of Shaka's fate, makes sense. She can't be allowed to become a rallying point for rebels seeking to use their loyalty to the King's ideals as an excuse to claim the throne. But . . .

'And Kani? What of Kani?' he asks. It has to be asked, for he needs to be certain she is aware of this added 'complication'.

'I will see to it that she is kept safe,' says Mnkabayi.

'The two are virtually inseparable these days.'

'I will see she's kept safe,' says Mnkabayi again, steel in her voice now, warning him not to push the matter further.

They walk on, the long grass brushing their knees. They're heading back to Bulawayo now.

'Waiting,' murmurs Mnkabayi.

Ndlela grins to himself, following her line of thought: from Kani to the Induna to . . .

'Why do you think he went with them, Ma?'

'To infuriate us.'

Ndlela glances at Mnkabayi and sees, by her expression, that she's only half joking.

'To infuriate us,' she continues, 'and to do some thinking.'

She pauses to take in the view of her cattle on the slopes behind them. 'Which might not be a bad thing for us,' she adds.

★

Enjoying the late afternoon sun, Mbopa ponders last night's farrago.

He has to hand it to Mnkabayi and Ndlela: they know how to sidestep a potential disaster and conceal the traces.

But still . . . Aiee! Why are they pandering to a madman?

★

Ndlela asks her why she's chuckling.

'Just thinking,' says Mnkabayi. 'The shadows are lengthening and you say you must return to inspect your troops before they go on duty, and I was just thinking how here we are, seeking to protect Shaka from one of our own!'

# 4
# The Hungry Man

**September 12, 1828**

There are four of them sitting side by side on a log, facing a roaring fire. They've had a good day of raping and pillaging, of chasing down Zulu cattle and burning huts. Six of their number have been tasked with hurrying the cattle away before they can be confiscated by their officers who, they feel, have done well enough out of these raids as it is. Now, with their shields and spears laid neatly behind the log, along with their sleeping mats and other baggage, they're eating their way through two hindquarters of beef prepared by the oldest of the trio, who's an expert in such matters.

This is the first night on which these men have had a chance to enjoy some of their spoils. And Zulu beef is good beef. As is Zulu beer, and they have a few calabashes of that too.

While the fire was being readied – the youngest warrior, of course, being the one sent to collect firewood – and the meat butchered, talk ranged from how other feasts would pale in comparison to this beef eaten on the field of victory, to head-shaking wonder at the madness of those Zulu greybeards who insisted on trying to protect their homesteads. And don't forget the wives – aiee, they were sometimes the worst, flailing like enraged leopards. Madness! Did they really think they could fight us off?

But where are their soldiers? It's a question that sees the conversation grow quieter, for not knowing the whereabouts of the Zulu army is always cause for concern. It makes a man constantly want to look ·behind him, keep his spear and shield close, wondering how much use these will be against Shaka's amabutho.

The smell of cooking beef had revived their spirits, however. That and the fact of one of them pointing out that maybe the swamps alone had defeated those same amabutho, as their ruler Soshangane had intended.

'Don't our sticky blades and sticky cocks prove this,' he had said with a laugh. No, the only thing they had to fear now was comrades from other Shangaan regiments smelling the roasting beef they were about to fall upon and devour.

Now, feeling bloated and sated, two of the warriors have slipped off the log to rest their backs against it and warm their feet. The other is guzzling beer, trying to cultivate a belch. The fourth, the youngest, stands up, suddenly feeling nauseated by the amount of unconsumed beef still laid out on a series of flat-topped stones.

He's not used to eating so much meat, and neither is his stomach. He now hurries away into the dark, and manages to kneel with his back resting against a tree trunk, his arms extended, his hands gripping the haft of his spear, in time to accommodate the first explosive cataract, which splatters his heels. A drum roll of flatulence signals another squirt.

A deep breath and a sigh, because the bloated feeling is dissipating. In its place, announced by another salvo, comes a sense of . . . accomplishment.

The Beef Cutter – the same warrior who'd prepared their meal tonight – had said, 'There she goes. That one's yours, what are you waiting for, Boy? After her!'

Straining to pass a few lumps now – and succeeding with a triumphant fart – it suddenly occurs to him that maybe the Cutter had known, maybe had guessed. Maybe he'd even been waiting to find the right one for him . . .

Strangely, this doesn't worry him. After all, if he did realise, the Cutter hadn't teased him, or told the others so they could all tease him. And if the Cutter had been waiting to find the 'right one' for him, that wait hadn't been in vain.

Enveloped in the fruity smell of liquid shit, he remembers how nervous he'd been . . . but also excited. Because it was finally going to happen!

That's if he caught her, of course.

And what a fool he'd look if he couldn't do that.

But he had. And now he feels the beginnings of another erection. With the girl just a pace ahead of him in the long grass, he'd dropped his spear and shield, and thrown himself on to her. And she was on her back beneath him before he even realised what was happening . . .

And, somehow, he just knew what to do. Slap her when she tried to scratch his face. Grip her wrists above her head. A knee between her thighs; then another, forcing her legs apart. Then the fur. The slot. The dryness only making his prick harder . . .

A good day.

★

Cattle, Zulu cattle . . .

They're the only things you're likely to see alive, but that's only because they're seen as umphango, loot – the treasure of the kingdom. The contingents are too small, too isolated, for this to be a full-scale invasion – and he doubts Soshangane could actually mount such an operation – but they are out to do as much damage as possible.

Villages and homesteads have been razed to the ground; even fields in the process of being prepared for sowing have been destroyed. Where they have tried to fight back, the menfolk have

433

been slaughtered, the women raped and then killed. Where they've fled, they haven't been chased – another indication that this isn't an invasion.

Fires and bodies, smoke and circling vultures, and the great northern war kraal untouched; deserted except for the elderly and the ill and a few udibis who stayed behind to look after them. Soshangane himself had come there and inspected them; but he'd left them alone, and stopped his men from setting fire to the kraal.

The great northern war kraal ruled over by Mnkabayi – and where regiments are permanently garrisoned – lies deserted.

The great northern ikhanda ruled over by Mnkabayi, because Shaka trusted her, and this was a war kraal of strategic importance – is also deserted.

Where were the regiments kept here to prevent incursions such as this one made by the Shangaan army?

Where was Mnkabayi herself? Yes, yes, she'd been in Bulawayo when they'd set off on their mission – how many years ago? – but, once she had heard the news of burning kraals and stolen cattle, she would surely have rushed northward with Mdlaka, the army's commander-in-chief.

Anyway, the generals in charge of the regiments would have been quite capable of using their own initiative.

But something had happened, for instead they had marched away.

Cannibals have been seen, haunting the secondary paths as if these were still the old days. Shangaan raiding parties. Pillars of smoke. Burning villages. Bloated bodies. A multitude of hoofprints.

And no Zulu regiments to meet them. Why?

Because they had been withdrawn to Bulawayo.

That's what one of the udibis had told him at the war kraal: the regiments had gone to Shaka's capital.

Why?

★

The young Shangaan returns to the campsite to find a stranger sitting on the log. One of the two warriors who was resting his back against the log remains in the same position, his body limp, his chin on his chest as though he's regarding the wound in his chest. The other is sprawled on blood-wet dirt on the opposite side of the fire. The third man, the Beef Cutter, has been thrown backwards; all the youngster can see are his feet dangling over the log, next to the stranger.

Who is stuffing his face greedily.

Swallowing his fear, the Shangaan lowers his spear and steps into the firelight.

Tossing a bone over his shoulder, the Induna holds up a hand that says *Wait!*

Despite the fear, the realisation he has caught the stranger unarmed, the lad obeys.

Leaning forward, the Induna selects some ribs. He hasn't eaten more than berries for four days now and he's starving. He starts gnawing.

The youngster feels a surge of indignation. He has the drop on the stranger, who's clearly a Zulu – how dare the man!

But the Induna's hand comes up again. Makes a flattening motion. *Wait! Easy! Easy!*

And again, after taking two steps closer, the Shangaan stops without knowing why.

The rib bones discarded, the Induna selects a chunk of beef.

He reminds the Shangaan of a hungry lion. The lad raises his spear.

435

In mid-chew, the Induna raises his hand, the palm facing outwards. *Stop!*

His eyes on the lad, the Induna finishes off the meat, then makes gentler patting motions with both hands. There's no rush. Everything is fine.

Then, rising swiftly, he snatches the long spear away from the youngster. Spinning the assegai round, he drives the blade into the lad's stomach and lifts the impaled Shangaan off the ground, carries him like that for a few paces, then lets him drop on to dead leaves and branches.

After pausing to eat a few more pieces of meat and finish off a calabash of beer, the Induna retrieves the shield and iklwa he was able to find at the war kraal, and then sets off on his way again.

# INTERLUDE
## He Broods About Betrayal – Perfidy – Knavery

*Betrayal? Cha! Betrayal is nothing. Nothing! A King expects betrayal, and he watches for it. It's just like eating, shitting, pissing. It comes naturally. You expect it, and watch for it, and wait to identify those involved – and then you strike. Sometimes it's a quiet disappearance; other times it's a public spectacle, with the miscreants confessing their treachery before all before being led away to face the impalers.*

*Then what happened here? How did James King sneak past his defences to gull him?*

*Because I was tired, so tired . . .*

*When you're the ruler of all you see – what comes next? More conquests? Why? That will only mean more treacherous vassals. And the longer you're away from the capital, the faster the termites eat, gnawing away at the loyalty of your advisors, unsettling the people with all manner of rumours.*

*Not that your people need much prompting. The more cattle your conquests bring them, the greedier they get. Just as, the higher they climb, the more venal your advisors grow.*

*And that question remains unanswered: what comes next?*

*Ennui.*

*And ennui has made his limbs leaden, his eyelids heavier, as he contemplates the days that lie ahead. Nothing to look forward to. Merely more plotting, more greed. Sweating beneath the ibandla tree, while listening to ceaseless bickering about silly, small things. Nothing to look forward to.*

*Nothing.*

*James King, however, had laid out a campaign of a different nature before him. It was a chance to deal directly with the British authorities – and who knew where that might lead? Hence the diplomatic mission.*

*And the second part of James King's plan: a few days after the mission left, Shaka would march against Faku's Pondoes and lead his victorious amabutho down the south coast. By eradicating the Pondoes and other bothersome pests Shaka would convince the British he was eager to work with them.*

*He was being tricked, of course — but King hadn't realised he would send spies well ahead of the main force. And they brought word back that the British and the tribes who served them were making ready to meet the Zulus, but as invaders, and not potential allies!*

*And Shaka also realised that, although nominally his hostage, Fynn was there to see he kept to King's timetable.*

*And who knows what deal King would have brokered if they'd reached Cape Town? Yes, while Sothobe and the others sat there, unaware of what was going on, their presence merely intended to show his British compatriots that King was Shaka's man — and maybe even that Shaka was King's man.*

*Then they'd hear news of the approach of Zulu amabutho coming to attack the colony, and King could prove how much sway he held over Shaka by getting word back to Fynn to persuade Shaka to withdraw his men.*

*But Shaka had acted first; and the diplomatic mission had failed because King's own tribe were suspicious of the trader's motives.*

*The fact that James King's plan was thwarted, in the end, matters not a jot, though. Shaka was tricked! He was shamed!*

*Which was why he had sent his regiments straight on to Mozambique, for they were somehow a part of — and witnesses to — his shame.*

*Is he losing his power? Is the greyness in his hair sapping his strength, and his wisdom?*

*A King can't afford to be seen as weak, since that will have his courtiers thinking about which of the heirs they should side with — thus speeding up the King's decline in authority.*

438

*Hai*, sometimes it seems as if he is ruled by his people, his children. There's so much he must do, yet so much he can't do.

'Sulking in your hut doesn't help.' His mother's voice coming to him from deep within his head.

'You wouldn't understand. You never could. And no one else understands . . .'

No one else understands how he feels like a rock, with a rock's energies. And how he struggles to fight this sensation.

There are mornings when he wakes up thinking today's the day. Let him stride forth, hold court, chat with his generals, visit his cattle. But by the time old Thenjiwe has finished dressing him, the heaviness has returned, that awareness of how pointless it all is, and he turns and drops back on to his sleeping mat, and rolls over to face the thatch.

*Ennui.*

After conquering the world – what comes next?

Part of the problem is that he doesn't know what to do now, how to respond to James King's perfidy. He's been told the crocodile is dying, but that doesn't quell his anger.

How can he punish the White Men? Wipe them out, and yet more will come.

It's as if someone is pinning his arms to his sides. He is trapped. Though the ruler of all he sees, he is trapped. And there is nothing he can do.

For the first time in his life, in his reign, there's nothing he can do to fight back.

# 5
## A Hundred Mouths

**August 15, 1828**

*I was the bearer of bad tidings. I was the portent. I was the messenger staggering home from the war, my wounds betraying the grim ending to the tale I have to tell, before I've even opened my mouth —*

— although there have been many of those lately: emaciated, hollow-cheeked ghosts wandering out of the swamps, without spears or shields, their eyes blank. Even if they've been too afraid, or too weak, to make it back to Bulawayo and are instead trying to reach their home kraals, they can't be ignored as they stagger along the roads of the kingdom, some even stopping to beg — these lions of Shaka.

*But bind up my wounds! Bind them tight, for in this instance I was sliced too. And my wounds were like a hundred mouths each screaming silently.*

*Do not complain, cur!*

*Are times so bad you must be rewarded — or even spared — for simply doing your duty?*

He had halted them as soon as Bulawayo came into sight. Jakot had already left the group. 'I will be the one who reports to Mbopa,' said Dingane; he would tell the prime minister they had succeeded in destroying the slavers, but had lost the Induna. Dingane was the prince, so it was his responsibility. And, because he was a prince, he could use his discretion and visit Kani first.

This was said with an eye on the udibi. 'Do not try to race me there,' warned Dingane. 'I know of the close bond you have'— a slight pause here, needing to replace an unthinking *had* with *have* — 'with both the Nduna and his wife. But telling Kani what's

440

happened is my responsibility. Besides, your misplaced guilt will only get in the way.'

'Wise words, Master,' said Njikiza, laying a hand on the udibi's shoulder, to indicate he'd see that Mthunzi obeyed Dingane's instructions. And the others, too, who were told they could boast about their success in defeating the slave traders, but were, for the moment at least, enjoined to say nothing about the fact the Induna had remained behind.

*Bind up my wounds! Bind them tight! A hundred mouths each screaming silently: my friend my friend my friend my friend!*

Yet reflecting: *Is this not a sign?* Thinking of when, after he had finished his report to Mbopa, the prime minister had started speaking about the way things were at KwaBulawayo.

He would mourn the Induna, he had said, yes, how he deeply would mourn the Induna, but a man could only carry a burden of a certain size, and then all else simply fell away; for a sore tooth no longer hurt after someone has stabbed you in the stomach . . .

*My friend my friend my friend my friend!*

*But look at what is happening now!*

'They need to be as sly as a hyena,' said Mbopa. And they need to be as careful as a skinner, one of those called in on feast days to make sure the animal is cut up and the hide removed without a single splash of gore or fragment of bone dropping to the ground – for such can be used against the nation, should any fall into a wizard's hands.

'Yet your aunt backs one who thinks he can simply send his hench-creatures to break into the isigodlo,' said Mbopa. Hai, the King is too strong to be toppled solely by force. You need cunning, among other things, but Mhlangana is the very opposite of cunning.

'How can your aunt expect loyal Mbopa to join her, when her plans so clearly involve Mhlangana?' asked the prime minister. 'How can she expect loyal Mbopa to decide his best interests would be served by marching with that fool, who can't be trusted not to turn on those who've helped him to power once he's sitting on the throne?'

★

*And Mbopa reminded me of another approach, made back in those dark days when Shaka was mourning Nandi . . .*

He'd managed to sneak out of Bulawayo, for some hours of solitude while sitting in the shade of a tree by a rushing stream was all he wanted. However, he'd just settled down, after drinking some water, when he saw Dingane coming along the path – and realised this was no accidental meeting.

Sitting next to Mbopa, Dingane had dispensed with the customary greeting and started speaking of those who were concerned about the future.

'And you have allied yourself with these worried gentlemen?' Mbopa asked him mildly.

The Needy One had shrugged. 'Let us rather say that I was prepared to listen to these loyal subjects.'

Loyal subjects? Did Dingane already see himself as King?

'And they *are* loyal, Mbopa,' said the Needy One, showing he had an idea of what was going through the prime minister's mind.

If they were so loyal, he had told the Needy One that day, why didn't these subjects take their concerns directly to the King?

Because their loyalty lies with the tribe, said Dingane.

'Many others have said that when they've sought to go against the King.'

'Yes, yes, I know . . . and is not the King the tribe? But what if the King's actions endanger the tribe?' asked the Needy One.

★

'Yet now you have grown silent,' observed Mbopa. 'Yes,' he continued, 'you and Shaka seemed to have become closer after you helped him defeat the Thembus. And he's always looked upon your complaints with a benevolence second only to that which he showed Mzilikazi, in the end. But somehow that doesn't account for your silence . . .'

What if the King's actions should endanger the tribe? Did I remember asking him that? Did I remember what I said?

'Should it ever dawn, that would be a day for hard decisions . . . That's what you said. And it will be night before we even realise it and where will we be, then? That's what you asked me that day,' said Mbopa.

'Well, it is night now,' said Mbopa.

'Night has fallen,' he said. 'Yet you remain silent. Why are you so silent?'

★

'Why not leave?' Dingane had asked. 'Why not run away?'

Because he is too old, too fat, Mbopa had replied, and he won't be able to outstrip the assassins who will be sent after him. Because fleeing will automatically declare him to be the enemy of whoever deposes Shaka. They will fear him and want him silenced.

Mbopa chuckled. The very attributes that keep him alive right now will see him become a hunted man should he avoid taking sides.

★

Whereas once the Needy One was a lone voice bleating amid the King's many victories, now he's fallen silent, leaving the cavilling and carping to others. Why?

And did he know Mhlangana had tried it again?

*What?*

'Mhlangana tried it again,' said the prime minister. 'He tried once more to kill Shaka!'

# 6
# Repercussions

She is reminded, she says, of Uzibandela, the Pathfinding Moon, when the new grass hides the trails, for she has certainly lost the track here.

Besides, she adds, her bones creak and her ears have been dulled by having to listen to so many years of blather.

'Hai, my Aunt, you seem to me to be in the best of health,' fawns Mhlangana, as well he might. He had meant to come to this encounter unrepentant – to even chastise the old lady for dragging her feet like a timid maiden. But, faced by Mnkabayi and Ndlela, his resolution crumbled.

They're on the hill of the isiguqo, a few paces away from the circle of stones. Mnkabayi is seated, and Ndlela looms behind her. Mhlangana stands before them, enjoying the full focus of his aunt's stare.

'Nonetheless,' says Mnkabayi, 'this matter confuses me.'

Mhlangana clenches his teeth, steels himself, knowing this is her way of announcing she's about to catalogue his many blunders.

'Indeed it does,' she continues. *For your bones are dull and your ears creak*, adds Mhlangana to himself.

'Ignoring the glaring question of *why* for now, let us start at the beginning again. Doubtless it all started off very well from your perspective, though – sallying forth armed with iklwas, resolution ablaze in your eyes. And why not, for you saw an opportunity and you seized it.'

'That was indeed our reasoning,' says Mhlangana.

'But you must have wondered . . .'

'Why Mdlaka had withdrawn his men? Yes, of course.'

'But you *knew* that he had?'

'Yes, my Aunt.'

'And so you sallied forth – you and Bamba and the other one.'

'Nolaka.'

'You sallied forth, and your expedition went unnoticed even though it was all done in daylight. Who was meant to strike the killing blow?'

'Nolaka. I trust him implicitly.'

'Clearly. And you yourself were there, right there, when he and the other one charged into the royal hut?'

'Yes, Ma.'

'And then things stopped going so well.'

'Perhaps, Ma . . . but I also believe the ancestors smiled on me.'

'Cha, cub! If they viewed your actions with benevolence, they would have seen to it that you had succeeded!'

'In a way I did.'

Ndlela gives a cough like someone who's accidentally swallowed a fly.

'And how do you arrive at that conclusion?' inquires Mnkabayi.

'Because I showed that it could be done,' replies the prince, stifling a smug grin.

'That *what* could be done? That you can lead an attack on an empty hut and stab at air? Do you know how much you risked?'

'Hai,' says the prince, 'the risk is there every day for as long as my brother remains alive. Besides,' he adds in a mumble, 'no one saw us.'

'If they had, everything would have been over – destroyed,

finished. All our plans, our hard work gone like that, you fool!' says Mnkabayi, snapping her fingers.

'We'll be finished, anyway, if we don't act soon. Enough planning, my Aunt! Enough talk! Let us now end this!'

'Enough planning, he says! Cha! Does your failure here not show you, once and for all, the need for thorough planning? Why, for one thing, did you think Mdlaka withdrew his men?'

'Perhaps to give us a chance,' says the prince.

'Did someone let you know this might be the case?'

'I'm not sure I understand, my Aunt.'

Mnkabayi sighs. 'Doubtless you have spies sniffing around the general – so did any of them warn you he would be recalling the royal guard because he wanted to open the gate to any who might be planning to do Shaka harm?'

'I . . . no, my Aunt.'

'Then this was merely supposition on your part?'

Mhlangana shrugs.

'A supposition that became a fact when the royal guard was removed,' continues Mnkabayi. 'Did it not occur to you to ask someone likely to know why this measure had been taken?'

'Who, my Aunt? Mbopa? But you yourself have said he's still not with us.'

'Mbopa's not the only one likely to know why the royal guard was absent. There was someone you could have come to, one you could have trusted completely.'

'Who, my Aunt?' Mhlangana frowns, sensing a trap but unsure of how to avoid it.

Mnkabayi rolls her eyes, shakes her head. 'Me, you idiot! If you had come to me before sallying forth – a brave impi of three – and said "My dear Aunt, the King's guard is no longer at its post", I would've been able to tell you that's because Shaka has left Bulawayo and they have accompanied him. Because that is what they do, my Nephew – they guard the King! They do not guard empty huts! Because who would attack an empty hut? Cha! But, then, look who I'm talking to!'

★

'He's right about one thing, Ma,' says Ndlela after the prince has been dismissed. 'The longer we hesitate . . .'

'I know. First I thought to go ahead and make plans, prepare the way, and then give my nephew time to recover . . .'

'But this has not happened, Ma.'

'And isn't likely to.'

Ndlela nods.

'The plans are ready, the men are coming, but now we must wait for him!'

The induna nods again. He knows who she's referring to, and knows she's right about the need to wait for him to come to his senses, as it were.

'And if circumstances force us to move before then? Before he comes to you?'

'You mean proceeding with Mhlangana alone?'

'Yes, Ma.'

'Then, old friend, the next one to die after Shaka will be me.'

★

Where is he? Is he well? Should she let Mthunzi go and find him, as he's been hankering to do? He's been pestering Mbopa three or four times a day, the prime minister remaining understanding and tolerant but always saying no. Mthunzi would have a lot of territory to cover; for who could know where the Induna might be by now? And, if he was dead, wild animals would have made his corpse disappear, so that Mthunzi's search might be endless.

448

There is an ache in her chest. Dread is her companion when she awakes in the morning, despair the cloak she pulls around her shoulders when the sun sets and the cold night moves in.

*Where is he?*

It's hard not to lose control whenever she hears of a messenger coming to the isigodlo. Will it be about him? Is he well? Is he safe?

*Where is he?*

Hard, too, to concentrate, to make her plans, to marshal her forces, because this is also about him, about insuring he survives the campaign.

But now he's missing.

Is he well? Is he safe?

*Where is he?*

# 7
## A Chat With Mnkabayi

**August 19, 1828**

DINGANE: My apologies for disturbing you in the depths of night, my Aunt, but I have serious matters to discuss with you. Matters not suited to the summit of a hill.

MNKABAYI [*thinking even she can become careless, for she had assumed her pilgrimages to the hill of the isiguqo would be seen as just that: pilgrimages in a trying time. But clearly someone has seen, and wondered*]: Hai, Nephew, you do not disturb me. I find tiredness abundant, but sleep scarce these days.

DINGANE: Matters of state, Aunt? Cha! But who cannot be perturbed about the way things are!

MNKABAYI [*chuckling*]: Feel free to speak openly with me, Nephew.

DINGANE: If my words sound treasonous, it is because tiredness has vanquished prudence.

MNKABAYI: You too, then, are kept awake by matters of state.

DINGANE: I thank you, Aunt, for not sounding surprised, for there are many who would say the Needy One is too concerned with preening himself, with counting his cattle and adding to his harem, to be worried about such trivial matters as a mad King seeming happy to see all he has wrought swallowed up by old foes and vassals who all these seasons have merely been awaiting a chance to avenge their subjugation. [*Sighing*] Then, of course, there's the state of my health . . .

MNKABAYI: You seem to me to be in good health, Nephew.

DINGANE: That's just it: I'd like things to stay that way.

MNKABAYI: That's understandable. But I'm not sure . . .

DINGANE: . . . how you can help me? Come now, Aunt – is it not true you are indulging in certain activities that will endanger my health in due course?

MNKABAYI: Hai! My legs are old, and you move too fast for me, Nephew.

DINGANE: Have you ever watched him, Aunt – when he doesn't think anyone's looking? Have you not seen the blankness that comes over him like a shadow? Have you ever seen him sad? Hai, when our father, your brother, died, the only thing he wanted to know was when our father's body servant would resume training us in the art of stick fighting.

MNKABAYI: He does seem like one that is separate from the herd.

DINGANE: But not because he was spurned! It's because he's not of that herd – he's a kudu among nyala. Because he and I are so close in age, and obviously rivals, I've spent a lot of time watching him to see how I could get the better of him. Instead, I saw this . . . this blankness, this emptiness . . . this lack. [*Laughing humourlessly*] At the time I thought this a sign of stupidity. But it's not that. I know Mhlangana's capable of doing stupid things, but my brother is also possessed of a low cunning. And I've seen how well he's managed to hide that blankness as the years passed. And he's become ever more cunning. Remember how quickly he latched on to Sigujana when he became King? I have no doubt he had it somewhere in the back of his mind to encourage our brother in his dissoluteness and to fuel his fears about the threat I posed. Then, once Sigujana had done away with me, he could do away with Sigujana and expect the backing of most of the elders, who would have by then deemed Sigujana well on his way to becoming out of control and doing harm to the tribe. But, of course, our long-lost brother Shaka intervened . . .

451

MNKABAYI: Indeed.

DINGANE: And not without your help.

MNKABAYI [*chuckling*]: I merely sought to smooth the path of the inevitable.

DINGANE: You're being modest, my Aunt. Considering all those visits to Nandi, those messages carried to and fro by Pampata, I think you did more . . .

MNKABAYI: If I did, remember that you were one of the beneficiaries of my interference, Nephew.

DINGANE: And for that I have never stopped being grateful. However, since we are talking freely, let us admit I was also being used. My acknowledgment of Shaka's claim was as important as your . . . [*grinning*] interference.

MNKABAYI [*softly; as if she hasn't heard him*]: A kudu among nyala? I think he'd prefer a more dangerous simile, like a lion amid duiker.

DINGANE: Dangerous is the word. And the fact that you know whereof I speak does little to allay my qualms about my continued well-being.

MNKABAYI: Why now?

DINGANE: What do you mean?

MNKABAYI: Why do you bring these qualms to me now?

DINGANE: Well, first of all, I couldn't believe you'd want to ally yourself with someone so volatile and untrustworthy as Mhlangana. This blankness whereof I speak – and which you acknowledge – is a disease that makes him dangerous to others. And I couldn't believe this was your choice of heir. And that's not taking into account the fact that, after Shaka, I am the eldest brother.

MNKABAYI: You know it's not as simple as that. The heir is the firstborn son of the King's chief wife, and Mhlangana's mother—

DINGANE: Cha! That's debatable. Our father, your brother, was known for changing his preferences when it came to his wives.

MNKABAYI: This is true.

DINGANE: And was Nandi ever his chief wife? No, never. Try as she might, she remained only his *first* wife, yet no one challenged Shaka's claim to the throne on those grounds. Or rather let us say no one dared to! But things have changed, haven't they?

MNKABAYI: How so?

DINGANE: Come now, Ma, you have clearly been biding your time – which is understandable. Despite what Mhlangana seems to think, killing a King is no easy matter. But if it was me, if I were you, I'd say Shaka going off to sulk at KwaDukuza provides you with an opportunity that must now be seized. Assuming, of course, the other aspects of your plot are in place.

MNKABAYI: of course. But you are wrong and you are right, Nephew.

DINGANE: How so?

MNKABAYI: You are right in that we *have* been biding our time, and with Shaka going to Dukuza . . . well, let us say he couldn't have done more to clear the way for us.

DINGANE: In which case you plan to strike soon and, if I remain here sitting on my hands, I will be next. Mhlangana will never leave me standing on my hind legs.

MNKABAYI: You are right about that, too. But you are also wrong to think we have been biding our time solely to wait on Shaka's movements. A pretext could easily have been found to get him to wherever we wanted him to be. No, there is another reason why I have been biding my time.

DINGANE: And what is that?

MNKABAYI: I have been waiting for *this*. I have been waiting for you to come to me of your own accord. I have been waiting for you to join us. This plan – my plan – cannot succeed without your participation. Hai! Do you not see? Championing Mhlangana was my way of drawing you to me. [*Chuckling*] I have my own health to think of, too, because were Mhlangana to take the throne, I would probably be eating dust soon after you. *You* are the one I want to see on the throne!

DINGANE: Me?

★

*Yes, you!* Does he still not understand? She needed him to come to her of his own volition, and because he feels it's his duty. Mhlangana is solely after power and personal gain, and will be dealt with in due course. So are some of the others involved, doubtless, but this is not just about increasing one's own herd or stature – this is about saving the nation. The People of the Sky will not now survive long if Shaka is left on the throne. That's why it's their duty to act, to do something: they must save the tribe. And they need an heir who understands this, understands the need to rebuild and repair, to bring their allies into line and punish those other tribes who have seen in Shaka's *sickness* – the word spat out – an opportunity to reclaim their territory.

★

DINGANE: But I am Dingane, the Needy One! The lazy one!

MNKABAYI: Cha! That's the way you like to be seen.

DINGANE: And the way I *have* been seen! Lazy, lazy, lazy, that's Dingane for you!

MNKABAYI: Idle, yes. Lazy, no.

DINGANE [*with a half-grin*]: There's a difference?

MNKABAYI: But of course! For an idle man is a thinking man, while a lazy man is an indolent one. A lazy man's eyelids are heavy, because he is sated in his indolence. An idle man is at rest, but never indolent. Hai, for that he is to be valued more than even a busy man. A busy man is never idle, never at rest, neither is he lazy; instead he acts without thinking, because he is incapable of the repose that thinking requires, and even fears such repose. And in so doing – in acting without thought – he may win the praise of his superiors, but he is also prone to make mistakes, milk bulls, reap weeds. No, Nephew, better an idle man than a busy one.

★

Dingane has watched Mhlangana, explains Mnkabayi, and she has watched Dingane – and watched over him. After Shaka had been stabbed she had sent the Induna, his old friend, to find him. Although she didn't think Dingane was that stupid, there was always the chance he had been behind the assassination attempt. And if he hadn't been involved, there was a good chance he'd be suspected anyway. Either way he needed protecting, especially in those mad days immediately following the attempt on Shaka's life. And so it was that she had seen to it he was protected, sending his friend the Induna to find him that night.

★

DINGANE: Aiee, Ma, you have truly spoken openly with me tonight.

MNKABAYI: That is so.

DINGANE: Now let me return the compliment. You speak of duty, of saving the tribe . . .

MNKABAYI: Yes?

DINGANE: And you are right. But when I came here tonight, I am not sure if I came out of duty or self-interest, merely a desire to save myself.

MNKABAYI [smiling]: Your doubt is reassurance enough for me, Nephew. In fact, your doubt tells me I've made the right choice. It also tells me you will do the right thing when you're crowned King of the Zulus!

# 8
## The Skirmish

**September 15, 1828**

The urge is strong to head straight to Bulawayo and see for himself what's going on, but he knows he must fight this and honour his promise to Shaka. Of course, there's also his wife and his family to consider, but fortunately the two concerns are yoked. Kani is likely to be with Pampata. As a result he's decided to make for Pampata's dela innyoni, her 'pleasure kraal'. Surely that's where Shaka will have sent her. If he's wrong, and Pampata isn't there, the Induna will reconsider his options.

But where are the amabutho? Why are raiders being allowed to run unchecked through the northern sector of the kingdom?

*Go to Bulawayo. Your King clearly needs you.*

No! Shaka has made him give his word, told him what to do under circumstances just like these. So he must first of all keep his word. The Induna rises to his feet.

The path curves away from him, heading out into the open. Above is a slope running up to a narrow kloof crammed with bushes. Below is a wall of stone and a gentle decline leading to the main track. This is a secondary trail and after a hundred metres or so it curls around the tip of a large outcrop that forms the precipitous left side of the kloof.

He's been waiting here, hidden amid tree-fuchsias and silver proteas and the shade of various trees as the sun has moved from ekuseni – the morning – to selili dlala – well-up. Meanwhile, on the main track, two groups of Shangaan warriors have passed by, herding Zulu cattle. But that was before the sun became old, and he's seen no other sign of the marauders for a while now.

Time to move.

Carrying his iklwa and shield, he jogs out into the sunlight. It's three days since he killed those Shangaan crocodiles and ate the beef they had cooked. Since then he's been kept too busy dodging Shangaan invaders to do much foraging. Fortunately he's been able to keep his waterskins full, but the lack of food is having its effect. Jogging seems even slower than walking; hunger and fatigue make him feel as if he's wading through waist-high mud. And the wound suffered during his sojourn with the Wild Cat People has opened up again.

*But got to keep on, got to keep moving on.*

★

'How fares our precious Pampata?'

'She is in pain, Ma! The King still refuses to see her.'

'You are sure of that? There have been no secret meetings?'

'No, Ma. I have been ever vigilant.'

'Good. And she has no reason to doubt your loyalty, Muvani?'

'None, Ma.'

'And the Nduna's wife?'

'She and the King's penis sheath remain inseparable.'

'Good.'

'But you say she is to be left alone?'

'Yes, yes. But she won't be a problem.'

'So it is time, Ma?'

'Yes, Muvani, it is time. Time we put an end to precious Pampata's misery. You will accompany her to her place of retreat. There you will kill her – and the other ladies-in-waiting.'

'And the Nduna's wife?'

'She won't be there.'

'Ah.'

'Kill Pampata and bring me her head.'

'It will be done, Ma.'

'The rest of her you can burn.'

'It will be done, Ma.'

★

He'll be crossing open ground, so he waits until the sun is at its zenith, as he knows that's when warriors are likely to seek out some shade to rest in, then he sets off, light-headed, tired and sore but forcing himself to move at a pace faster than walking. However, when he's about halfway along the path, a group of Shangaans appears around the headland at the opposite end of the path.

He stops.

The Shangaans are moving in single file, and the first few warriors instantly come to a halt, causing the line to bunch up.

He looks at them.

They look at him.

He knows how an insect must feel when it's trapped in a spider's web. He can't go forward. He can't flee to his left and go leaping down the low wall of rocks there, because a larger group of Shangaans has appeared on the main track down below. He can't go back . . . well, he could, but it wouldn't take them long to run him to ground and by then he'll be even more tired. He . . .

'Si-gi-diiii!'

A Zulu war cry.

The Induna – and the Shangaans – stare up the slope to see a Zulu warrior raising his shield.

And the Induna goes charging up the slope before the Shangaans can react. The sight of another Zulu warrior reinvigorates his muscles, and his thighs soon swallow the gradient. But he's not as fast as he could be, and the Shangaans are closing the distance as he reaches the warrior . . .

. . . and is stunned to find that the warrior can't be older than fourteen summers, and therefore is too young to be a warrior.

But the Induna scarcely has time to register this fact when other warriors, also too young to be warriors, spill out of the bushes at the kloof's opening.

★

'You have received no news of your husband?'

'No, Ma.'

'Yet you seem . . .'

'Unconcerned?'

'Not quite that, Kani . . .'

'Aiee, Ma, it is as we have discussed before. I *am* concerned, but something also tells me he lives. He lives, Ma!'

'I have the same feeling, Kani. As you doubtless know, your husband has performed many valuable services for me, and I believe I have come to know him well. And I have the same feeling: I too believe he is alive.'

'Thank you, Ma. It means a lot that someone else should think the same way as I do . . .'

'Nonetheless, as you have said, you can't help but be concerned, even frightened. Yet you have put aside these feelings to look after your friend Pampata, which I find very laudable.'

'I thank you again, Ma, but she is, as you say, my friend . . .'

'Which means you want the best for her.'

'Yes, Ma.'

'As do I, and that's why I've summoned you, Kani. We need to get Pampata out of Bulawayo.'

'She won't leave the King, Ma.'

460

'Yes, but it's because of the King we need to persuade her to leave the capital.

'We *have* to persuade her to leave, because Mhlangana is plotting against Shaka. We can protect the King by making sure he's well guarded, but I have reason to believe Mhlangana will then target Pampata instead.'

'But she can be guarded too, can't she?'

'Yes, and that will be the trap we'll use to catch Mhlangana. But, for that to happen, it's best if Pampata is well away from here and safe among her ladies-in-waiting. Hai, let me go further and be brutally honest with you, Kani – Pampata out of harm's way will be one less thing to worry about. Does that make sense?'

'Of course, Ma. But how can we ever persuade Pampata to leave Bulawayo?'

'I have given the matter some thought, Kani, and I think I have an idea, but it will require your cooperation.'

'I am yours to command, Ma. I too think we must get Pampata out of harm's way for now.'

'Very well, then. Now listen closely . . .'

★

Some of the boys may be as young as ten, but someone has drilled them well. Or perhaps they've learnt from watching the warriors they have served as udibis. Passing the Induna, urged on by the youngster who called out to him, they spread out into a line, ready to meet the Shangaans lumbering up the slope.

'Pull them back there!' calls the Induna, pointing to his left, where the wall of the cliff curves away from the kloof. 'Pull them back!'

The youngster nods in understanding and starts pushing back the other boys to create a wall of shields from one cliff face to the other in front of the kloof.

461

The Shangaans chasing him have kept close to the precipice of the promontory and that's why the Induna joins the human wall on its right flank – to help the boys meet their charge. The Shangaans are out of breath, and some have dropped their shields, the better to chase the Induna unencumbered. They also hesitate when they see they're facing children, so it's the latter who start moving forward over the last spear-length, some wielding their iklwas like seasoned warriors, some more jabbing hesitantly rather than stabbing. It is these latter the Induna moves to assist.

Then the Shangaans are retreating, and the Induna has to dart in front of the youngsters and order them back. More Shangaans are coming up the slope; if the young Zulus break ranks in chasing the first batch, they're sure to be slaughtered by the second lot. After herding his young charges back into position, the Induna turns to see warriors from the main path scrambling up the wall of rocks. Checking their left flank, he sees the boys have curled around towards them. They're clearly eager to join the fray but, in the process, they're leaving a gap between the line and the precipice, which can be exploited.

Running over to the youth who seems to be in charge, the Induna quickly explains why they need to close this opening. And, anyway, these eager young lions will get a chance to feed their assegais soon. The boy nods and calls to the others to reform, then he steps out in front of them to make sure they remain in place.

Yes, decides the Induna as he examines the enemy's disposition, their blades will be bloodied very soon. The other Shangaans have got the remnants of the first onslaught turned around, and now they're all coming up the slope spread out in a long line, moving more slowly to conserve their breath. All segments of the Zulu wall will be fully tested this time . . .

*And they're children!*

And two already lie dead among the five Shangaans they managed to kill in the first charge; and a third is wounded and wailing – and now the Induna notes he's being dragged away by two girls.

Not just boys, then. But girls too!

One of the warriors who's clambered up from the main track is trying to call back the line of Shangaans. But he's being ignored. These men aren't going to be beaten by children. Five spear-lengths away they break into a run, bellowing a war cry.

Some simply knock the smaller children out of the way. It's these the Induna moves to meet: his isihlangu hooking aside his opponent's shield, then an underarm thrust into his ribs. But he can't hold back all of them, and many have turned round to stab the nearest child in the back, or bury an axe in a young skull. This leaves them exposed to the Induna and the older boys follow-ing his example, but too many Zulu youngsters are going down.

'Fall back!' calls the Induna. 'Fall back!'

And there's a Shangaan almost upon him, his spear raised hori-zontally. Instinctively backing away, the Induna trips over a body. He's bringing his shield across to protect himself, when a long hunting spear sails over him to hit the Shangaan in the throat. Scrambling to his feet, the Induna realises it's been thrown by one of the girls. The two of them exchange a smile, and then he rejoins the ragged line of shields, while the girl turns and, picking her way through rounded boulders, makes her way higher up the kloof.

Surveying the slope again, the Induna is relieved to see the Shangaans have retreated. They've left many of their number eating dust, and not a few writhing in blood; but there are many more Zulu children screaming and thrashing about, or lying still.

★

'You have heard all that?'

'Yes, Ma.'

'Aiee, I do wish it could be otherwise—'

'But it can't be, Ma. We've been through this before. She can't be allowed to become a rallying point.'

'True.'

'Even were she to withdraw from public life, we will never be able to trust her, for thoughts of avenging her beloved will never be far from her mind.'

'You are right, Ndlela. And better by my hand than Mhlangana's! Who knows what indignities he'd make her endure. But it is done. The order has been given. Now, tell me, what news of my regiments?'

'It is as you wished it. The Mpholo regiment stands ready to deal with any threat from the north. The Mbelebele is to its east, the Phezi to its west, both close enough to reinforce the Mpholo if need be, and also close enough to Bulawayo to be deployed here if necessary.'

'I hope it doesn't come to that.'

'Neither do I, Ma. But not because I think there's a chance of things going wrong here. It's the reports we've been receiving from the north that worry me. Soshangane seems to be treating Zulu territory as his own.'

'Cha! We'll sweep him aside and clean up the mess. We'll show the people how easily such things can be fixed once we have a King who doesn't spend every day hiding in his hut. But, tell me this, have the stories started circulating?'

'Of turmoil up north? Yes, Ma.'

'And we have our witnesses safely tucked away?'

'Yes, Ma.'

'Now the only thing to do is not to think too much about just what it is we are intending to do, and let events take their course.'

# 9
## Strange Regiment

Xosha is the name of the youth leading this strange regiment of children, and the Induna's relieved to see he's survived the clash with the Shangaans. He's not sure he himself is up to herding a group of izingane, children, even if they seem to know what they're about. However, he intervenes when Xosha instructs four of the youngest boys to remain behind to defend the kloof as best as they can – to sacrifice themselves, in other words – while the rest of them follow the girls in scrambling up to the top of the escarpment.

He can understand the reasoning. He is even impressed by the necessary callousness in choosing the youngest, because the older boys are more adept warriors. But he won't have it. He's already seen enough death on his long journey from the Barrier. The Shangaans, he reckons, will spend a long while licking their wounds; there will be no need for a heroic last stand to buy them time.

Besides, the larger group is herding cattle, the men will want to get the izinkomo away as soon as possible.

'And they might think we are still hiding up there, ready to roll boulders down on top of them if they attack,' adds the Induna.

Xosha agrees and begins urging all the others up the kloof. Unfortunately, the seriously wounded will have to be left behind, since too many of the survivors are just too small to carry them as well as their own shields and weapons. Xosha's in the rear and, when he reaches the escarpment, he turns and gazes down the defile to where the Induna continues to linger among the wailing and weeping wounded. He's about to call out to the older man, when he realises why the Induna has remained behind. After a pause, he rejoins the others on the heights and starts hurrying along those hobbling in the rear.

They might be children, but they have just fought as Zulu warriors, so let them die as Zulu warriors. Quickly, as is the custom, the Induna moves from boy to boy. 'Are you ready to begin the Great Journey, Little Brother?' he asks. When the boy nods, the Induna disembowels him. If the child is unconscious, his acquiescence is assumed.

When the Induna is finished, the Shangaans are still arguing among themselves, below.

★

*They are so happy, so, so happy. And by 'they' I mean Mnkabayi, whose domineering presence always warrants the plural pronoun. So gratifying to think I've been the source of so much joy. But it's more than that (so much more!) – it's glee. And that, in turn, makes me happy, because I do so enjoy glee in others. It makes them careless, leading them to lower their guard.*

*And now they are saying – that is, Mnkabayi is saying – 'Ahh, Mbopa! We always knew he could be persuaded. We always knew he was like a maiden playing hard to get, with her isoka!'*

*And how she and Ndlela must be laughing.*

Mbopa steeples his fingers and grins.

★

Bringing up the rear, he is running – forcing himself to run. Blood streams down his thigh again and he's received various new scratches and cuts from dying Shangaans. That he's been almost continuously on the move for many days, sleeping little, eating less, doesn't help. Pausing to check that they still aren't being followed, he seizes the opportunity to catch his breath, reaching deep down into reserves that are all but sapped.

When he turns to continue on his way, he suddenly realises he recognises this place. It was up here, on these moor-like heights, that his udibi had found where Zodwa had hidden his sister Sibongile. The cavern is somewhere over there . . . And that smoke from the valley beyond must be coming from the village where the two had stayed.

Another umuzi destroyed!

They cross the escarpment and scramble down a narrow cleft. With two youngsters posted on the heights to watch for pursuers, the others drink gratefully from the stream that winds its way among the scree at the foot of the gorge. Soon they're joined by two boys old enough to belong to a regiment, who come scuttling down the slope of the opposite cliff.

They can no longer go that way, they tell Xosha, for there's a battle taking place in the next valley. Upon hearing this, the Induna rises to his feet painfully and hobbles over to them. That the two newcomers don't show surprise at his presence doesn't occur to him until much later.

'What do you mean?' he asks. 'Are our men fighting back?'

It's Xosha who replies. No, he says, it's Beje's Khumalos, who have come down from their vastness, to fight the Shangaans for a share of Zulu plunder.

The Induna shakes his head. The news just keeps getting better and better!

★

*I can hear her telling Ndlela: 'See how well our Dingane has performed his first task! Such a good boy, such an obedient little prince, for bringing Mbopa over to our side.'*

Ha! Just how stupid do they think he is? Just how stupid does *she* think he is!

He has been making his own plans.

Mbopa shakes his head. Did she really think he'd sit on his arse doing nothing while she put a dangerous, vicious monster on the throne?

He wasn't about to do anything to save Shaka, but he'd do everything to save himself. Didn't she realise that?

Yes, of course she did. But she thought it meant that convincing him to join her would be easy. It was always a possibility, and he had strung her along, playing his game of wait-and-see, making the way a little easier for her now and again, but keeping her guessing all the same. Because he was doing other things to save himself.

And those measures – he smiles – remain in place despite the fact that he's allowed Dingane to persuade him to join Mnkabayi.

*I'll give you this, old witch, and consider it my lobolo for our nuptial: you had me fooled there. I couldn't understand why Mhlangana, he thinks. Why that one?*

*And know this – I would have moved fast to remedy things once you had replaced Shaka with Mhlangana. That prince wouldn't even have lasted as long as Sigujana! Instead I would have put Dingane on the throne.*

*So, my dear Mnkabayi, you who are everybody's favourite meddling aunt, it didn't take much persuading on Dingane's part!*

He scratches his chin. The question now is how deeply has the Needy One been drawn into Mnkabayi's coven?

'I am being used,' he muses, 'and I will be happy to be used if it means I strike the killing blow. But when the time comes to discard me – and, as a King-killer, I must be made to vanish sooner or later – will Dingane go along with them without demur? Or will he realise, and remember, how valuable an ally I can be?

'And with the Induna missing, presumed dead, he'll need all the friends he can get. And I will merely advise, whereas Mnkabayi will meddle and seek to control.'

And if Dingane is disobedient, there's always the psychotic Mhlangana to wield as a threat . . .

★

They've noticed how he's tiring and have adapted their pace accordingly. Anyway, Xosha has sent out smaller groups in various directions to mislead potential pursuers; and it seems as if the Shangaans have passed on through and are heading north again. So they can afford to move more slowly, although who knows how many supposedly vanquished tribes have joined the Khumalos, and are now roaming about in search of easy pickings.

★

*Saving Shaka . . .*

Mbopa hasn't considered that a viable option for a while – and it's not because of the great crime the King committed against him. Ever since the King demanded that the First Fruits be celebrated only by himself, Shaka has been losing his grip – on the affairs of his kingdom and also his sanity. The end of this particular journey has been in sight ever since then.

Mbopa has quietly set about building up his own army, establishing his own power base. At the time of the assassination attempt – and already thinking ahead – he assumed command of the Nyosi or Bees regiment, saying he too wanted to have a hand in hunting down the would-be killer or killers. Since then he's ensured the Bees have been kept policing the kingdom's eastern border. They took part in the campaign against Faku, and it required a lot of manoeuvring on Mbopa's part to ensure they weren't among the regiments sent straight to Mozambique.

After a suitable amount of time had elapsed, he sent the Bees back into Pondo territory to collect all the cattle that had been taken from Faku's people. With the regiments hastening to obey

470

Shaka's summons, these beasts had been left along the route the army had taken through the country between the Umzimkhulu and Port Natal. Fear of Shaka had meanwhile prevented the Pondoes from 'reclaiming' the animals.

These cattle remain forgotten – not surprising in the light of subsequent events – and having them in his possession, and hidden away, means Mbopa has a fair amount of capital with which to bribe sundry generals and headmen.

So he is by no means unarmed or unprepared.

'They want me on their side,' Mbopa tells himself, 'though my participation isn't indispensable (I'm not so vain), but it will make things a little easier because the people trust Mbopa. They know how much I have endured and how loyal I have remained. And, because I am thus trusted, Mnkabayi and her minions, too, think they can trust me.'

He chuckles.

But they can't.

# INTERLUDE
## He Contemplates The Difference Between
## The Sun & The Moon

*The thing is, it was really very simple. It only began to sound compli-*
*cated when he tried to explain it to someone else — and Mnkabayi was the*
*only person he had tried to discuss it with.*

*Never mind the fact that the Zulus have been helping shipwreck survivors*
*for generations: the White Men arrive at Thekwini and then come to see*
*the mighty Shaka. What seem to be differences — the colour of their skin,*
*the kinds of clothes they wear as if they are ashamed of that colour, the*
*language they speak — turn out to be cosmetic, and they're welcomed.*

*But, in his dealings with these savages, Shaka began to catch glimpses*
*of a deeper difference, or so he thought, and one these White Men them-*
*selves weren't aware of. It was a difference that had to do with — and here*
*words always began to fail him — with knowledge, power . . .*

*And so he had invited the White Men to the First Fruits, where he*
*hoped the Night Muthi would help him learn more about this difference,*
*this otherness.*

*Yes, yes, he had resorted to sorcery, despite his animosity to sangomas;*
*but it was by then his only option — the only way left of getting more than*
*glimpses.*

*And?*

*And, much to his chagrin, it hadn't seemed to work.*

*At least not until the night he was stabbed and Fynn was tending to*
*him, and he gripped the White Man's wrist to stop himself from scream-*
*ing in pain, and there had been a connection of sorts.*

*He couldn't understand much of what he saw, can't even remember*
*much of what he saw, but this remains . . .*

*A woman gives birth to three daughters, and one remains while two* move on. They leave footprints that span centuries, becoming mud huts and towering cities, battlefields and bustling caravanserai, becoming canoes, pirogues, dhows and other craft capable of venturing further and further out into the oceans. Three become many, but the many will always be kin to those three – and their mother.

And some of the many find themselves in a cold land of dark forests. The ancestors of the White Men's ancestors, they begin to revere the sun as a source of warmth and hope. And, in turn, the sun takes possession of them, gradually burning off their humanity . . .

Mnkabayi had suggested that Shaka felt this difference, this otherness, lay in the fact that the White Men were of the sun, while the People of the Sky were of the night. As a result, the White Men believed all was knowable, for didn't the sun eventually illuminate everything? And their shadows . . . You had to watch those shifting shapes because, for the present, these savages would be affable, seeking only peace, but then the sun will shift, and the shadows will shift, and they will become vindictive and underhand.

That's why these savages could never be trusted, Mnkabayi had said. 'And they will fear us, fearing the night for the mysteries it holds, secrets beyond the reach of the sun they revere,' she had said.

She was right but, as he's discovered, there's even more to it than that.

Gradually he has come to understand the Night Muthi hadn't failed him. Instead, it had tried to show him he was looking for the wrong thing.

To him, the White Men had come to seem like creatures created by another, more powerful entity. It had got the colour of their skin and a few other things wrong, but there were enough similarities for the two nations to meet amicably. What was this entity? What power, what new horizons, could it offer a tired King?

But he was wrong.

They are truly like albinos, Mnkabayi had told him – cursed in themselves and a curse to others.

473

*But there was more . . .*

*A mother. Three daughters. Footprints across time.*

*The sun may have changed their skin colour, but it hadn't burnt off their humanity after all. Those were only Mnkabayi's words getting in the way of his memory.*

*No — a mother; three daughters; footprints across time — these people were brothers at last returning home.*

*And now it's not the differences that terrify Shaka. It's not the differences that contribute to his malaise, this tiredness, this dread . . . it's the similarities.*

# 10
## The Thing In The Reeds

**September 17, 1828**

The People of the Sky have what has to be one of the odder creation myths around. Here's how Koto of the Langeni tribe, whose father's sister was Nandi, the mother of Shaka, explained it to Henry Callaway in the 1860s: 'Unkulunkulu came into being and gave being to man. He came out of a bed of reeds.' In other versions it's said Unkulunkulu, the Great Spirit himself, emerged from the reeds first, before calling on man and woman to follow him – 'and at their word there came out all those works which we see, both those of cattle and of food – all the food which we eat'.

That's it: humanity emerged from an umhlanga, a bank of reeds. And that's the tale recounted in countless books on Zulu myths and legends.

However, H. C. Lugg, who lived and worked among the Amazulu for all of his life, has an interesting theory. First he points out that the Zulus claimed all tribes had emerged from reeds. Then he observes that the word 'uhlanga' could refer to a reed, but also to any other hollow tube such as a length of bamboo or, later, an empty cartridge case hung from the neck as a snuff container.

He notes that Callaway and other missionaries who set about collecting information about Zulu beliefs were obviously well versed in biblical history and the bulrush story of Moses. When they then heard the word uhlanga, they naturally equated it with 'umhlanga', or reed bed. 'But,' writes Lugg, 'there is nothing more abhorrent to the Zulu mind than to imagine that his creation was associated with fish, frogs and other aquatic life.'

On the other hand, the Zulu custom of hlonipha – the 'language of respect' – means the use of euphemisms is widespread. For example, if a King is named Induku, or Stick, another word has to be used when referring to a stick. The same applies 'in matters referring to the toilet or sex', says Lugg. The penis is referred to as the umphambili, or 'front portion', or indeed as the 'induku' – stick. And Lugg believes 'uhlanga' – hollow reed – was being used in the same way.

And, doubtless puzzled by the bizarre lack of basic biological knowledge implied by the question, those interrogated by the missionaries were politely trying to tell them that humanity emerged from the penis.

Whichever version is correct, and were he in a position to consider such things, the Induna would be forced to agree that the abomination crouching in an opening in an umhlanga could just as well have sprung from someone's festering penis as from the surrounding reeds.

Right now, though, he's still too dazed, entangled in the blurred memories of those final few kilometres . . .

. . . *trudging along, your head bowed, no longer caring what your young companions might think, your pain a barking dog holding your pride at bay. Just get there. Just make it . . .*

Then, long after the mountains had swallowed the sun, the arrival . . .

. . . *drawing back, raising his spear through his giddiness, because there were women, so many women of all ages, and his time among the Wild Cat People came back to him, and he was among them again, among those harridans, ready to fight. But then he was aware of calming words. There was the smell of cooking meat; also of uhlelen-*

*jwayo, a gruel made of crushed stalks that have not borne mealies and sweetened with imfe, wild sugar cane. He was among Zulu women; good, kind Zulu women. And he dropped his spear, and dropped on to some mats. Could barely manage a few mouthfuls before falling asleep . . .*

The Induna frowns, pretending to be more anaesthetised than he really is, and tries not to notice the ugliness sitting cross-legged on the other side of the shallow stream that separates them. A man must first make sure his hut can withstand the harshest storm, before turning his mind to other things within the kraal.

The fuzziness in his head brings to mind the muthi Duthlle had fed him to keep him docile, before that other long trudge, and this suggests he's been drugged here too . . .

*. . . and by Zulus! Why? Why would his own people . . . ?*

But let those questions chew the cud for a while. Working out exactly when he had been drugged is more important for now – not least because he needs to know how much time he's already wasted.

Conscious of the thing's eyes on him, glistening, and knowing, he remembers waking up in the early afternoon the day after their arrival. A veritable feast had been awaiting him. He had gorged himself, swallowed lakes of beer and then, just as he was beginning to pay attention to his surroundings, he felt tiredness creeping up on him again. Suddenly, the urge to keep moving, and the promise he had made to Shaka – these things seemed of little consequence. As did the fear he felt for his wife's safety, and the safety of the King, of Mthunzi, of Njikiza, even of Dingane.

'Are you now completely with us, Nduna?' asks the deformity across the way. 'That is to say, we trust that parts of you don't still remain strewn along the many paths you've had to traverse lately?'

The Induna narrows his eyes. Is it – he – a hairless monkey? Cha! But the vervet this one so closely resembles, with his tiny toes and hands, his short skeletal limbs, doesn't have brown skin beneath its fur; neither are its facial features as human-like.

Or is he looking at his first tikoloshe? There is after all the water, and amatikoloshe hide in rivers. But this is no river! The rustling stream in front of him wouldn't even cover a man's feet. And those small, malevolent creatures are supposed to be covered in ochre-coloured fur and have black piggy eyes, a dog's snout, and a tail that doubles as its penis. Anyway, these creatures who ride out at night astride hyenas are merely tales told by sango-mas to frighten the gullible!

Or – almost unthinkable this – is he dealing with some kind of malformed child, with the body of a child just out of its infancy, yet the compressed, crushed, wrinkled face of a man who has seen at least forty summers, maybe even fifty?

The small hand makes a sweeping motion. 'Please! Feel free to break your fast while we speak, because you must regain your strength.' A grin. 'And rest assured there will be no more muthi placed in your food. Although that was done partly for your own benefit.'

'For my own benefit?' asks the Induna, looking up from the pots placed in the gap between himself and the stream.

'Yes, so we could cauterise that,' says the other, a small finger indicating the Induna's thigh.

The warrior's hand drops to the wound. There's a poultice there now – and pain when he presses against it . . .

. . . *and he has a brief memory of waking up screaming as a red-hot*

478

*assegai blade was pressed against the wound; waking up screaming and being held down as the smell of burning flesh filled his nostrils.*

'The wound will heal now,' continues the man-child. 'And the poultice contains a special potion to deaden the pain. Hai! But I forget – you know of this muthi,' he adds. For the Induna has experience of the Wild Cat People, has he not?

Well, a few of their number, preferring a more regular infusion of semen, have left the tribe, and some have found their way to this merry group – where they have shared the secret of the potion with the inyangas.

'We will give you a supply when you leave us, and you will need it to keep going, trust me. But, in the meanwhile, please eat! As I've said, you need not fear any more sleeping draughts.'

Keeping his eyes on this man-child, this monkey-man, this abomination, the Induna selects a piece of lumpy porridge and pops it into his mouth.

The creature doesn't laugh so much as cackle. 'Now I can see you are wondering whether you can throw yourself across this stream and be upon me before I can call for help. Do not delude yourself there. You have your udibi, I have my women.'

At this the Induna feels a blade tap his left shoulder, and he twists his head to look over his shoulder. The woman who stands smiling down at him has a long isijula, or hunting spear, held firmly in her hands.

He's seen her somewhere before . . .

It's only when he glances again at the midget, then back at the woman, that the memory drops into place.

Lombi!

'You!' He addresses the midget again. 'You were the one who stole the spear. And you,' he says, turning to the woman, 'you smuggled him out with the spear right under our very noses, strapped to your back like an infant.'

The clapping of small monkey hands. 'Well done, Nduna. Although, of course, it wasn't the real spear, thanks to your cunning. But our paths have also crossed at other times and I have been a little more successful on occasion.'

'Who are you?'

'They call me General Hlakanyana – those who look to me for protection and the chance to enrich themselves.'

Hlakanyana? The child who, while still in the womb, told his mother it was time she gave birth to him. Who ate all his clan's meat, and left bones in each hut so everyone would blame everyone else. Who, when captured by cannibals and put into a pot by their mother, persuaded her to let him out and threw her in instead, cooked her and fed her to her own sons. Who murdered an elder who had the temerity to reprove him for bad behaviour, by trapping the old man in a hut with an open sack filled with snakes, scorpions, spiders and other venomous horrors.

Many are the tales told about Hlakanyana, who cut his own umbilical cord and robbed, lied and murdered his way through the world.

If this little deformity, who somehow avoided being strangled at birth, wants to adopt the name of a character from a tale told to children, that's just fine by the Induna. And the fact that this Hlakanyana claims he has bested the Induna on previous occasions is a matter the warrior will deal with another time – but deal with it he will.

Why has he gone to so much trouble to ensnare him? *That's* the important question for now.

'Yes, let us get down to business,' says Hlakanyana. 'I saw in your eyes when I mentioned that our paths have crossed that, despite all you have seen and endured on the road, a part of you would like to see justice done, as if nothing has changed.' He leans back. 'Well and good, for if justice is still important to you, then I haven't wasted my time in searching for you. And that wasn't my initial plan, understand?'

Oh no, Hlakanyana had resolved to herd his little tribe as far away as it was possible to get from Shaka's territory. Then the tales told to him by the women from the Wild Cat People led him to reconsider. Their accounts of the powerful Zulu who thwarted Mantatisi could only refer to the Induna. He was still alive, then, and just the man Hlakanyana needed.

He sniggers. 'Is that not a sign of how dire these days have become – that General Hlakanyana should require the assistance of the Nduna, and that the Nduna should agree to help him! Aiee!'

The monkey hand flattens the air, as if seeking to calm the outrage that tightens the Induna's muscles. 'And you will, Nduna. You will agree to this most unlikely of alliances, once you've heard what I've had to say.'

Then, of course, there's the fact that, when he speaks of an 'alliance', it doesn't mean they'll be standing – here Hlakanyana chuckles – shoulder to knee in the face of the coming tempest. Once they've finished their duologue, it's highly unlikely the Induna will ever see him again!

'We'll see about that,' thinks the warrior, reaching for some more porridge. He's mildly surprised to find himself still hungry.

'I have worked for many masters,' continues Hlakanyana, 'although none remain to tell anyone more about me than I'd like known. For perpetual silence has been my final task for them.

Of course, I allowed . . . hmm, whispers to circulate, so that others might come demanding my special talents.'

And so it was with Mhlangana, he adds, as the Induna piles black beans, imbuya – a spinach-like vegetable – and the coarse yellow flesh from some amaphuzi – a form of pumpkin – into a bowl.

'He is ambitious, vain, ruthless and fancies himself far more intelligent than he is. In short, he was perfect for my purposes.'

'Purposes?' echoes the Induna.

'I like killing, Nduna. It is my meat, and the suffering of others is my sweet amasi.' Which is not surprising, he explains, in one who had no mother to prepare amasi for him, that special treat comprising milk curds so beloved of children.

'Hai, spare me your look of disgust! Let a man kill another man, it is murder. Let a King kill thousands of men, it is policy. But I am not here to debate or justify and, as far as Mhlangana's concerned, there is no need for debate, or' – a smile – 'justification, for this lizard is a friend to neither of us. More than that, he'd have us both eating dirt if given the slightest chance.'

The Induna can no longer feel the blade of Lombi's spear. Clever that, not letting the tip of her blade touch him, for that would give him some idea of where she's standing, should he try to disarm her.

The man-monkey goes on to name some of those he killed for Mhlangana, adding that he was the one who murdered the prince's servant, Eqa, a few months ago.

'As a warning to the prince?'

'You might say that.'

'Had the two of you had a falling out, then?'

The features on that infant-like head scrunch together in a smile. 'No, the falling out, as you say, came much earlier. It started when that fool Kholisa came crawling to the prince. As you will recall, he was setting himself up to take Nobela's place as the most powerful sangoma in the kingdom. Then you and Mgobozi shamed him in public and, I suppose, he decided a more subtle approach was called for.'

Mhlangana was the ideal patron, and Kholisa had impressed him with all manner of fatuous, addle-headed ideas. And Hlakanyana's services were therefore less and less frequently required. And things had come to a head over the Umkhontho Wamadlozi. That accursed spear! 'Did you know Nandi wanted it, too?'

His mouth full of wild fig, the Induna nods.

Hlakanyana's failure to deliver the real Umkhontho into Mhlangana's hands had resulted in a major rift. 'I have no doubt he would have had me killed, but I'd already had my doubts about the spear's authenticity, so made sure I was nowhere to be found when poor Bamba presented it to the prince.'

Instead there had followed an uneasy truce, when Mhlangana had quickly let it be known he did not in fact blame Hlakanyana for failing to acquire the genuine spear. 'I had found occasion to warn him of what had happened to my previous employers,' explains the midget. 'Not my standard practice, naturally, but I had already learnt this was an unstable man and a stupid one, too, who had to have his nose rubbed into it before he got the message.'

Meanwhile Kholisa had become Mhlangana's man, the one whose magic would lead the prince to the throne.

'Yet, when things started to go wrong, who did the prince send for? General Hlakanyana, of course. I was the one who fed the poor creature, tried to tend to its wounds, scout out the paths it would take when it set out to kill.'

A shrug. 'It was demeaning work.'

Not only has the woman made sure her blade isn't touching him, she's also standing in such a way the Induna can see neither her shadow nor her reflection in the water.

Looking up, brightening, Hlakanyana continues: 'I did learn one thing, though. There was someone extremely powerful helping him. Unfortunately I could never find out who this person was. Despite the failure of the plot, I have no reason to doubt that person is still helping the prince.'

At any rate, the plot's failure had put Hlakanyana's life in danger. It was time for a tactical withdrawal. Then, when he heard of the attempt on Shaka's life at the end of the First Fruits, he reckoned he would be spared the chore of killing Mhlangana.

'Because who but Mhlangana would have been behind such a stupid plan?' he asks. 'Hai, one doesn't just kill a King, not if one wants to live long enough to enjoy the fruits of one's labours.'

He'd thought it was only a matter of time before the prince was identified as the one behind the plot to kill Shaka, and thus sent to the impalers. But apparently it hadn't been Mhlangana, and so Hlakanyana had withdrawn even further, to consider his options. And duly found himself in the service of Faku, who, tired of being bullied by Shaka, was seeking to strengthen his position by winning over the other tribes and clans in the region.

'Ah!' says Hlakanyana, as another woman places a pot full of ubisi next to the Induna. 'Fresh milk! Drink and enjoy, for our cows produce very sweet milk!'

The warrior reaches for the pot, and takes a sip. The man-monkey is right: it *is* sweet.

At any rate, continues the creature, as soon as he heard about the trouble Shaka's army was experiencing in Mozambique and the growing discontent at home, he returned to Zulu territory, knowing here was another chance for Mhlangana and whoever was helping him to seize power.

'That's right, Zulu. Mhlangana means to kill your King. And if he succeeds, you can be sure all those loyal to the King will be next to die. That means Mnkabayi, Ndlela, Mbopa, Pampata, and who knows who else. And if I were Dingane, I wouldn't be complacent either. And then there's you – your life will also be worthless.'

The Induna looks up.

'Oh, yes, I have seen to it that certain rumours have been spread and by now the prince is likely to know you're still alive and at large.'

'You spoke of an alliance between us,' observes the Induna.

'Yes, but my part is finished. Even General Hlakanyana grows old and stiff, and isn't as nimble as he used to be or else, believe you me, I would be going after that lizard myself! But that is not to be.'

The Induna frowns, wondering why his head feels as if it's about to float off his shoulders.

'I have already done what I can to thwart Mhlangana's plans, the rest is up to you.'

The Induna shakes his head. Touches his left cheek, which feels numb. Or maybe it's his fingers that are numb.

'It's up to you now, Nduna,' continues the midget. 'It's up to you to catch and kill Mhlangana and save your King's life, as well as the lives of the many others who will die if Shaka dies. It's up to you.'

The world is starting to tilt. The Induna tries to stand, but Lombi's hand on his head pushes him down again.

'I did not lie when I told you there was no muthi in your food, but I said nothing about the milk.' Hlakanyana rises, looking more simian than ever. 'Do not worry, though. You will not sleep long, for you have much to do. But by the time you wake up, we will be gone.'

# 11

## The Happy Prince

**September 18, 1828**

Mnkabayi has just finished her breakfast and is waiting for the others to arrive. She is using this time to compose herself, for she hasn't felt this happy for a long while.

Late last night a young girl had been brought to her. She had been out courting, she explained, and while making her way home had come across a badly injured woman. After getting the girl to make her comfortable and light a fire, the woman had sent her to find Mnkabayi. 'Her name is Muvani, Ma, and she says she must speak to you at once,' said the girl.

Hoping nothing had gone wrong with the plan to kill Pampata, Mnkabayi immediately sent for Ndlela, who of course fussed like a granny when Mnkabayi insisted on going to see the injured woman herself. But, as Muvani was one of her servants, that was the least she could do.

After she had led them to the donga where the fire was burning, the girl was sent home. Mnkabayi doubted she needed any warning to say nothing of this occurrence, as a girl of her age staying out with her boyfriend this late probably faced her parents' wrath, were they to hear of the escapade.

Blood covered Muvani's midriff and her hands, and from her ragged breathing it was clear she was dying.

With Ndlela's help, Mnkabayi lowered herself to the ground so that she lay on her side next to Muvani.

'What is it, my Daughter?'

Whimpering and groaning, and gasping in pain as she squeezed Mnkabayi's hand, Muvani told her how she had fallen upon Pampata and the others, as soon as they reached the dela innyoni. Pampata fought back fiercely and had severely wounded Muvani, before Shaka's beloved was made to eat dust.

Somehow Muvani had managed to make it back to Bulawayo. 'I am sorry, Ma,' she hissed. 'S-sorry I could not' – a breath like rustling leaves – 'could not bring you Pampata's head.'

Mnkabayi had squeezed Muvani's hand. 'As long as she is dead. And she is dead, isn't she?'

'Y-yes, Ma,' said Muvani. 'And there . . . there's something else I must tell you,' she whispered.

★

Mbopa, Dingane and Mhlangana arrive, to be ushered into the hut by Ndlela.

'Willing', 'eager', 'enthusiastic': these are the adjectives that apply to Mhlangana this morning. It's as if he's scraped years of sullen surliness off his countenance. Not that this change is noted by his companions, who all have much on their minds. Besides, the prince is trying hard to hide his good humour.

At first, though . . . aiee! At first, when Ndlela told him Dingane had come over to their side, it had felt as if a spear had been driven up his spine, the blade scraping against every vertebra and causing sparks before embedding itself in the back of his neck. Fortunately, though, he had succeeded in maintaining his composure.

Fortunately, indeed, because, as he had stalked away from Ndlela's hut, his pace began to slow as a smile formed, then suddenly he had to restrain himself from howling out loud with laughter!

Let Dingane join them, because that would just make things so much easier. There would be no chance of a repetition of what had occurred when Sigujana had been made King.

488

Sigujana hated Dingane, and it would have been easy to persuade him to arrange an accident for his brother. But, at the time of their father's death, the Needy One had been away living with the Qwabes. He was still absent when Shaka assumed the throne – and then, when he finally made his appearance, a little guile and a lot of sycophancy had seen him allowed to remain on his hind legs.

This time, though, Mhlangana will know exactly where to find his brother when the time comes . . .

But what's Mnkabayi going on about now?

'So it is done,' she says.

Mhlangana quickly scans the faces of the others for a clue as to what exactly has been done. Ndlela's face remains placid, but both Dingane and Mbopa show surprise. The Needy One seems especially taken aback.

'Pampata?' he says disbelievingly. 'Dead?'

*What? Can this be so?* thinks Mhlangana.

Mnkabayi nods.

'You are sure, completely sure?' asks Mbopa.

'Yes, she eats dust.'

'And what of those who did the deed?' says Mhlangana, thinking fast.

An irritated stare from Dingane. 'Haven't you been listening, Brother?'

Eager to ensure the enmity between the two is kept to a low hum, Mnkabayi interrupts before Mhlangana can respond: 'Yes, it is as I said. Those who did the deed will not be around to implicate us.'

*Us? You mean you, you old hag! Cha! But this is no time for such pettiness. Pampata dead? That is something,* thinks Mhlangana. *There's no turning back now.*

489

Nonetheless, seeking to irritate Dingane further, and perhaps provoke his aunt, who looks altogether too pleased with herself this morning, Mhlangana asks about those who saw to those who had seen to Pampata.

Dingane doesn't disappoint: he rolls his eyes and shakes his head. Mnkabayi, however, merely smiles, taking his question seriously. 'Of course they didn't know why they were taking care of those who . . .'

'They were ordered to take care of?' suggests Mbopa.

'Precisely.' The smile is still there as she regards Mhlangana. 'Satisfied, Nephew? May we continue?'

'Certainly,' says the prince, waving his hand in an imperious *be-my-guest* gesture and earning a disgusted *Cha!* from his brother.

★

Fat Mbopa speaks next. At last the plunder taken from the Pondoes has been collected together. It will be transported to KwaDukuza tomorrow, and there presented to the King by a contingent of troops who fought in that same campaign. The prime minister will accompany them. Even if his attendance hadn't been mandatory, he would have still wanted to be there, just so he could provide a ready answer should Shaka ask why the cattle that comprise the loot are so puny and so few. As it is, Mbopa's presence means he'll be able to see how things are at the kraal and, more specifically, if Shaka is still there alone with his chief body servant, Thenjiwe. Then the soldiers will relieve those on duty, and Mbopa will return to Bulawayo with this same party.

'What about the soldiers who remain behind?' asks Mhlangana. 'Will they be of a mind to give us trouble?'

'Rest assured, I'll be able to talk them over.'

'Hai, cannibal! Perhaps you overestimate your powers of persuasion, for I know they certainly do not work on me!' Mhlangana looks around, expecting laughter, then shrugs on hearing none. *What a glum bunch!* But his concern is real. What if the men decide to defend Shaka?

'I do not think much persuading will be necessary,' Mbopa says. 'Do not forget, they are among the men who were sent straight from fighting Pondoes to make war on the Shangaan.' They have witnessed at first hand the suffering endured in the swamps, and doubtless they couldn't stop praising the ancestors when they were called back.

'Hai! They may even wish to join us!' suggests the prime minister.

'Which cannot be allowed to happen,' snaps Mnkabayi. The army has, by and large, adopted a wait-and-see policy, and therefore must not be given the slightest chance to claim credit should their plan succeed.

'I understand that,' says Mbopa. 'I was merely endeavouring to put the prince's mind at rest.'

*Fuck you, fat Mbopa. Your day will come,* thinks Mhlangana.

'Speaking of the army,' says Dingane, 'I trust Mdlaka has already left . . .'

Yes, confirms Mnkabayi; he and his bodyguard left for Mozambique early this morning, to recall the regiments at last. It's part of that wait-and-see policy, and also a way of salving Mdlaka's conscience. The commander-in-chief can later say he wasn't there when Shaka was overthrown, so could do nothing to stop it.

'And so he can reap the rewards, while pretending to have had nothing to do with the actual deed,' grumbles Mhlangana.

'Nonetheless, his expertise will still be needed in the seasons to come,' says Mnkabayi. 'What of your own men, Nephew, are they moving into place?'

The prince nods. He feels a little uneasy about this aspect of the operation. On the one hand, it's good his men will be largely responsible for bringing down those whose loyalty to Shaka is unswerving, and who will therefore constitute a threat in the disorganised days immediately following the mad King's execution. On the other hand, though, he's worried that it's the regiments belonging to Dingane and Mnkabayi that have been tasked with keeping order at Bulawayo. Only a few of his men will be present, here, but he decides not to say anything for now. He has anyway ordered his men to head straight back to Bulawayo as soon as they're done with the killing.

'Good,' says Mnkabayi. 'And you, Dingane? Are your men ready?'

'They are, Ma.'

'As are ours,' adds Ndlela.

Mnkabayi looks around the group. 'Is there anything else we have to discuss?'

Ndlela coughs politely and says, yes, there is.

★

Mnkabayi has orchestrated this, and it's become even more important, in view of what she heard last night. 'What is it?' she asks.

It involves Mthunzi, the Induna's former udibi, and also Njikiza, explains Ndlela. They have both been pestering him to be allowed to go and help protect the King.

'They have been snapping at my heels also,' adds Mbopa.

'Well, then, they must be sent on an errand,' decides Mnkabayi.

As they have planned, Ndlela suggests despatching them to investigate alleged sightings of Pondo scouts in the coastal region.

Mhlangana has to struggle to hide his grin. *Oh, beloved Aunt, you are making things too easy for your poor, despised nephew!* he thinks. He has so long wanted to see that smug sycophant and his cronies brought down. Since disease has allowed the Induna to elude him – and here's hoping he died a lonely, miserable death – he can at least see to it that the big fool and the Shadow of the Shadow join their master sooner than expected. Oh, yes, indeed, let the Shadow become a shade!

And, in a burst of inspiration, he sees how he can improve on Ndlela's suggestion and ensure that they are finally made to eat dust.

Speaking with the humility of one tentatively making a suggestion, and nothing more, he wonders if that isn't a little too vague. Might not being told spies have been seen, therefore go find them, strike Mthunzi and Njikiza as a little odd? Might it not even arouse their suspicions? Why not give them something more concrete to reflect on?

And this is where he can help. Bamba, one of his indunas, has a brother-in-law who lives in the coastal region. Why not tell them this man has spotted the spies, and thus send them to his homestead to investigate?

Of course, the brother-in-law will have to be forewarned in order to play along, but that won't be a problem. He can send Bamba to him today; and Bamba will have been and gone before the intended victims arrive.

Mnkabayi gives Mhlangana's suggestion a moment's thought, then says yes, that *is* a good idea – see to it.

★

The meeting over, with only Ndlela remaining, Mnkabayi sits down to savour Muvani's final revelation last night. 'There's something else,' she had whispered, seeming to rally, as if the joy she knew her tale would bring Mnkabayi had strengthened her momentarily.

It was the Induna! On their way to Pampata's dela innyoni they'd heard whispers and rumours that the Induna is alive, and making his way towards Bulawayo, killing every Shangaan who stands in his path.

'It could merely be wishful thinking,' she observes, as though musing aloud.

Ndlela hesitates, then says: 'It could be.'

'One doesn't want to get one's hopes up . . .'

'Always a good strategy, Ma, yet . . .'

'Yet?' she asks, looking up like an eager young girl for a moment.

'It could be true.'

'It could.'

'You spoke of a feeling, Ma, a special feeling, a sense of knowing . . .'

'Yes! And Kani had the same feeling.'

'This is so. And now you have made sure she is safe, Ma. And you have done the same for the udibi.'

'He has to be, Ndlela. He has to be alive!'

★

The prince has Nolaka, the Leopard Man, summoned to his hut. Of course he's not going to send Bamba, even if it is the man's brother-in-law; for the induna's behaviour has been worrying him of late. It could be that he is going soft on him, so better to send Nolaka instead.

Who initially seems disappointed when Mhlangana outlines his plan.

494

Noticing this, the prince chuckles and says Nolaka is not to worry. He'll still have ample time to rejoin the other platoon, the one tasked with the more pleasurable . . . well, task.

'I only wish I could be there with you!' chuckles the prince.

# 12
## A Slight Digression

**September 21, 1828**

A brief but violent thunderstorm has turned the sea and horizon into a single blur of grey, hiding the *Elizabeth Susan* at anchor in the bay, behind a deluge of watery liquid arrows. But now the sun slices through the clouds, and the denizens of Port Natal have emerged from the wattle-and-daub structure that still forms the centre of the settlement.

Wearing a Zulu kilt, and with a blanket around his shoulders, Fynn stands next to Jakot, reflecting on how little the sun has done to dispel the gloom.

*Gloom.* He thinks how onomatopoeic that word is, and how its sound mirrors their present attitude. He ponders how different it is to their initial enthusiasm, his own initial enthusiasm, and his dreams of meeting the great King who had cowed all around him. Dreams of piles of ivory, of rivers glittering with gold, all just waiting to be scooped up. And for him, for Fynn himself, there was the allure of blank spaces, uncharted territory.

And now gloom. Such a gloomy place. Like the Slough of Despond.

Farewell's company is short of capital, and he continues to regard Fynn as a traitor who went over to James King's side as soon as Shaka chose him as his new favourite. He also, rightly in this instance, blames the ailing King for destroying all his patient negotiation with Shaka and his quiet pleading with the authorities at the Cape, and being responsible for their current predicament. No investors now, meaning no ships lining up in the roadstead. No gewgaws with which to soothe matters with

Shaka; and nothing to barter with. How much finer were the beads they then had to offer than the ones the Zulus received from the Portuguese! To think that had been a boast of theirs! And here they are, thinks Fynn, watching the evaporation rising from the wet ground like a veil; here they are with empty bellies, because they are barely able to feed themselves.

Jakot, who's wearing a collarless shirt and tattered trousers that reach only to his calves, wishes the White Man would move away and leave him to enjoy this cessation of the sky's anger, as well as the smells awakened by the rain. Because Fynn stinks of sweat, smoke and rot. It's a sewage stench that brings to mind the streets of Cape Town.

Francis Farewell and John Cane are standing over by the newly prepared vegetable beds which have now become huge puddles of coffee-brown water. Farewell whistles loudly towards the ragged huts a few metres away, where reside some of the refugees they protect from Shaka.

A motley assortment of scarred old-timers with crooked legs and some limping men and a few maidens emerge. The sores and disfigurements on display are enough to make a man vomit, but the urge to do so is partly ameliorated by the maidens. By some of them, at least – and one in particular as far as Henry Ogle's concerned.

He's built his own kraal a few kilometres away, but happened to be caught here by the storm. He's quite the unumzane these days, all but worshipped by his 'tribe', and he reckons it's time he took a third wife. And this one might just do. She has a bum like a cushion, ideal for some good thrusting – bet she likes it rough, or will get to like it rough under the right tutelage – and tits that could suffocate a man, porridge smackers made to slide over his cock.

He's about to call out to her when a cry from a man with an arm permanently bent like a wing turns her round and has her quickening her pace in the opposite direction.

'What the blazes!' exclaims Farewell, as both men realise all of their wards are similarly making themselves scarce. And they're not heading for their huts either, but pushing their way through the bushes beyond.

Then, as Cane joins them, smoking marijuana in his pipe, they glance over to where Jakot and Fynn are standing, and see the reason for this sudden exodus.

Two Zulus have made their appearance. One is carrying a spear, while the other – the giant they know to be some kind of hero among the People of the Sky – simply carries a huge club.

'Now what?' mutters Farewell, as these warriors make their way towards Fynn and Jakot, who has seized on the appearance of Njikiza and the udibi as an excuse to put some nostril-cleansing distance between himself and Fynn.

Since their encounter with the slavers, things have grown more cordial between him and the new arrivals. A certain amount of chaffing still goes on, but even the Watcher seems to regard Jakot with respect these days. In fact, Mthunzi is somewhat startled to note a certain amount of sheepishness in the big man's demeanour as they now exchange greetings with the Xhosa.

A further indication of the change in their relationship is the fact that the udibi gets down to business right away. 'We have been told Faku's Pondoes are abroad,' he declares. 'Is this true?'

Something – a hunch, a gnawing suspicion; the udibi doesn't know what exactly, only that the Induna would call it 'Sky Knowledge' – has led him to suggest to Njikiza earlier that they first visit Thekwini. It's not too far out of their way, and Fynn has been having dealings with Faku regularly. If anyone knows

whether the Pondoes have been planning a foray into Zulu territory, it will be him.

The udibi's question arouses in Jakot a twinge of fear, for Faku's
Pondoes are not to be trifled with. Therefore he says he will ask
Fynn.

Old habits die hard, and the udibi watches their exchange
closely to see if Fynn's expression and attitude contradict whatever Jakot chooses to tell them subsequently. He sees Fynn shake
his head vehemently, sees Fynn glance in their direction and then
reply to Jakot, his face showing insistence and certainty.

'He says no,' says Jakot, when he returns to them. 'He says
Shaka's last campaign pushed Faku further down the coast, where
he bumped into the Bhacas, and now the two tribes are busy
growling at each other.'

'He is sure?' asks Mthunzi, looking past Jakot to examine Fynn.

'Yes. He has been in a bad mood, because now Faku is beyond
the reach of even his feet, and anyway the path to there is haunted
by bandits. And he says Faku won't be returning just yet.'

After thanking him, the Zulus turn to leave, but Jakot falls in
step alongside the boy. 'The Nduna?' he asks. 'Has he returned?'

The boy shakes his head.

'Aiee,' hisses Jakot.

★

And there they stand together: Farewell, Ogle, Cane and Fynn.
Even James King has risen from his sickbed to stand leaning against
the doorpost of the wattle-and-daub structure, with a blanket
draped over his shoulders. There they stand – the traders who,
on land granted them by Shaka, King of Kings, created the settlement that later became Durban, a city that, by the twenty-first
century, would cover more than two thousand square kilometres
and have a population of around three and a half million.

Since they're all here together as it were (although King has tottered inside again), and our tale is nearing its end, a slight digression is surely in order to trace the course of these men's lives.

★

James King skippered the *Salisbury*, which Farewell chartered to seek a site on the south-east coast from which the Farewell Trading Company could commence commerce with Shaka. On their return to Cape Town after (re)discovering, by accident, exactly the kind of sheltered bay Farewell was looking for, King sets about trying to sell the idea of establishing a British settlement there to Earl Bathurst, Secretary of State for Colonies – but without mentioning Farewell in any of his correspondence.

Farewell feels betrayed, and the two will never now be able to put aside their differences. But someone like King, who's willing to brave the storms that bedevil this stretch of coast, not to mention the sandbar across the entrance to the bay, is not to be shunned.

King's fortunes change for the better after the assassination attempt on Shaka, but the failure of the diplomatic mission sent to negotiate directly with the British government leaves him a broken man. He and Farewell are no longer on speaking terms, and he dare not visit Shaka. But these things no longer matter, for King has contracted dysentery and will die before the month is over.

★

Francis Farewell is, of course, the one who had the idea of dealing directly with Shaka and thereby cutting out the Portuguese at Delagoa. When King betrays him, he gets on with putting together his own speculation. When the Governor of the Cape, Lord Charles Somerset, gives his permission for the establishment of a trading post, so long as it remains a private venture

500

and there's no annexing of any territory on behalf of the Crown, Farewell optimistically raises the Union flag as soon as a flagpole has been fashioned for it. When times are tough – and they often are since there's no government backing for this venture – and the settlement is reduced to a handful of ragged, hirsute skeletons relying on the Zulus for food, Farewell continues making regular visits to Bulawayo, along with Fynn, always taking pains to please and entertain Shaka.

The fact that relations with Shaka are currently strained is worrying, as are the reports of dissent at the King's court, but Farewell believes that if they survived Nandi's death, they can survive anything. Besides, he sees no reason why any prince who might succeed in overthrowing Shaka wouldn't want to continue to do business with them.

There's one thing no amount of perseverance, business acumen or just plain guile can overcome, though: the tempestuous seas between here and Cape Town. They've already claimed many a ship heading to Port Natal with much needed supplies or returning to the Cape with holds full of ivory. And Farewell's been thinking of opening up an overland route between Port Natal and Port Elizabeth, which will in turn open up more business opportunities along the way, starting with trade done with Faku's Pondoes.

Finally, in September 1829, after a brief stay at Cape Town, Farewell strikes out for Port Natal to open that hoped-for trail. He's accompanied by Walker (a naturalist), Thackwray (an 1820 settler) and a number of servants.

When they reach the Umzimvubu river, Farewell visits Nqeto, chief of what remains of the Qwabes after Shaka had punished them for siding with the Thembus. The three White Men are made welcome and a cow is slaughtered in their honour. But, at dawn the following morning, Farewell, Walker and Thackwray are massacred in their tent and their bodies mutilated.

★

Henry Ogle was a member of the advance party that crossed the sandbar at the mouth of Thekwini on the *Julia* in May 1824. He was also among those who accompanied Fynn on the first landing. When a storm blew up that night, and the party was attacked by hyenas, it was Ogle who risked his life to wrest a pair of his trousers from one of the predators, because there was a Dutch sixty-dollar note in the pocket.

Aged twenty at this time, he was a 'mechanic', which in those days meant handyman or jack of all trades. And he and the others proceeded to build the large wattle-and-daub structure where the Durban Post Office now stands.

In 1826, at Fynn's urging, Ogle accompanies Farewell and King to Bulawayo to congratulate Shaka on his recovery after the assassination attempt. During the visit, the Englishmen persuade the Bull Elephant to grant them a chunk of land that extends 160 kilometres inland and stretches 40 kilometres along the coast, and which includes the high bluff that protects the bay from the storms that bedevil this littoral.

Eventually, the area immediately around the bay and on the bluff will have a population of around four thousand people, including refugees fleeing the Zulu kingdom.

While the others come and go, Ogle remains, later taking part in several skirmishes against the Zulus. In May 1838, he's one of only nine White Men who stay behind to rebuild the settlement after it's been destroyed by rampaging impis.

Having seen Port Natal begin its growth into the city of Durban, he dies on February 20, 1860.

★

502

John Cane was, in the words of one historian, 'a stormy petrel of early Natal whose life was recklessly expended for little advantage'.

A sailor on the trading route between England and the Far East, Cane liked what he saw at Batavia, as the Cape was known during the Napoleonic Wars, and stayed on to become an assistant to a local wine merchant. Hearing of Farewell's trading venture, he signs on as one of the 'mechanics'. Like Ogle, he's soon a virtual chief, possessing his own land, his own village and a collection of wives.

He's killed in a clash with the Zulus in 1838.

★

As for Henry Fynn, who loved travel for travel's sake, who had developed an interest in Shaka before joining Farewell's party, and who went to seek out the Zoola king within days of landing at the bay the Sky People called Thekwini, his is perhaps the strangest story of all. Putting aside its dubious authenticity, his diary may have eventually made him the best-known of the traders who operated from Port Natal, but it only tells half the story.

Having met and befriended Shaka, Fynn was one of the first White Men to set about trying to record Zulu customs, and he did so as objectively as possible. His occasional expressions of horror and disgust are understandable, since these were violent times. He also set out to trade with the Pondoes and established good relations with their king, Faku.

In short, as one historian puts it, he travelled where very few other White Men had ventured, depending for his life 'not only on his physical endurance but also on his ability to allay the fears and suspicions of hostile local communities'.

Then he changes, becoming a stereotype of colonial oppression.

He travels to the eastern Cape in September 1834 and, when war breaks out on the frontier in December that year, he joins Sir Benjamin D'Urban's staff as an interpreter. Three months later, he's sent to ensure Faku's neutrality in the war.

In January 1837, Fynn becomes 'diplomatic agent' to the tribes in the upper Kei region. It's a post he holds for eleven years, but what does it say about his performance there when, in 1845, the Cape Governor, Sir Peregrine Maitland, passes him over when the post of diplomatic agent in Natal becomes vacant?

Instead, the position goes to Theophilus Shepstone, despite the fact that, at forty-two, Fynn is fourteen years older than Shepstone and has twenty-six years of frontier experience behind him, including ten spent in Natal.

Further proof of Fynn's 'diplomatic prowess' surfaces when he's appointed 'resident agent' to his old mate, Faku of the Pondoes, in 1848. By inciting a Pondo attack on some suspected Bhaca cattle thieves, Fynn sets off a series of incidents which eventually involve the governments of both the Cape and Natal.

In 1852, he returns to Natal, which has been a British colony for nine years by then. He serves as a magistrate until 1860, when ill health forces his retirement. He dies in Durban on September 20 the following year.

\*

There they stand in the colander-filtered light breaking through the storm clouds, watching as Jakot hesitates, then goes off after the Zulus, grabs the udibi's arm and starts talking to the warriors earnestly.

'What is the blighter up to now?' wonders Farewell, before returning his attention to what's left of the vegetable garden.

Resigned to the fact that the comely maiden won't be returning any time soon, Ogle signals to Cane and they make their way over to the wattle-and-daub structure to carry King back to Ogle's kraal.

Fynn, meanwhile, remains standing with his head bowed, his eyes fixed on the footprints in the mud. He had the dream again last night. That same dream he's been having, from time to time, ever since he treated Shaka after the assassination attempt. It's the kind of dream that stains your mind, haunting you long after you've woken up . . .

# 13
## Dreams & Awakenings

*The same dream . . .*

Or perhaps a play in three acts, but each one is connected, so
. . . still the same dream. Recurring, haunting, taunting him for
night after night, then vanishing only to restart a few months
later. He's had it almost every night since about mid-August now.

The dreams may have started a few days later, but he has no
doubt their genesis lies in the night Shaka was stabbed.

He remembers being tired. They had been the first White Men
to witness the culmination of the First Fruits, and he'd been fasci-
nated – and annoyed by the boredom of the others in his group,
which they could scarcely be bothered to hide. This was not the
way representatives of the Crown should behave – and it was
also dangerous. Who knew how Shaka might have reacted should
such disrespect have been noticed . . .

He remembers being relieved when Farewell and the rest
were allowed to leave and Shaka asked him to stay behind to
witness – and enjoy – the less public conclusion of the First
Fruits.

He remembers being relieved and flattered. But the early mornings, long days and late nights had taken their toll, and he also
remembers feeling tired – terribly tired – that fateful night. Had
left the feast early, when the young warriors had started dancing. He had seen enough, heard enough, learnt enough. It was
time to return to Port Natal, and he and his servants were due
to depart the following day.

Fynn remembers having just settled down in his hut when
they came for him. And he'd gone from tired to shocked to disbe-

lief as his servants trembled and he groped about for his medicine chest. Shaka stabbed! It was beyond belief.

He remembers asking for more light and for everyone to step
back, and the Induna was there, trying to help him, and he remembers beginning to babble, talking to calm himself and remind
himself of the procedures he needed to follow.

And he remembers Shaka clutching his wrist, probably as a
way to stop himself from crying out as the White Man examined his wounds. He remembers Shaka clutching his wrist, then
. . . nothing.

Nothing . . . until one of the King's warriors gently woke him
up and told him Shaka had regained consciousness. A miserable
dawn: greyness above, greyness below in the faces of the people
around them, in their gait, their whispers.

Somehow he had managed to stop the bleeding. But he
couldn't remember anything of what happened after Shaka had
gripped his wrist.

Then, after days of pondering this lacuna in his memory, the
dream had started . . .

★

The same dream . . .

No, not quite. There are spectators now. General Hlakanyana
is there, perched on Lombi's shoulders and looking more than
ever like a man-monkey. And he has to pass by them . . . pass
them to reach the man by the hut. And they are not alone, for
they have an escort with them, obviously there to watch over
them. Babies, chubby babies with chubby arms and legs, sitting
astride dogs. Only . . . the Induna sees each baby carries a long
spear made of gall and despair, the blade fashioned from cold
inevitability, and a small round shield woven from time and
torment. And each baby has the head of a dog: long snout, brown

507

fur, eyes that dart here and there, seeking the scents picked up by their flaring black nostrils, their pointed ears still in repose. And each dog has the face of a baby, chubby features, with flattened nose and ears.

*(Someone is . . .)*

★

The same dream. He's standing in a clearing surrounded by savannah. In front of him is an old woman who is naked except for the multiple bead necklaces around her neck. The long grass whispers in the wind and, as Fynn watches, the old woman collapses. Early on, when the dreams were still fresh, he'd move forward to catch her, stop her from falling – and would wake up to find his arms outstretched. Then, for some reason, one night he hesitated . . . and watched how the old woman became a young girl even as she fell in slow motion. Became three young girls, one dropping to sit cross-legged before him, the other two each moving diagonally past him, so the further they went, the further apart they became. And, as he turned, he saw how one of the girls became two in her turn. Later he realised he had turned to call after them, because he knew their names. But they were names no man awake could ever pronounce. And so it went on for many nights, until Fynn was even able to urge his dream-self to remember those names, but it was to no avail. The scrawls on the paper he kept by the bed offered no clue the following morning. A mixture of letters and numerals: Eli, E1i, El1, for the first young girl, the one who remained in front of him; Eltoo, Litwy, for the second; Ltree, Lthrice, E3ell, for the third.

Then there came the night his desperation to remember their names became something else, and the second act of the dream began . . .

★

The same dream; the one he's been having on and off for so many seasons now.

Rain falling. Speckled puddles. Huts seeming to sag into mounds of waterlogged thatch. And the rain is falling sideways, a swarm of mosquitoes, stinging your skin. You tilt your head, wipe your face.

You move forward, your vision blurred as droplets catch on your eyelashes. You wipe your face once more. An instant of clarity before the swarm surrounds you again.

Another irritated sweep of your arm, a brushing off that miraculously reveals the body in front of the hut.

A big man lying on his side, with his back to you.

Moving forward, knowing instinctively it's no use.

*(Someone . . .)*

He is dead, this man. There's nothing you can do to save him.

Observing this as a third party might, having blundered on to this scene, you see yourself drop to your knees.

Nothing.

There is nothing.

*(Someone is . . .)*

Nothing you can do.

Nothing.

*(And someone is shaking him.)*

★

His desperation to remember those names becomes a fear-filled scramble to find firewood. The Earth itself has listed and night is flooding in over the gunwales . . . and he must find wood to make a fire. He knows the African night is a time for staying close to roaring flames, but he's never known such fear, or such desperate scrambling. And it's no good. He gets the fire going, finds more wood than it should be possible for any man to find

509

lying around in grassland, but it's never going to be enough, and he can't keep the night at bay. He remembers telling Shaka how strange it is that, while the Zulus welcome it, the full moon is feared by his people, and regarded as a sign of lunacy. And he now laughs hysterically as the night begins to infect him. And, when the darkness begins to recede, he remains infected. Suddenly he's naked, and he laughs hysterically as he examines his hands, his limbs, his body – for he's now the colour of coal. He throws himself into a pool of sunlight and feels the night evaporate.

Then he stands up and enters the third part of the dream . . . he stands up and finds himself in a drawing room, in front of a painting of his mother. In the painting there's another picture behind her left shoulder. As he moves closer, the portrait becomes bigger, and he can see the woman in the other picture is his grandmother. Don't ask how he knows; he just knows it. And, as he moves still closer, entering in effect the portrait of his mother, he sees there's another picture behind his grand-mother's shoulder. It's of his great-grandmother. And, as he moves closer, he sees there's a portrait behind her – his great-great-grandmother – and another portrait behind her, and so on. Portrait after portrait, of a mother and her mother and her mother . . .

★

'Aiee, Mbopa, you have returned with an alacrity likely to render speechless those who mock your girth,' says Mnkabayi.

'Have no fear, Ma, I can move fast when the occasion demands it.'

'And what was it about this occasion that . . . ?'

'Please allow me to reassure you, Ma. I bring only good news.' Mbopa shakes his head, because he still can't believe it. 'Aiee,' he continues, 'we couldn't have foreseen a better outcome.'

That has Mnkabayi sitting up, her eyes glistening with antici-pation.

They arrived at Dukuza with the trophies, and Shaka had kept them waiting for a long, long time before emerging from his hut. You could hear their stomachs grumbling, adds Mbopa.

'And, when my nephew finally left his hut, how was he?'

'No better, Ma – and a lot worse, I'd say.'

Shaka had waited until the rare and valuable crane feathers and genet and monkey skins were all laid out before him. There were even some gold artefacts the Pondoes had probably retrieved from shipwrecks. There were also ostrich headdresses, and kilts decorated with highly-prized otter tails.

When the men had retreated to their ranks, continues Mbopa, there was a moment of expectant silence. Then Shaka had gone into a rage, kicking aside these valuable prizes and castigating the men for being cowards. That was a serious accusation, one that could see them all sent to the impalers. And the fact that their ranks appeared to shrink away from his anger only enflamed that anger more.

Then, suddenly, it was over. Shaka stood there breathing heav-ily, his hands at his sides.

'What did you do then?' asks Mnkabayi.

He took a chance, replies Mbopa. Suspecting the King was about to return to his hut, he began shouting at the soldiers, gesturing at them with his isinkemba, a broad-bladed spear with a short haft. Then he suddenly threw the isinkemba onto the ground in front of them.

'They saw this as a sign that I had ordered their execution,' says Mbopa.

'As well they might. What happened next?'

'They fled Dukuza.'

'And what did my nephew do?'

This was where Mbopa had taken the chance. He'd had to throw the isinkemba in Shaka's presence, and hope the latter didn't turn on him and countermand the order implicit in this action. And it was only when the King said nothing that the troops fled.

'Shaka said nothing, even though this left him without a body-guard?' asks Mnkabayi.

'Not a word, Ma.' Although he did give his prime minister a strange look before re-entering his hut – but Mbopa doesn't mention that.

It was Thenjiwe, the King's body servant, who brought up the matter of the guard, just as Mbopa was leaving.

'What did you tell him?'

'I told him to sharpen his assegai blade for tonight, and that tomorrow I would bring another contingent.'

'Very good,' chuckles Mnkabayi. 'You are right, this is an outcome we would never have dared to hope for!'

'Yet it has come to pass, Ma.'

'So it has, Mbopa, so it has.'

★

Someone is shaking him, rocking him back and forth.

He sits up.

Turns.

Pampata!

They embrace. Then he's on his feet, crouching, looking around. They're in a clearing surrounded by interlocked branches and singing birds. His eyes find the path that leaves the glade.

General Hlakanyana and his retinue have left, says Pampata.

'His day will come,' murmurs the Induna.

'Hai, but he saved my life,' responds Pampata. Besides, they have more important matters to deal with right now. They have been left with weapons and supplies – it's time they were on their way to Bulawayo.

The Induna straightens, runs a hand over his face.

'Is anything the matter?' asks Pampata.

No, he says. Surprisingly, the muthi they used to dope him has left no sluggish after-effects. In fact, he feels quite energised.

They have also left some medicine for his wound, adds Pampata.

'But come now,' she says, 'we must be on our way.'

'Wait!' says the Induna.

'Oh yes, I forgot – Kani is fine. She awaits us at your homestead.'

'That is good and that is where we will go.'

'But Shaka needs us!'

'Hai, but the King has issued us with specific instructions, and you know the penalty for disobeying him.'

'But things have changed! Don't you see?'

'Nonetheless . . .'

'Do you know who that . . . that man-monkey saved me from?' asks Pampata. 'Do you? I'll tell you who! Mnkabayi!'

The Induna takes a step back. That cannot be!

'I know about you and her . . . Well, I know she has always shown an interest in you. But it's true!' Pampata goes on to explain how the one Mnkabayi had tasked with killing her had been Muvani – who happened to be one of Hlakanyana's agents. And as soon as they had reached the dela innyoni, Muvani had held Pampata fast while she summoned reinforcements from the surrounding bush to kill the concubine's handmaidens and ladies-in-waiting.

*It can't be*, thinks the Induna, staring at her.

Then she had been brought to General Hlakanyana's hideout.

To allay any suspicions Mnkabayi might have had on receiving no news about Pampata's fate, Muvani and a younger girl travelled back to Bulawayo, where Muvani pretended to be mortally wounded, while the girl fetched Mnkabayi. After Muvani had told her story – dropping in the rumour about the Induna – and Mnkabayi had left them, the two females had hurried back to General Hlakanyana.

'I know!' says Pampata. 'I know how much you respect her. I was taken in by her, too – as was my beloved.'

'Be that as it might, we remain under Shaka's orders,' says the Induna.

They will fetch Kani and the others, and he'll take them to the White Men at Thekwini, where they should be safe. Then he will return to Bulawayo.

'But it might be too late by then!' says Pampata.

'Do you now doubt the King's wisdom?'

'No, but—'

'Do you not think he had a good reason for issuing the instructions that he did? Do you not think he issued them precisely because things might change?'

Kani's words come back to her: *But, my Sister, haven't you thought that, with you safe, our Father will have one less thing to worry about?*

And Pampata nods.

*It can't be! Not Mnkabayi!* The Induna softens his tone. 'You are right. The King needs us now more than ever. But let us not add to his burden by questioning his wisdom.'

'I know, I know,' sighs Pampata.

'You must trust me on this, and I must be able to trust you in return,' whispers the Induna.

A sad smile. 'You will not need eyes in the back of your head. For I will not try to sneak away.'

'Good. If we leave now, we should reach my kraal by daybreak,' decides the Induna.

★

Having dismissed Mbopa, Mnkabayi sits pondering his news a while. It truly is a propitious sign, yet that only increases the apprehension she feels. Raising her right hand, she examines the slight tremor. It's not due to old age, for she has been spared such infirmities – so far. No, not old age, but not unexpected either. Of course, she will not reveal her trepidation to the others, but is willing to acknowledge it's only natural. Which is one of the reasons why she must constantly appear self-assured and calm, so as to quell their anxiety.

It's only natural . . . this knot in her stomach, and the what-ifs circling her mind like vultures, the sleepless nights that have grown ever longer as the day approaches.

Only natural, because killing a King – that's no small thing.

Only natural . . . and anyway a little fear will stand her in good stead tomorrow.

And let her take her own advice and not think too much about just what it is they're about to do, but simply let events take their course.

★

*It can't be! Not Mnkabayi!*

Remembering Hlakanyana's words: *That's right, Zulu. Mhlangana means to kill your King. And, if he succeeds, you can be sure all those loyal to the King will be next.* And the man-monkey had included Mnkabayi's name in the list.

*I have already done what I can to thwart Mhlangana's plans,* Hlakanyana had said. *The rest is up to you.*

And who had told Pampata that Mnkabayi was behind the plot to kill her?

Hlakanyana!

Even though Mhlangana is Hlakanyana's quarry, the Induna wouldn't put it past that monstrosity to try and stir up things in other areas, just for the sake of it because it's in his nature.

He won't argue with Pampata, however. He needs her obedient and docile so that he can keep the promise he made to Shaka, by ferrying her to safety.

★

*Don't think too much about it . . .*

But her thoughts turn down a path she'd rather avoid.

A panting, whimpering girl drenched in sweat that is stained orange by the fire, trying to peer over the mound of her belly. A final scream, loud enough to shatter the moon. Then the midwife is lifting the blood-drenched baby from between the girl's legs. The umbilical cord is cut and put aside, for the girl has insisted the usual rituals be performed, even if this isn't exactly a 'natural' birth. Afterwards the inkaba, or navel cord, and the umzanyana, the placenta, will be buried in the girl's hut, near to where the baby was born. Now, though, the baby is placed in her arms. And she holds the infant, her vulnerability. And vulnerable isn't something she can ever afford to be. But it's a beguiling vulnerability this, bringing with it a host of emotions she never thought she'd ever experience. And when gentle hands remove the baby from her arms, and a voice says 'It's better this way', she resolves to keep track of the infant, follow his progress, perhaps help him where she can.

Now, Mnkabayi wonders, if she were to meet that young girl today *(It's for the best . . .)*, would she advise her differently? *(For the best . . .)* Or tell her to let the child go, let herself lose sight of him – her vulnerability. Would that have been better?

Because, aiee, they do not know what is coming . . .

★

516

He had the same dream again last night: the old woman in the savannah, coloured beads around her neck, becoming three young women amid a jumble of letters and numbers, Eli, E1i, El1, Eltoo, Litwy, Ltree, Lthrice, E3ell. And one of the girls sitting cross-legged in front of him, the other two moving away, heading north, the third female becoming two women. The desperate scramble for firewood as night comes, infecting him, then the cleansing . . . and the room of portraits extending ever back in time.

The same dream except that, when he had woken up this morning, he'd found two names scrawled on the piece of paper. He knows they belong to the two women that the third girl became, but he doesn't know why he should suddenly have 'remembered' them, or have brought them back into consciousness with him.

Manju and Nasrin.

What do they mean?

# 14
## The Drunk Induna

**September 24, 1828**

By travelling through the night, they've timed their journey so that Phepho and Sola can catch up to them and they would reach KwaBulawayo just after midnight, to give themselves a few hours to rest. (For who knows what other lies they'll have to face?)

Mthunzi is the first awake. He's slept fitfully and now the early morning chill taunts his wound, causing the left side of his midriff to ache. They're camped behind a low rise crowned with boulders. Leaving the others wrapped up in their wildebeest cloaks, he creeps up to where he can see the royal capital laid out on the gently sloping plain; its concentric circles, circular huts, and with the sacred cattlefold and gathering place in the centre.

He checks the sky, judges it to be seku lukwikwi, dark dawn. But this dawn has brought with it heavy clouds that hide its stars. It's going to be an overcast day. And those clouds are moving imperceptibly, like snails, so there's likely to be rain as well.

Pale, milky light: the time of dawning. Mthunzi yawns as he watches the herd boys gathering. Then watches them taking the cows out. He feels like a scout come to survey the lie of the land, the disposition of the enemy's forces, an inholi come to hlola, reconnoitre, while hidden regiments wait with hungry iklwas.

It's an unpleasant feeling, for it bespeaks of a giddy world, a world askew. A world where lies and deceit have buried truth and honour and declared themselves the rulers of all human intercourse: governing, guiding, leading and misleading. A baneful, malevolent, parlous world, where praise songs have become threnodies, and where laughter is only ever malicious.

Has the moon been stolen? Do they now live in the terror of the dark night and the dread day thereafter, when amatikoloshe ride out on their hyenas and the dank breath of witches and wizards sidles across the land like a fog on crocodile feet?

It's the tiredness, he tells himself; and the scar. It's as if a millipede has burrowed under there and is pressing thorn-sharp feet into his flesh, and it's all he can do not to scratch it. For he knows that, if once he starts, he won't be finished until the wound is opened afresh.

And there's the fact that they've felt it necessary to pause here outside the Zulu capital, their home – what does that say about the way things now are?

Mthunzi remembers Jakot's words at Thekwini. The Xhosa had come running after him, had grabbed his arm. He'd been about to pull away, snarl a rebuke, then he had seen the anxiety in Jakot's eyes, an intensity so uncharacteristic of the man.

★

'You'll remember how the nature of our interaction changed after that encounter with the slavers,' the old general tells the young men who are listening to him spellbound. 'We would never ever fully trust him, certainly not in the way Dingane would one day, but neither would we be so rough with him in future. We had seen a different side to the Swimmer, and he had thereby earned a modicum of respect from us.'

'In a way,' says Zamo, 'he needed to be something of a scoundrel in order to survive. After all, his life was in constant jeopardy. Should Shaka decide to attack Thekwini, and he happened to be there at the time, he would have been shown no mercy even though nominally in the King's employ. In fact, 'that's why he could expect no mercy: he would have been seen as a traitor, just like those others who had fled to the White Men for protection.'

'This is so,' agrees the general.

'And if he were with Shaka's men and they were attacked by Soshangane's savages, let us say, none would have first stopped to check if he was a Xhosa and not a Zulu, before driving the blade home.'

'Cha! But that's what Shaka should have done in the first place,' interjects Fanele.

'What is that?' asks the general.

'Attacked the whites at Thekwini, chased them away before they got a foothold on our land! For, see, it is no longer our land!'

'Many believed that then, and many believe it now,' observes the general. But the Induna had agreed with Mbopa: the White Men were coming, and nothing would stop them. Kill some here, others would land there. Better to parley with them, reach some kind of agreement. It was a view substantiated by Jakot's revelations when he first turned up at Bulawayo, and one the general would also come to share.

Was it the right path, though? The general shrugs: who knows.

'Cha!' says Fanele. 'The answer's right here. See where we are now! See what we must do! Talk has not stopped the red ants from coming.'

'Perhaps you are right,' concedes the general. 'But we are talking about a decision made a long time ago, and one that cannot be undone.'

'Yes,' agrees another of the officers, 'tell us, instead, what Jakot said, General.'

★

'Put your distrust aside for once,' had said Jakot, 'and know this: Fynn does not lie! Can't you see? They have grown wary of Shaka, as they aren't sure what's happening up there. And where is the ivory?'

He was right about that – very little of that commodity was currently coming from the Zulus.

'They are short of money, and bicker among themselves, and that's why they want the Pondoes to come! Fynn especially since, as you know, he has spent much time with Faku. They want the Pondoes to come, so that their ships can then be sent away fully loaded again.'

*That's* why they can trust Fynn when he says Faku and his people are now far south.

'Hai,' growled Njikiza, a bit of his old contempt for Jakot evident in his voice, 'that's just the reason why he might lie! He wants the Pondoes to come, so let them come and catch us unawares.'

Finally releasing Mthunzi's arm, Jakot had turned to Njikiza, conceding that he had a point.

'But,' he added, 'you can trust *me*! Fynn thinks he understands the Pondoes, but he knows nothing! We Xhosas know how deceitful those animals can be! And, if they come, my life will be worth nothing! Not because I have served Shaka but because I am a Xhosa. So I will not lie about a matter such as this.'

'Because your own skin is precious to you,' observed Mthunzi.

'This is so,' agreed Jakot. But, he added, turning back to Njikiza, the Whites at Port Natal wouldn't have been able to contain their joy had they worked out some deal with Faku that saw the Pondoes invading the coastal region of the Zulu kingdom. And he himself would have known about it, and would have wasted no time in warning Shaka.

'And I would have done the same had I myself seen so much as a single Pondo scout in these parts,' he told the big man.

Mthunzi and Njikiza exchanged a glance: they were clearly right to have come here first. But where, then, had those reports of Pondo activity come from? From this man whose kraal they were supposed to visit? But why would Mbopa have taken a single report so seriously? He had, after all, been delegated to collect the plunder from the recent campaign against Faku, and had been talking with soldiers returning from that region almost every day of late.

Jakot had been right when he told Mthunzi: 'Whoever has sent you chasing after Pondoes has an ulterior motive. They clearly wanted to get you away from Bulawayo, and you have to ask yourselves why.'

★

A giddy world. A world disfigured and splay-footed. A world rattling with questions and suspicions.

Then Mthunzi realises he's been watching a strange phenomenon, without realising it. People are beginning to gather below in Bulawayo's great circular centre. What's this? And so early, too?

It's grown lighter and, at the top of the circle, set a few paces to the side of the ibandla tree where the King will customarily stand when addressing a gathering such as this, Mthunzi spots a wide platform fashioned from planks laid across a number of barrels left by the White Men after their various visits.

He turns and, keeping low, moves away from the rocks. 'Njikiza,' he hisses once, then twice . . . and the big man rises out of his dew-spangled cloak, reaching for his club.

Mthunzi beckons the Watcher to join him. Let the others sleep for a while longer.

He points out the platform as well as the fact that soldiers with spears and shields are mingling with the people instead of lining the fence that encircles the great cattlefold. After giving Njikiza a few moments to take it all in, Mthunzi asks him what he makes of it all.

'Someone is about to address our people.'

'But it's not going to be the King,' says Mthunzi, because the dais has been placed adjacent to the ibandla tree, not under it.

'No,' agrees Njikiza with a sigh, and Mthunzi knows the Watcher is thinking the same thing as he is. Shaka isn't suddenly 'recovered' and about to set things right . . .

And the soldiers standing among the people?

'That *is* strange,' says Njikiza. 'I would suggest they have been specially placed there.' Discipline hasn't deteriorated so badly among the regiments that individual soldiers are likely to wander into a crowd such as this, acting as if they're part of the general gathering, even though they're fully armed.

'And see there . . .' The Watcher points to where a large semicircle has been deliberately left clear in front of the platform. This space has been 'cordoned off' by two ranks of warriors, who hold the crowd back, and now men are filing into it from the gate behind the ibandla tree.

Mthunzi and Njikiza are, of course, too far away to recognise anyone, but there are enough grey heads and tottering figures leaning on iwisas to suggest this section comprises elders, advisors, district heads and even perhaps some generals.

It's Njikiza who now examines the sky. Although it's growing lighter, the clouds remain heavy. Unless a wind comes up, they're unlikely to see the sun today; instead there'll be thunder, lightning, rain.

'I think we should go and hear whatever is about to be said,' murmurs Mthunzi.

'I agree,' says Njikiza.

★

As Phepho (the Tornado) and Sola (the Grumbler) were the fastest runners, they were sent off to Duba's kraal, where they hid themselves among old anthills rising near a clump of bushes. They moved into position after dark on the day Mthunzi and his men were meant to arrive. All was quiet. Then, in the early morning mist before the cattle were taken out, they saw man-shapes approaching the kraal. Some of them spread out and took up positions around the homestead. Duba must have been awake and waiting for them, however, for almost instantly Phepho and Sola heard raised voices: one man castigating the other, the other shouting back in indignation, like a little dog barking in self-defence.

Aware of the pickets, who they soon saw were more concerned with ensuring no one escaped the kraal, the two crept closer through the long thatch grass. The mist was fraying and thinning, and they saw some of the warriors were carrying Pondo shields, which were also oval but bigger and more flimsy than the Zulu isihlangu.

Duba was now declaring it wasn't his fault, as he couldn't wish them to be there . . . 'Them being us,' Sola had told Mthunzi, once they caught up with the other three.

Despite the fear in his voice, Duba had also been able to manoeuvre his interlocutor out of the kraal, as if that would be enough to protect his family. It also meant the Tornado and the Grumbler could now see who was admonishing him.

It had been Nolaka, the Leopard Man, who was one of Mhlangana's indunas. And suddenly he stabbed Duba in the left armpit.

'Must have lost his temper,' observed Sola.

'That one being just like some maidens,' remarked Phepho, 'losing his temper as often as they lose their virginity.'

Mthunzi had nodded, for Nolaka was possessed of a brutality he reserved not for the battlefield – which he had seldom experienced – but for everywhere else. It's doubtful he would have ever attained – never mind retained – his current rank under any master other than Mhlangana.

With Duba lying on the ground and dying, Nolaka's voice rose above the screams of the man's wives, ordering some of his men to set fire to the entire settlement.

Now Mthunzi orders Phepho, Namasu and Sola to remain where they are, while he and Njikiza approach Bulawayo. If anything happens to them, the other three are to . . . he scratches his head . . . well, seek out someone they can trust, or just go to ground until they can work out what's happening.

*Mbopa's orders. Mhlangana's men.*

'And some of them carrying Pondo shields,' adds Njikiza, as they follow the road that leads to Bulawayo's main gate.

And was Duba not one of Bamba's brothers-in-law?

Bamba: another one of Mhlangana's indunas.

'Clearly we were meant to be massacred by Faku's jackals,' adds Mthunzi.

'When, instead, a leopard was involved,' says the Watcher. 'But what's this?'

They're about fifty paces from the gate when twenty men of the guard come surging towards them. Njikiza and Mthunzi stop, move apart, the latter tightening his grip on his iklwa. Njikiza is still resting his giant club against his right shoulder, only now his insouciance is a mere pose. Both men have woken up their shields, as Zulu soldiers say, meaning each isihlangu is ready to move and fend off any spear thrown towards them.

The twenty men meanwhile form up in two rows, about five paces from Mthunzi and the Watcher, their shields raised, their spears lowered. Their long hair and isihlangu patterns show them to be Hlubis. But it's the man staggering in their wake that Mthunzi and Njikiza now have their eyes on.

It's Bamba. And he's drunk, very drunk, and can barely remain upright. 'Fasimbas!' bellows Mhlangana's induna as he forces his way through the middle of the Hlubis, followed by his udibi, who's nine summers old and carrying a calabash.

'Fasimbas!' he says again, sneering. 'What are you doing here, *Fasimbas*?' He comes to a swaying halt in front of Mthunzi and Njikiza.

'We were sent to seek Pondoes,' replies Mthunzi calmly.

'Pondoes!' Bamba extends his arm to the udibi, who hands him the calabash. He takes a swig of beer, burps, rubs his stomach and returns the calabash to the boy.

'Pondoes,' he says again. 'And did you'– another burp that becomes a hiccough – 'did you find any Pondoes?'

'No,' replies Mthunzi.

'Well, then,' says Bamba, parting his arms and swaying backwards. 'Go back to the swamps, Fasimbas, and die alongside your comrades!' He makes a shooing motion with his hands. 'Go. What are you waiting for? Off to the swamps with you!'

When Mthunzi and Njikiza show no sign of moving, Bamba wheels around, staggers sideways, recovers his balance and tells the Hlubis they can go now, as he himself will deal with these . . . these *Fasimbas*.

The men begin to back away, still keeping formation, with their eyes on the Zulus. Bamba shakes his head and orders them again to return to their post and to hamba – make haste. With something resembling a combined *have-it-your-way* shrug, they turn and jog back to the gate.

Watching them, Bamba takes the calabash from his udibi again. Throws back his head, and drains the contents. Returning the container to the boy, he tells the udibi to go and fetch him some more.

He then turns to Mthunzi and Njikiza, staggers sideways again, before holding up his left hand. 'Don't club me just yet, Watcher of the Ford! Hear me out first,' he says, then pauses as if an idea has just struck him. He raises his hand in a *just-a-moment* gesture this time. Takes three steps away, bends over and throws up. After spitting a few times, he leans over to the left and allows natural momentum to carry him back towards the two men.

'The swamps,' he says, addressing Njikiza. Clearly he reckons that, given the man-mountain's quick temper, the Watcher is likely to use his club before Mthunzi lowers his iklwa. 'That thing about the swamps, that . . . that was for their benefit,' he says jerking a thumb over his shoulder. 'Although I myself am considering a trip in that direction soon, for those swamps suddenly seem more salubrious than *these* swamps.'

He waves his hand in front of his face, like one chasing away a bothersome fly. 'But what I do is neither here nor there, neither nor . . .' This time he doesn't move away to vomit, and Njikiza and Mthunzi have to leap backwards to avoid being splattered.

'But you . . .' continues Bamba, wagging his finger at them after the inevitable spitting. 'You must get away from here.'

'Why?' asks Mthunzi.

'Because . . . because the King is finished,' says Bamba. A burp becomes a gulp, and suddenly tears are flowing down his cheeks. 'The King is finished.'

Finished? What does he mean?

'What do you think I mean?' bawls Bamba.

'Where is he?' asks Njikiza.

'Does it matter? There is nothing you can do to change things. There is nothing anyone can do.'

'Let us be the judge of that,' says the Watcher.

'Hai, if I were you, I'd be more concerned with my own hide.'

'What do you mean?' asks Mthunzi.

Wiping the tears from his face, Bamba tells them that messengers arrived yesterday evening with news of the massacre at Duba's kraal. And how Mthunzi, Njikiza and others were seen fleeing the carnage.

'We didn't—' begins Mthunzi.

'I know that, but few others do,' interrupts Bamba. 'So you are hunted men,' he continues. And now isn't the time for them to set about proving their innocence.

'My master, who is soon to be your master . . .' Bamba shakes his head. '*Our* master . . . And I have yet to drink enough beer to make that prospect palatable.'

But, anyway, Mhlangana is convinced they are the killers. However . . .

'Yes?' prompts Mthunzi.

'You can't save the King, but you can still help your master.'

'The Nduna?' asks Mthunzi.

Bamba nods, before running a hand over his face. Of course, they won't yet have heard! 'It is said your master is still alive—'

Mthunzi and Njikiza glance at each other. *The Induna alive!*

'—and heading this way. But,' adds Bamba, seeing the joy in their faces. 'But waiting for him, or going to find him, is not the way you can help him.'

'What do you mean?' says Mthunzi.

'Many will die in the days to come. My master . . . *Our* master
. . .' Again the pause, and the pained expression.

Mhlangana has sent out his men to slaughter those loyal to
Shaka and those likely to support any heir more kindly disposed
to themselves, resumes Bamba. It is a list the prince has composed
with a certain amount of glee. And, as the failed ambush at
Duba's kraal has shown, Mthunzi and Njikiza are on that list. As
is the Induna.

And Mthunzi and Njikiza can best serve the Induna by seeking refuge at his homestead, where they can protect his wife and
await news of events at Bulawayo.

Who knows, perhaps the Induna will make straight for his
kraal. Certainly, he'll have heard what's afoot and may decide to
first ensure that Kani is safe.

So there they have it, says Bamba, after throwing up yet again.
They can either go and try and protect the King, an attempt
doomed to failure, or they can lie low at the Induna's kraal, and
watch over Kani.

★

'What did you decide to do, numzane?' asks Klebe.

Reasoning that Shaka can't not have known what was afoot,
and would anyway have had his bodyguard with him, they decided
to make for the Induna's kraal, explains the general.

There's a pause as they sit in the sun, contemplating the old
man's words beneath a cloudless sky which is a depthless, delicate blue.

Then one of the other young officers breaks the silence. 'And
this was the day, wasn't it?' he asks.

Growls and mutterings about the fellow asking a stupid question. But the old general who, as a young boy had been the udibi
to one of Shaka's greatest indunas, understands why the man feels

the need to ask such a question. They are, after all, speaking of a momentous day for their nation, and therefore one that needs underscoring.

'Yes,' says the general, 'this was the day.'

# 15
## A Giddy World

Omiso, so named because he was born during a drought, sits up, arching his back, and stretches. He presses his palms into his eye sockets, trying to erase the weariness weighing down his eyelids; the somnolence that comes with being on watch. Leaning forward against his knees, he yawns . . . and stares. Someone is coming. A woman? Omiso grins as he rises to rest on his haunches and reaches for his iklwa. A woman! And not old, judging by her posture and the speed of her pace. No, definitely not old. The tip of his tongue roves across his upper lip.

A woman . . .

*

She moved in front of him, slapping her palms against his chest, and pleaded with him, begged him! 'Wait, please wait,' she insisted. 'We must think about this,' she said. His eyes staring far, far past her, rage turning his features as hard as stone, he stepped to one side. Then, heedless of her rank and status, he used his shield to sweep her out of the way – and moved forward in long strides. Pampata recovered her footing and charged after him – and threw herself on to his back, wrapping her arms tightly around his neck, clamping her thighs to his flanks as well, so he couldn't toss her off easily. She was hoping to slow him down, prevent him from moving out of cover of the trees to where he – they – might be spotted. And she succeeded, causing him to stagger sideways, before starting to turn round and round as, remembering her rank again, he tried to gently dislodge her.

*

A woman. He sniffs: the smell of burning, mingling with scorched flesh, still lingers like the memory of a spoilt meal. A brief glance down into the ravine. Their orders were to strike hard and fast, so they didn't have a chance to reward themselves for their exertions. Not that there was much to choose from, he reflects as he turns his attention back to the woman. Children, mainly; although the way they fought belied their age. Not that age matters when a man has war raging in his blood and would celebrate his survival, his victory.

She's getting closer – is definitely on her way here . . .

★

The Induna had built his homestead in a ravine. The first huts were constructed along the stream that bisected its steep sides, while the five dwellings for Mgobozi's widows and children lay further along, where the Induna – with the udibi and Njikiza – had dug away a portion of the bank and reinforced this excavation with a woven latticework of reeds.

The slope on the opposite side of the stream was almost concave, a shallow incline that suddenly curved up steeply to form a precipice. It was here the Induna had his cattle kraal, the rock face making up its fourth side. He'd also diverted part of the stream so that it ran through the lower end of the byre. Next, roughly opposite the newer huts, were the vegetable gardens tended by Kani and the widows.

On the top of the precipice rising above the cattle kraal were two squat rocks, the second one higher than the first, conveniently forming a backrest. This was where the Induna liked to take his leisure whenever at home. From here he could overlook the ravine where it curved to follow the stream, and watch his cattle grazing on the plain beyond, where flat-topped trees stood watch over fan love and thatch grass. You could also spot anyone moving along one of the paths that cut through the veld: some running north–south, past the ravine and the homestead hidden there, taking wayfarers towards the coast or inland laden with the wares they'd received from the savages at Thekwini; some running east–west, looping around the ravine, with the trail branching off to follow the stream into the gorge barely noticeable to those striding towards Bulawayo, or returning from the capital.

As luck would have it, Pampata and the Induna had approached the homestead from the north, heading through a defile and entering a wood of tambotis, marulas and tangled sagebush. By then they were both running, after they'd spotted the ghost of smoke: a smudge of grey that told of fierce fires now dying down . . . assegai thrusts . . . screams silenced . . .

The Induna was still thinking straight then, and had led her down a narrower trail that took them towards a parapet of rocks. Here he told her to keep low. Putting aside his shield and spear, he'd crawled forward until he could dispel any lingering, tenuous doubt that the smoke wasn't coming from his own homestead down in the ravine.

He pushed himself backwards and dropped down next to Pampata, his forearms resting on his knees, his eyes staring straight ahead, his lips parted slightly. After a quick glance at him, Pampata rose to a crouch and crept forward to see for herself. And in doing so, glancing up from the dissipating smoke, she spotted the sentry sitting on the Induna's rock. Whatever had happened might be over, but they hadn't left yet. They were clearly expecting the Induna . . .

And expecting him to do what he did even as Pampata returned to his side — rise up and stride off to seek vengeance.

★

533

Is she returning home and wondering about the smoke? *(Did they miss one?)* Is she a neighbour coming to investigate? *(But why alone?)* Or is she a mere wayfarer? But Omiso is dim, and these thoughts are like flies that hover and bother him for a few seconds before moving away (to find a less repellent heap of shit). And there was no time, and they had fought back ferociously. If their orders had been to take prisoners, they would have been forced to disobey them, and the two youngest women had fought most fiercely, so there had been no question of delaying their demise. But bheka! *Look!* See what the ancestors are about to deliver up to him.

Those breasts, those thighs . . .

★

'Will you stop and listen to me,' said Pampata into the Induna's ear.

A sullen pause, then a nod.

'Kani was my friend too, but what has happened has happened! It's over. There's nothing you – we – can do to change that.'

The Induna stood as still as a menhir.

'Can I get off now?' asked Pampata. Another nod – and she slid off the Induna's back. Turned him gently towards her.

'Look at me.'

The Induna obeyed, studying her from below heavy brows.

'Kani was my friend too,' she repeated, 'but we must face facts.' And there were two possibilities here. The first was that Kani and the others had merely been taken prisoner – possibly to be used as hostages. Let the Induna hand over Pampata, and his wife could go free.

*If only that were true!* Pampata is happy to consider that option, even if it puts her own safety in jeopardy, but she doubts that's what happened. For one thing, it's unlikely anyone yet knows she's with the Induna. Which leaves them with the second possibility: that they're already all dead. And the Induna has to . . . well, think about things.

Because what if those are Zulus there? And, really, she doesn't think there need be any doubt on that score. And if they *are* Zulus, what does this say about the peril Shaka is in?

'He would never place me under your protection, then order *that!*' she exclaims, pointing in the direction of the burning homestead.

The Induna runs the back of his hand across his lips. 'What about Mbopa?' he snarls. 'See how our Father repaid him for his loyalty!'

It's not the same thing . . . that was a mistake. How often has she held Shaka close while he wept and cursed those who had been overzealous in obeying his orders, and thus turned a rebuke intended merely to frighten into a massacre? But to point out these things right now will make her sound like a betrayed woman still foolishly trying to excuse her lover's actions.

Pampata takes a deep breath. 'Let us go and see what is going on,' she says. 'But let this be where your vengeance begins, not ends. Those over there, who we are going to kill, are not the ones who ordered this deed. So let us remain alive to find their masters!'

★

'Hello, sweetness,' leers Omiso, who's scrambled down the slope. 'And what are you doing here?'

Pampata shrugs, lowers her head.

He eyes her full breasts, imagines tasting her nipples, then studies the beadwork isigege covering her loins, wondering about the warm, moist crevice it hides.

He switches his iklwa to his left hand, his shield side, and tickles the girl's chin. 'Come now, pretty one, don't be shy. Do you belong here?'

The answer to that question will determine how long she has to live, and she shakes her head, thereby increasing the amount of breath she'll be allowed to breathe.

'Well, then?' says Omiso, raising the girl's chin so he may see her face.

He is a mere soldier and there is little chance of him recognising her.

'I have come to see if it's true,' says Pampata, in a sudden burst of inspiration.

'If what's true?' asks Omiso, his finger circling the girl's left nipple, watching it emerge from its areola.

'If it's true Mhlangana's men are as virile as some claim.'

A grin smears itself across Omiso's face. He's heard of no such rumour and the thought that there *is* one pleases him almost as much as it does to have this shapely wench offering herself up to him.

'Oh yes!' he says. 'You will not be disappointed. And you will see, too, that some are more virile than others.'

*But why is she backing away from him . . . ?*

He's just about to lunge forward and grab her, when he feels the sharp point of an iklwa dig into his lower back. Then a voice is telling him to turn around.

He obeys. Finds himself staring at the Induna.

*Oh shit.*

'Where are the other dead men?' asks the Induna.

Piss running down his leg, Omiso raises a trembling finger and points, past the Induna's shoulder, to a distant slope covered with trees and bushes. It's part of the same chain of mountains that Pampata and the Induna came through earlier.

'Can you see where he's pointing?' asks the Induna, keeping his eyes on Omiso's face.

When Pampata murmurs that she can, he slips his iklwa into Omiso's gut and twists the blade, before withdrawing it. A sucking sound, then he stabs Omiso again before the latter's knees buckle.

Pampata starts babbling something about these being Mhlangana's men, even though they carry Pondo shields, but the Induna ignores her as he makes his way up the slight incline to where the first hut is – or rather was, as now it's simply a circle of hard-packed earth floor surrounded by knee-high, fire-blackened thatch.

To get to Omiso and Pampata, he'd had to run past several of these huts, forcing himself to ignore the corpses, but now he stands over Kani and stares at the body which once offered him solace and joy, noting the numerous stab wounds that show how fiercely she fought back. No fewer than seven dead men lie scattered about, testament to how fiercely they all fought. Even Mgobozi's eldest widow is clutching a spear in her arthritic fingers.

And his children . . .

Tears streaming down his cheeks, he seeks out his three sons and two daughters. His youngest boy is wearing his iziphandla – a pair of armbands made of insimango, monkey skin. He remembers how excited the child had been when allowed to accompany his father and older brothers to fetch the monkey itself; how impatient he had been during the drying of its hide; how he hadn't left Kani's side until she finished making the armbands; how proudly he had worn them, as they were a sign that he was growing up. His middle son lies under the body of a warrior, having killed him while himself being killed. The Induna drags the man off the child's body.

His eldest son, a lad of twelve summers, lies across the bodies of his sisters. He clearly died protecting them, and seems to have accounted for three full-grown men. The Induna squats next to the boy's corpse and leans over it to touch the cheek of each daughter. One is still wearing her umgexo, a necklace made of snail shells that the Induna's udibi had helped her find. Gently slipping his fingers between her throat and the umgexo, he pulls the necklace loose and subsides on to his heels, knocked backwards by an onslaught of grief.

★

*He isn't aware of how long he sits there, staring at the necklace draped across his palm, drowning in tears . . .*

*Numb . . . no feeling.*

*Flies, blood-drenched sand, the smell of burnt thatch, of flesh already beginning to rot. His own flesh – flesh of his flesh – rotting there in the sun. His love left to decay.*

*Doesn't know how long he's been sitting there before he hears Pampata calling to him.*

★

She has crossed the stream to where the cattle kraal is. It's empty now, of course, with the cattle out grazing.

*Shaka, oh Shaka, what is happening? Barefoot Thorn Man! Sky that Thunders in the Open! Will you be able to thwart your enemies?*

Then she spots them.

And she's on her feet, calling out to the Induna.

'Look!' she shouts, when he appears between the destroyed huts, and she points at the collection of pots arranged near the entrance to the cattle kraal.

Sleeping mats, items of clothing, ornaments and other belongings lie scattered about, for these men were like locusts out to destroy everything. But here is an array of empty pots.

538

'There are more of those men still here,' she says as she splashes across the stream.

'There are more of them,' she repeats, when she reaches the Induna. 'They've gone to fetch the cows to milk them, and who knows how soon they'll get back!'

# INTERLUDE
## He Dreams Of His Cattle

*Is there anything more beautiful than a herd of Nguni cattle grazing on a hillside on a sunny day? It is poetry, words becoming colours and shapes and horns.*

*Animals mirrored in animals. There's ulukhozi, with black rump and black hump disintegrating into spots down his white front legs, splattered backwards towards his scrotum, then the black neck above white dewlaps: markings that resemble the black eagle. There's inkwazi, the fish eagle, with its black rear and white head. There's insingizi, with a patch of white on its flank and the edge of its haunch, resembling the ground hornbill which has white feathers that become exposed when it takes flight. There's the brindled cow which brings to mind a hyena, and so is called lingampisi.*

*And there are more – bulls that resemble ash, white cows with dark splotches that look like kraals seen from afar, beasts the colour of wild mushrooms or sugar beans or millet.*

*And there are the horns, which have been bent, shaped and turned in different directions by deliberately burning each horn with a hot iron. There are the wide horns, their sharp tips curving upward . . . the elephant horns, curving down like tusks . . . horns that curve forward and then back, like two arguing women throwing up their arms in exasperation.*

*How he misses his cattle.*

*But so deep is this hole, so heavy this weight, that even they can't lure him out to enjoy their company. Or to check their health . . . their hooves . . . their dung.*

*Anything runny or too dry – too painful – is a bad sign. Thick porridge firm enough to form a pat, that's what you want to see. And that plop-plop heard while the animal defecates is one of the most beautiful sounds a stockman can hear.*

*How he misses his cattle.*

*And overseeing a favourite cow's first milking. Maybe even doing it oneself.*

*The herd boys bring the cattle home just before midday, when a grass cord is then passed through the nostrils of the cow to keep it still. Her calf is allowed to suck for a short while, then is pushed away. And, squatting on his haunches, the pot between his knees, the boy begins the milking.*

*Simpler days: taking the cattle out at first light, offering a chance for him to be alone, to escape his tormentors for a while. To dream of the day when his herd will outnumber all others.*

*But cattle never belong to you alone, for they also belong to the ancestors who live in a man's hut and in his isibaya . . .*

*. . . and just as a woman conceives and gives birth in the tenth month, so does a cow, so a cow is like a human . . .*

*. . . and the isibaya is like a hut: the gateway is the door; the centre of the byre is the hearth; the upper end, opposite the gateway, is the umsamo, which is the place where the spirits reside in a man's hut . . .*

*But to sit on a rock watching, just watching, your herd − is there a greater pleasure?*

*I don't want to be this way. I fight, I struggle, but I cannot get back to that rock.*

# 16
## The Final Calumny

Each holding one of her hands, Ndlela and another warrior help
Mnkabayi up on to the raised platform. She moves gingerly
towards the opposite edge, testing the rigidity of the planks, but
they're laid across four rows of six barrels each and so seem firm.
She also intends her slow, almost unsteady shuffle and bowed
head to be taken for signs of infirmity and trepidation. The iwisa
she leans on adds to the illusion. When she reaches the edge of
the platform, facing the councillors and district heads and generals here at her feet, the double row of warriors behind them, and
then the multitude, men and women of all ages, she pauses a
moment, like an old woman getting her bearings. Soldiers stand
among the multitude, as though part of that multitude. They're
there to keep order and ensure Mnkabayi's words are accurately
conveyed to the rows assembled on the far side of the huge cattlefold. Usually, when Shaka holds court, what's said beneath the
ibandla tree is passed back fairly accurately to those standing out
of earshot – but on this day there can be no error. Her words
cannot be lost, or misconstrued.

*The cattlefold,* she thinks, *the sacred cattlefold, and these people too
are like cattle: two-legged cattle now rising on tiptoe, craning to see me,
their ears straining to hear me, and who will then chew on my words and
produce the milk I desire. Beautiful cattle – proud, strong bulls and fertile
cows – but they need protecting, need to be herded, or else their strength
will be wasted, their udders will run dry, and their calves will be stolen
by predators.*

Speaking into the hush, she says: 'My children, my people!
The ancestors are angry. An mkhokha, a spirit full of wrath and

pain roams our land. And it is too late to perform the usual rites. Simpler to hold up your hands to these clouds above us and try and stop the rain from falling.'

She throws back her head and regards the leaden sky a moment, then addresses the crowd once more: 'Aiee, this darkness! This is the darkness that covers our land.'

★

They approach along the other side of the stream, three men and two udibis herding five cows. The cows aren't at all happy, as they haven't been milked and their udders are swollen.

The men wear the Zulu umutsha, and each carries an iklwa and shield. The tallest of the three is called Geneca, and he's the leader of this detail. He gazes up the slope, and looks around. Where is that fool Omiso? Then he returns his attention to the cows. Get them in the kraal, get them milked, then get away from this place. Soon the scavengers will be coming and a few spears won't keep them from seeking even fresher flesh.

He also reckons that the sooner they rejoin the others, the better, because who knows what's happening at Bulawayo, or how their master might be faring.

Leaving Geneca to harangue the others, the shortest of the three warriors crosses the stream and ambles up the slope towards the ruined huts. Geneca spots this act of skiving off, but lets him go. The fellow's not the most popular warrior in the regiment, and men have been known to court a charge of insubordination by arguing with their induna about having this creature assigned to their platoon whenever they're given a detail. He's generally loathed and shunned. The fact that he doesn't mind being called Crocodile — and even seems proud of the appellation — only increases this sense of abhorrence.

After a glance over his shoulder to make sure Geneca's still busy with the cows, the short man turns his attention to the bodies scattered amid the smouldering thatch. Like Omiso, he's annoyed that they didn't get a chance to enjoy the fruits of their victory. Unlike Omiso, he's now going to remedy that.

He stops by a hut that collapsed inward, thus smothering the flames meant to burn it down. A pair of buttocks and legs protrude from what used to be the entrance. Shapely buttocks. The way they curve out to join the top of the thigh is enough to give him a hard-on.

After checking yet again that the others are still occupied at the cattle kraal, he returns to the buttocks and picks up the legs, an ankle in each hand.

Tightening his grip, he pulls.

And pulls.

But there's a resistance.

He frowns.

And pulls harder, leaning backward.

And almost topples over as the buttocks and legs separate from the torso.

Clearly the woman had been mortally wounded and tried to crawl into the hut before it was set on fire, and then had had the upper half of her body burnt.

Crocodile stares down at the buttocks, considering it; thinking about flipping them over.

Cha! But he can find something better.

Turning, he moves towards the next hut along.

And spots her.

Oh yes! How could he have missed her!

See how many men she had brought down before dying – and he was almost one of them.

544

And see, there, a few metres from the hut there's a donga that's taken a gouge out of the sloping side of the ravine. Get her in there and no one will see them.

He'd better hurry, though, as they'll be finished milking soon.

Kani's lying on her back, assegai thrusts criss-crossing her body, the killing blow a gaping wound in her side. He picks up her ankles and drags her to the edge of the donga. Then he leaps into it.

The wall of the donga facing the hut comes up to his chest. Grabbing Kani's ankles again, he tugs her down into the hollow.

He's not wearing a penis sheath – never wears one – and within moments he has Kani on her back and has forced her legs apart with his knees. Leaning forward, he reaches beneath his isinene, grabs his prick and sets about trying to enter her, the dry scraping sensation almost enough to make him ejaculate straight away.

★

'You have been told of the horrors taking place to the north, but why is that happening?' she asks. 'Our soldiers, our brave soldiers – what have their sacrifices accomplished? For now the Shangaans and the Khumalos have come out of hiding to slaughter our people.'

A babble of shock and surprise passes over the crowd like a gust of wind over a lake.

'How long before Faku joins them? Hai, how long before treacherous Mzilikazi comes seeking vengeance?' asks Mnkabayi, enjoying the effect these 'revelations' are having.

'Our men, Shaka's lions, have died – are still dying – and yet still the invaders come! Our men, Shaka's lions, are brave – never doubt that – but an mkhokha, a spirit full of wrath, haunts us and robs our regiments of their power. It sees them win every battle, yet never defeat their foe.'

Mnkabayi pauses a moment for these words to sink in – and to be transmitted further back among all those anxious faces.

Then, she continues: 'And you, my people? Who can go to sleep at night saying they do not fear what tomorrow might bring?'

After a pause she adds: 'Pestilence and famine are among us.' But it's not the kind of famine that leaves the stomach empty, for it's something far worse. 'It's a famine that leaves us bereft of hope, of laughter and happiness; a pestilence that eats away at our being, bringing with it mistrust and betrayal,' she says.

'And so this spirit, the mkhokha, covers our land. There is blood in the milk, owls in the night . . . venom in the words of those who were once friends.'

★

Geneca gazes up at the sky, checking the horizon in the direction of Bulawayo. The grey clouds are moving this way. It's time they were done. 'Hurry up,' he tells the udibis. They must just fill the pots, then let the rest of milk splash onto the ground.

Leaving the other warrior in charge, he sets off across the stream to find Omiso and Crocodile.

Climbing the slight incline, he passes the burnt hut, and the bodies of the warriors these insane women brought down. They had to have known they were doomed, so why didn't they just accept the inevitable? Why did they have to make things tough for everyone, not least themselves?

Standing there with his hands on his hips, still aware of those worrying clouds behind him, he glances around. Where are Omiso and Crocodile?

★

'Hai! Do not blame the King! Do not blame Shaka! Do not blame our Father, the Bull Elephant. He suffers as much as we do, and that is why I am here,' declares Mnkabayi. 'A sacrifice is needed, and that is why I am here. I have come to offer myself. Do not blame our King! Blame me! For I was the one who stood by and saw this mkhokha left unappeased – left to become the horrors we face today.'

She shakes her head. 'No, do not blame Shaka! He couldn't help the dream he had.'

That dream . . . let them think back, and be reminded.

'Do not blame Shaka,' she says. 'It was my fault.' She raises her arms. 'This is all my fault!'

★

Shaking his head, Geneca glances into the donga . . .

*Crocodile?*

Anger rising, he moves closer to the edge of the depression.

And stares. Just when you think you've seen it all! He swallows, working up to a rebuke, a bellow of disgust, a roar of repugnance. And he's only just beginning to realise Crocodile isn't actually moving, when one of the dead warriors lying behind him rolls over and – in one movement – launches himself at Geneca's back.

The two go crashing into the red sand alongside Crocodile and Kani.

The Induna straightens up so he's sitting on the small of the other man's back, his knees on either side of him. Straightens and pushes Geneca's face into the dirt. As the latter's left heel comes up, the Induna turns, grabs the foot with both hands and twists, breaking Geneca's ankle. Lifting his head, as if about to roll sideways and throw the Induna off him, Geneca screams.

The Induna's hands close around the back of the warrior's neck, forcing his face into the sand again. And Geneca sends his left hand out, reaching for his iklwa. Keeping one hand on his neck, the Induna leans forward, grabs Geneca's wrist and twists the man's arm behind his back. Pushes it higher and higher, until another bone breaks.

But fear and adrenalin kick in, and Geneca manages to toss the Induna sideways.

Screaming, his left arm still bent behind his back, he tries to reach the spear with his right arm, pushing himself forward with the foot that still works. It's a vain attempt. The Induna kicks his head, drops his knees on to Geneca's back, grabs his right ankle and twists, tearing ligaments and separating the fibula and tibia from the talus. Then, rising to his feet, he breaks Geneca's right arm, too, by standing on the elbow and bending the fore-arm backwards.

*

'Yes, it is so,' she declares. 'Our Father had another dream about his sisters . . .'

Mnkabayi pauses. Let all remember that other occasion, when Shaka woke up one day saying he'd had a dream that had told him some of his warriors were sneaking into the seraglio at Bulawayo to have sex with his sisters, and his concubines.

While the people looked on, the males and females suspected of this crime were gathered together in front of the ibandla tree. But, before the massacre could begin, Shaka suddenly turned on his mother Nandi, who was supposed to watch over his concubines. She hadn't been doing her job properly, he shouted, and started punching and slapping her. Then, as his ageing mother lay on the ground, he kicked her in the stomach – once, twice

– before he ordered the other miscreants to be taken to the Place of Execution.

*Let them remember . . .*

'It is so,' she says again. 'Our Father had another dream about his sisters, and he came to me for advice. He had dreamt, he said, that one of his sisters was with child – and that he himself was the father. He was extremely worried by that for, as all know, he wanted no heir! But there was something else . . .'

She pauses, lowers her head, bangs the tip of her iwisa against one of the planks.

'There was something else,' she repeats. 'The dream had also told him his beloved mother Nandi was protecting the girl, protecting her even though she knew of her son's antipathy to fathering his own assassin.'

★

Without pausing for breath he digs two fingers into Geneca's nostrils and drags the man towards the rear edge of the donga.

As the Induna turns and straightens, the third warrior leaps into the donga.

He clearly thinks the Induna will go for the iklwa lying in the sand, and he therefore has a good chance of getting in the first thrust.

He's wrong.

The Induna lunges straight for him, and punches him in the face before he can bring his assegai into play. Staggering backwards, his eyes watering, his nose feeling as if it's been flattened, the warrior feels the knuckles of the Induna's left fist connect with his chin, knocking his head sideways. Then, as he's folded up against the wall of the donga, the Induna snatches away his iklwa and drives the blade into the warrior's stomach.

His scream of pain becomes a howl as the Induna methodically breaks both his ankles, then the man passes out.

The Induna drags him to the opposite corner of the donga — away from Kani — and props him up so that, when he comes around, he can see Geneca.

Next the warrior pulls the short man off Kani's body. Although facing the huts, Crocodile had been too busy trying to force his way through the dry stiffness encountered by his cock, and had only become aware of the Induna when the latter landed next to him with a thump. By then, of course, it was too late.

After positioning Crocodile on his back in the middle of the donga, the Induna casts about for a spear. There's one!

He picks it up, then settles on his knees alongside Crocodile's corpse. A few moments of hacking and stabbing, and he's opened the man's gut, revealing his intestines.

He stands up and sees that Geneca has regained consciousness and is watching him. A little something to draw predators and scavengers to the donga, explains the Induna.

'Enjoy yourself, Nduna, for you have not long to live.' Geneca coughs, trying to squirm into a more comfortable position, no easy feat given two broken ankles and two broken arms. 'Not long,' he whispers.

His hands and forearms red, his iklwa blade dripping with gore, the Induna shrugs. 'At least I will be able to choose the manner of my death.'

Pointing the blade at the other warrior, who's also regained consciousness (more or less) and is whimpering and trying to cover his wound with his hands, he adds: 'You two, meanwhile, can only watch and wait.'

★

She tells Shaka's children how she went with Shaka to accost Nandi. He had come seeking her advice first and, although she could see the dream had rattled the King badly, his anger growing as he recounted it, she thought she could ensure that her nephew kept his temper with his mother, thinking the mere fact that she was present would be enough.

But she was mistaken.

'I was wrong, my people,' she tells them. 'That is why I am to blame for the hardships that dog us now.'

By the time the pair had arrived at Nandi's kraal, Shaka had convinced himself Nandi was harbouring a concubine pregnant with his child. He stormed into his mother's hut, demanding to know where the girl was. Nandi, needless to say, was bewildered, but Shaka slapped her hard and told her what he believed.

And things happened so quickly! Nandi was denying Shaka's accusation for the third or fourth time, when Shaka suddenly drove his iklwa into her mouth – so that her lies might cease.

A hiss of shock from the crowd.

Nandi was dead before she hit the ground, before Mnkabayi could even move.

And Shaka had then torn the kraal apart in seeking the pregnant girl. When he didn't find her, and deciding, for some reason, that she had fled to Faku's Pondoes, he calmed down. Was forced to consider what he had done – and what now had to be done.

Fynn was bullied into saying he had tried to treat Nandi and had failed. And then Shaka set about slaughtering hundreds of his own people, his children, hoping that would appease Nandi's mkhokha.

But nothing helped.

*Nothing!*

And that is why Mnkabayi is here, because perhaps offering herself as a sacrifice might at last allow Nandi's spirit to rest in peace.

'For, after all, it was my fault,' she says. 'I stood by and did nothing. Do not blame Shaka!'

★

Pampata had hidden behind the wall of reeds that provided a natural barrier between the cattle byre and the nearest vegetable gardens. After the remaining warrior had left to go and find the others, she had emerged brandishing an iklwa and taken the two udibis captive.

Now she watches as the Induna washes his hands and forearms in the stream, and asks him what they are to do with the boys.

He looks up at the quaking youths, one of whom is only nine summers old. They can't simply be chased away; the older one will probably regard it as his duty to warn the other warriors hunkered down amid the trees on the slope over to the east.

'I have an idea,' he says, rising.

While Pampata guards the udibis, the Induna removes two long poles from the fence surrounding the cattle kraal. They're not as thick as those preferred by the Cat People, but they'll do. Once the boys' arms are tied in place, he adds his own innovation, using a length of leather cord to hobble each udibi, so they can only move at a slow, shambling pace and will find it almost impossible to climb an incline if they're still intent on warning the men on the slope.

Then he points them towards the mouth of the ravine and tells them to get moving – and to keep moving across the plain. If he sees them again, they'll rue the day.

As they shuffle away, the Induna starts looking for two undamaged shields and as many spears as he can find, ignoring those embedded in the bodies of the slaughtered women.

When he reaches Omiso's body – he had dragged it away from where it might be spotted by his comrades and left him face down next to the last hut in the row – he pauses. The dead man's isibaya is indeed the kind used by Faku's Pondoes. As are quite a few of the other shields left scattered about.

It will probably be Mhlangana's men who 'discover' the massacre and produce these shields as proof of the identity of the culprits.

And Mnkabayi? What role did she play in this?

A swirl of thoughts and questions assail him, made more volatile, more confusing, by the agony of his loss.

It's a fever worse than the one caused by the spider bite.

It's a jackal howl reverberating through his body.

A gaping wound, its jagged lips speaking their names, and taunting him amid a haze of pain.

A vulture plucking at your sanity.

The swirl coalescing into a single thought: kill them; kill them all.

★

'Do not blame Shaka,' she is saying. 'Do not blame our King, our Father, for I was the one who knew and yet didn't try to heal the spirit's pain. So let it be me!' she insists. 'I must die!'

Cries of *No, Ma!*

Cries of *No, Ma! Not you!*

*No, Ma! No!*

Cries of *The King! The King! The King!*

Cries of *Let the King sacrifice himself!*

*Let Shaka be the one who is offered to the mkhokha! That is the only way the tribe can be saved!*

Cries of *Shaka! Shaka! Let it be Shaka! He has brought this horror upon us!*

And Mnkabayi bows her head, as a way of showing she acquiesces to the crowd's superior wisdom – while hiding her smile.

★

Pampata hands him a large beer pot filled with milk.

'It won't be long before the rest miss their comrades,' she says. It's her way of reminding him they might not have time to bury Kani and the others.

She's right, of course, and the Induna takes a long draught from the isanqulu, giving himself time to get used to the fact this is the way things have to be.

He swallows, wipes his mouth, says he will escort her to Thekwini as planned. And then . . .

'No,' says Pampata. 'Let us first go and find those up there, before they find us.'

# 17
## The Escape

They come for him in the afternoon.

The sky is as grey as an elephant's hide. Though the rain has stopped, there's every indication it will resume again soon. Wet thatch is the colour of ripe maize and puddles reflect the swollen clouds. The tips of leaves and the blades of grass glisten and, in passing, Dingane notices how a spider's web has caught a rainbow. All around, in whichever direction you look, a fine mist, a shade lighter than the glowering sky, has swallowed up the surrounding mountains and valleys.

KwaDukuza consists of five huts arranged in a circle, surrounded by a palisade of poles lashed tightly together. The circle, in turn, is set near the edge of a large clearing encompassed by a broad swathe of untidy red bushwillows, their heavily scented flowers floating amid broad, wavy green and yellow leaves, buffalo-thorns with shiny green leaves and reddish-brown thorns, marulas with their edible berries, and a tangle of creepers and underbrush.

The track approaching Shaka's retreat comes in from the side, running parallel to the wall before reaching the gate itself.

There are three of them: fat Mbopa, the King's prime minister, and Dingane and Mhlangana, the King's brothers. All three wear the isinene and ibeshu that form the umutsha, and amashoba; none wears any form of ornamentation. Each also carries a broadbladed iklwa but no shield.

Every step they take seems to draw the mist closer. Not even birdsong can be heard. The veld is quiet, as if waiting.

It's a sullen silence, unsettling. For Mhlangana it feels as if they're crossing an unsteady log lying across a swollen stream.

You could even say it's annoying, this silence, since it enables a man to hear his own thoughts: with reminders of what-ifs and possibilities better lost in the clamour of action, victory and acclaim. And Mhlangana believes this part of the operation should have been left to Mbopa alone. He is here only because Dingane is here, and he will not have his brother stealing a march on him; but for all that – although he'll never admit it – Mhlangana is scared shitless.

★

Red blades, sticky hafts . . . a clearing alongside a path. A patch of blue sky. A shallow slope to recline on. Half-empty water-skins; they didn't even have a chance to look for some beer. Thirsty work, and a man has the right to expect beer after a strenuous day. But at least they have beef to eat. Seven men and one udibi; the latter cuffed for talking back when told to make a fire, and asking if the ones they're waiting for won't spot the smoke. They're bored with waiting, which can be as tiresome as killing women and children. Let the enemy come and find them!

Mhlangana's heard the rumours about the Induna's return and he has instructed Nolaka, the Leopard Man, to wait here until tomorrow, in case the Induna arrives. Then they're to make haste to KwaBulawayo.

'Hurry up with that fire,' Nolaka tells the udibi, who's trying to control his snuffles. 'And you,' he tells the man who hit the boy, 'go and find some more firewood.'

He looks around as the man moves off down the path. Seven men, in all, counting himself. Soon to be six, though, he reckons. Boniso over there, at the end of the row, is lying on his side, his back to the rest of them; he thinks he's hiding his wound from them, and the fact that it's only his hands that prevent his intestines from unspooling. How he made it up here is anyone's guess. And now, shivering and sweating, what he's hoping for is anyone's guess, because there's no doubting he's found his final resting place.

Leopard Man casts a glance in Ivory's direction. So called because he seems to believe his opinions are as valuable as the ivory the White Men crave, he sits on the other side of the path, beneath the branches of an umnqumo tree, tossing berries down the slope.

*Ignore him.* Nolaka checks the other three: Fula and Dakwa are dozing and Nkantsha – or Marrow, a nickname he's earned because of his love of that delicacy – is getting the beef ready for grilling.

Which reminds him. Where's Geneca? How long does it take to round up and milk a few cows?

He's considering kicking the feet of one of the sleeping warriors and sending him off to see where the others are, when the man who he earlier chastised and sent to fetch firewood backs straight into him.

For a second Nolaka thinks the man is actually attacking him, then he glances over the warrior's shoulder, and sees the haft of a long hunting spear protruding from the man's chest. Stepping aside to allow the warrior to continue falling, Nolaka raises his gaze and sees the Induna charging toward them.

'To arms!' bellows the Leopard Man.

★

No! No, no, no! The King is here because he wants to be alone, says Thenjiwe, intercepting them. They must go! The King doesn't want to see anyone.

And what's this? They're each carrying an iklwa. This won't do! Shaka's chief body servant turns to the prime minister – surely Mbopa, of all people, knows weapons aren't permitted here.

557

'Fetch the King,' says Mbopa.

Thenjiwe seems on the point of arguing, then he turns and runs over to the King's hut.

'Master, Master,' he hisses.

Shaka, who's been lying staring at the wall, rolls over.

'You are in danger, Father,' says Thenjiwe, in answer to the King's glare.

'They are here,' he hisses. 'And they have spears, Father!'

He drops on to his knees and starts scratching at the thatch. 'But we can escape,' he babbles, scratching, scratching, scratching.

His fingernails ripped, his fingertips bleeding, Thenjiwe pauses as Shaka scrambles to his feet.

'You are in danger, Father!'

When Shaka stops at the fire circle rubbing his face, Thenjiwe thinks he's reconsidering his plan. They can go out the back and through the fence, and that's where he'll hold them off while Shaka makes his getaway. Finding an iklwa blade nearby, Thenjiwe begins hacking at the thatch.

When next he looks round, though, Shaka has left the hut.

★

Seven men resting. Trying to approach them through the undergrowth is impossible, as they'd soon be heard and then trapped amid low branches and thorny creepers. Having one of them circle round, so they can attack from two directions at once will take too long. That leaves only one option. Each has a shield with three spears strapped to it, besides another assegai already in hand. The Induna will go first. Pampata will follow. As soon as the Induna engages with the first warrior, she'll charge up and along the incline to attack those on the far side. The path curves, where they are now, and the Induna goes down on to his stomach to peer through the foliage one more time. The man moving up and down the path worries him: not because he recognises him as the Leopard Man, but because there's a chance he'll look this way and spot them as soon as they emerge from cover.

Then he sees Nolaka castigate one of his men before sending him along the path in their direction. For a moment the Induna considers staying hidden and bringing this one down. But trying to pick them off one by one is unlikely to work; and also Nolaka is no fool. The repeated non-appearance of men he has sent on various errands is likely to arouse his suspicions. Then, instead of a sleepy group of soldiers, they'll be dealing with men fully on the alert.

The warrior pauses, scratching his crotch. Clearly he has no enthusiasm for whatever task he's been assigned.

The Induna transfers his iklwa to his shield hand and removes a long hunting spear from the isihlangu.

'It's time,' he tells Pampata. And, without waiting for her response, he charges round the bend and throws the hunting spear with all the strength he can muster.

The man doesn't even see him; his head is bowed and he appears to be trying to examine one of his testicles. And, behind him, Nolaka is looking the other way. And the spear pushes the warrior backwards into him.

By the time the latter shouts 'To arms!', the Induna is almost upon him.

*And Shaka had been a shadow among shadows. 'You have come,' he murmured, his voice hoarse. And he had leant forward, into the firelight. Heavy lips bisecting a deep philtrum from a cleft chin. The hint of polished pink porcelain, fringed by tiny folds of dryness, in vermilion lips. 'You have my trust, Nduna. Your loyalty has never been in question. Which is why I would ask this of you . . .'*

Nolaka dives to the right, reaching for his iklwa.

The warrior working with the meat is the next to react. Rising, he throws a severed hindquarter at the Induna. But Pampata's on the slope opposite him and she leaps at him, stabbing him in the ribs . . .

. . . while the Induna sweeps aside the meat with his shield, and wheels to face Nolaka. But he's already scrambled up the slope to put some distance between them . . .

. . . and, in turning, Induna's left his right flank exposed. But, rudely awakened, Dakwa has only managed to lay his hands on an iwisa . . .

Over on the other side, Pampata puts the wounded warrior out of his misery. And turns just in time to meet Marrow's lunge with her shield. But then, like a rhino lowering its head, he pauses and charges again. This time Pampata's forced backwards and trips over the dead man's body. However, Marrow's momentum carries him after her, and all she has to do is raise her spear – the haft pressed into the dirt – and let him impale himself . . .

. . . the rounded head of the iwisa comes down on the Induna's shoulder. Fortunately, it's his shield arm and, despite the flaring pain, he swings the isihlangu outward, knocking Dakwa off balance . . .

. . . a brief glance in Nolaka's direction shows that he's still waiting for his chance, and the Induna follows the momentum of his shield, wheeling to drive his spear into Dakwa's back.

Then he dives sideways, dodging Nolaka as he pounces. In the process, however, he collides with Fula, who's finally risen to his feet. He's a big man with a boulder of a paunch and the impact serves only to bring the Induna up against his shield, much too close to the man.

'Do something!' Nolaka orders Ivory, who's standing a few paces off the path, amid the dried leaves, watching the proceedings.

★

Shaka stares at Mbopa, noting the iklwa gripped in his prime minister's hand, then shifts his attention to his brothers standing a few paces away. They're also carrying spears and they try to meet and hold his gaze but fail, pretending instead to be distracted by an itch or, in Mhlangana's case, something at Shaka's feet.

Mbopa's thinking of Ndlela's words. Mnkabayi's induna had caught him alone last night. 'You and I have never been friends, cannibal,' he'd said, grabbing Mbopa's arm, 'but I would have you know why this must be done.'

Releasing his arm, the older man had told Mbopa to forget all he's heard. 'An heir cannot kill a King,' he had continued, 'but that is not why you are doing this thing. Shaka has done you a great injustice, I know, but that is not why *you* must do this thing!'

No, he had continued, this thing must be done because Shaka has abolished the old Zulu coming-of-age ritual, saying service in the King's army is the true test of manhood. But, because they haven't gone through the coming-of-age ritual, those youngsters who now fall in battle are not-quite-men, not-quite-boys and therefore they cannot join the ancestors. Instead they're left lost and alone, travellers with bloody, torn feet, racked by pain and the knowledge that they will never make it home, yet forced to keep on walking, to keep on trying . . .

'Forget all else,' Ndlela had hissed to Mbopa. '*This* is the great evil the King has done us. *This* is why Shaka must die. *This* is why you must drive your blade home on the morrow . . .'

There's a rumble high above them as the sky melts and it starts to rain. Shaka tilts his aching, throbbing head backward, and feels the first few tentative raindrops splash against his forehead, his eyelids, and run down his cheeks like tears.

Then Mbopa steps forward and stabs him in the stomach.

★

Marrow's still alive, vainly trying to grab hold of Pampata as she frees herself from his weight. And her spear's stuck in him. Removing another iklwa from her shield, she stabs him in the throat, then turns her attention to the others. She's now accounted for two. Nolaka's gone crashing into the bushes; another is standing there transfixed. Then there's the big man . . .

*'When the time comes,' Shaka had said, 'you will do what you can to protect Pampata. Nothing else matters. You must get her to safety!' And Pampata had said: 'But, beloved . . .'And Shaka had held up a hand. 'Heed me! I speak as your King now!' Addressing the Induna: 'You must give me your word that you will keep her safe, as well as yourself!' And the Induna had said: 'Gladly! I am yours to command. You have my word, Father!'*

'Nduna!' calls Pampata, rushing forward, and knocking the frightened udibi out of her way.

At the shout, the Induna frees his all-but-useless arm from the shield and pushes himself away from Fula . . .

. . . and swivels round, kicking out with his right leg and catching Nolaka's isihlangu with enough force to cause the latter to take a step back . . .

. . . but now Fula grabs him in a bear hug from behind. Lifts his feet off the ground.

'Good work,' grins Nolaka. 'Keep him there while I see to the bitch.'

*'But, Majesty . . .' Pampata had protested, dropping to her knees. 'Heed me,' said Shaka, 'for this I have seen. This I have seen.' Then he dragged his hand over his mouth and over his chin, forcing a sheen of*

sweat to fall into the darkness. *'This I have seen,'* he said again, his eyes tired and bloodshot. *'Our fates are entwined. What happens to one happens to the others.'* Addressing Pampata in a softer, more gentle voice, he continued: *'So you see, my Sister, if you are kept safe, I will be safe too!'*

The Induna twists this way and that, but Fula only tightens his grip, crushing him against his paunch.

Then, as Nolaka edges past them, the Induna feels an iklwa blade scrape across the top of his head, and Fula's arms fall away.

'Sorry,' says Pampata. Wanting to be sure of her kill this time, she's driven her iklwa blade through the back of the big man's neck to emerge out of his throat . . .

. . . but Nolaka's coming at her and there's no time to unclip the last spear from her shield. Instead she parries his first thrust. And his second . . .

. . . then Fula crashes down alongside him, and Nolaka realises the Induna is free.

*'Your word, Nduna. Do I have your word?'* Yes, Father. *'And you will know when the time is right. You will know.'* Yes, Father.

'Leave her,' says the Induna. 'Let's see how you fare against a real man.'

Nolaka straightens, and uses the pause to try and get his breath back. 'You and me?' he asks the Induna.

The Induna nods.

'No trickery?'

'No trickery,' says the Induna.

'She can be trusted not to fall upon me when I am likely to win?'

'Hai!' interjects Pampata. 'Do you know who I am?'

Nolaka looks at her sharply. 'No, should I?'

Then he feels a burning sensation in his left side. He looks down in time to see the Induna stab him again.

'You said . . .'

'Cha!' says the Induna, stabbing him a third time. 'This is better than you deserve after what you did to my family.'

'And you?' asks Pampata, addressing Ivory. 'What say you? Are you a coward fit only for slaughtering women and children?'

'No,' says Ivory, throwing down his spear next to Nolaka's body. 'This . . . what happened today . . . it was too much . . .'

'Yet you . . .' begins Pampata; then turning to the udibi she shouts: 'Stop your snivelling, Boy!' Addressing Ivory again: 'Yet you did nothing to stop the killing.'

'What could he do?' murmurs the Induna. Answering Pampata's look of surprise, he adds: 'Had he done so, there would merely have been one extra corpse lying down there.'

'This is so,' whispers Ivory.

'Hai, but do you think to win mercy by voicing your regrets?' demands Pampata.

'No.' Ivory shakes his head. 'Although keeping me alive is a better punishment, for that way I'll never stop hearing their screams. I am ready to die by your hand, Nduna, for today . . . today we did not act as true Zulus, but were as bad as the savages we despise. But at least let me die a Zulu's death.'

The Induna nods. Motions him to step on to the path. Glancing at Pampata, he says: 'You have been wounded.'

'A few cuts, nothing to worry about.' Pointing to the udibi, she adds: 'This one has gathered the makings of a fire. Do we have time for us to cook some meat?'

The Induna gazes up at the sky. It's no longer blue, but the colour of stone. The rain they will have experienced at Bulawayo is coming this way. He'd like to resume their journey as quickly as possible, because the sooner he delivers Pampata into the care of the White Men, the sooner he can return to the capital and see what's been happening. But he has to also consider Pampata's well-being; they haven't eaten anything today and, although he himself is not hungry, she must be starving.

Very well, then, he says; for they can but try to beat the rain. Does she have any flints?

Pampata nods and sets about rearranging the kindling the udibi has collected.

The Induna indicates that Ivory should walk ahead of him. 'I will not try to run,' he says, as the Induna lays a hand on his right shoulder.

'I know,' says the Induna, tightening his grip and running his blade through the back of the man's neck. Taking him by surprise, not letting him see the blade coming – these are the few crumbs of mercy the Induna can scrabble together today.

He turns.

Finds himself looking down at the udibi.

At the haft of a spear that ends in his own stomach.

An explosion of pain and blood as the youngster pushes the blade deeper, and deeper again, so that the blade and even part of the haft emerge out of the Induna's back.

'NO!' screams Pampata, rising. 'WHAT HAVE YOU DONE?'

The udibi faces her, cringing, clearly expecting an assegai thrust in his turn. But she pushes past him.

The Induna is on his knees, leaning forward, only the haft embedded in the dirt keeping him upright.

'No!' says Pampata. 'No! No no no no!'

Moving to his side, she crouches down and gently places a hand over his mouth and nose. No breath. He's dead.

'What have you *done*?' she wails at the udibi.

Looking around she finds an iklwa – and the boy cringes again, bringing his arm up as though that will be able to shield him.

But Pampata picks up the spear and moves off in the opposite direction.

Thunder and lightning, and the wind picking up. A jog-trot through rain that is propelled sideways. Panting and sobbing at the same time, while remembering Shaka's words. Knowing that now nothing can save her beloved.

At last she comes upon the precipice of a narrow kloof over-grown with shrubs and bushes.

It's over. All over.

But they can't be allowed to find her body. Her beloved would not wish her body to be paraded about by his enemies.

Standing on the very edge of the precipice, Pampata gazes down at the iklwa blade pressing into her stomach like a finger. 'This is going to hurt,' she thinks, the blade itself blurring and the bushes below coming into focus like a green froth.

This. Is. Going. To. Hurt.

Now her eyes are focused inward, guiding her memory of all that's happened. A King trapped in his own pain; an ageing lion swatting at all who come near, because he's afraid of the mock-ery that will ensue should he prove no longer able to bring down a buck or zebra; so no longer trying, and instead merely lash-ing out with his claws. Mnkabayi, so trusted by Shaka, and elevated to a status she would have enjoyed under no other ruler, meanwhile plotting to move against Shaka. *Why? Why? Why? He only ever respected you!* Kani's murder, and the death of her children, and Mgobozi's widows and children – all slaughtered by the henchmen of an insane prince. *Why them? Are you behind this too, Ma?* And Dingane . . . ? What role has he played in all that's happened? Is he with them – with Mnkabayi and all the other traitors – or does he too eat dust now? The Induna's death, and what that means, recalling Shaka's words: *Our fates are entwined. What happens to one happens to the others.* He too is gone, isn't he?

This realisation alone is enough to silence all thoughts of pain; it is, after all, greater than any pain she might inflict upon herself.

Almost before she knows it, Pampata has driven the iklwa blade into her stomach. A searing pain pushes the breath from her body. Gasping, her eyes watering, she twists the blade, rips it to the right . . . and topples forward into myth.

★

It takes the udibi and Njikiza about four days to piece together what happened. Although Shaka's assassination has shaken the kingdom to its core, and shock, fear, bewilderment and, yes, even relief are the order of the day, the tale of two herd boys found hobbled, with their arms tied to poles placed across their shoulders, spreads fast.

The two men eventually trace the boys to one of Mhlangana's regiments. After Njikiza bashes some heads, they get to speak to the lads, who in turn direct them to the udibi who killed the Induna. They question him and then leave, neither man having the slightest thought of punishing the boy. That would be like blaming the leaves for rustling, when one's ire should be directed at the wind.

They survey the damage wrought at the homestead, then find the clearing where the Induna fell. Shields and spears and items of clothing lie scattered about on flattened, blood-smeared grass. But there are no bodies to be seen, for the scavengers have torn them apart and dragged the pieces away.

As for Pampata, the boy said she had run off in that direction, towards the sea. But neither Mthunzi nor Njikiza need to know about the promise Shaka had extracted from the Induna for them, to understand that Pampata would have realised it was all over. And she would have made her escape by taking her own life, as soon as she came upon a secluded spot where her body would not be found.

When Dingane is told what happened to his old friend, the Induna, he takes the news stoically. Even later, alone in his hut, he allows his rage to merely smoulder, for he knows he can't safely reveal the depth of his loss to anyone. He's feeling uneasy enough, as it is. Among those Mhlangana sent his men to kill, because of their supposedly unassailable loyalty to Shaka, there were more than a few headmen and generals who would have happily transferred their allegiance to Dingane. Now this! His brother has gone too far. They are meant to rule together, but the Needy One will ensure that it's a state of affairs that won't last long.

As for Mnkabayi, when she hears of the Induna's death, she's as distraught as only a mother can be.

★

Shaka is buried in an unmarked grave whose location is known only to the two brothers, who rule together for a while. Needless to say, both soon begin to plot against each other, but Dingane strikes first and has Mhlangana murdered. In this he is aided by Mnkabayi. But it's Jakot, the Swimmer, who soon becomes his chief advisor, especially after Mnkabayi's death (from old age) and a group of Voortrekkers, led by Piet Retief, manage to drag their ox wagons over the Drakensberg towards the end of 1837.

These are not like the English who the Zulus continue to do business with at Port Natal, says Jakot. Or the missionaries who have arrived, for that matter. Instead, they are of the same savage tribe who abducted and abused him – and others of his people. More importantly, they're seeking to escape British rule and want land – Zulu land.

Dingane must do whatever he can to stop them, says Jakot. In the campaign that follows the Zulus enjoy some early successes, mainly through surprise attacks on Trekker camps. Significantly, only the Trekkers are attacked; other whites are left alone. But then the newcomers regroup. And on December 16, 1838, about fifteen thousand Zulu warriors led by Ndlala KaSompisi attack a Voortrekker laager on a plain alongside the Ncome River. Thousands perish, while the Trekkers, who number 470, suffer only three casualties, none serious; whereupon the water runs red with Zulu blood and the Ncome becomes known ever after as Blood River.

The Zulu army thus broken, Dingane goes into hiding. Led by Andries Pretorius, the Voortrekkers install Mpande as King, who sees to it that Dingane is tracked down and killed in January 1840.

The last of Senzangakhona's sons proves a better ruler than expected. All the same, dark days follow for the People Of The Sky: days of poverty, subjugation and internecine struggles. Then Cetshwayo KaMpande becomes King.

As for Mthunzi and his exploits during these days – well, that's a tale for another time . . .

★

Shaka places his hands on Mbopa's shoulders, to steady himself, and gazes into the old cannibal's eyes. He starts to open his mouth, but there will be no famous last words – it will be left to others to supply those. Instead, his lips part to expel blood. Black-red, viscous blood.

Mbopa stabs him again. Shaka grunts and is forced back a step. Then he staggers past the prime minister, blood pumping from his wounds, and glistening on his chin.

For a moment it seems as if he's heading towards his brothers.

'Again! Stab him again!' urges Mhlangana.

'Shut up! It is done,' says Dingane, as Shaka's legs begin to give way and he veers to the right, fetching up against the thatch of the hut.

Keeping his eyes on his brothers, he sags to the ground. Then he coughs up some more blood and slowly, gently, as though being helped by invisible hands, lies down on his side.

For a while this King of Kings, who had no need of grapeshot and ships of wood to bring the world to him, this Bull Elephant, this Defiler and Defyer, this Spear Red to the Haft, this Sky that Thunders in the Open, Where There is Neither Mimosa Nor Thorn Tree, watches the raindrops shatter against the dark dirt . . . then he's walking among the heavenly herds, at last at peace.

# Coda

Cha! There are those who will say none of this ever happened.

Having seen Shaka assassinated once already, they are still trying to kill him with malicious lies, political toadying and smug ivory-tower sophistry – but he lives on.

Shaka lives on.

Bayede!